Dear Reader,

Thank you for choosing a Sophie Lark book! My readers mean everything to me, and I love connecting with you through these stories.

My promise to you:

- **Powerful escape** from stress. My books are like movies you can see in your head, complete with illustrations and a soundtrack. You will feel like you're there.
- **Powerful couples** who trust each other. By the end of the story, my couples are true partners and soul mates who make each other better.
- **Powerful love** you can believe in. You deserve it in your life—never settle for anything less.

Most of all, I hope to make you laugh along the way...as long as you forgive me if I also make you cry.

Love you all,

Sophie Lark

P.S. Stay rowdy

ALSO BY SOPHIE LARK

Minx

Brutal Birthright

Brutal Prince

Stolen Heir

Savage Lover

Bloody Heart

Broken Vow

Heavy Crown

Sinners Duet

There Are No Saints

There Is No Devil

Grimstone

Grimstone

Monarch

Kingmakers

Kingmakers: Year One

Kingmakers: Year Two

Kingmakers: Year Three

Kingmakers: Year Four

Kingmakers: Graduation

KING MAKERS

YEAR ONE

SOPHIE LARK

Bloom books

Series cover design by Emily Wittig
Cover design by Nicole Lecht/Sourcebooks
Cover images © morita kenjiro/iStock, diversepixel/Depositphotos,
ProVectors/Getty Images, VikaSuh/Getty Images
Internal images © Line Maria Eriksen

Published by Bloom Books, an imprint of Sourcebooks
P.O. Box 4410, Naperville, Illinois 60567-4410
(630) 961-3900
sourcebooks.com

Originally self-published as *The Heir* in 2021 by Sophie Lark.

Cataloging-in-Publication data is on file with the Library of Congress.

Printed and bound in the United States of America.
WOZ 10 9 8 7 6 5 4 3 2 1

This one is for anybody in love
with their best friend
XOXO

Sophie Lark

SOUNDTRACK

"Love Chained"—Cannons
"Best Friend"—Saweetie ft. Doja Cat
"Daisy"—Ashnikko
"Fire for You"—Cannons
"Crazy in Love"—Sofia Karlberg
"Wicked Game"—Chris Isaak

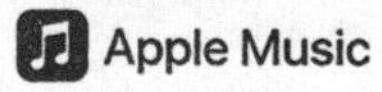

CONTENT WARNING

The Kingmakers series is dark mafia romance in a University academic setting. Expect all the violence and plotting a bunch of conniving, young adults from crime families will commit. Due to violence and sexual content, these books are intended for mature readers.

This book may contain, but is not limited to, the following potential triggers:

- Violence
- Other man drama
- Nonconsensual drug use
- Dubious consent
- Attempted murder

WELCOME TO THE WORLD Of KINGMAKERS

Think of "Kingmakers" as your next binge-worthy TV show in book form...

Every great show needs a villain.

Dean Yenin wants to destroy Leo Gallo and take everything he loves.

At the end of the first book, half of you will loathe Dean. 🤬

But half of you... might just love him 😈

Which side will you be on?

Whichever you choose, by Year Three, everything will change...

KINGMAKERS

YEAR ONE

LEO

ANNA

DEAN

MILES

ARES

CHAY

ZOE

LUTHER

MISS ROBIN

OZZY

HEDEON

ENZO GALLO

GIANNA LUCAS

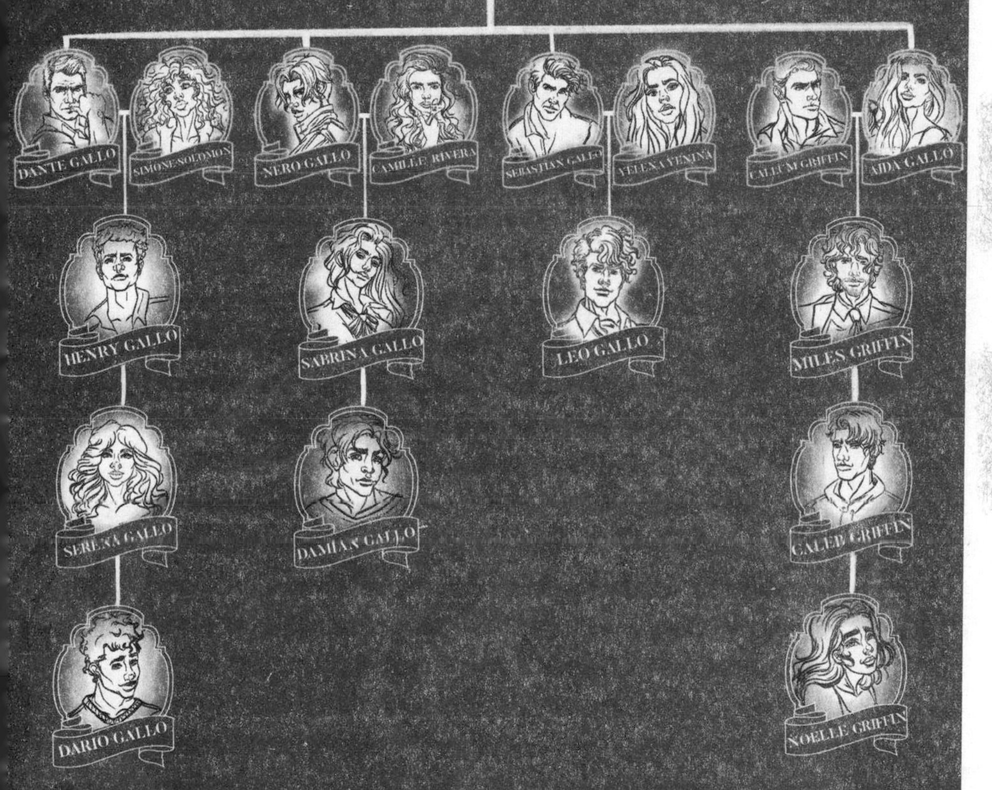
DANTE GALLO
SIMONE SOLOMON
NERO GALLO
CAMILLE RIVERA
SEBASTIAN GALLO
YELENA YENINA
CALLUM GRIFFIN
AIDA GALLO
HENRY GALLO
SABRINA GALLO
LEO GALLO
MILES GRIFFIN
SERENA GALLO
DAMIAN GALLO
CALEB GRIFFIN
DARIO GALLO
NOELLE GRIFFIN

GALLO
Family Tree

AIDA GALLO

GRIFFIN
Family Tree

YENIN Family Tree

Lee Gallo
AND
Anna Wilk

PROLOGUE

CHICAGO, ILLINOIS

IT'S MY LAST CHRISTMAS AT HOME. ONCE I LEAVE FOR KINGMAKERS, I'll only be able to visit over the summer.

Christmas has never been my favorite season—I'm more of a Halloween kind of girl. But knowing this is the last time all of us will be gathered around one table to eat turkey and pull crackers is making me more nostalgic than usual.

Leo…not so much.

He can't wait to leave. He's so done with high school, I'm not sure how he's going to make it through five more months of classes plus final exams.

Actually, I don't know how he passed any of his classes. He's not much for following instructions.

Right at this moment, he's supposed to be helping me set out the place cards so everyone can find their seat at dinner. Instead, he's swapping the order for maximum drama.

"You're supposed to sit each family together," I remind him.

Leo only grins. "What's the fun in that?"

With twenty-four people en route, it's lucky the dining room in my parents' house resembles the great hall in a medieval castle. The fireplace is large enough to stand up in, and the table stretches about an acre end to end. If my mom and dad sat at opposite ends, they'd hardly be able to shout to each other. But she always sits right next to him.

"Don't even think about moving that one." I point to the card with *Nessa* written in my mother's pretty, cursive script.

"I'm not suicidal," Leo says, leaving that particular card exactly where it sits, right next to the one reading *Mikolaj.*

Leo is dressed more formally than usual, meaning he's wearing trousers with his halfway tucked-in T-shirt. But his dark, wavy hair is messier than ever, and when he bends his knees, his slightly too-short pants show several inches of eye-searing Christmas socks.

I smile to myself. "Are you growing again?"

If he is, he'd better stop. Leo's approaching the height of your average NBA player, which means he already doesn't fit very well into airplane seats or compact cars.

"Let's see." He comes around to my side of the table, wrapping his arms around me in a hug so he can rest his chin on the top of my skull. "Nope. We're still exactly one head apart."

"Maybe I grew too."

"How am I supposed to judge anything if you won't stay the same?" He smiles down at me, not letting go.

I'm not complaining. Leo gives the best hugs. I mean, the best out of anybody, ever. For one thing, his body temperature seems to burn at about 102 degrees. Also, he squeezes like he means it.

Until my dad enters the room. Then Leo lets go of me quick.

"Almost finished?" my father says dryly. Pretty much everything he says comes out dry. Or menacing. Or both.

You have to know him well to spot his moments of softness. He has a narrow vein of emotion, but it runs down to his core. No one loves deeper than he does.

However, that love is almost exclusively reserved for me, my mom, and my two younger siblings. He's not the biggest Leo fan.

As Leo is well aware.

He shoots me a sideways smile.

"Look how beautifully Anna set the table."

Smooth recovery. Leo knows the best way to mollify my dad is to compliment me.

I do think it's one of my best efforts. I've brought in armfuls of white Christmas berry from the garden, filling the air with the scent of evergreen. The ghostly berries and tall white tapers are offset by the black tablecloth and bronze plates. It's elegant and slightly gothic. Basically, the exact opposite of Leo's socks.

"Anna's taste is almost always excellent," my dad says.

When he's safely out of earshot, Leo mutters, "He means with the exception of me."

I laugh. "I'm pretty sure he was talking about my clothes."

I dressed up too, but like Leo, I have my own definition of what that means. My favorite tulle gown with its trailing, transparent layers and short, puffy sleeves looks like something a vampire would wear if she died when she was twelve years old.

"But black's his favorite color." Leo grins. "His *only* color, as far as I've seen. Does he know other colors exist? Have you ever seen him wear blue for instance? Or the ultimate horror...pink?"

I bite my lip to hide my smile. "Don't make fun of my dad."

"I would never." Leo places his palm over his chest in pretend penitence. "I told you, I'm not suicidal."

"Sometimes you make me wonder."

"Oh, look!" He grabs my arm, pulling me over to the window.

Snow has started to fall. It drifts down in huge, puffy flakes, obscuring our view of the overgrown backyard.

We stand in silence, watching.

One of my favorite things about Leo is that even though he buzzes at ten thousand beats a minute, he knows when to be quiet too.

"Let's go stand in it," he says.

We sneak out through the conservatory, knowing my poor

stressed mother is sure to assign us another task if she catches sight of us.

The back garden is always like its own secret world but never more so than when it's blanketed in snow. The silence is complete, the twelve-foot-tall stone walls and towering trees blocking out any noise from the city beyond.

My parents fell in love in this house. My father almost died in this garden. I was born in one of the rooms upstairs. When I think of leaving, my heart feels stretched to its limit, torn in two directions.

Looking at Leo gives me the same feeling.

You can't get everything you want. Not when you want two opposite things at once.

I want to keep everything I love perfect and unchanging, preserved under glass like a snow globe. But I also feel the pull of the great wide *something more*.

"What are you thinking about?" Leo asks me.

He asks that question often, whenever he can't tell just from the look on my face.

I don't mind. Not when he's the one asking.

Leo's the only person who gets open access to my mind. I can tell him anything, and I don't have to translate it, minimize it, or change it so it's what he wants to hear.

Or at least...that's how it used to be.

Lately when I look at Leo, I still get that swell of warmth and excitement. But I also feel like I might burst into tears. Like when you hear a song so beautiful your chest hurts, and you want something you can't name...something that may not even exist.

I don't understand what changed between us.

He's right here, right next to me.

He's giving me that grin that's been lighting me up almost every day of my life.

But lately, Leo's grin is torture as much as pleasure. The smile hasn't changed, only the way it tears me up inside.

Something deep within me whispers *Tell him.*

"What is it?" Leo says.

He tilts his head, examining my face.

I look into his eyes: tawny brown, but that could never capture all the depth of color dancing there. Leo's eyes are lit from within, golden lights as wild as whatever lives inside him.

Softly, he says, "You have snowflakes in your eyelashes."

So does Leo. Also snowflakes in his hair, pale stars nestled in the dark waves. They melt the moment they touch his warm, brown skin.

Leo looks like he toasted just a little longer than the rest of us, like he burns a little hotter.

He's not like anyone else.

Even surrounded by people I love, Leo's special to me, precious. A bond so tight it hurts.

If I asked him for something right now, for anything, he'd give it to me.

But I don't know what to ask.

Promise me this won't be our last Christmas.

Promise me you'll never change.

Impossible things. Stupid things. Things that no one can promise.

Promise me I'll never lose you.

Even that, no one can say. Either of us could die tonight, struck by lightning. Or in our case, probably something a bit more personal.

So instead, I ask of him, "Promise me that we'll always be friends."

Leo's smile spreads slowly across his face, illuminating each feature in turn until his eyes are aflame.

"Anna." His voice is low and secret. It warms me to my toes. "You know I couldn't stop. Even if I wanted to."

The joy that burns inside me is fierce and hot and dangerous.

That's what I cling to, like a bright bead of gold that I swallow while it's still molten hot: Leo will always be my best friend.

Headlights sweep across the yard.

Leo turns. "Looks like everyone's arriving."

"Everyone" means every single one of our aunts and uncles and all the cousins. They've traveled here to commemorate our last holiday at home, even Dante and Simone, all the way from Paris, and Raylan and Riona from their ranch in Tennessee, with their four redheaded sons.

Simone and her daughter, Serena, come up the walk first, their arms full of wrapped gifts. Serena looks impossibly beautiful and stylish in her Parisian coat and high-heeled boots. I'm not surprised to see the three oldest Boone boys fighting over who gets to take the packages out of her hands.

Only Teddy, the youngest, remains immune to the charms of our gorgeous foreign cousin, much more interested in tearing around the house with my little brother, Whelan.

It's not Serena's fault she's so stunning—her mother is a supermodel after all. And I can't even hate her for it because she's so damned nice.

"I brought you some of your favorite macarons." She presses an elegantly wrapped package into my hands, then kisses me on both cheeks.

Her older brother, Henry, does the same, taking my arm to help me back up the icy walk.

"No kiss for me?" Leo says with a slightly strained smile.

"How about a hug." Henry releases my arm.

The competition for tallest member of our family has been running hot ever since Henry passed Uncle Seb and then Leo threatened to pass Henry.

Henry grabs Leo by the shoulders, locked in a kind of steely examination that finally ends as our eldest cousin sighs. "Yeah, you definitely caught up."

"Caught up and passed you!" Leo chortles.

"Let's not get carried away. We're eye to eye."

"Then how come I can see the top of your head?"

"Pinch yourself. You're dreaming."

Serena links elbows with me instead.

"Don't worry," I tell her. "I already know you're taller than me."

"I missed you!" she says in her silvery, soft voice, melodic as a Christmas bell.

I lean my head against her shoulder, already full to the brim with the buoyant warmth of seeing the people I love and liking them even more than I remembered.

"No hugs for me? And no help with the packages either," Uncle Dante grumbles, alone and forgotten behind us.

Aunt Simone laughs, kissing her husband on the cheek and squeezing his bicep the size of a ham hock. "If these can't carry packages, then what are they good for?"

"You know what they're good for," he growls in her ear.

"Gross, Dad," Henry says in a resigned tone.

"If your dad wasn't irresistible, you wouldn't exist," Simone reminds him.

"Yeah, but we're here now, and we've had enough of you two sucking face," Simone's youngest pipes up.

"Don't say 'sucking face,'" Simone corrects Dario. "It's crude."

After a glance at his glowering father, Dario ducks his head and says, "*Désolé, Maman*," then races off to join Teddy and Whelan.

"I want to hear Dante say something in French," a merry voice calls.

Aunt Aida comes up the walkway, her mischievous face flushed and beaming.

"His French has really improved," Simone says at the same time that Dante grunts, "Not a chance in hell."

"How does he survive in Paris?" Uncle Nero inquires, always eager to join his sister in teaming up against their eldest sibling.

"I bet he points a lot," Aida says. "Or pretends like he didn't really want that thing anyway."

Dante rolls his eyes. "Could you two wait until we're inside before you start bullying me?"

"Bully you!" Aida stands on tiptoe to give her brother the kind of hug that might rival one from Leo. "Not until after dessert."

The rest of our relatives stream into the house, Leo's parents the last to arrive, along with my grandparents, whom they picked up along the way.

By the time we're done with the rounds of kisses and greetings, the entryway is at least ten degrees hotter, and the sofa has disappeared beneath a mound of discarded coats and scarves.

My mother's running everywhere, stacking gifts, bringing drinks, and separating Whelan and Dario, who have already begun to squabble. My father helps her, trying not to grimace at all the rowdy boys running around his house and all the hugs he's forced to endure.

"Don't you just love all this Christmas cheer?" Aida teases him as Dario lets out a particularly ear-splitting shriek.

I think my aunt Aida is the only person on this planet brave enough to rib my dad.

But then her husband is also pretty scary.

Uncle Callum looks only slightly less tortured than my father. As soon as could possibly be considered polite, my dad says they need to "discuss something," a.k.a. disappear into his study to drink their whiskey in peace.

Funny that those two tried to murder each other once upon a time. Now they bond over jazz music no one else likes and the unfortunate sociability of their wives.

"Do we have the weirdest family that ever was?" Leo murmurs in my ear.

Uncle Nero is showing my aunt Aida his newest knife. Aida gives it a practiced flick and sends it spinning across the kitchen to sink hilt deep into the turkey. The Boone boys hoot and howl like a pack of redheaded baboons. Aunt Riona looks slightly less impressed.

"I spent seven hours on that turkey!"

"His name was Lawrence," Teddy Boone sadly says.

"I told you not to name him." Uncle Raylan rests a hand on Teddy's shoulder. "You do this every year."

Leo's my cousin, sort of. His aunt Aida married my uncle Callum. It wasn't exactly a voluntary marriage—the Griffins and Gallos were rival Mafia families who tried to destroy each other for generations. Now we all eat pumpkin pie and only jokingly threaten to murder each other.

But the iron roots of our family tree remain.

The Griffins and Gallos decided to graft their branches before they burned each other to the ground.

But not all our blood feuds have been laid to rest. Not even close.

An hour later, we're all seated around the formal dining table, with the exception of the youngest cousins, who eat in the kitchen. Nero's daughter, Sabrina, was so incensed at being relegated to the kiddie table for one more year that she swiped a box of chocolates and a bottle of wine and disappeared entirely. She's probably up in the attic, which was also my favorite place to sulk.

I've been amusing myself with the results of Leo's place card swapping that have Serena seated directly between Creed and Marshall Boone, who are well on their way to a fistfight, and Aunt Aida next to Grandma Imogen, who looks appalled at the triple-decker turkey-cranberry-stuffing sandwich Aida is building.

Henry was supposed to be sitting near me, but I notice he's now three seats down on the other side of Uncle Dante.

"How's your residency going?" Uncle Raylan asks him.

"Excellent." Henry takes a heaping spoonful of corn and passes the bowl down. "Other than I get no sleep and I have no life."

"That's what you get for being the smart one," his sister, Serena, teases him.

"I thought *I* was the smart one," Marshall Boone remarks.

"*You!*" Creed Boone scoffs. "You're not even the sixth-smartest one."

"I heard Leo got an offer from Duke," Aunt Riona interrupts to stop her boys from squabbling.

"Yeah, but I'm not going," Leo says, without even thinking about it.

"What?" Aunt Yelena says a little too sharply.

Quiet falls across the table. You can hear the birch boughs popping in the hearth.

Leo glances at his mom, who's sitting directly across from us. Aunt Yelena is tall, even taller than Aunt Simone. When calm and composed, she resembles a Viking princess. Right now, lips pale and violet eyes crackling, she's a full-fledged Valkyrie.

Uncle Seb slips an easy arm around her shoulders. She shakes him off.

"What do you mean you're not going to Duke? When did you decide this?"

Russian accents are scarier than Polish. That's what I'm thinking as even my dad's head snaps up.

It's not the most comfortable thing in the world to have twenty pairs of eyes turned in your direction, especially when one of those pairs of eyes belongs to your extremely pissed-off mom. But Leo squares his shoulders and answers firmly.

"I already told you. I'm going to Kingmakers."

My heart jerks in my chest.

I've never heard Leo say it for sure—that he's definitely going.

I want him at Kingmakers with me.

It's no normal school, or even one you'd find on a list of colleges.

Kingmakers exclusively serves the children of criminal families from around the globe.

Many glances are shared in many directions across the table. The two oldest Boone boys lean forward, excited. They love a good fight.

Uncle Seb tries to murmur something to his wife, his big hand rubbing slow circles in the center of her back. Yelena's not having it.

"No, *zhizn moya*," she hisses. "That's enough of this foolishness."

Aunt Yelena draws herself up to full height in her high-backed chair until she towers like a snow queen, eyes glittering like chips of violet ice.

"You are not going anywhere *near* your cousin, let alone sleeping in the same school as Dean."

Leo is an only child. I've seen how Yelena gets pale and quiet when the littlest ones are around, how she's softest with the babies. My other aunts fell pregnant easily. They used to ask when she'd have another. She'd laugh and say, "When Leo's less trouble." But soon she stopped laughing, and people learned to stop asking.

Leo is her light and joy. Usually, she'll give him anything.

But apparently not this.

Leo hesitates, sensing the static in the air.

"Mom, I'll be fine. They haven't had a death at Kingmakers in years. I can handle myself."

"Oh yeah? Have you been in a lot of street fights?"

The soft sneer comes from Uncle Nero. His attack is unexpected—Uncle Nero doesn't often involve himself in other people's business, and he's the last one to throw stones for risky behavior.

Feeling teeth where he most expected support, Leo hisses back, "Yeah. I've been in a few. You don't need to be in a hundred, Nero, to prove that you can do it."

Uncle Nero's face darkens at that disrespect.

Leo's eyes meet mine, full of hurt and frustration.

But the last cut comes, swift and cold, from my father. "How many of those fights were against a Russian with a knife?"

Leo presses his lips together, jaw tightening. No matter how frustrated he might be, he's not going to argue with my father.

It doesn't matter. My dad's not even close to finished.

"Do you think Dean is sitting down at a table like this tonight?"

He gestures down the length of the room, stuffed end to end with liquor, delicious food, and friendly faces. My father sits at the head, pale and stern as a ghost.

"Look how far our family has wandered and forgotten about a blood feud. Leo, your life is in danger as you sit here. If you don't think that the son of Adrian Yenin has planned many ways to kill you at Kingmakers, you have already underestimated him. He will try to destroy everything you love." He casts a long and burning look at my mother, who slips her pale hand into his, completely black with tattoos. "He's had eighteen years to plan his revenge. That's what I would do."

The silence that falls is complete.

I'm begging for someone to break it so I can breathe.

I glance at Aunt Aida, certain that she at least won't let me down. But even Aida is somber.

In fact, she's gazing across the table at her youngest brother, Uncle Seb. The exchange that passes between them is puzzling. Uncle Seb mouths something that looks like "I'm sorry," and Aida whispers back "Me too."

All the adults at the table are exchanging guilty glances, even my grandparents.

And then, with a jolt, I understand.

They're remembering all the ways *they* fucked up.

All the reasons we're in this mess in the first place.

And even if they're right that Leo can be just a little bit reckless...

I'm not going to let them gang up on him. Not on Christmas Eve. Not even my dad.

So I grab Leo's hand beneath the table and squeeze it hard. My voice cuts across the room, high and clear.

"You're all afraid because you remember the scars from the bad decisions you made when you were younger." Some of those scars are literal, like the six bullet wounds on Uncle Nero's back. I stare him right in the eye, and Uncle Seb too. "Leo's eighteen. Where are his scars? He doesn't have any, because he knows what he's doing! He makes good choices. He's the most popular kid at our school. Everyone loves him. Maybe he'll mend things with Dean!" I'm becoming reckless, but I don't care, because I believe it as I say it. I believe in Leo. "He'll figure out a way to fix it. I've seen him do incredible things. You should trust him."

Leo stares at me, open-mouthed. For once, he's speechless.

I am too.

I don't think I've ever talked that much at once at a family gathering.

It's received with the usual dignity.

Marshall Boone rolls his eyes. "When it comes to Leo, Anna's never biased."

Creed Boone reminds me, "You slept with Sailor Moon sheets until you were fourteen years old."

Did I think I loved these people?

Now I'm understanding why so many murders happen around the holidays.

It doesn't matter. Leo gives me a grin that makes it all worth it, squeezing my hand and mouthing "Thank you" before letting go.

"Besides," he says to his dad, reclaiming his confidence, "Dean can't *actually* kill me. They're pretty strict about that whole eye-for-an-eye murder rule."

"You're saying if he kills you, they'll kill him back?" Uncle Seb snorts. "Never go to war with someone who has nothing to lose."

"Don't be simple," Nero snaps. "There's plenty of ways to get away with murder."

Leo better hope Uncle Nero doesn't think of one later tonight if he's still sore about that snippy comment.

Aunt Aida's finally ready to lighten the mood. "Do we have to wait for pie?"

"I'm only here for pie," Marshall Boone says, seizing a stack of plates. What do you know? Pie is what it takes to get Marshall to be helpful.

I gather the glasses, threading them through my fingers like the stems of a bouquet. Leo rises to do the same.

My head feels light and floating, full of bubbles. I drank two of those glasses of champagne, and now I'm wondering if Leo might like to come look at the snow with me again, now that the moon is out.

He pauses in the doorway, his fingertips resting on my hip.

"Did you want to tell me something earlier?"

"What?" I say, heat in my face.

"Earlier." Leo looks in my eyes, his golden and close. "I thought maybe you wanted to tell me something."

The moment resurfaces, the whisper in my head… *Tell him.*

My lips part, like they know what to say.

"Kiss her!"

The shout splits us apart.

Aunt Aida's laughing at the mistletoe over our heads. She's had too much to drink. Or maybe not—she kind of behaves the same either way.

"Kiss her," she teases Leo, her expression mischievous and taunting.

And in that moment, when I look up into Leo's face, I think *Oh my god, he's actually going to do it. Right here, with everyone watching.*

The dining room disappears.

Leo's eyes are all I see, gazing into mine.

His full lips part. He dips his head.

And drops a kiss on my forehead.

The kind of kiss you'd give to a little sister. Or a cousin you've known all your life.

Humiliation sweeps down, a red, boiling curtain. I hear Marshall's hoot, and I'd give everything I own to punch him in the jaw.

But then he might see tears on my face. Or Leo might see something much worse.

All I can do is turn and run.

Leo finds me an hour later, long after the ice has entered my soul. I've been sitting out in the gazebo, punishing myself for being that fucking pathetic.

He takes off his jacket and wraps it around my shoulders. "Tell me you haven't been sitting out here the whole time."

"I haven't." The lie comes out easy. Scary easy, considering I never lie to Leo.

"Good." His face melts with relief.

Oh my god. He can't tell. I always thought he'd be able to tell if I lied to him.

"You're cold, though." Leo puts his warm palms on the outsides of my frozen arms and rubs vigorously.

"You've got a fat lip."

He touches the place where his lower lip is split, right down the center. "Oh yeah. I beat the shit out of Marshall."

My face flushes. "What for?"

"You saw. He was asking for it."

Without his coat, Leo's only wearing his T-shirt, but he doesn't seem cold. He leans forward on his knees, huge hands crossed loosely in front of him, plumes of steam coming out of his warm lungs.

His breath touches my face. The coat hangs around me like a cocoon, toasty warm, covering me neck to knee, the cuffs hanging over my hands.

It's the best feeling in the world. The absolute best.

If I don't want to lose it, I know what I have to do.

Leo glances over at me. He bites at his split lip, worrying the cut with the tip of his tongue.

"Sorry about earlier."

"What do you mean?" A slight toss of my head.

"With the mistletoe—"

"That was nothing," I interrupt, looking only at the blank snow, not meeting his eyes.

"Oh." Leo hesitates, less certain. "I thought maybe—"

"No." I'm firm, while inside I'm screaming. "I was just embarrassed. Everybody looking. Sometimes Aida—"

"I know. She's an asshole."

"It doesn't matter." *Lie lie lie lie lie!* "Seriously, don't worry about it. I'm sick of all of them. I can't wait to get out of here."

"Me too." Leo sighs with relief.

He's glad I'm letting it drop. Glad we can just pretend the whole thing never happened.

But inside me, something is ripping.

In fact, it's already gone.

Whatever rogue part of my heart was rebelling, beating, begging for more, I've torn it away and encased it in ice.

What it wants can never happen.

It would destroy everything I love.

So it has to freeze and die.

When I'm calm and composed once more, I look at Leo. "Are you really coming with me? Even if Dean—"

"I'm coming." His eyes are locked on mine with that stubborn certainty I know so well. It means Leo's going to do what he wants to do, even if our entire family is set against him. But then he blinks and says, "If you want me to."

I know what I *should* say to Leo—what his parents would want me to say.

Leo could have a real career in basketball. He got offers at plenty of schools besides Duke.

The blood feud with the Yenins is no joke. They killed Leo's great-grandfather. They shot Nero. For Leo's safety alone, I should keep him far away from Kingmakers.

But to do that, I'd have to tell another lie.

Leo waits for my answer, his head cocked to the side, his hands thrust in his pockets, his white T-shirt as crisp and glowing as the falling snow against the burned brown of his bare arms.

I fling my arms around him.

Nose pressed in the soft waves of hair around his ear, I whisper, "Whether it's wrong or right, I'm always going to want you with me."

CHAPTER 1
LEO

WE'RE TWENTY-THREE MINUTES INTO THE STATE CHAMPIONSHIP game.

We're playing Simeon, an athletic powerhouse stocked with muscle-bound behemoths who look like they started shaving in the second grade and might have been born with a basketball in their hands.

Every one of their players is better than every kid on my team.

Except for me.

And I am all I need.

I'm paired up against Johnson Bell, their power forward. He's six seven, a full two inches taller than me. He's fast, and he's strong, I'm not gonna lie. And most of all, he's fucking cheap.

This motherfucker has been chippy with me all game. Chopping at my arms, charging me, slashing me with his uncut fingernails like he's trying to embody the wolverine plastered across his chest.

He knows as well as I do that the head coach for the Kentucky Wildcats is sitting right in the front row at center court, watching us both.

Bell wants to be a star.

I already am a star. And I don't give a fuck about that scout. I'm not going to Kentucky—or anywhere else on this continent.

But I *am* going to win this game.

Bell takes the ball up the court, trying to drive past me. He does some fancy dancing with his giant feet in his vintage Jordans. It doesn't faze me for a second. I keep my eye on his navel. Like my dad always says, you can't go anywhere without your belly button.

Without even looking at the ball, I slap it away from him with my left hand, knocking it over to my right. I plow past him in the opposite direction, sprinting for the basket.

Their guard tries to block me, and I pull up short, sending a gorgeous arcing shot over his grasping fingers. I'm seven feet behind the three-point line, and it doesn't matter a bit—the ball drops through the net without even grazing the rim.

The roar of the crowd hits me like a slap. My eardrums vibrate. My heart thrums in my chest.

There's no feeling quite like being adored by a thousand people at once.

The buzzer sounds, signaling the end of the first half. I go jogging back across the court while my teammates slap me on the back. We're up six points.

While my team hustles down the tunnel toward the locker room, the dance team is running in the opposite direction up to the court. Anna and I pass each other in the darkened hallway.

She's all dolled up in her drill gear—blond hair pulled up in a high pony, face painted, and every inch of her sprayed with glitter. It always makes me laugh to see her in her dance clothes, since bright and tight is the opposite of what she wears normally.

She gives me a fist bump as we pass, saying in her low voice, "You're gonna win, Leo."

"I know." I grin back at her.

Anna is my best friend. We grew up together, closer than siblings. Our fathers run this city together. Our mothers went through their pregnancies together, Anna and I born only two months apart. She's older than me, which she loves to rub in my face every chance she gets.

Anna is the only person I've met more intense than me. Sometimes she scares me a little. But mostly she's my balance, my rock.

Here at Preston Heights, I'm the fucking man.

Everybody wants a piece of me. They all want to sit by me or talk to me. All the girls want to date me.

They think they know Leo Gallo.

Anna is the only person who actually does.

She knows exactly who I am, and she doesn't try to change a damn thing about me. Unlike my parents.

I saw my mom and dad sitting two rows behind the Kentucky coach, just a little to his right. They never miss my games. They're always here, cheering me on. Celebrating my wins even more than I do.

It's my dad who taught me how to play. He was a college star himself, before he and Uncle Cal got in some kind of scrap and his knee got all fucked up.

Doesn't mean he can't still work me on the court, though. My dad taught me everything I know. He practiced with me, drilled me, taught me how to read my opponent, how to watch the flow of players on the court, how to outwit and outplay every guy I came up against. How to destroy them mentally and physically. How to beat them before I even made my first move.

My father's pretty fucking smart. You don't become the don of Chicago any other way. And you sure as hell don't stay there being stupid.

He taught me how to play basketball.

But what I actually want is for him to teach me how to run the world.

I'm not trying to be an athlete. I'm trying to be a king.

I'm still gonna win this game, though. Because I win everything, always.

We head back to the locker room so the coach can tell us how we fucked up and how we're supposed to fix it in the second half.

I'm barely listening to him. I've watched more game tape from before I was born than this guy has ever seen. He's just a teacher who happens to have the best damn player in the country on his team.

I gulp down a lukewarm cup of Gatorade while listening to the pounding beat of "Billie Jean" emanating from the gym. I've seen Anna practice this number a dozen times, but I still ache to be out there watching her live, in costume, in front of all these people.

Her parents are sitting right next to mine—Mikolaj and Nessa Wilk, the boss of the Polish Braterstwo and the princess of the Irish Mafia.

Anna's parents started out as enemies, a lot like mine. And just like mine, they're weirdly obsessed with each other. I guess Anna and I should be glad we both come from families with parents that love each other, but Jesus, you shouldn't have to tell grown adults to get a room.

Anna is to dance what I am to basketball—the fucking best. She makes the rest of the girls on her team look like they've got clown shoes strapped to their feet. She's always front and center, grabbing your eye from the second she starts dancing and refusing to let go until long after the music fades away.

I'm pulled back toward her, even though I know Coach will be pissed if I don't stay till the bitter end of his motivational speech. I wait until he's at a particularly rousing point, then I pretend like I think that was the end of it, leaping to my feet and shouting, "That's right, Coach. We got you! Let's get out there and win this fucking thing!"

The locker room breaks out in whoops and howls, everybody stomping the floor and chanting like we're Spartans going off to war.

We run back out to the court, me ahead of everybody else, wanting to catch the end of Anna's dance.

Her team is dressed in some kind of bizarre Day of the Dead skeleton getup. Their faces are painted like bejeweled skulls with flowers in their hair.

Anna is captain of her dance team and head choreographer. Watching her numbers is like watching a fever dream. They're wild, intense, and hard-hitting. The pounding bass of the song shakes the bleachers, and the girls look like they're possessed, none more than Anna.

You'd think she doesn't have a bone in her body. She flings herself around, strong and precise and tight as a whip.

I take back what I said about the other girls—Anna is a ruthless drill sergeant, and they absolutely know how to hit their marks. It's just that no one comes alive like Anna. She looks supernatural as she whirls through her triple pirouette, then drops down in the splits. The crowd screams just as loud as they did for me.

The dance team are champions in their own right. They took nationals all three years that Anna was captain, even beating out those bitches from Utah who had been formerly unbeatable with their bleached blond hair and mile-wide smiles.

I almost forget that we're in the middle of a game.

I forget everything but the low, flashing light and the throbbing beat and wild, brilliant dancers. They're supposed to be hyping up the crowd, keeping the energy high during the break. They've done much more than that—they've brought a new level of darkness and intensity to the proceedings. They've made it seem as if this game truly is a matter of life and death.

The song ends, and the overhead lights burst on. I remember that I'm in a high school gymnasium. I smell the sweat and rubber and floor polish once more. I see my parents looking proud and anxious and Uncle Miko and Aunt Nessa looking how they always do—Miko somber and intent, Nessa bright-eyed and eager.

Anna is leaving the floor, giving me a wave on her way out. A boy in a varsity jacket intercepts her. I don't recognize him—he must go to Simeon. He blocks her path, trying to engage her in conversation.

I can't hear what they're saying, but from the smirk on his face and the way he grabs her arm without permission, I'm guessing it's something along the lines of "Hey girl, you're pretty flexible. I'd like to see you wrap those legs around my head."

It's the kind of thing guys used to say to Anna at our school, until they learned their lesson.

I grin, knowing exactly what's about to happen.

Anna grabs his hand off her arm and bends his wrist back, all the pressure concentrated on his pinkie. Even from across the gym, I hear the varsity douche scream like a little girl.

Anna brushes past him, whipping him in the face with her ponytail as she passes. The guy cradles his hand, muttering something under his breath.

I cast a quick glance at Uncle Miko.

He watched that whole exchange the same as I did. Now his ice-blue eyes are narrowed to slits, his jaw rigid with rage.

All I can say is that kid is pretty fucking lucky to get off with nothing more than a sprained wrist. If he put one more finger on Anna, he wasn't likely to make it home tonight.

Grinning, I jog over to the bench to slug down a last gulp of water before the ref blows his whistle.

Moments later, the game is back in full swing, and we're running harder than ever. My team is amped, but so are the Wolverines. They're running a full-court press, fueled by fury that the game is even this close when they're supposed to be the best team in the state.

They are the best team. But they don't have the best player.

Johnson Bell is fighting hard for that title.

He's a big dude, thick with muscle, sweat dripping down his face just two minutes into the third quarter. I'll give him credit, he's the toughest opponent I've faced this year. But tough just isn't good enough.

Still, it's hard carrying the rest of these assholes all on my own. Kelly Barrett misses an easy layup, and Chris Pellie turns the ball over twice. I have to make four more baskets just to keep the game even.

As the third quarter comes to a close, my team is up three points.

I'm driving to the hoop when that fucker Bell comes up hard behind me. I jump to shoot, I'm up in the air, and he knocks my feet right out from under me. He sends me pinwheeling, crashing down in an awkward sprawl that slams the air out of me.

The crowd gasps and then starts to boo, at least on the home team side. The Wolverine fans laugh and jeer at me.

That makes me angrier than anything. I *hate* being laughed at.

Bell gets the foul, but I want him kicked out of the fucking game. You don't go at somebody's feet—it's dangerous, and it's goddamn disrespectful. I haul myself up, breath wheezing in my lungs, and whirl around to face him. He smirks at me, his big dumb face showing nothing but pride.

I'd like to murder him.

But all I can do is take my shots.

I sink them both. That doesn't relax me in the slightest. Blood throbs against my temples. All I see is Bell's smug face.

The Wolverines inbound the ball. Their point guard brings it up the court, then passes to Bell. I guard him, tracking him closely. He dribbles carefully, knowing I'm fast as fuck and I'd love to steal the ball back in revenge.

He doesn't know I've got something better planned.

If he wants to play dirty, I'm happy to roll around in the mud.

I pretend to go in for the steal, and instead I shoulder-check him hard in the face. My shoulder slams into his nose. I hear his grunt and the instant patter of blood dripping down on the boards.

"Oops." I grin.

Bell's eyes are already swelling up as he takes his place at the free-throw line.

He makes the first but misses the second, blinded by the pain in his face. I laugh to myself quietly.

The buzzer rings to signal the end of the third quarter.

The coach immediately hauls me to the side, chewing me out for hitting Bell like that.

"How many times have I told you not to lose your temper? Don't you know the Kentucky coach is right up there in the stands watching you? You think he wants some hothead on his team?"

"I think he wants the best." I push past the coach so I can wipe my face with a towel.

The last quarter is a fucking brawl. My team is pissed, the Wolverines even angrier. The ball turns over again and again as we battle for every single point.

The coach calls a time-out so he can set the next play. Pulling us into a huddle, he says, "Barrett, you're gonna set a screen for Brown. Pellie will inbound the ball to Brown, Brown will take it up the court, and once he gets past half-court, Gallo will come and set a high screen. Brown will drive to the hoop, and if you have a shot, then take it. If you get covered, give the ball to Miller instead."

I can hardly bite back my retort to that cockamamie bullshit.

Me, set a screen? You've gotta be joking.

I carried this team to the state championship on my fucking back.

I don't even bother to argue with the coach. He's the one who's gotten emotional over that foul, and now he's not thinking straight.

Instead, I wait till Chris Pellie gets his hands on the ball, and I hiss at him, "Forget what Coach said. You pass the ball to me."

Pellie's eyes get big in his face, so he looks like a little kid.

"Wh-what?" he stammers.

"You heard me. Throw me that ball, or I'll break every finger you've got."

Pellie gulps.

He takes his position behind the line.

Everybody is set up. The ref still has the ball. I'm walking over all slow and casual, standing upright, like I'm barely gonna play.

The whistle blows. Teeth bared and eyes terrified, Pellie chucks me the ball. The moment it touches my hands, I drop down into cheetah stance and take off like a fucking rocket.

I blow past the point guards before they can even blink.

Five seconds left. Four…

I can hear the coach screaming and waving his arms on the sidelines, red with fury that I disobeyed him. It only makes me chuckle. That's what he gets for trying to hold me back.

I'm going coast to coast like Danny Ainge in his '81 game. I'm flying down the court in six strides with these long legs that were meant for nothing better than this.

The Wolverines don't know what to do. You're not supposed to take the game into your own hands. Not with four seconds left. Not in the state championships.

I don't slow down for a second. I can't lose my momentum.

I should go right. It's my dominant hand, and that's where the center is standing, a big dumb oaf, the slowest dude on the team.

But there's Bell standing to the left of the hoop. The motherfucker who shoved me and slashed my arms to bits like a bitchy little kitten and then took my legs out from under me.

He's gonna pay for that.

I charge him like a bull.

If he held his ground, I'd have to go around him. But he doesn't plant his feet. He's lost his nerve, lost his focus. His feet stumble back.

I bend my knees and spring upward into a Herculean jump, higher than any I've taken before. Fueled by adrenaline and spite, I go right over that six-foot-seven motherfucker. I vault him like a hurdle, my legs going over his shoulders and my crotch right over his face. He falls backward onto his ass.

You know what "posterized" means?

Think of every poster you ever saw featuring Jordan or Kobe making the most beautiful dunks of their life.

For every epic, timeless poster, there's some idiot trying to guard that all-time great, their hands up and their face scrunched with dismay while the god of basketball sails right over them.

I posterize Johnson Bell with my balls in his face.

It's so beautiful I could cry.

Roaring like a lion, I slam the ball down in the hoop in a loud, aggressive, spectacular dunk of death.

As the ball bounces against the ground, the buzzer shrills.

I can barely hear it beneath the collective scream of the crowd. Every person in the gym has leapt to their feet, pumping their fists and howling.

My whole team swarms me, whooping and slapping me on the back. I look down at Bell sprawled out on the boards, and I say, "When they give me the ring, I'll carve your name inside it to remember the guy who licked my balls while I dunked the game winner."

Bell leaps to his feet, flinging himself at me with both fists swinging. My teammates shove him back while I laugh in his face.

I'm high on triumph. It's running through my veins, more intoxicating than any drug.

I look around, not for my parents, because I already know they're cheering for me. I want to see if Anna was watching.

It's impossible to find her—the fans are covering the court. My dad claps me on the shoulder and pulls me into a hug.

"You know the Kentucky coach was here watching."

I roll my eyes. "Yeah, Dad, I know."

My mom kisses me on the cheek, not caring how sweaty I am.

"Well done," she says in her understated way.

You can still hear the hint of a Russian accent in her voice and the full measure of Russian stoicism where you could win the goddamn Olympics and they'd give you a nod and a "Could be better" as their compliment.

I just grin, because I know my parents adore me. I'm their only child. The center of their world.

"Not bad," a low voice says.

I turn around.

Anna is standing there, dressed in her torn-up jeans and leather jacket once more. She's washed some of the makeup off her face, so she no longer looks like the corpse bride, but plenty of black liner remains, smeared around her pale blue eyes.

That's the moment when I really feel like I won—when I see the smile she can't possibly hold back lighting up her face.

I sweep her up in the biggest hug and swing her around.

When I set her down, she says, "Hi, Uncle Seb. Hi, Aunt Yelena," politely.

"Did you choreograph that dance, Anna?" my dad asks her. "That was incredible!"

"Most of it," Anna says. "I took a few of the eight counts from Mom's burlesque ballet. With a few modifications."

Aunt Nessa smiles. "I thought it looked familiar. I can't believe you remembered that. That was forever ago. You couldn't have been more than…six?"

"Anna remembers everything," Uncle Miko says. Then, frowning, he demands, "Who was that boy?"

"What boy?" Aunt Nessa is oblivious.

"Nobody." Anna tosses her head disdainfully.

"Next time, you break his wrist," Uncle Miko orders, his lips still pale and thin with anger.

"Power is not only in what we do but in what we don't do," Anna quotes calmly.

"Don't use my own words against me." Uncle Miko sounds stern, but I know him well enough to catch the hint of a smile on his face.

"Was there a problem?" my father asks, frowning.

"No," Anna assures him. "Unless you consider an overprotective father to be a problem."

My dad grins at Uncle Miko. "You shouldn't have married such a pretty wife if you didn't want beautiful daughters."

"I know." Uncle Miko frowns. "A serious strategic error."

"Don't let Seb tease you," my mom says. "He'd be even worse if we had girls."

She's joking, but I hear the sadness in her voice. My parents wanted more kids. They tried for years and did four rounds of IVF. In the end, they were given the extremely helpful diagnosis of "unexplained infertility."

They had to be satisfied with me—the accidental pregnancy that was never followed by another.

"What should we do to celebrate?" my dad says, changing the subject swiftly and tactfully.

"We should go for dinner!" Aunt Nessa says. "Someplace fancy, to celebrate you champions."

Anna and I exchange a quick glance.

It's not that we don't want to go for dinner with our parents. But there's gonna be ten different ragers to celebrate the championship and the end of the school year.

Catching the look, my mom says, "Why don't we all get ice cream, and then you two can meet up with your friends?"

"That sounds great." Anna smiles. "Thanks, Aunt Yelena."

"Have you been to Pie Cone?" my mom says, linking arms with Aunt Nessa. "All the ice cream is pie-flavored. Key lime pie, pumpkin pie, blackberry crumble…"

"Oh my god." Nessa laughs. "You already sold me at 'ice cream.'"

CHAPTER 2
DEAN

The underground fight club of Moscow is literally underground, in what was once an abandoned metro station. Now it functions as a spot for raves, drug deals, and bare-knuckle boxing tournaments run by the Bratva.

The shouts of the crowd echo down the tunnel where the train tracks are overgrown with weeds and clogged with discarded hypodermic needles. You can still see the remains of faded billboards plastered on the curved walls, advertising products that haven't been sold since the fall of the Soviet Union. Over that is layer upon layer of graffiti in dripping spray paint.

It's chilly down here, at least ten degrees colder than at street level. I keep my hoodie on until the last moment so my muscles stay warm.

"Who are you fighting?" Armen asks me.

He's smoking a cigarette, even though he's supposed to fight in a minute himself.

"Chelovek," I say.

"He's pretty big," Armen remarks.

"Pretty fuckin' slow too."

Armen takes a long drag, exhaling the blue smoke up to the vaulted ceilings, then crushes the butt under his heel.

"I'll bet on you," he says, as if he's doing me a favor.

"I'm not betting on you," I tell him.

Armen laughs. "That's why you're rich and I'm broke."

"Dmitry!" Boris shouts. "You're up."

I'm the first fight of the night. When I'm fighting, I use my Russian name. I use it for most everything when I'm in Moscow.

I strip off my hoodie, baring my body to the cold. The chill feels like an electric current against my skin. I can smell the scent of Armen's cheap cigarette and the damp mold of the subway tunnel. Also the sweat of the fifty or so men crowded on the platform and the tang of alcohol from the flasks in their jackets.

There's no ring. We fight in a chalk circle. If we step outside the circle, the spectators will shove us back in again.

Boris is the event organizer. He's not Bratva himself, though he works for them. He's skinny with a shaved head and spacers in both ears, wearing a long coat with a fur collar. His best attribute is his loud, raspy voice that cuts over the noise of the crowd, no microphone required.

I step into the circle, bouncing lightly on my toes. I'm wearing only a pair of trunks now and flat sneakers. My hands are taped.

Chelovek strolls into the other side of the circle. I haven't fought him before, but I know who he is. He's got a thatch of ginger hair shaved into a Mohawk and a tattoo of a snake-ridden skull sprawled across his chest. He goes by Ryzhiy Chelovek, which basically means Copper Top.

We're about the same height, a little over six two. While I'm lean and wiry, he's beefy to the point of softness. In real boxing, he'd be way outside my weight class. In the underground fights, they just call this a "thick and thin."

We face off against each other. He raises his fists up under his chin, shoulders hunched. I stand exactly as I am, with my arms at my sides.

I haven't fought Chelovek before. I've seen how he moves, though. In fact, I can tell what sort of fighter he'll be just by the way he walked into the ring: brash, swaggering, and overconfident.

Sure enough, as soon as Boris blows his whistle, Chelovek comes at me with both fists flying, thinking that if he can land a solid punch, I'll go down hard.

I duck the blows easily. *Left, right, left, left, right, right.*

Jesus, he's so predictable. I can see each punch coming from a mile away.

He's already breathing hard. Either he smokes like Armen or he's been neglecting his cardio. Probably the latter. That's why he's so soft around the middle.

I duck down and give him a sharp punch to the gut, testing his muscle tone. He grunts and exhales hard. He's neglected his crunches too, apparently.

I can hear the spectators shouting their bets. Those who bet on Chelovek initially are now trying to hedge. But the numbers aren't as much in his favor anymore.

I can see my father's friend Danyl standing at the edge of the ring. He's got his hands tucked in his pockets, smiling toothily. I'm sure he knew better than to bet against me.

Of course my father isn't here himself to watch me win. He never comes to my fights. It takes a lot more than that to get him to leave the house.

I block another haymaker from Chelovek, and he hits me in the side with a left hook. I feel an unpleasant bending of the ribs, and I hunch over enough that his next blow catches me on the ear, making my head ring.

That pisses me off, but I don't let my anger get the better of me. I shove it down, like coal in a furnace. I want the rage to fuel me without letting the fire run wild.

I watch for my opening.

Left, right, left, left—

This time, I interrupt Chelovek's sequence with an uppercut to the jaw. His teeth click together hard, and his head snaps back. He stumbles back on his heels, dazed and pained.

I pursue the advantage, hitting him twice in the body and again in the head. Now I know his ears are ringing worse than mine.

Chelovek spits a little blood onto the platform, raising his fists once more, steadying himself.

He comes at me slower now, more carefully. He learned his lesson. Or at least he thinks he did.

I could wear him down like this. Let him tire himself out while I duck his blows. He doesn't have the stamina to keep it up for long.

But I made my own bet on the fight. I've got to knock him out in the first round.

Only twenty-two seconds left, according to the count I'm keeping in my head.

If I want the KO, I'll have to set a trap.

Chelovek is annoyed and embarrassed. He wants to hit me. If I offer a tempting bait, he'll jump at it.

I send a couple of quick jabs at his face, popping him lightly on the nose to piss him off even more. Then I hold my fists high, exposing that same right side to his left hook.

Sure enough, Chelovek swings hard for my ribs. He hits me in the same place as before, and this time I hear a pop and feel the sickening hot burn of a rib cracking.

It doesn't matter. I've already sent a right cross rocketing down toward his jaw. I hit him in the exact spot where the jawbone meets the skull. I can feel the bone separating. I watch the whole bottom half of his face pop out of alignment.

Chelovek doesn't feel it. He's already unconscious before he hits the ground. He goes down like a tree, straight and wooden, unable to even put his hands up.

The winners shout in triumph, and even those who lost their bets can't help howling.

I stand tall in the ring, refusing to acknowledge the pain in my side.

Boris grabs my fist and hoists it aloft.

"Once again, Dmitry Yenin takes the win! That's six matches now, still undefeated!"

Boris stuffs a wad of bills in my hand, my winnings from the fight.

I don't care about forty thousand rubles. I won ten times that amount betting on myself. I'll collect it from Danyl later.

Still, I stuff the money in the pocket of my shorts.

I wince a little as I bend down to pick my hoodie up off the concrete.

Armen is smoking again while bouncing lightly on his toes to warm up. He's taken off his hoodie and sweatpants, revealing a truly stunning pair of silk shorts emblazoned with a gold tiger across the crotch.

"Not bad," he says to me. "Glad I put a whole two thousand on you."

"Bet Chelovek wishes he did too."

"I think Chelovek wishes he never crawled out of his mother's cunt." Armen leaks his wheezy laughter.

"Good luck," I tell him.

"You're not staying to watch me fight?"

"Nah. You got everything you need to win."

"Really?" Armen says.

"Yeah. Except speed, stamina, and technique."

Armen stares at me for a second, then bursts out laughing again.

"Get the fuck outta here," he snorts.

"You got those shorts at least."

Armen grins. "That I do."

I head back down the tunnel, walking along the deserted tracks. I hear Boris's whistle signaling the start of Armen's match and the shouts as his backers cheer him on. The noise fades away as I round a curve in the tunnel.

I pass the staircase that would take me back up to street level. I prefer to walk down to the old Park Kultury station and go up from there. This is a more direct route, cutting under the Moskva River. Plus I like it down in the tunnels. It's dark and quiet. At some points, you can hear the vibration and rushing sounds of the trains passing by on parallel tracks that are still operational. Other spots, you can hear the river itself running overhead.

I've got my phone out so the screen casts just enough light to see the tracks ahead of me. "Major Tom" plays quietly on my earbuds, my steps falling in time to the beat.

I shut the music off when I hear a scuffling sound up ahead. Not a rat. Something worse than that.

Fucking junkies.

There's three of them, two men and a woman. If you can even call them that. They look scraggly and feral, and I can smell them from twenty feet away.

Who knows what the fuck they're doing down here. They've got a duffel bag on the ground in the middle of their little huddle, and it looks like they're pulling things out of it. Probably stolen from somebody on the subway or on a crowded street up above.

If they're smart, they'll let me pass by.

Two of them have the right idea.

But the third stands up, twitchy and bright-eyed.

"Hey," he says. "Where you goin'?"

I ignore him, continuing to walk past.

"Hey!" he shouts a little louder in his raspy voice. "I'm talkin' to you!"

His lank, unwashed hair hangs around his shoulders. He's wearing a jacket with nothing underneath, his skinny chest bare. He's got scabs on his face and body, and I can tell from the stiff way he walks that his feet are swollen. The effects of krokodil.

The government has tried to stamp it out a dozen times, but it always pops up again. It's just so cheap to make. You can cook it in your kitchen with shit bought from pharmacies and hardware stores: hydrochloric acid, paint thinner, and phosphorus scraped off the side of a matchbox.

It's an imitation of heroin, just as addictive. The only downside is the way your flesh rots away from the injection site and your brain starts to atrophy inside your skull. Which doesn't lead to the best decision-making.

Which is why this fucker thinks it's a good idea to talk to me.

"That a new iPhone?" he demands, eyeing my phone greedily.

I stop walking, turning to face him slowly.

"You want to fuck off now," I tell him. I slip the phone into my pocket so my hands are free. While I'm doing that, I close my fingers around the smooth handle of my switchblade instead.

Without that faint blue light, the tunnel is even dimmer. It doesn't matter. I'm sure I can see better than the three junkies.

They're all standing now, fanning out silently so the woman is in front of me, the two men trying to flank me.

"Give us the phone," the second man hisses.

The problem with fighting these three is that I have no idea what diseases they might be carrying. One scratch from an uncut fingernail and I could get hepatitis.

As they close in around me, I plan to end it quick.

The guy on the right charges first. I send him stumbling backward with a kick to the chest. The second guy isn't as lucky. I press the button to flick out my blade while it's already whistling through the air toward his torso. I stab him in the liver with medical precision, then jerk the blade back before I get any blood on me. It still splashes down on the toe of my sneaker.

He drops to his knees, groaning.

That takes the steam out of the other two.

The girl raises her hands, blubbering, "We don't want any trouble."

I tell her coldly, "Then fuck off like I said."

She grabs the duffel bag and scrambles off down the tunnel, the opposite direction I was walking.

The guy I kicked looks at his fallen friend, then at me. He runs after the girl, abandoning the man I stabbed.

I ignore him too, continuing on down the tunnel.

He'll probably bleed to death, but the thought doesn't disturb me any more than the knowledge that every butterfly you see will be dead in a month's time. That's the cycle of life—junkies die young, from the drugs, the company they keep, or trying to rob the wrong person in a tunnel.

I continue on my way until I reach the staircase up to Krymskiy Proyezd.

Spring in Moscow is hell.

There's a word the Russians use to describe it: *slyakot*, which means "slush mud." That's partly why I stayed down in the tunnels—so I wouldn't have to navigate the torrents of thick brown mud, stiff with ice crystals.

The roads in Moscow are always shit. But in the springtime, you have to worry that you're about to step through a slush drift into a pothole that will break your ankle. The sidewalks become crowded with shuffling, slipping pedestrians, and the traffic is worse than ever. The melting snowdrifts are black from a whole winter's worth of car exhaust.

Without any proper drainage system, the melted snow sits in stagnant puddles. It's *rasputitsa*—the time of the year "when roads stop existing."

I hate Moscow.

I'm an American. I was born in Chicago. My mother is American.

Yet my father brought me here, back to the city he never loved. Back to the environment so miserable that it drove my mother to drink herself half to death, until the only way to save herself was to leave.

I'll be leaving soon myself.

Going to the one place my father will support—the one thing he won't view as abandonment.

Finally, I reach Korobeynikov Lane, where the slush has been painstakingly cleared from the street for the benefit of the elite residents of Noble Row. It's a long sandstone building divided into six luxury residences, worth about twenty-one million each in American dollars.

That's where I live with my father.

I would assume that the other five houses on Noble Row are bright and clean inside, full of sparkling chandeliers and gleaming woodwork.

That's not how our house looks. Not on the inside.

It's dark, crowded, and filthy, because my father won't allow any maids. He won't let anyone in the house but me. Not since my mother left.

He's holed up in there like Howard Hughes, only leaving when he absolutely has to handle his business in person. And he's barely managing that these days.

I open our front door, struck in the face by a waft of stale and dusty air. It smells like the carpets haven't been vacuumed in six years, which they haven't. It smells like the windows are never opened and the walls are full of mice.

It's dark inside, almost as dark as the train tunnel. The heavy drapes that hang floor to ceiling are all pulled shut. It's as quiet as a tomb.

You can still see the remnants of my mother's decorating from the time when we first moved here, when I was a toddler and she still had the motivation for projects.

I don't actually remember that time, other than a few snippets—a few bright flashes nestled in my memory like jewels. My mother with paint streaks on her face, laughing and telling me not to ride my tricycle in the house. My father coming home dressed nicely in a suit, bringing me a little bag of Tula gingerbread, asking me to guess in which pocket it was hiding.

I can see the work she did—the blue floral wallpaper in the dining room. The gold chandelier shaped like elk horns. The soapstone fireplace with its pile of white birch logs, never burned, never touched since.

All those rooms are filled with shit now. Piles of books stacked taller than I stand. Piles of newspapers too. Magazines, old bills, and receipts. And then the boxes: things my father ordered and never even opened.

So many boxes. Telescopes and globes. Toasters and binoculars. Stationery, photography equipment, power tools, and shoes. I couldn't guess what's in half of them. I don't know why my father started ordering all this crap. And I don't know why he piles it up on tables and chairs, never even bothering to look at most of it.

I climb the long, curving staircase up to his office. He expects me to check in when I get home at night.

I knock on the door, waiting for him to say "Enter" before I turn the knob.

He's seated behind his vast walnut desk, dressed neatly in a dark suit with a cleric collar. His ash-blond hair is combed back. He has carefully shaved the side of his face that grows hair.

His hands are folded on the desktop in front of him—one smooth and pale, one red and scarred. That hand doesn't work as well as the other. The tissue is so tough and knotted that he can't even grip a pen.

My father is jarring to look at.

He's so handsome and so ugly at the same time.

The left side of his face is beautiful almost to the point of femininity—his eye a particular shade of blue that almost looks violet, striking against his fair skin and white-blond hair.

The right side is a mass of blistered, discolored flesh, like a dry river bottom baked and cracked by the sun. His hair is burned back to show a patch of shiny skull, with no eyebrow on that side. Even the eye itself is milky and pale. He can't see out of it. His mouth twists up at the corner as if he's smirking, though he never actually is.

The scars run all the way down the right side of his body. Down his arm and leg.

He looks like a strange kind of cyborg—part human, part something else. Not robot—monster instead.

I've only ever seen him without a shirt on one time. He hates to be viewed that way. He hates to be viewed any way, really.

He's only become more sensitive about his appearance over time.

When I was small, he would let me sit on his lap and touch the roughly wrinkled skin on his right hand.

By the time my mother left, he wouldn't let her near him. They slept in separate rooms so she wouldn't even see him changing.

My father is a powerful man. He holds a high position within the Bratva—the *derzhatel obschaka*, the bookkeeper. The head accountant for all illegal dealings within the city of Moscow.

He has a team of men who work under him. He's subservient to only two men at the Moscow high table.

And of course, like any criminal, he has enemies.

But it wasn't his enemies who did this to him.

It was family.

All his deepest wounds have come from the people he loved.

He loved my mother once. Maybe he even loved me.

Not anymore.

He looks at me with his one good eye and that milky orb.

I used to think that my father's dual appearance represented the good and evil inside him. The days when he was kind and brought me gingerbread and the days when he raged and threw my mother's decorations against the wall, smashing everything inside the house.

Now I think there is no devil and angel inside people.

There's only the appearance of good and then what people actually are: weak and flawed. Destined to hurt you in the end.

My father looks at my boxing trunks.

"You fought today?"

I nod.

"Did you win?"

"Of course."

"Of course," my father mimics me. "You are arrogant."

"It's not arrogance if it's true. I've never been beaten."

My father snorts softly. "I sounded like you once. Stupidity must be universal at that age."

His good eye flits down to the toe of my shoe, where the junkie's blood makes a dark stain on the dingy canvas.

"Your blood or his?" he says.

"Neither. Someone tried to rob me on the way home."

My father nods without interest in hearing more. "They didn't know who your father is."

He's not bragging, just making a simple statement of fact. No one would attack the son of a Bratva on purpose.

He shoves something across the desk toward me. An envelope: heavy, expensive, and slate gray in color.

"What's that?"

"Open it."

I crack the wax seal keeping the flap closed and slip out the dual sheets of stationery, skimming down the ornate script.

"I was accepted," I say.

"Danyl Kuznetsov recommended you."

"I'll call to thank him."

"You'll do more than that. He expects two years of labor from you after you graduate."

I nod. It's a reasonable demand, considering the value of the favor.

Most students accepted to Kingmakers are from legacy families—those where the father, the grandfather, and the great-grandfather all attended the school.

My grandfather was part of a KGB task force, instructed to hunt down Bratva. He only rose through the ranks of the organization once he defected. The Bratva hated and distrusted him at first. He forced his way into their world. He advanced through violence and ruthlessness.

Kingmakers is beyond exclusive. They're scrupulous about who they allow through their doors. Only those who can be trusted with the secrets of Mafia families from around the world are allowed to enter.

I scan the letter once more.

"They accepted me to the Heirs division."

I wasn't sure if they would. Moscow is divided into three territories with three separate bosses. Technically, my father isn't one of them. But in our section of the city, the actual boss has no children, and neither does the next man down.

If I do well at Kingmakers, there's nothing stopping me from ascending to the position of *pakhan* in time.

I look at my father's face, searching for some hint of emotion: pleasure, anticipation, pride.

I see nothing.

"I'm tired," I tell him. "I'm going to bed early."

He nods and turns back to the papers spread across his desk.

I go down the long, gloomy hallway to my bedroom.

I strip off my clothes and stand under the boiling hot shower spray for as long as I can. Then I take my exfoliating sponge and roughly scrape every millimeter of my skin, cleansing the sweat from my fight, the filth from the subway tunnels, and any possible hair or skin cells that might have touched me from those fucking junkies.

I soap myself over and over, rinsing and then starting once more.

I always make sure that I'm perfectly clean, that I smell of nothing more offensive than soap. I do my own laundry, washing my clothes, my towels, and my sheets every time that I use them.

I can't stand the thought that I might accidentally smell as musty and unkempt as this house.

The scent clings to everything I own.

I hate that smell.

I hate coming home.

When I'm finally clean, I slip beneath the fresh sheets I put on the bed this morning.

I take a book from my nightstand, the one I've been reading the last three nights: *Midnight's Children*.

Cracking the spine, I read until the physical exhaustion of the fight finally overtakes the frantic bustle of my brain. Then I set the book down and let my eyelids drop, trying to remember only the words on the page without letting my mind wander.

I don't want to think about anything in my real life.

That's what books are for.

To take you away.

CHAPTER 3
ANNA

THREE MONTHS LATER

It's my last night sleeping in my own bed at home.

Tomorrow, I leave for Kingmakers for the entire school year.

Once we're at the school, we can't come home again until the next summer. It's part of the security measures necessary when you're bringing in children of rival Mafia families from all across the globe.

There's no cell phones allowed on the island. No laptops or iPads.

You can use landlines to call out, or you can write letters.

It's strange, and it's old-fashioned. It makes me feel more like I'm going to another world rather than simply to another country.

I've never been away from my family before.

We live in a mansion way out on the edge of the city. This house is already like our own secret world, away from everything else. The walls are so high and the trees are so thick that you wouldn't think there was anyone else within a hundred miles.

I love our house intensely. It has everything I need.

I've explored every inch of it from the time I was small. It's so old that it has dozens of tiny rooms and passageways. I used to climb into the dumbwaiter and lower myself down all the way to the kitchen. Or go through the secret hallway that runs from my father's office out to the astronomy tower. There's laundry chutes and a hidden staircase from the ballroom to the wine cellar.

And then there's the attic, stuffed with items left behind from five previous generations of occupants: tarnished silver mirrors, old gowns, record albums, jewelry, photographs, crumbling letters, yellowed lace tablecloths, candles melted away and chewed by mice, ancient cribs, and dusty bottles of perfume that still carry the remnants of fragrance.

I used to spend entire days up there, poking around in the moldy boxes, examining objects and putting them back again.

My younger sister, Cara, loves it even more than I do. She likes to go up there with a lamp and a bag of apples so she can write in her little notebook in the middle of two hundred years of history.

Cara thinks she's a poet or an author or something. She's always scribbling away on some new project. She never lets us see it, though.

Her work is probably pretty good, or as good as it can be coming from a fourteen-year-old. Cara is brilliant, though most people don't know it since she's so quiet. She got all our mother's sweetness but not her friendliness.

Whelan is the opposite. He's loud and outspoken and brash and sometimes a little asshole. We all adore him regardless, because he's the baby. But he can be sneaky and mischievous. His explorations of the house usually end with something broken or him howling because he got his head stuck between the iron railings over by the old carriage house.

My room looks down over the walled garden. It's a dark room with high Gothic windows, deep crimson walls, a massive fireplace, and ancient velvet canopies around the bed. It was the room my mother slept in when she first came to stay in this house.

My father kidnapped her. Snatched her right off the street. Then locked her up in this house for months.

Slowly, bit by bit, without realizing or wanting it, he fell in love with her, and she fell in love with him. Simultaneous Stockholm syndrome.

It's a strange love story, but everything about my family is strange.

When you grow up as a Mafia daughter, you learn the history of your people the way the Roman emperors must have done. You learn the triumphs and failures of your ancestors, their bloody struggles and their revenge.

My parents have never shielded me from the truth.

For that reason, I always planned to attend Kingmakers.

My mother told me that when she was kidnapped, she was an innocent. Deliberately sheltered from the reality of the criminal underworld.

Her father was the head of the Irish Mafia, but she went to a normal school with normal kids. She was completely unprepared to be abducted, held captive, and offered as bait in a trap intended to murder every last member of her family.

"I don't want that to happen to you," she told me, her green eyes clear and somber. "I don't want you to be weak like I was. Confused and unprepared."

My father trained me to defend myself. To understand the language, the negotiations, and the stratagems necessary to operate in the underworld.

In high school, I may have looked like a normal girl. I ran the dance team, and I attended parties. But I was raised to be a mafiosa, not a ballerina.

I slip out from under the heavy covers and walk over to the window. I never bother to pull the drapes, so the moonlight is streaming in. I can look down to the overgrown garden with its stone statues and fountains, its cobblestone paths slippery with moss.

A tall, slim figure dressed in black walks from the garden into the glass conservatory.

My father.

I leave my room, running down the wide, curving staircase, then across the dark and silent main floor of the house to the conservatory.

The house is still, other than the usual creaks and groans of old wood settling. It's chilly, even though it's the end of summer. The thick stone walls and the heavy trees all around keep it cool no matter the time of year.

The conservatory is warmer, still trapping the last heat of the day. The heady smell of chlorophyll fills my lungs. It's dark in here, only tiny pinpricks of starlight penetrating through the thickly crowded leaves. It's two o'clock in the morning.

I can hear my father, even though he's almost silent. I know how to listen for the sound of human breath.

Likewise, he hears me coming no matter how quietly I walk.

"Can't sleep, *mała miłość*?" he says.

"Won't, not can't."

"Why is that?"

"I don't want to waste my last night at home."

I've pushed my way through the trees and hanging vines to the bench where my father sits. He's still wearing the cashmere sweater and slacks that are his usual work attire. With his sleeves pushed up, I can see the thickets of tattoos running down his arms, all the way across the backs of his hands and down his fingertips.

He's told me what some of the tattoos mean. And he's added more since I was born. Any remaining space on his body he filled with tattoos commemorating the dates of his children's births, tattoos for each ballet my mother choreographed, and tattoos that immortalize experiences between the two of them, unknown to me.

I have five tattoos myself: a swallow for my mother, a wolf for my father, a quote from my sister's favorite book, a sprig of aconite for my brother, and a fifth that I've never shown to anyone.

"Are you nervous for tomorrow?" my father asks me.

"No," I say honestly. "I am glad Leo's coming, though. I'd be lonely without him."

"I'm glad he'll be there too." My father nods. "I know you don't need anyone to protect you. But everyone needs allies. In your first week, be careful who you allow in your circle. Every bond you forge can open a door or close another in your face."

"I understand."

"Don't let Leo drag you into anything. He's not strategic."

"He leads with his heart," I say. "But his instincts are usually good."

"He has a temper." My father frowns, his pale blue eyes narrowed and homed in closely on my face.

"Dad, I know what Leo's like."

"I know you do." My father puts his arm around me, pulling my head against his shoulder. "I love you, Anna. And I trust you."

My heart beats hard against my ribs. There's something I want to say to my father, but I'm afraid…something I saw in my acceptance letter that I hardly dared believe.

I lick my lips, trying to find courage.

"Dad…"

"Yes?"

"In my Kingmakers letter, it said I was accepted to the Heirs division."

"Of course," he says in his cool, clipped voice.

"Was that… Did you…tell them to do that?"

He sits up so we're looking at each other once more. I resemble my father more than I do my mother. Same pale skin without a hint of freckles. Same blond hair. Same glacial blue eyes.

Those eyes are terrifying when they're fixed on you.

"You are my heir," my father says firmly. "You're my eldest. It's your birthright."

"But Whelan—"

"It's my choice to consider gender or birth order," my father says. "Before you were even born, your mother and I agreed."

My heart stopped for a moment. Now it beats twice as fast as normal, trying to catch up.

"Good." I fight to quell the slight tremor in my voice. "I'm glad."

"It will all be yours if you want it," my father says.

"I do," I whisper. "I want it."

My father nods. He puts his hand on the back of my neck, pulling me close so he can kiss me on the forehead.

"You will have everything you want in this world, Anna. I knew it from when I first held you in my arms. I knew you would take it all and hold it tight."

We sit quietly, not speaking.

I love my mother. I love her intensely. It's impossible not to. She has all the good qualities I lack. Endless kindness. A complete lack of selfishness. An internal joy that lights the room, that buoys up everyone around her.

I'm not like that. Sometimes I'm sad for no good reason. Sometimes I want to sit in silence, thinking about the passage of time and how painful it is to remember the best and worst moments that have come and gone so swiftly.

Then I'd rather be with my father, because I know he feels the same way. He and I are alike inside as well as on the outside. For better or worse, I'm not sweet, and I'm not always happy.

The only time I see that part of myself in my mother is when she choreographs her dances. Then I see that though she may not be dark herself, she understands sorrow and fear. She sees the beauty in damaged and disturbing things. That's why she understands my father and loves him. It's why she understands me.

Dance is how we bond. It's how I've channeled my worst and most destructive impulses. I keep control of them so they don't destroy me.

But there won't be a dance team at Kingmakers.

I'm not sure what I'm going to do with the feelings that build up inside me. They mess with my head. They make me want to do things I know I'll regret.

"You should go to bed," my father tells me. "You don't want to be tired as you travel."

"I can sleep on the plane."

"Unlikely," he says, "if you're sitting next to Leo."

I smile. Leo is always full of energy and excitement—particularly when doing anything new. He'll probably talk all the way to Croatia.

"It will be difficult at the school," my father says. "You can handle that. But if anything goes seriously wrong..."

"I'll call you," I promise.

We fly from Chicago to Frankfurt at ten o'clock the following morning, from Frankfurt to Zagreb, and then Zagreb to Dubrovnik.

My family and Leo's both come to the airport to see us off.

Aunt Yelena looks pale and strained. I know she doesn't want Leo to go to Kingmakers. She thinks it's dangerous.

She would know. After all, she was Bratva. They send more children to Kingmakers than anyone.

It's supposed to be a kind of sanctuary. A temporary détente between the grudges and rivalries of the various families. But for the children of criminals, rules are made to be broken. Even the school's motto, *Necessitas non habet legem*, means *Necessity has no law*.

Our acceptance letters came with a list of strict school rules, along with their accompanying punishments. Our parents had to sign the contract for the rule of recompense, and so did Leo and I. We had to press our prints in blood to the bottom of the page. It means that we submit to the authority of the school.

If we get ourselves in trouble, we'll be disciplined by the chancellor. He is—quite literally—judge, jury, and executioner. Our parents can't intervene or retaliate.

As usual, Leo seems completely unconcerned by any of that. He hugs both his parents, lifting his mother off her feet and kissing her hard on both cheeks.

Aunt Yelena blinks like she's forcing her eyes not to tear up.

"Be careful, Leo," she says.

He shrugs that off, not even bothering to pretend like he'll try.

"Love you, Mom."

Cara puts her arms around my shoulders and squeezes me tight, while Whelan does the same with his arms around my waist.

I feel the worst about leaving Cara. She doesn't let many people in. I know she'll be lonely without me, even if she never complains.

"Why can't I go?" Whelan demands.

"Because you're six," my father says calmly.

"That's not fair!"

"It's the epitome of fair. You can go at eighteen, exactly like your sister."

"It's not fair that I'm not eighteen," Whelan mutters under his breath, knowing not to push our father too far.

Whelan is the only one of us who got my mother's freckles and green eyes. They look much wilder on him because he's a little demon in human form. His copper-colored hair is always sticking up, and you can't tell what's freckles and what's dirt on his face. Even though he's stocky, he's fast as hell and surprisingly strong.

Cara is slim like me, medium height, with pale blue eyes. She's got darker hair than the rest of us, so brown it's almost black. She didn't speak until she was four, and even now you might be forgiven for thinking she still hasn't learned to do it.

"Can you call me on the weekends?" she asks me quietly.

"I think so."

"Just write if you can't."

"I will," I promise.

My mother hugs me too. She always smells clean and fresh, like the inside of a flower blossom.

"I'm starting to regret this already," she says. "Because of how much I'll miss you."

"I'll try to find somewhere to practice on campus."

"I never had to worry about you practicing." My mother shakes her head. "Sleeping, on the other hand..."

I smile. "I'll try to find time for that too."

Leo and I board the plane, sitting next to each other in the second row of first class. Nobody else our age is flying from Chicago to Frankfurt. We're the only Mafia children from our city going to Kingmakers this year.

We do know one person who's already there: our cousin Miles.

He's a year older than us and left last September. He came home over the summer, but we're not on the same flight going back out, because freshmen start a week later than everybody else.

Technically Leo and I are cousins, though not by blood.

His father's sister is married to my mother's brother.

It's complicated, and nobody at school could ever understand it when we tried to explain. They all just accepted that we were family, which was fine because that's how our own family views us. I've always called his parents Uncle Seb and Aunt Yelena, and he's always called mine Uncle Miko and Aunt Nessa. He loves my little siblings and is the same toward them as he is to me: teasing, friendly, and occasionally exasperating.

Like right now on the plane. Leo seizes my packet of pretzels—having already eaten his own—and tears them open with his teeth.

"In your dreams." I snatch them back. "I'm hungry too."

He grins. "Then why haven't you eaten them yet?"

"Because I'm not a rabid animal that inhales food in five seconds."

"You would if you were as big as me," he says, trying to steal them back again.

He's fast as fuck, but so am I. I manage to keep the torn packet away from his grasping fingers, just barely.

"Paws off," I say. "And don't be thinking you're going to put your elbow over that armrest either. I don't care how big you are, you're not using any of my precious personal space on this flight."

"You've gotta be kidding. Look at these legs!" Leo sprawls out his massive thighs, each the size of a small tree trunk. His leg presses up against the outside of mine, and I can feel the warmth of his flesh through my jeans. I shove him back, my face getting hot.

"You should have bought two seats, then."

"My dad's too cheap," Leo says sourly. Then, grinning at me again, "Bet Papa Miko would have gotten you two seats if you asked him nicely."

"Probably. But I wouldn't ask him, because I'm not a spoiled baby like you."

I lift a pretzel to my lips. Leo manages to snatch it out of my hand, tossing it into his mouth. He crunches it up deliberately loudly, just to annoy me.

"I'm going to flick you every time you try to fall asleep," I inform him.

"No fucking way am I falling asleep!" Leo says. "I'm too excited."

Ten minutes later, he's snoring with his heavy head flopped over on my shoulder.

Leo and I switch planes in Frankfurt with a six-hour layover. Refreshed from his nap, Leo convinces me to pop out of the airport so we can find a proper biergarten, where he orders us two massive foaming pints and a sizzling platter of sausages served with thick black bread.

Once we're up in the air again, the beer seems to hit me much harder than normal. My head feels pleasantly light on my shoulders, and I'm warm and relaxed.

I've got the window seat. The airplane seems like a ship floating over a sea of clouds with peaks tinged pink from the setting sun.

"Look," I say to Leo.

He leans across me so he can peer out the window. His shoulder presses against my chest, and his soft, dark curls brush my cheek.

His hair smells nice, like sandalwood. Below that, I smell the richer and more dangerous scent of his skin. It has the same effect on me as other scents that are both stimulating and upsetting: smoke from a fire, iron and blood, spilled gasoline. It makes my heart rate jump.

"Beautiful," Leo says, glancing back at me with his face right next to mine.

The sun hits his irises, illuminating every fleck of gold in the brown. His eyes are lighter than his deeply tanned skin. He's burned darker than toast after a long summer of boating and shirtless basketball games on the lakeshore courts.

I notice details. Things that make one person different from anyone else. Leo has a lot of things like that. More than anyone. There's nobody who looks quite like him.

I push him off so he's not so close to me. "Alright. Back to your own side."

Leo brought a deck of cards. We play some ridiculous game that involves betting on a hidden card that your opponent can't see. Leo's good at trying to convince me of what he's got, but I have a better poker face. It's hard to keep from laughing too loud when the cabin lights dim and everyone else tries to get some sleep.

We have to switch planes again in Zagreb at some ungodly hour, and we both fall asleep on top of our duffel bags, barely waking up in time to sprint down the concourse to our last flight.

Sweaty and grumpy, we finally fly into Dubrovnik. It's a port city on the edge of the Adriatic Sea, right at the very southernmost tip of Croatia.

The plan is to stay the night here, then take a boat to Visine Dvorca the following morning.

Dvorca is a tiny rocky island in the Adriatic Sea. There's one small town on the island, with a few hundred locals scratching a living on the hillsides, raising sheep and goats, cultivating little farms and vineyards. Most of their produce is sold to the school.

My father told me that. He didn't attend Kingmakers

himself—he's not from a legacy family. But his adoptive father, Tymon Zajac, was.

My father visited Kingmakers twice with Zajac to meet with the chancellor. He said he'd never been to a place with such a sense of history. The school has stood on the same spot for seven hundred years. The most brilliant and ruthless criminal minds of centuries have passed through those halls.

In fact, Kingmakers influenced my father to buy our house in Chicago. Both buildings are ancient, remote, and castle-like. And both are stuffed with secrets.

Because of the high rocky cliffs and the currents that dash against the island, there's only one place where a boat can make harbor. And that's what makes Kingmakers so defensible. You can't sneak up on the island unannounced. You can't approach the school without warning. You have to take the single wide-open road up to the front gates, just as we'll do tomorrow.

For now, Leo and I will be spending the night in a hotel in the Old Town part of Dubrovnik. The Grand Villa Argentina is perched on the cliffs above the blue ocean. The red roofs of the Old Town are spread out below, leading down to the medieval-looking Ploče Gate with its squat stone towers.

"I wonder if they'll let us come into Dubrovnik often?" I ask Leo. "There's not much on the island. What if we need new clothes or something?"

We were only permitted to bring one suitcase each.

"You won't need clothes," Leo says grimly. "We're supposed to wear those stupid uniforms."

"It's to prevent us wearing gang colors or whatever the fuck, I guess." I shrug.

"That wouldn't matter for you," Leo says, "since all you wear is black. How are you gonna adjust to having to wear green sometimes? And gray and silver?"

The school uniforms are mostly black, with a few pieces in

shades of charcoal, silver, sage, and olive. It's all fairly muted, but of course Leo can't resist an opportunity to give me shit.

"I don't only wear black," I inform him.

"Midnight and onyx are also shades of black," he teases.

"Did you look those up ahead of time for that joke? Admit it, you didn't know the word 'onyx.'"

Leo snorts. He loves trying to wind me up, but what he really wants is for me to hit him back. He wouldn't respect me if I didn't. Everything is a competition to him.

"There's probably some other kids from the school here by now, don't you think?" he says.

I wish we could have flown out with Miles. He would have been our guide the whole way. He could tell us where to eat dinner right now. He always knows the best place to get anything.

Of course Leo and I grilled him about what Kingmakers is like, but it's hard to get a straight answer out of Miles. He's sarcastic as fuck and not one to show emotion. He wouldn't admit if something were seriously scary or difficult. He acts like nothing affects him.

I say, "We can't be the only ones who got in today."

After stowing our bags in our adjoining rooms, we head down to Old Town to look for someplace to eat.

Old Town sits within high stone walls, preserving the city in its original medieval state—or as close to it as you're likely to find. It's stuffed with baroque churches and monasteries and stone palaces with two-foot-thick walls. The streets are roughly cobbled, and the squares are paved with flat slabs of marble. The air smells of salt, thyme, wild orange trees, and the spray of dozens of fountains that keep the greenery lush.

We find a little restaurant with outdoor dining and sit down at the wobbly table shaded by a bay leaf tree. The waiter brings us hot tea and a warm basket of flatbread without us even asking.

Leo tears into the bread like he hasn't eaten in weeks.

"What should I get?" I ask the waiter.

Enough tourists come here that he speaks English quite well.

"We're famous for our seafood," he says proudly. "We have fresh-caught oysters, mussels, squid, and cuttlefish risotto. Fish stew—we call it *brudet*. Also beef stew—that's *pašticada*."

"I'll have oysters, please."

"Anything that isn't fish?" Leo asks. He doesn't like seafood.

"*Peka* is baked meat and vegetables," the waiter says.

"Sounds great." Leo nods.

"He mentioned beef stew," I remind Leo.

"I don't like stew either."

"Can you bring us some sides as well?" I ask the waiter. "Whatever you think we'll like."

"Of course." He hurries away to ring it all in.

To Leo, I say, "You picky motherfucker. What are you gonna do if they only have one option for dinner at Kingmakers?"

"Fucking starve, I guess." Leo grins, without a hint of concern.

As we wait for our food, Leo leans back in his chair, long legs stretched out, arms crossed over his broad chest, surveying everything around us.

I like to look at the sky and the water, the orange trees and the stone facades of the buildings. Leo is primarily interested in people.

There's a table of boys off to the left of us, laughing and joking. Some of them are speaking a language I've never heard in my life, while the others are Russian. I can understand a little of the latter—Russian is close enough to Polish to get the gist. Leo, I'm sure, is catching every word.

"Are they talking about the competition?" I ask.

He nods. "They all want to be captain of the freshmen team."

Every year, Kingmakers runs a competition called the *Quartum Bellum*—the War of Four. All four years of students participate, even the freshmen. Of course the seniors usually win, but not always.

Kingmakers is divided by year and also by specialty. Leo and I are in the Heirs division. There's also the Accountants, the Enforcers, and the Spies. The Accountants handle the finance and investment arms of the business, the Enforcers do most of the day-to-day operations and security, and the Spies are for subterfuge and subverting law enforcement.

The Heirs, of course, are meant to be the bosses. But there's no guarantee that you can become boss or stay boss even within your own family. The primary purpose of our training will be leadership. Because even after you're appointed, you still have to convince your men to follow you.

To practice exactly that, we participate in the Quartum Bellum.

All you win is bragging rights and maybe a plaque on the wall. There's no real-world advantage.

But we all want it.

I know I do.

I can guarantee that Leo wants it worse than anyone.

The boys at the table seem to be boasting about their future exploits.

I can see Leo's eyes getting bright. He's dying to interject himself into their conversation.

Instead, the group turns their attention to the kid sitting alone at the next table.

He's dark-haired, silent, hunched over his bowl of beef stew. His hair is shaggy, his skin deeply tanned, and his clothes are shabby. His sneakers look like he's been wearing them about three years too long, the soles almost separating from the tops.

"Hey, Ares," one of the guys calls. "What division are you in anyway? Have they got one for chauffeurs and bag boys?"

Ares glances over at them, eyes narrowed.

"I'm not going to be a chauffeur," he says quietly.

They asked the question in Russian, but he answers them in English, his voice slightly accented.

"I'm surprised your parents could afford the tuition," another kid says. "How many goats did they have to sell? Hopefully not the one you use for a girlfriend?"

Ares stands up, pushing his chair back roughly.

The table of boys stands up as well, full of malicious energy and spoiling for a fight.

They might not have realized quite how tall Ares is—I see a couple of nervous glances as they realize he's bigger than any of them. But it's still six against one.

Until Leo says, in perfect Russian, "*V chem problema*?"

The boys turn, startled. They probably thought Leo and I were just some American couple on vacation.

"*Bratva*?" a black-haired boy mutters to his friend.

The second boy shakes his head. "*Amerikantsy*," he says. *Americans*.

"Didn't you read the list of rules?" I say to them sharply in English. "No fighting allowed."

"We're not at school yet," the first boy says, smiling at me wolfishly.

He's not one of the Russians. He was speaking the other language, the one I've never heard before. He's got jet-black hair and a scar that bisects his right eye, and he'd be good-looking if his expression weren't so arrogant.

"We will be soon enough," Leo says. "So we should try to get along."

Leo's been in plenty of fights, but for all his cockiness, he doesn't like bullies. He never has. He punches up, not down. It's one of my favorite things about him.

"Who are *you*?" the black-haired boy demands.

"Leo Gallo. My father's Sebastian Gallo, head don in Chicago."

"If you're Italian, then how come you speak Russian?" one of the other boys says, looking him up and down.

"My mother's Russian," Leo says.

The boys exchange looks. One of them mutters, "*Dvornyaga*," which I think means something like "mongrel" or "half-breed." I see a spark of fury in Leo's eyes, and I have to dart between him and the other boys to prevent him rushing forward.

The black-haired boy scoffs. "Is that your girlfriend?" he sneers.

"We're cousins," I say before Leo can respond. "Who the fuck are you? *Sagat*?"

The boy scowls, not understanding the reference, but one of his minions snorts. The black-haired boy silences the laugh with a look, then turns his glare on me.

"I'm Bram Van Der Berg, son of Bas Van Der Berg," he says, haughty and proud.

Oh, Dutch. That's why I couldn't understand him—the Penose Mafia in Amsterdam is home-grown, and they speak their own bizarre cryptolect called Bargoens.

No wonder Bram is so high on himself. The Penose are known for being smart and vicious and for holding a grudge until the end of time. That's why nobody fucks with them—they'll track you down and put a knife in your back ten years after you forgot you offended them.

I don't want to give Bram the satisfaction of knowing that his family is just as famous as he thinks. But on the other hand, I can't pretend to be that ignorant.

"Oh yeah," I say slowly. "I've heard of your dad. Doesn't he make waffles or something?"

Like most Mafia families, the Van Der Bergs run an up-front business to help launder the money that pours in from less-savory sources. In Bram's case, it's a chain restaurant so successful that I've even seen them in America. The mascot is a chubby little Dutch boy proudly holding up a plate of syrup-drenched waffles.

"Were you the model for the sign when you were Baby Bram?" I mock him.

Bram's face flushes, and now it's his friends who have to hold him back from taking a swing at me. I wouldn't give a fuck if he did. I know I'm not as strong as these boys, but I've never met anyone with faster reflexes than me. Not even Leo can catch hold of me when I don't want him to.

Leo knows that. He doesn't jump to intervene. In fact, out of the corner of my eye, I see him grinning.

If I was going to guess, Leo's favorite thing about *me* is probably that I don't take shit from anybody. It feeds his desire for chaos. Plus Leo's a steamroller. He can't be friends with anybody who gives in to him too easily—they'd be chewed up and spat out in his wake in a matter of days.

Bram is not nearly as amused as Leo. His top lip is curled, practically snarling at me. I can tell he wants to push this further. But the odds aren't quite as good anymore—Leo, me, and Ares against Bram and his five buddies.

It's Leo who speaks up first, cutting the tension.

"Why don't you come sit with us?" he says to Ares. "I've never heard of—where did you say you were from?"

"Syros," the boy says softly.

"Come educate me," Leo says, his bright smile flashing in his lean, tanned face.

"Yeah," Bram scoffs. "Go sit with the Americans. Maybe they'll pay for your dinner."

"You don't have to pay for my dinner," Ares says as he follows us back to our table. Glancing over where he was sitting, I can see that he only ordered a small plate of stew and that he already ate all of it, not a bit left in the bowl. There's no way that was enough food for a guy his size.

"We're not gonna pay for your dinner," I say, wanting to spare his dignity, "but you should eat some of our food. We ordered way too much."

Sure enough, before we've even sat down, the waiter carries out a heavy tray full of mussels, Leo's beef, and a half dozen side plates of what looks like spinach pastry, marinated salad, pickled vegetables, and fragrant rice stuffed full of nuts and raisins. It smells phenomenal.

Ares sits across from me, looking awkward and embarrassed. He's tall and broad-shouldered, lean and rangy. His skin has an olive tone, but when he looks directly at me, I see that his eyes are a surprising shade of blue-green, like a turquoise sea.

"I'm not afraid of them." He gives a little jerk of his head back toward Bram and his friends, who are seated at their table once more, laughing and talking with obvious jeers in our direction.

"Of course not," Leo says. "We didn't come over to save you. Just the level of doucheyness caught our attention."

Ares chuckles. "I was on the same flight over with them. Can't say I was enjoying my first introduction to Kingmakers students."

"Do you know anyone else coming?" I ask him curiously.

"No." He shakes his head. "I barely know anybody. What Bram said is true—my family's tiny and poor. Syros is tiny and poor. We're Mafia in name only. My father works as a tour guide. I only got accepted because the Cirillos have been going to Kingmakers since it was founded."

"You're one of the first ten families," I say with interest.

"Yeah." Ares shrugs. "The smallest and least impressive, though."

"Who gives a fuck! That's still cool!"

"Anna loves history," Leo tells him. "She probably knows more about Kingmakers than the rest of us combined."

"No, I don't," I correct him. "I've never even seen it, and I'm sure some of the other kids have."

"Anyway, tell us more about Syros," Leo says.

"It isn't very interesting." Ares takes an enormous bite out of a spinach pastry. "Just a little Greek island. Not as pretty as Mykonos or Santorini. You said you two were from Chicago?"

"Yeah." Leo nods proudly. He loves Chicago more than any place on earth.

"Have you ever been there?" I ask Ares.

"I hadn't even been on a plane before today," he admits.

I can't help laughing at that. "Are you serious?"

"Yeah." He smiles a little. He has a nice smile—slow and warm. I think Ares is a gentle giant. I like him immediately, though I don't know how gentleness will fare where we're about to go.

"There must be something cool in Syros," Leo says, spearing a huge chunk of beef and stuffing it in his mouth.

"Well, I really do have a whole farm full of goats," Ares says. "But not for what Bram said. They're fainting goats. If you startle them, they stiffen up like a board and keel over. It's kind of adorable."

"Do you have siblings?" I ask.

"Two brothers and a sister. I'm the oldest. I feel bad for leaving them."

"Me too," I say.

We talk about our siblings for a few minutes while Leo listens, mildly jealous. He always says he wishes he had a brother, but I don't know how he'd actually handle that, since Leo loves to be the center of attention at all times.

The waiter carries away our rapidly emptying plates, then brings out chilled dishes of *rožata,* which is some sort of custard pudding. Bram and his buddies got bored and left, so there's no one throwing unpleasant sneers in our direction anymore.

We drink several cups of sweet, fruity brandy, the sky darkening and the ancient stone walls glowing from the row of lanterns all along the sea wall. The night air is fragrant with orange blossoms and sea salt.

Leo and I get a bit tipsy, pleased to finally be in a country with a reasonable drinking age.

Ares relaxes too, though he's not drinking as much as we are. It's funny that he's named after the god of war. There's nothing aggressive about him. In fact, without the candlelight brightening his face, I think he'd look sad and anxious. He's probably nervous about sailing off to Kingmakers tomorrow, as we all are.

"Let's get another round!" Leo says, finishing his brandy.

"The boat comes at seven in the morning," I remind him.

"All the more reason to stay up all night," Leo says. "I hate getting up early."

"Your logic is impeccable."

"Come on," Leo coaxes me.

I glance over at Ares, who doesn't seem to mind the idea of another drink.

"Alright," I say. "Just one more."

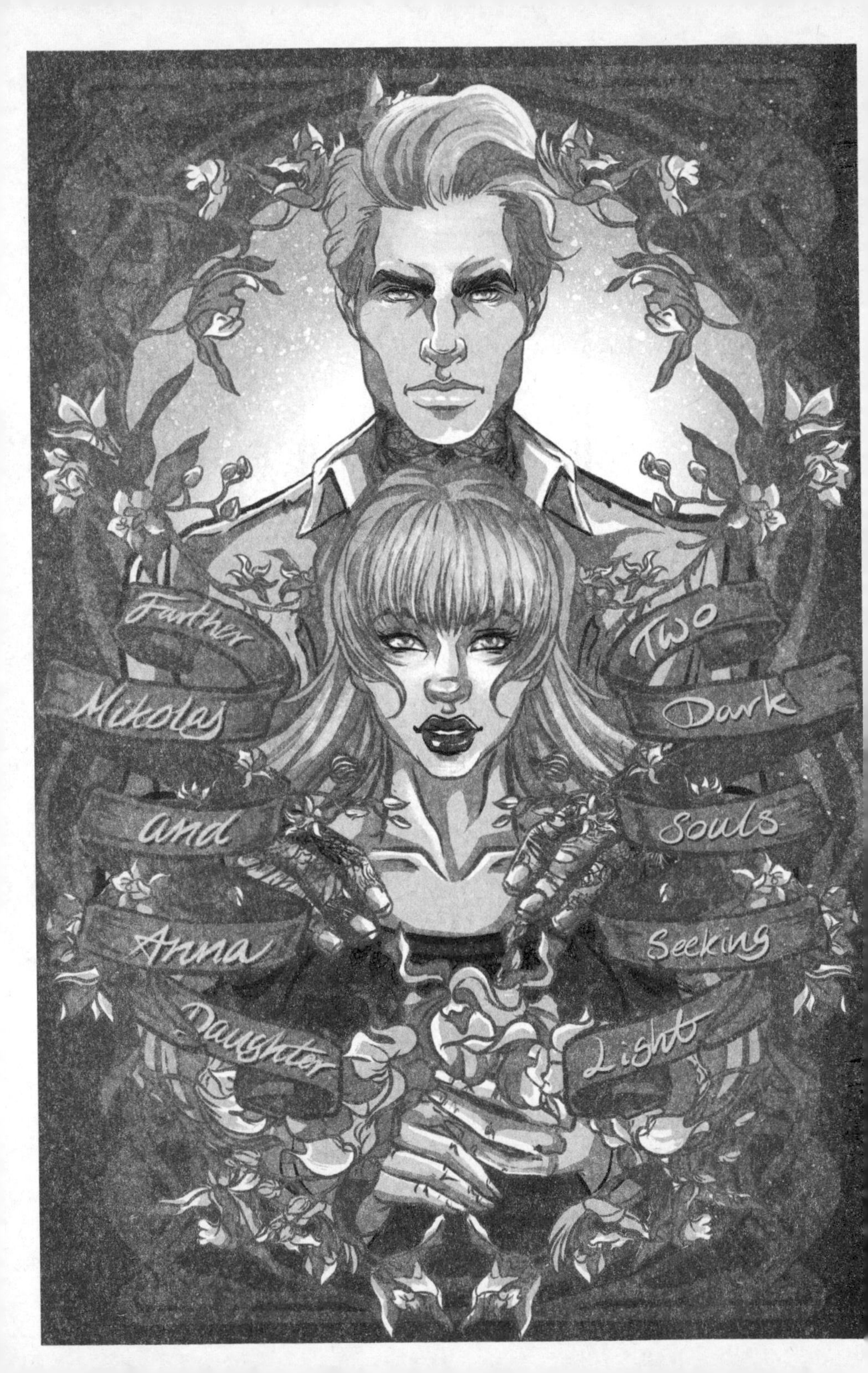
Farther
Mikolaj
and
Anna
Daughter
Two
Dark
Souls
Seeking
Light

CHAPTER 4
LEO

"LEO!" ANNA SHOUTS, YANKING OFF MY BLANKET AND DRAGGING me out of the bed so my ass bumps on the floor.

The impact makes my skull throb. I don't know what was in that brandy last night, but I'm experiencing a hell of a hangover. The bright Mediterranean sunshine streaming in through the window is about ten times more cheerful than I want to experience at the moment. I'd much rather plunge back into the lovely dark silence of a huge pile of blankets over my head.

"What are you doing?" I groan, shaking the hair out of my eyes.

"We're supposed to be boarding in ten minutes! Didn't you hear me banging on your door?"

"Anna," I grumble. "Can you do me a favor? Can you please just...shush? You're so loud."

"Get up!" she hollers, making my head ring like a bell. "We're gonna miss the boat!"

"Okay! Jesus," I say, picking myself up off the floor.

Anna thrusts a glass of lukewarm tap water into my hand, and I chug it down. It tastes weird, as water always does in a foreign place. My stomach churns.

"How come you're not hungover?" I ask her.

"Because I didn't drink as much as you."

"But I'm twice as big as you. I should be able to drink twice as much."

"Good hypothesis. How's the field test working out for you?"

"Not great," I admit.

I fell asleep in my clothes. I pull my dirty T-shirt over my head and then unbutton my jeans and drop them down. Anna turns around quickly, facing the door.

"You've seen me naked before," I tease her. "And I've seen you..."

"Not in a long time," Anna says coolly.

We used to go skinny-dipping together in Carlyle Lake, Anna thin and pale no matter how late it was in the summer and me brown as a nut. But it's true, we were only kids at the time. I haven't actually seen Anna nude since she...well...filled out.

"How'd you get in here anyway?" I ask her. I'm pretty sure I wasn't drunk enough to forget to bolt the door.

"I picked the lock," she says. "It's hardly Fort Knox."

Anna is an encyclopedia of hidden skills. I've long since learned not to compete with her on random tasks. At least not with any confidence of whether I'll win.

I'm heading to the shower when Anna shouts, "We don't have time for that!"

"Okay, okay," I grumble, rifling through my duffel bag. I stare stupidly at the clothes, realizing that it's almost all white dress shirts, gray or black trousers, charcoal sweater vests, and sage-green pullovers.

Fucking uniforms. I forgot about that.

Grabbing items at random, I put on a white button-up and a pair of gray slacks, both horribly wrinkled from being stuffed in my bag without proper folding. I rake my fingers through my hair, give my teeth a five-second brush, rub on some deodorant and a spritz of cologne, and in less than two minutes I'm ready to go.

"With time to spare," I say to Anna.

She rolls her eyes at me, marching toward the door, her green plaid skirt swishing behind her. She already has a run up the back of her stockings, and she's wearing the same big, clunky vintage Docs that she's owned since junior high.

"You're looking very *kawaii*," I say, grinning at the sight of her in a skirt.

Anna whips around, narrowing her ice-blue eyes at me in their ring of heavy black liner.

"Don't start with me," she hisses.

"I'm just saying—"

"Don't say anything. Not a fucking word."

I'm guessing she's sensitive because Anna's ability to express herself through her clothing matters to her. Even though it looks like she wears the same depressing shit every day, I know her well enough to differentiate between her fetish wear ensembles, her Victorian vampire look, and her punk-rock goth. It's a good indication of her mood. For instance, the more chains she's wearing, the more I know I better not fuck with her that day.

"My lips are sealed," I promise, throwing my duffel bag over my shoulder and following her out of the room.

We have to run to make it down to the dock in the remaining seven minutes. Thank god we picked a hotel so close to the water.

Our boat is leaving from the very last berth. They've only just started loading, and the dock is still crowded with students from all over the globe.

I can guess where some of them are from: One boy has a traditional dragon tattoo extending down his arm from beneath the rolled-up sleeves of his dress shirt, the scaly, curling tip of the tail wrapping around the base of his thumb. His friend is probably Yakuza too, though not a very obedient one. He's missing the tip of his right pinkie, which means he's had to commit *yubitsume,* the apology ritual where the offender has to amputate his own finger.

Next to those two, I see a girl with flaming red curls who wipes the sweat from her face, saying loudly, "Jaysis, it's quare warm today, isn't it?"

The dark-haired girl she's speaking to stares back at her blankly. "What?" she says in an accent I can't quite place. It might be Galician.

"It's fierce hot!" the Irish girl reiterates. "Anybody got a mineral?"

"I thought we were all supposed to speak English," the dark-haired girl says tartly.

"I bloody well am!" the Irish girl cries.

I glance over at Anna to see if she's enjoying this exchange, seeing as she's half-Irish herself. She doesn't seem to have heard a word of it. She's gazing up at the ship instead. It's bigger than I expected, and not at all the bus-like ferry I was imagining. Instead, I see a four-masted barquentine with a navy and gold hull and crisp white sails.

"Why's it so big?" I say out loud. There's less than a hundred freshmen, and the trip isn't that long.

"The water around Dvorca is rough as hell," a boy with close-cropped dark hair answers me. "If you tried to sail over in some fishing boat, you'd get tossed around like corn in a popper. Some parts of the year, you can't come and go from the island at all."

"How do you know?" another kid demands.

"I've had five siblings go through Kingmakers," the boy replies, shrugging. "I've got a pretty good idea how it all works."

"Where're you from?" I ask him.

"Palermo," he says. "I'm Matteo Ragusa."

"Catholic?" I ask.

"You know it." He grins.

"I'm half-Italian too." I put out a hand to shake. "Leo Gallo."

"Chicago, right?" he says.

"Yeah, how'd you know?"

"Two of my brothers live in New York. There's plenty of Italians at Kingmakers. More Russians, though."

"I'm also half-Russian," I tell him.

He laughs. "I won't hold it against you. Can't say the same for the rest of them." He jerks his head toward our fellow students.

"What's wrong with Russians?" Anna demands.

"Everything," Matteo says, laughing. "They're blunt and rude. Mean as hell, though not as mean as the Albanians. Then you've got the Italians. You know we're all hotheaded and a little bit lazy. Then you've got the Irish—"

He breaks off, seeing Anna raise one darkly penciled eyebrow.

"Just kidding around." He raises his hands in defense. "You've got twenty different kinds of Mafia families, with a hundred kinds of prejudices and grudges. Yet somehow we're all supposed to get along for four years. Until we go out in the real world and get to battling again."

"I'm not worried," I say, mostly to annoy Anna. "I get along with everybody."

Anna snorts, tossing her head.

People who don't know me very well are always impressed by me. Anna knows me best of anyone, and she's never impressed. I've done the craziest things to try to force her to admit that I'm funny or skilled or a fucking badass. But she'll never admit it.

I don't know what kind of guy would turn her head. While I've gone through a dozen girlfriends, she never seems to fall for anybody.

A whistle blows, and one of the deckhands motions for the students to start boarding.

"Here we go," Matteo says nervously.

I spot Ares joining the queue, carrying one small and battered backpack in place of a suitcase.

"Morning," I say, looking him over for signs of a hangover.

Like Anna, Ares looks a hell of a lot better rested than me. *Fuck, am I the only lightweight?*

He grins at me. "You made it."

"Just barely."

"Come on," he says. "We better get on board if we want a good spot up at the bow."

Anna and I join Ares in the line, and we all scale the gangplank up onto the ship.

Those with bigger suitcases left them in a pile on the dock for the deckhands to load below. I see a French girl arguing furiously with one of the crew, because she brought at least three matching Louis Vuitton suitcases, while our acceptance letters stated we were only allowed one bag each.

"How am I supposed to fit everything I need in *one suitcase*?" she demands, as if the idea is obscene.

"I'm only puttin' one on the ship, so you better tell me which one, or I ain't taking any of 'em," the deckhand says sourly.

I don't see how that drama plays out, because I'm stepping up onto the deck of the ship already swarming with uniformed students. Plenty of them have already ditched their vests or jackets, wilting beneath the blazing sun. At least there's a sea breeze.

"Why do we have to wear wool?" I complain to Anna.

"It'll be cooler on the island," Ares says. "Out in the ocean, it gets chilly in the winter. Not freezing, but close to it."

Ares spots a piece of netting strung between two masts like a giant hammock.

"Come on," he says, chucking his backpack up into the net. "Let's sit up here."

Anna and I follow him up. Even though we're only five feet in the air, we have a much better view of the activity on the deck as the sailors prepare to cast off. We can see more of the port and the wide, dark expanse of the water leading out of the bay.

Once all the students are on board, the sailors cast off the ropes tethering us to the dock and start unfurling the sails. The huge white sails immediately fill with wind, and the booms swing around to form the right angle to carry us out onto the open water.

We all look back at the dock, but there's nobody waiting to wave us off. Parents were instructed to say their farewells from their home country. We're already on our own. Leaving Dubrovnik is only symbolic.

The city looks foreign to my eyes, and the place we're going is only more so.

There's nowhere on earth like Kingmakers. A secret school only known to a few dozen families. I won't get any degree or diploma from this place. Just the accumulation of knowledge passed down through generations of criminals. How to operate in the shadows. How to find loopholes in the law. How to outwit and outplay governments and police forces. And how to barter, negotiate, and battle with one another.

The wind fills the sails with surprising force. The wooden planks groan as the ship is shoved hard across the water. Despite its size, the ship picks up speed rapidly. The planks aren't groaning anymore—they've adjusted to the pressure and the temperature change. Now the boat seems to transform, to become as light as a bird skimming over the water.

Soon we're passing out of the port, out into open ocean. The red-roofed medieval buildings of Old Town are disappearing behind us. We're cutting through the fishing boats, moving out where there's no one else around.

Seagulls rise up from the fishing nets, circling around our ship briefly in case we have something better to offer. When they see how quickly we're moving, they abandon our masts and head back where they came from.

"Look!" Anna cries, pointing down to the water. "Dolphins."

Swift gray bullets race alongside the ship, leaping in and out of the frothy wake.

"That's good luck," Ares says.

"Do you know how to sail?" Anna asks him.

"Yeah," he says. "I had a little skiff in Syros."

At first, I'm loving the cool breeze and the waves and the view of the dolphins. But soon Anna pulls out a book and starts reading, and Ares lies back against the mast, using his backpack as a pillow and laying a spare T-shirt over his eyes so he can take a nap.

What was exciting and stimulating becomes repetitive and boring. I'm tired of the view. I want to see what everyone is doing down on the deck.

I swing down from our makeshift hammock. Matteo was right—the water only gets rougher the farther out we sail. I have to use all my balance to cross the rolling deck.

Some of the other students are seasick, with several kids lined up to puke over the railing. I can't say my stomach is totally steady, especially not with the lingering effects of my hangover, but at least I'm not that far gone.

Up at the front of the bow, I spot a group of boys playing some kind of dice game. I wander over for a closer look.

Bram Van Der Berg is there, along with two of his friends from the night before. Also a couple of boys who look Armenian and one Asian girl.

After watching for a minute, I can tell the game is just a variation of street craps. I can't be sure, but I think one of the Armenians is using a loaded die. He certainly seems to be rolling an eleven more often than would be statistically probable.

Bram and I eye each other warily across the circle. He hasn't shaved, and his face is rough with stubble. I probably look scruffy too, but hopefully in less of a just-got-off-a-ten-year-stretch-in-solitary kind of way. I can tell he's watching to see if I plan to resume the hostilities from the night before.

I assume there's going to be a whole lot of jockeying for position in the first few weeks at Kingmakers. Every kid here thinks they're the alpha, and they probably were, wherever they came from. But we can't all be alphas at the school. There's going to be a new hierarchy.

I intend to be at the top, like always.

Bram probably thinks the same thing. He narrows his eyes at me, tossing back his longish hair and muttering something to his friends. The other Penose give me venomous looks.

Bram's the next shooter. He rolls the point number three times before hitting a seven, ending the round. He scoops up his winnings, grinning.

"Hey, Dmitry," he calls. "Why don't you come join?"

He's calling to a tall blond boy who's standing at the railing looking down at the water. The boy took his shirt off because of the heat. A Siberian tiger is tattooed to the right of his spine, done in the classic style as if it were crawling up his back. Because he's so pale, the tiger looks snow white with black stripes.

Dmitry turns slowly to face our group.

He looks right at me and seems to recognize me immediately.

I get a similar jolt.

He's strangely familiar, even though I know we've never met.

His eyes narrow, his jaw tightens, and his lip curls up in a sneer.

"No thanks," he says coldly. "I don't like the company."

"What?" Bram says, glancing back and forth between us. "The *Amerikanets*?"

"What's wrong with Americans?" I say. I keep my voice level, but I'm looking the blond boy right in the eye.

Bram and I sized each other up last night, and it was clear that we both thought we were hot shit. Whose shit is hotter remains to be determined. With Dmitry, it's something else. He doesn't eye me like a rival. He's glaring at me like an enemy.

"It's not Americans," he says, voice dripping with disdain. "It's *you*."

Something in his voice, coupled with his coloring and the familiarity of his features, makes it all click at once.

I'm talking to my cousin. He's calling himself Dmitry, but this is Dean Yenin, I'm sure of it.

Not that Dean considers us family.

His father and my mother are twins. They were best friends growing up. Until my mom chose my dad over her own family.

Dean's grandfather (who I guess is technically my grandfather too, though I never met the bastard), tried to kill everyone I know and love at my parents' wedding: my uncle Nero, my aunt Camille, Uncle Dante, my godmother Greta, even my father. He succeeded in murdering my grandpa Enzo, so I've only ever known him from a portrait that hangs in my father's office.

And in return, my father rained down bloody retribution on Dean's family. Dean's grandfather is dead, strangled to death by my dad. And his father, Adrian, is burned up worse than Vader from what I've heard.

So we *are* enemies, maybe more than anyone else on this boat.

I knew Dean was coming to Kingmakers.

I knew this was coming.

But it's something different to meet him face-to-face after never even having seen a photo of him.

He's the main reason my mother didn't want me coming here. She's tried to reach out to her brother over the years—tried to repair their relationship so they could at least have a measure of forgiveness, even if they could never be close again.

He never responded to her, not a single word.

It's clear from the expression on Dean's face that my mom was right. The Yenins weren't just avoiding us. They fucking hate us still.

"Is that any way to talk to your cousin?" I say to Dean.

I won't give him the satisfaction of glaring back at him. Instead, I paste a grin on my face, like I don't take him seriously. I know that's the best way to really piss him off.

Sure enough, he takes another couple of steps toward me, closing the space between us. Instinctively, everyone else steps back. They all know the feeling of a fight about to happen. That anticipation in the air, the electricity between two people itching to do each other harm.

"Don't call me that," Dean says.

It's funny how even the simplest words can cut if they're said sharply enough.

Dean hasn't raised his voice, but he makes it perfectly clear that he isn't fucking around. His fists tighten at his sides, and his shoulders swell as his body shifts into a more aggressive stance. He's got the look of a fighter, as if he's most natural in that position. If I were anybody else, I'd probably take a step back, cringing like a little bitch.

But I'm not somebody else.

I'm me. And I don't back away from anybody.

"Don't call you what?" I say. "*Coz?*"

Dean takes another step forward until we're within arm's reach of each other. I'm taller than him by three inches, but he's got a decent amount of muscle packed on his frame. I'm watching him carefully, though I don't let it show. I stand there as relaxed and casual as ever.

"We're not family," Dean hisses. "Your whore of a mother *betrayed* her family. She's not a Yenin anymore. She's just a piece of treacherous trash."

I want to hit him so bad my fists are throbbing. I can't let that go unanswered.

"The Yenins broke a blood oath," I spit back at him. "I don't know how the fuck you're even here. You should be excommunicated. Whose cock did your father have to suck to get you back in?"

We rush each other at the same moment. I throw the first punch, right at his stupid fucking face. But to my surprise, he slips the hit so my fist barely glances off his jaw. I've never missed like that before.

At the same time, he hits me with a left hook that fucking rocks me. Dean may not be quite as big as me, but he's fast as hell and strong. My head is ringing, and my hangover headache comes roaring back.

I swing at him again, and this time he can't quite duck it. At six five, I've got a fuck of a longer reach than he's used to. I pop him in the cheek, raising an instant red welt under his eye.

In retaliation, he slugs me in the gut, hard enough to regurgitate whatever was in my stomach if I'd eaten any breakfast. Jesus, he's got a sledgehammer for an arm.

The howls of Bram and the other students draw the attention of the sailors. Two of the deckhands tear us apart before we can finish the fight. They're big, burly men, and they fling us down on the deck, shouting for us to knock it off.

The bigger of the two, a man with a glass eye and two sensuously entwined mermaids on his forearm, points a sausage-like finger at me and growls, "Raise your fists again, and I'll chuck you in the fuckin' ocean. No fighting on board."

He stands there, arms crossed over his broad chest, watching us both until Dean picks himself up off the deck and resumes his sullen position at the railing and I head back toward the bow.

I climb up in the net once more, making Ares stir and mumble in the midst of his nap. Anna glances up from her book.

"What the hell happened to you?"

She's staring at my face.

I swipe my hand under my nose, blood smearing across my knuckles.

"Little family reunion," I say.

"Dean?" Anna asks, eyes wide.

"Who else?"

"Why'd you have to go and fight him?"

"He started it. I was willing to be friendly."

Anna frowns. "For how long, two seconds?"

"He called my mom a traitor!"

"Of course he did! You know what he's probably been told. Did you even try to talk to him?"

"It's not my job to *talk* to him!" I scoff. "*His* family are the traitors, and if he says another word about my mom, I'll break his fucking jaw for him."

"You'd better not," Anna says darkly. "You know the rules."

"He's the one—"

"They won't care!" Anna cuts across me. "This is exactly what Aunt Yelena was worried about."

"Oh, get off it," I grumble. "I heard enough of that before I left."

I hate when Anna acts like she's on my parents' side about me not going to Kingmakers. She should be happy that I came here with her instead of taking my full ride to Duke. Does she want to be here alone? I thought she'd be thrilled that we were both experiencing this together.

The thought of going to some school without her, any school, made me sick to my stomach. She's my best friend. We've always done everything together.

I know Anna cares about me. But sometimes I think she doesn't need me the same way I need her. She's got siblings and I don't. I would never admit this in a million years, but sometimes I'm jealous of Cara and Whelan. I hate that Anna loves them almost as much as she loves me. I don't want her attention divided.

I know it's ridiculous, because they're just kids. But I want to be first in her eyes, the way she is in mine. Closer than blood.

"Leo, you can't act like that at Kingmakers," she says, her blue eyes fixed determinedly on my face.

"Act like what?" I say stubbornly.

"You can't act like you usually do."

I hear the edge of fear in her voice, and that's what makes me smother my flippant retort. Anna isn't scared of anything usually.

"I know," I admit. "I know it's not high school anymore. I'll be careful."

"You promise?" Anna says.

"Yes. I promise."

"Alright." She gives me a small smile, leaning back in the hammock and picking up her book once more.

She's reading an ancient, battered copy of *Lord of the Flies*.

"Let me guess," I say. "Your suitcase is full of books you've already read."

Anna smiles just a little.

"Not full," she says. "But yeah, about half of it."

"They have a library at Kingmakers, you know."

"I don't care," she says. "This belonged to the other Anna."

Anna is named after her aunt, who died a long time before she was born.

Anna has a strange reverence for this namesake she never met. She talks about the other Anna like she's her guardian angel. Like a piece of her soul lives inside Anna herself.

I'm jealous of the other Anna too. A girl who died thirty years ago.

That's how stupid I can be.

I've never been able to be rational when it comes to Anna.

"How much longer till we get to the island?" Ares asks from beneath his T-shirt.

"I dunno," I say. "All I see is ocean."

Just like Matteo warned, the water gets rougher as we draw closer to Kingmakers. Long before we spot the island, the ship is pitching and tossing, and I can tell the crew is approaching in a kind of zigzag to avoid rocks or sandbars beneath the surface or maybe just because of the way the currents run.

More of the students succumb to seasickness, and I can smell the vomit even from up in the net. I must be turning green myself, because Anna says, "You better not puke on me."

Ares looks completely undisturbed.

"I used to go out in fishing boats all the time," he says. "Boats a lot smaller than this. You bob around like a cork."

When we finally spot the island, it juts out of the water like an accusing finger pointing up toward the sky. The limestone cliffs rise up for hundreds of feet in a sheer pale sheet, with waves crashing against their base, sending up so much spray that we can feel it all the way over on the ship. Far up on the cliffs, I spy the stone walls of Kingmakers itself.

Part castle, part fortress, Kingmakers is built directly into the cliffs, so it rises up in three levels hewn out of the rock. Constructed in the 1300s, it has most of the Gothic elements you'd expect, including six main towers, a portcullis, military-style gates, and a winding German-style zwinger, which forms an open kill zone between the defensive walls.

The limestone walls are white as bone, and the steeply pitched roof is black. The pointed archways and the stained-glass windows are dark as well, as if there's no lights on inside. To divert rainwater off the roof, the drainage spouts are carved in the shape of grotesque gargoyles, demons, and avenging angels.

The students fall silent below us, gazing up at Kingmakers just as Anna and I are doing. The school has us all transfixed. Even in the Mediterranean sunshine, there's nothing bright or welcoming in its towering stone walls.

Our ship has to skirt the island to approach on the lee side. Even then, it takes our captain several attempts, doubling back and trying again, to shoot the narrow gap into the harbor.

We pull up to the only dock, the crew throwing down their ropes with obvious relief. As they unload our bags, the students climb into open wagons with bench seats running along both sides. Each wagon is pulled by two massive Clydesdale horses that stand even taller than me at the shoulder, thick tufts of hair hanging down over hooves the size of dinner plates.

"Are we going on a hayride?" One of the girls in our wagon laughs.

"I don't think they have any cars on the island," Anna says to me. "Look."

She inclines her head toward the unpaved road winding through the tiny village clustered around the bay. Sure enough, I don't see so much as a moped anywhere.

Once the wagons are loaded up, the drivers climb up on their tall bench seats and flick the reins to tell the horses we're ready to go.

Our driver is a skinny, deeply tanned man wearing suspenders and a pair of trousers that are more patches than pants.

"Do you work at the school?" I ask him.

"Yup." He nods.

"How long have you worked there?"

He glances over at me, squinting in the bright sun. "Feels like a hundred years."

"Did you go there yourself?"

He snorts. "You writin' a book, kid?"

"Just curious."

"You know what curiosity did to the cat."

I grin at him. "I'm not a cat."

"No," he says. "I didn't go to Kingmakers. I was born on this island. I've lived my whole life here."

"Do you ever go to Dubrovnik?"

"What's Dubrovnik?"

He says it so dryly that it takes Anna stifling a laugh for me to realize that he's fucking with me. I laugh too, and the man grins, showing teeth that are surprisingly white next to his tanned face.

"I go once in a while," he says. "But I like it better here."

It doesn't take long to leave the little village behind us and to begin ascending the long, winding road toward Kingmakers. We drive through orchards and farmland, then up through rockier ground where goats and sheep graze. I see olive groves and a vineyard so heavy with grapes that you could almost get drunk off the scent alone.

All the while, we're climbing steadily, drawing closer to the colossal stone gates of Kingmakers.

On one side of the gate stands a winged female figure brandishing a sword. On the other is an armored man holding an axe. We pass between the two figures onto the grounds of the school.

Up close, the castle is even larger than I expected. It's almost like its own self-contained city with greenhouses, terraced gardens, courtyards, palatial buildings, towers, armories, and more. I don't know how the fuck I'm ever going to get to class on time.

Anna sits next to me, silent but looking everywhere at once.

"What do you think?" I ask her.

"It's beautiful."

Trust Anna to skip right over "strange," "terrifying," and "intimidating" to land right on "beautiful." I guess, considering the house she grew up in, Kingmakers probably feels more like home to her than it will to anybody else.

Since I grew up in a normal house with sunlight and stainless-steel appliances, I find Kingmakers just a little bit spooky.

As the wagons pull into the main courtyard, we're met by a dozen students who look like they're probably seniors. They're all neatly dressed, with their shirts tucked in, ties in place, and hair properly combed. They look cool and comfortable and like they're ten years older than us instead of only three.

By contrast, we tumble out of the wagons in various states of undress, sunburned and sweaty, with our hair salty and tangled from the sea breeze. The seniors smirk at one another.

A tall Black girl steps forward. She's slim and elegant, with her hair twisted into a thick braid that hangs over her left shoulder.

"Welcome to Kingmakers," she says coolly. "I'm Marcelline Boucher, and I'm a senior year Accountant. This is Rowan Doss, Pippa Portnoy, Alfonso Gianni, Johnny Hale, Blake Wellwood, Grant McDonald..."

She points to her fellow students, listing off their names in such rapid succession that I can't remember any of them a moment later.

"We're here to take you to your dorms. So you can get...cleaned up." She raises a disdainful eyebrow at the lot of us. "I'm going to read your names. Grab your bag, and join your guide. And pay attention! I'm not going to repeat myself."

She barks the last line at a couple of freshmen who were whispering to each other. They snap to attention under her fiery stare.

Marcelline pulls a list out of her pocket and begins to read off our names.

Anna's in the first group and the smallest—there are only three female Heirs in our year, including her. She retrieves her suitcase and goes to stand beside Pippa Portnoy, a petite girl with a sly expression and thick, dark bangs hanging over her eyes.

The next two groups are enforcers—almost all male, with a dozen students assigned to each guide. The Accountants are called next, then the spies, and finally we're down to the male Heirs. Marcelline reads off the names, pointlessly since we're the only ones left.

"Bram Van Der Berg, Ares Cirillo, Erik Edman, Leo Gallo, Hedeon Gray, Valon Hoxha, Kenzo Tanaka, Jules Turgenev, Emile Girard, and Dean Yenin."

Fucking great. I'm going to be sharing a dorm with the two most obnoxious people I've met so far.

At least Ares will be there too. He gives me a fist bump as we line up next to our guide, a Polynesian guy with his hair shaved into a Mohawk and several piercings in both ears.

"I'm Johnny Hale," he reminds us. "I'm supposed to help you get settled in. Remind you of the rules. Make sure you get places on time the first week. But I'm not your fucking babysitter, and I don't give a shit about your problems. So follow the rules, and don't expect me to bail you out if you don't. Any questions that aren't fucking stupid?"

He glares at us, challenging us to come up with a query that fits his criteria. Nobody dares to try.

"Good," he grunts. "Let's get going."

He leads us across the courtyard in the direction of the towers on the northwest corner of campus. We pass through a couple of greenhouses and then what looks like an armory.

"Gym's in there," Johnny says. "That's where your combat classes will be held too. You can work out any time outside of class hours—it's open all night. There's an underground pool too. And showers so you can clean up after."

"Are all the dorms over here?" I ask him, wondering how far away Anna might be.

"No," Johnny says. "They're scattered all over. The Enforcers are in the gatehouse. Spies in the undercroft. Accountants over by the library. You lot will be in the Octagon Tower. The girls are separate from the boys. You're not allowed in their rooms, so don't get any bright ideas. There's four guys for every girl at Kingmakers. You're not supposed to be dating, and the odds aren't in your favor anyway. Half the girls here probably have some marriage contract lined up already, and if you get one pregnant, her family can have you castrated. So just keep that in mind."

I can't tell if he's joking or not. Bram looks green at the thought.

"We're in here," Johnny says, shoving through a heavy wooden door studded with metal reinforcements. The thing looks like it weighs as much as a refrigerator, but Johnny pushes it aside easily.

He's leading us into the second-tallest of the towers on the northeast corner of campus. Unlike the others, which are cylindrical, this particular tower is indeed octagonal. Its strange shape creates odd corners in the main common room and awkward angles for each of the dorm rooms. At least our rooms are high up with good airflow and a stunning view of the limestone cliffs.

"Two to a room," Johnny says. "Pick your own roommate. I don't give a fuck."

It's an obvious choice to go with Ares. We only have to make eye contact and grin at each other to confirm it.

I expect Bram Van Der Berg to room with his Albanian friend Valon Hoxha, but to my surprise, he gives a quick upward jerk of the chin to Dean, saying, "You wanna share?"

Dean eyes him warily.

"Alright," he says. "As long as you're tidy."

"Of course." Bram nods.

They take the room down the hall from Ares and me. I can't tell if it's a good thing or a bad thing to have both my antagonists teaming up. At least it puts them in the same place, so I can keep an eye on both of them at once.

Valon Hoxha looks disgruntled at being abandoned without so much as a second thought. He's forced to turn sullenly to the blond Norwegian Erik Edman instead.

"You have a roommate already?" he mutters.

"Nope," Erik says. "And I don't snore, so you better not either."

Jules Turgenev turns to the French-Canadian Emile Girard. "*Serons-nous colocataires*?"

"*Pourquoi pas*?" Emile shrugs.

That leaves the boy with the dragon tattoo, Kenzo Tanaka, to room with the sullen and silent Hedeon Gray, who I believe is from London.

Ares and I take the room at the very end of the hall. It's the farthest walk away from the stairs, but it has the best view and hopefully will be a little quieter than the bedrooms closer to the common room.

It's a small space with two beds on opposite sides of the room, two dressers, and no closet. No desks either—I guess we're supposed to do our schoolwork in the library. If there even is any schoolwork. Do we write papers at Kingmakers? I have no idea.

That's when the strangeness of this place finally hits me. I realize that I have no fucking clue what class is going to look like tomorrow. This is not a normal college. I can't picture what we'll be learning or how.

"You care which bed you get?" Ares asks me.

"Nope."

"I'll take this one, then," he says, throwing his backpack down on the bed set against the right-hand wall of the room.

"Suits me," I say, flopping down on the left.

The bed is hard and narrow. My feet hang off the end.

"Well, shit," I say, realizing how poorly I'm going to fit in this room, especially with a guy as big as Ares. "Maybe we should've picked smaller roommates."

Ares laughs. "It wouldn't help you fit on that mattress any better."

At least the rooms are clean—the stone floor is swept, and the walls have been freshly white-washed to remove whatever scuffs or scribbles the former occupants might have left.

"Does the window open?" I ask Ares.

"Yeah," he says, trying it. "Careful, though. It's a long way down."

He peers through the bubbled glass down the steep walls of the tower to the courtyard below.

"When do you think we get dinner?" I say.

I skipped breakfast, and they didn't feed us anything on the boat. My stomach is growling.

"Should we ask Johnny?" Ares says.

I weigh my hunger against Johnny's obvious irritation at being asked to care for us freshmen in any way.

"Yeah." I grin. "Let's ask him. But be prepared to run if he decides that's a stupid question."

CHAPTER 5
DEAN

I WAKE EARLY, BEFORE THE SUN IS EVEN UP. I KNOW AT ONCE THAT I'm not in my old room at home. I can tell because the air isn't musty and enclosed, with that awful lingering scent of neglect I could never seem to shake. Instead, I smell sea breeze and the fresh herbs growing in the terraced garden below my window.

Bram is still snoring in the bed across from mine. It's weird sharing a room with another dude, especially one I barely know. Bram is an ally, though, and that's all that matters. I only just met him in Dubrovnik, but I've seen that he's tough, aggressive, and reasonably intelligent, and that's what I want in a friend.

In Moscow, I always got up early to go for a run while the streets were still empty. I could probably run all over this island in a couple of hours. But I don't know the rules well enough to know if we're allowed to leave the school grounds.

Better to just use the gym our guide showed us the day before.

Slipping out of bed quietly, I open my top drawer and pull out the gym attire I purchased along with the rest of my uniforms. I'd already neatly folded my clothes and stowed them away in the dresser the night before.

When Bram asked if I wanted to room together, I told him bluntly that he'd better keep it tidy if he wants to share space.

"I don't want to see one goddamned sock on the floor," I told him.

He shrugged, tossing back his dark hair out of his face. "Fine by me. Guess I'd better learn to clean up after myself anyway if we don't have maids here."

Like most spoiled Mafia children, I'm assuming he has a full-time cleaning crew at his parents' house.

Anyway, he's kept to his word so far, and if he doesn't, I'll chuck his clothes out the fucking window. I can't stand mess. It makes my flesh crawl. It makes me want to rip my own skin off.

I pull on the plain gray sweat shorts and white T-shirt that we're expected to wear whenever we do combat training or anything else physical. Even the white tube socks are mandatory.

I don't really give a shit. I've never cared much about clothes.

Once I'm dressed, I slip out of the dorm down to the empty courtyard. There's no one around, the first gray light illuminating the edges of the balustrades.

It takes me a minute to find the armory again. I take a wrong turn and end up on the opposite side of the building, over by a cluster of orange trees surrounding a flat, open platform that might once have been used for weapons training.

I would have walked right by, except I hear music playing.

We're not technically supposed to have electronics at the school, though I guess it doesn't much matter—there's no internet connection on the island. Still, it piques my curiosity. I creep over to the orange trees and peer through the branches, looking to see who's making the noise.

It's a girl. A blond girl, dressed in a black leotard and torn-up tights.

She has on a pair of extremely battered pointe shoes, and she's dancing on the cracked stone platform like a music box ballerina up on its stand.

The music isn't classical—it's something wistful and moody that I haven't heard before.

"Love Chained"—Cannons

The girl is tall, which makes her legs look a mile long, especially up on tiptoe. She's slim, but I can see the lean muscles flexing on her shoulders and back and on her thighs and calves.

I see the muscles working, but her movements look utterly effortless. She seems to float across the rough stone. She bends and swoops like a bird in flight.

The early morning light gleams silver on her skin and on her long sheaf of pale hair that whips around her face as she spins. The open back of her leotard shows several tattoos on her shoulder blade, triceps, and wrist.

Her eyes are closed. She's completely lost in the music, making up the dance as she goes along, or so it looks to me.

I've never seen dancing like this. It's vulnerable, it's raw, it's emotional. The song is sad and yearning, about a love unrequited. It's not the kind of thing I would usually listen to. I don't give a fuck about love, and I certainly don't listen to maudlin, whiny music.

But in this moment, this girl seems to be embodying the emotion of the song to such a degree that I can't ignore it. I can't not feel what she's feeling.

My heart is tight in my chest. My hands feel cold, and I realize I haven't blinked once since I first laid eyes on this girl.

She's been dancing with her back to me.

Now she turns, and I can see her face fully for the first time.

She's stunning. The most beautiful girl I've ever seen. Her features are painfully sharp, with high cheekbones, a pointed chin, and a pouting mouth that turns down slightly at the corners, the top lip the same fullness as the bottom.

She wears too much makeup—white powder that makes her look even paler than she actually is, dark lipstick, and a mask of smoky shadow around her eyes.

Maybe she wants to look tough instead of pretty. It's impossible. No amount of makeup can hide the loveliness of her features.

She opens her eyes at last, and I can see that her irises are a pale, clear blue, like glacial ice, like blue diamond.

Even through the leaves of the orange trees, those eyes fix on me at once, and her dreamy expression burns away in an instant, replaced by cold fury.

I've already drawn back and turned around, striding away from her as quickly as possible. I didn't mean to watch her like a pervert hiding in the bushes. I didn't mean to look at her at all. It just happened. The music pulled me in, and then I was transfixed by the strangeness of what I saw.

Now I shake my head, trying to physically shake the memory out of my brain.

It was just a girl practicing a dance, which is stupid and has no place at Kingmakers. She must be a freshman. Otherwise, she'd be working on something useful instead of prancing around.

I jog over to the armory, where I meant to go in the first place.

Pushing through the doors, I'm hit with the not-unpleasant scent of sweat, iron, and rubber mats. It reminds me of the gym where I trained in Moscow, and that makes me happy.

I spend the next hour punishing my body relentlessly. I alternate between hitting the heavy bag and the speed bag, jumping rope, and doing compound lifts in drop sets. The gym is impressively equipped. There's nothing I want that they don't have.

As the sun comes up, I'm joined by a few other students looking to get in an early morning workout—though not quite as early as mine. By this point, I'm dripping in sweat, and every muscle on my body is throbbing.

I'm working even harder than usual, trying to banish the image of that girl from my mind.

I don't know why I'm still thinking about her. Because she was pretty? I've fucked plenty of pretty girls before.

I chug down a glass of cold water from the cooler, then head in what I hope is the direction of the showers. It's irritating trying to find anything in this place—there are no signs like there would be at a normal college. Even the doors to the changing rooms lack the usual male and female stick figures.

It doesn't matter. I'm the only person in here anyway.

The changing room is large and echoing, with double banks of lockers and a dozen showers in one open space.

I strip off my sweaty clothes, folding them neatly and stacking them on top of my sneakers, leaving the pile on a bench for the moment. Then I turn on one of the shower heads, twisting the nozzle till the spray runs hot and steady. I'm about to step under when I realize I forgot to grab a towel.

I hurry across the cold tiles, starting to get chilly now that the sweat is drying on my skin. Though it's still more summer than fall, all the interior spaces of Kingmakers are well-insulated by the thick stone walls, and the wool uniforms are starting to make a lot more sense. It's never entirely warm inside this place, especially when you're naked.

I pull a scratchy, thin towel out of the linen cupboard and hurry back toward my shower. I'm practically jogging, rounding the corner of the nearest locker bay with my head down.

I thought I was alone in here, the loud spray of the shower echoing around in the space, drowning out any other sounds.

So I wasn't expecting to plow headlong into another person. We hit hard, my bare feet slipping out from under me on the tiles as I crash down on top of a stranger.

The other person is just as naked as me. I quickly realize from the long, slim legs sliding between mine and the soft, round breast on which my palm lands—not to mention the startled shriek of outrage—that I've collided with a girl.

Despite how tangled we are, she leaps up again as quick as a cat hitting water. She crosses her arms over her bare breasts, but not before I get a glimpse of a pair of milk-white tits, the pale pink nipples stiff with shock and fury.

She doesn't seem to realize that covering her breasts has left her pussy bare. I have to physically wrench my eyes up to her face to avoid fixating on those delicate pussy lips, clean-shaven, the same shell-pink color as her nipples.

It's the girl from outside, the one who was dancing. I know that before I even get a proper look at her face.

She recognizes me too.

"Did you follow me in here?" she demands. "I saw you spying on me!"

"I wasn't *spying*. You were dancing outside. Anybody could see you."

"Why were you hiding in the bushes, then?"

"I wasn't hiding! There were trees in the way. There's a difference between standing on the other side of a tree and hiding behind a tree."

"I don't think there is," the girl says, her pretty face twisted up in a scowl.

"I didn't follow you!" My face feels hot, and my heart squeezes painfully in my chest, a mix of embarrassment and discomfort, which are two emotions I thought I'd squashed a long time ago. "I was exercising. What are you doing in here anyway?"

"What am *I* doing?" she cries, half scoff and half shout. "What the fuck are *you* doing? This is the girls' room!"

"No, it isn't," I say, though I don't actually know for sure.

"How do you know?" she demands.

In truth, I was guessing. Based on…not much, really. The fact that the changing room looked big and gloomy and smelled like a bunch of dudes might have showered in there.

I'm about to admit that when I catch the flicker of uncertainty in the girl's blue eyes, and I realize that she's guessing too.

"You don't know either," I say.

"I…well…" In her discomfort, the girl drops her eyes, which inevitably run down the length of my naked body. I haven't bothered to cover up, so my cock is hanging there in plain sight, slightly swollen from unexpectedly rubbing up against a sleek female body.

Her cheeks flush pink, and she whips her head to the side with comical speed.

"Are you going to put some clothes on?" she demands.

"No," I say calmly. "I haven't showered yet."

"I have to shower too," she says.

"So?"

"So there's no separate stalls."

"Go in the other changing room then."

"You don't know if that's even the girls' room!"

"Neither do you."

We glare at each other, equally as committed to being stubborn as we are unsure of whether we're actually in the right.

Neither of us wants to cave. But we can't stand here naked forever.

"I'm showering right here," the girl declares, tossing her head so her blond ponytail swings back over her shoulder. Dropping her arms from their protective stance across her chest, she snatches up the towel she dropped on the ground and marches over to the showers.

I stare at her back, trying hard not to let that turn into staring at her ass, then I pick up my own towel and follow after her.

She's already standing under *my* showerhead, soaping up her hair with a hefty lather of shampoo. Ignoring her, I turn on a second nozzle and step under it before it's even warm.

I scrub myself with equal vigor and an equal attitude of *I don't give a fuck.*

The trouble is it's hard not to look over at the girl as soap suds run down her naked body. Her little breasts bounce on her chest as she shampoos her hair. I can't stop thinking how slippery smooth her skin must be, remembering how her bare thigh slid between mine as my cock pressed against her flat, tight stomach.

I turn around and face the shower nozzle so she won't see my cock stiffening up all over again.

I'm only halfway through showering when I hear a sound that makes my blood run cold: the voices of two girls chatting and giggling as they stroll toward the showers.

I turn around right as they reach me.

The girls stop dead in their tracks. They look a little older than me, maybe sophomores or juniors. They've got towels wrapped round their bodies, and they're wearing identical expressions of surprise and amusement.

"Well, hello," one of them says to me.

"Are you lost?" the other asks.

Well, fuck. Guess the ballerina was right after all.

I grab my towel and hustle out of there without answering.

They don't even wait till I turn the corner before bursting out laughing. Their giggles echo off the stone ceiling, reminding me what an idiot I am about a hundred times before I reach the door.

I draw a few more amused glances walking back to the dorms dressed only in a towel, with my duffel bag slung over my shoulder and my gym clothes tucked under my arm.

I'm embarrassed, but I can't say I entirely regret the experience.

It definitely had its pleasant moments.

CHAPTER 6
ANNA

I CAN'T BELIEVE I'VE BEEN AT THIS SCHOOL ONE DAY AND I'VE already rubbed my naked body all over some stranger.

My face is still burning an hour after my shower.

I hope that fuckhead doesn't go and tell all his friends, but I'm sure he will. He probably did the whole thing on purpose. I know he was watching me, and it *was* the girls' room. That asshole.

It's not how I wanted to start my first day of classes. I'm already running late. Though honestly, that's mostly because I lost track of time dancing. They don't offer dance classes at Kingmakers, and there's no way I'm going to spend the next four years only dancing over the summers. I'll practice on my own.

I don't even see it as practice. I see it as a necessary part of my day, like eating, sleeping, and walking around. If I miss a few days, I feel stiff and anxious. My body and my brain feel neglected. I need dance to level out my emotions.

Maybe I'd better find a less public place to practice. I didn't think anyone would be around that early in the morning. But I guess in a school this big, there's always going to be someone around.

After changing into a fresh uniform, I head to the dining hall. I know Leo was just giving me shit, but the truth is that I do feel distinctly uncomfortable in the assigned clothes. What I wear is important to me. Not for other people but for myself.

I like dark colors. I find them calming. I'm sensitive to busy patterns, loud noises, uncomfortable textures. And I hate wearing anything that clashes with my mood. Sometimes I want to feel like I'm in a dark fantasy dream. Sometimes I want to look like I'm a ghost from a graveyard or a Victorian beggar. Sometimes I want to feel like a rock star.

Never would I ever wear something fuzzy and pink. No shade on the girls that like it—it just isn't me.

At least the uniforms are relatively subdued. Mostly tones of black, gray, and dark green, with a little silver or white. It could be a lot worse. Imagine if the school colors were fluorescent orange and blue.

We can wear whatever shoes we like, so I didn't have to give up my favorite boots. I paired them with the same green skirt from yesterday, a black pullover, and black tights. Not too bad—something I might possibly have worn in the normal world.

There's nothing normal about Kingmakers, and I love that. I never pictured myself on a bright, sunny college campus, joining clubs and making friends, going to frat parties on the weekend. I always wanted to come here.

My father told me all about it when I was small—or told me everything he knew at least. He had a deep reverence for Mafia traditions, since he wasn't raised in that world but instead was initiated as a teenager by his adoptive father.

He told me, "I had nothing, Anna. Nothing at all. I was poor, miserable, desperate. Trying to scratch a life for myself in Warsaw but knowing that I would likely live and die as poor as I started, just like my parents. The only person who brought me happiness was my sister. She was brilliant, you know, like you. She wanted to become a doctor. I planned to work and pay her way through school. We dreamed of someday buying a house in a nicer neighborhood… Well, you know what happened instead."

I nodded, sitting next to my father on the rim of an empty stone fountain in the walled garden behind our house. Even though I was only six or seven at the time, he had already told me exactly what happened to the other Anna.

She was attacked and raped by three Braterstwo while walking home from school one day. She was only sixteen at the time. She killed herself that same night.

"I had no weapons, no training. But I was bent on revenge. I stalked those men. I tracked them. I killed the easiest one first. It was the first time I had ever raised a hand to someone, and I slit his throat without hesitation. You have never killed anyone, Anna. But someday, if you intend to take my place, you will have to make that choice. It may fill you with horror or shame. Or perhaps, if you are like me, you'll find that you feel no remorse, as long as you are justified."

I nodded again slowly, looking up into my father's face.

I have always loved my mother with a love that's almost like worship. She's pure kindness and light. She's a divine goddess on earth, casting joy on everyone around her.

But I was made from my father's bones. Not divine—fully mortal. My father is the one I take after. When I look into his face, I see myself.

So I already knew, even at six years old, that I wanted to be a boss someday, like him. And that when the time came to kill, I could do it without hesitation. Feeling that I was justified.

"I killed the second man too," my father said. "But when I went to kill the third, I failed. I was captured by the Braterstwo. I was brought before their boss, Tymon Zajac. I thought he would torture and murder me. It's what I expected. Instead, when he heard what his men had done, he shot his own lieutenant in the head, completing my revenge."

My father swallowed hard, a muscle jumping in the corner of his jaw. Even all those years later, I saw what that meant to him—that the other Anna had been fully avenged. I knew he believed her soul could never be at peace otherwise.

I thought that perhaps her soul wasn't at peace, though. I thought she might be haunting me. She died before I was born. Maybe her soul had even been reincarnated in me.

The thought didn't frighten me. In a strange way, it seemed comforting. If the other Anna had become a vengeful spirit, it would only make me stronger.

My father continued, "What I learned in that moment is that the Braterstwo had honor. They had a moral code. They were not simply criminals, as I'd believed. Tymon Zajac looked at me. He didn't see a poor, skinny child. He saw that I was like him. Or that I could be like him someday. He offered me a position at his side. He taught and trained me. And he told me the history of the Braterstwo, the Bratva, the Italian Mafia, the Penose, the Yakuza. Each has its own genesis and development. But like any ecosystem, we have grown, collaborated, battled, and aligned over time. And like many ancient families, we have ancestors in common. Many of the criminal families today can trace their ancestry to the thieves' guild of the medieval era. That guild had its headquarters at Kingmakers."

I had finally interrupted him then, too interested to listen quietly any longer.

"What does it look like?" I demanded, even though he'd told me before.

My father gave me a description of the island and the castle fortress, which he had described for me many times but I always wanted to hear it again. If he left anything out, I reminded him.

"Then there's the towers—" he said.

"*Six* towers!" I cried, not wanting any detail omitted.

"A library—"

"In the tallest tower!"

"That's right," he said and smiled.

My father's smile is not like my mother's. Her smile is so warm that it lights up the room. Her eyes crinkle up, her cheeks flush pink, and you feel like she's laughing, and you have to laugh too.

My father's smile is thin and subtle. It doesn't show his teeth. But it runs over you like an electric shock. He is just as mesmerizing as my mother in his own way. They are Hades and Persephone: the king of the underworld and the queen of summer.

I always knew I would come to Kingmakers. And now that I'm here, it doesn't disappoint. Every stone, every doorway seems stuffed with antiquity and intrigue. I want to get to know every inch of this place. I want to imprint my own history on its walls so that a piece of me will remain here long after I'm gone.

As I walk into the dining hall, I see Leo already sitting with Ares, each attacking a massive platter of bacon and eggs. I dish up my own plate from the silver chafing dishes set out for us, and I grab a pot of mint tea as well.

So far, I've found that the food here is simple but extremely good. Fresh-baked bread, meat and produce from the farmland directly around Kingmakers.

"There you are!" Leo says as I sit down. "You almost missed breakfast."

"Morning," Ares says, pushing a stone tureen of cream in my direction for my tea.

Ares is dressed neatly in a crisp white button-up, tucked into ironed trousers. His shoes don't look new, but he's polished them carefully. I wonder if he likes the uniforms because it makes it less obvious that he's not as wealthy as the rest of the students.

Leo, by contrast, has not ironed any of his clothes, and his shirt is only half tucked in. His dark curls look like he just rolled out of bed, and he's shoved up his sleeves so he can attack his food more easily, showing his bare brown forearms with veins running up both sides and his large, long-fingered hands.

As he spears a sausage with his fork, his forearm flexes, and I feel strangely warm. Leo is sprawled out in his seat like always, too big to fit comfortably in normal furniture. His long legs are perpetually stretched out under tables and across aisleways, his broad shoulders always taking up more than their fair share of space.

Leo's loud too. He talks and laughs with so much animation that every eye in the room is drawn to him. Leo is the sun, and everyone wants the sun shining on their face. Girls flutter around him like moths. Even boys can't deny his charm. Everyone wants to be friends with him. Everyone wants to be near him.

I have to admit, it's flattering to be the best friend of a man like that. Everybody wants to spend time with Leo, and he gives that time and attention to me more than anyone.

But lately I can't enjoy our friendship like I used to. It used to be so pure and simple. Leo was my brother, my confidante, and my partner in crime all rolled into one.

We sailed through every phase of life without anything coming between us. When we went through puberty, I laughed at Leo's voice cracking and deepening, and he teased me mercilessly about my awful braces and how quickly I shot up in height so that he was the only boy in our class still taller than me.

He started dating girls from our school and then girls from other schools, and I was never jealous, because while they might be his girlfriends, I was his best friend.

I went on a few dates myself, but I never felt that thing you're supposed to feel, that spark of infatuation. The boys were sometimes nice and sometimes obnoxious, but either way, I didn't appreciate them putting their clumsy hands on me. I never wanted to take things further than an awkward kiss at the end of the night.

I never knew if Leo was taking things further. I assumed he was, because he's a boy and wildly popular—he could fuck a different girl every day of the week. But that was the one thing we didn't talk about. Leo seemed strangely reticent, and since I had no sex stories of my own, it was pointless to bring it up.

Our families saw us as cousins, as brother and sister even. I thought I felt the same.

Then last year, something changed.

All of a sudden, I felt a tension that was never there before. I started noticing things about Leo that I didn't want to notice.

When he throws his arm around my shoulders, I breathe in his scent and my heart starts to race. I notice how warm his skin is and how surprisingly soft. I see how he bites the corner of his lip when he grins, and I get this uncomfortable squeezing in my gut that was never there before.

I tell myself it will stop.

My emotions have never been as stable as Leo's—it's something I admire about him. His confidence and optimism are boundless, whereas I'm often sad or anxious, sometimes for no reason at all.

This just-enough swell of emotion, rolling over me like a wave. A bizarre impulse that will fade and die, just like how it rose up out of nothing.

I have to ignore it, even smother it.

Because whatever happens, I can't risk my friendship with Leo. Nothing is more important to me.

"What's up with you?" Leo says. "You look grumpier than usual."

"I'm not," I say, chewing a piece of bacon.

But I can't fool Leo.

"What's wrong?" he persists. "You have a bad dream or something?"

He knows I have nightmares. He knows everything about me. Well…almost everything.

"No." I gulp down the hot mint tea. "I just had a weird thing this morning."

I don't want to tell Leo what happened because I know he'll laugh his ass off at the image of me running into some dude buck naked. He'll never let me hear the end of it. But he's sure to hear about it anyway, if Kingmakers is anything like high school. A story like that doesn't stay quiet for long.

Before I can say a word, Leo's face darkens, and he glares across the dining hall.

"There he is, that fucker."

"Who?" I turn to look.

"Dean Yenin."

Leo is staring across the hall not at a stranger but at the very boy I ran into this morning. I recognize him at once, even though he's now fully dressed in a green sweater vest and trousers.

I whip my head back around, cheeks flaming.

"That's Dean?"

I never asked Leo what Dean Yenin looks like. The silver-blond hair, the fair skin, the violet eyes—I'm a fucking idiot. It's Aunt Yelena's nephew, clear as day.

Had I not been so embarrassed and annoyed, I would have realized. Now that I'm paying attention, I can even see a faint bruise under his eye—a remnant of his fight with Leo on the deck of the ship.

"That's him," Leo says grimly. "Wonder if we'll have classes with him today."

"Probably. The heirs will mostly be together, won't we?"

"What do you have first?" Ares asks us.

I take my schedule out of my bag. We didn't select the classes ourselves—it was all determined ahead of time, mailed to us in one of those thick slate-gray envelopes that can only mean a missive from Kingmakers.

The Kingmakers letters are handwritten every time. I wonder if that's because nothing is stored on a computer at this place. They must have a dozen employees with perfect penmanship, because my schedule looks like something torn out of an illuminated manuscript.

It's not exactly easy to read. Leo squints at the ornate cursive, trying to figure out what the hell his first class even is.

"I think I've got…history," he says at last.

"Me too," I say.

"Me three." Ares grins.

"Well, you'd better hurry up, then," Leo says. "We only have five minutes, and I have no clue where the keep is."

I fold up one more slice of bacon and stuff it in my mouth, washing it down with a gulp of tea.

"Do you think we're supposed to clear the dishes?" Ares asks.

"Nope." Leo nods toward a man in a crisp white apron who's cleaning off the neighboring table. "Looks like that guy's doing it."

Ares hesitates, seeming like he'd rather help, but Leo and I are already slinging our bags over our shoulders.

"Come on," Leo says. "I don't know what they do if you're late—string you up on a rack, probably."

The draconian punishments of the school were spelled out in our rules and regulations list. But so far, it's all theoretical, so it's easy for Leo to joke about it.

I don't feel quite as sanguine. I've never known anything to be a joke in the Mafia world.

Our acceptance letters clearly spelled out the rule of recompense.

Students from all over the world come to attend Kingmakers. There's a heavier concentration of Italian, Irish, and Russian students, because those are the territories closest to the school. But with children from all countries and families and plenty more grudges than the one between Leo and Dean, they have to be strict about violence.

They know that fights will break out—it's inevitable with so many young hotheads used to solving every problem with their fists.

The one thing we have in the back of our minds at all times, reminding us never to go too far over the line, is the rule of recompense.

If any student injures, disfigures, or maims another student, the same injury will be applied to them.

There's no arguing. No appeal. To prevent an endless cycle of retaliations between families, the punishment is applied immediately and swiftly.

If you break someone's arm, your arm will be broken too. If you put out their eye, they'll pluck yours right out of the socket. And if you kill someone… Well, that's the last thing you'll do.

That's why my father was worried about Leo coming here with me. He knows Leo has a temper. And it wouldn't be the first time Leo has pulled me into trouble right along with him.

"Come on!" Leo grabs my arm and tugs me along since I'm too slow gathering up my book bag. "Where do you think the classroom is?" he asks Ares.

"I think most of the classes are in the keep," Ares says.

The keep is the largest building at Kingmakers. It's five stories high, with staircases built into the thickness of the stone walls. This would be the last stronghold of the castle if all the other outer walls fell to invaders.

I don't think anyone has ever actually attacked Kingmakers—it's too far out in the middle of nowhere. But if someone were to try, before the era of drone strikes and bombers, it would have been almost impossible to scale the cliffs or breach its fortress walls.

We find our classroom just in time, located on the second floor of the keep. It's a large, airy room, the walls covered with antique maps and the blackboard already crowded with chalk diagrams of family trees and endless notations in a fine, spidery script.

Leo, Ares, and I slip into three of the remaining desks in the front row. The professor closes the door only a moment after, striding to the front of the class.

She's a tall, dark-haired woman, about forty, wearing a perfectly fitted suit and a pair of elegant horn-rimmed glasses. Her husky voice instantly claims the attention of the room.

"'If you don't know history, then you don't know anything,'" she says. "'You are a leaf that doesn't know it is part of a tree.' Who said that?"

She looks around at us, her demand echoing in a room that has fallen so silent that you can almost hear our individual heartbeats.

"Was it...Churchill?" an Irish boy with untidy brown hair asks hesitantly.

"No," Professor Thorn says. Her lips curve up in a small smile.

"It was Michael Crichton. Authors tend to note the repetitive cycles of events. They look for patterns in behavior, cause and effect. What about this one? 'A man who has no sense of history is like a man who has no ears or eyes.'"

She waits for us to respond. This time, no one has the temerity to guess.

"That was Hitler," she says with a wicked smile. "I don't think he took his own advice."

She turns and writes on the blackboard in that fine, flowing script.

"La Cosa Nostra," she says, speaking aloud the words as they unfurl from the tip of her dusty chalk. "Giuseppe Esposito was the first Sicilian Mafia member to emigrate to America. He fled there, along with six of his men, after killing the chancellor and vice-chancellor of his province, along with eleven oligarchs. The Italian Mafia spread from New York to New Orleans and then to Chicago. Several families rose and fell from power—first the Black Hand, then the Five Points Gang, then Al Capone's Syndicate.

"This semester, we will study the history of the Italian Mafia in Italy and America. Then we will move on through the various families represented at Kingmakers until we have covered each and every one by the end of your fourth year."

She frowns at us, perceiving the thrill of excitement in the students of Italian descent.

"Don't be too happy," she says sternly. "Every semester, the students who fail are the ones who think they already know everything that I'm about to teach them. Trust me, you don't. Every year, you freshmen prove yourselves shockingly ignorant of your own history, the history of your country, and the history of your friends and enemies. You've probably been told more legends than truths by your relatives. Memory is fallible. And no one is more prone to self-serving reconstructions than those who believe they can write their destiny at will."

I can feel Leo getting restless next to me. I don't even have to look at him to know that he's probably gazing around the room to see what the other students think of this speech or trying to peer out the windows that run down only one side of the classroom.

Whereas I feel electric excitement at Professor Thorn's words. I've always loved history. You live a thousand lives when you learn about the people who came before you, and you can take their lessons as your own.

I spend the next ninety minutes scribbling furiously in my notebook as Professor Thorn recounts the origins of the Cosa Nostra in Sicily.

Leo doesn't bother taking any notes, safe in the assurance that he can copy mine later.

That doesn't bother me. I'm more annoyed by the fact that Leo is so clever that he can get away with barely paying attention to the professors' lectures, scoring almost as high as me on exams without even trying.

Ares writes slowly and steadily in his notebook. His stubby pencil disappears inside his large hand, bent so far over his notebook that his nose almost touches the page. I can't tell if he's as fascinated by the lecture as I am or simply very focused.

Behind Ares, Hedeon Gray stares at the professor with an irritated expression. I don't think I've seen him make any other face yet. He's good-looking but perpetually sulky.

Professor Thorn has a fascinating narrative style. Her history lesson is not at all dry. How could it be, when the history of the Mafia is studded with conniving deals, double crosses, and, of course, murder?

I barely look up from my notebook the entire ninety minutes. In fact, I'm surprised when the professor breaks off midsentence, saying, "That's all the time for today. I'll see you tomorrow morning."

With that, she turns and strides out of the room without bothering to bid us goodbye.

Leo practically rockets up out of his seat. "God, I thought that would never end."

"I liked it," I say.

"Of course you did." Leo rolls his eyes. "You like learning."

I laugh. "Is that supposed to be an insult?"

"What about you?" Leo demands of Ares. "Were you actually enjoying that?"

Ares shrugs. "I didn't know barely any of it. I'll probably have to study a lot."

Leo snorts. "Nobody cares about grades here. It's all about who wins the challenges."

We have to change clothes before our next class. It's a combat class, which means gym uniforms and sneakers.

I make sure to turn into the correct changing room, deliberately averting my eyes from the spot where I collided with Dean next to the showers.

The gymnasium is located in what used to be the armory. It's a dim, cool space. The floors are soft with thick mats. Ancient medieval weapons hang from hooks on the walls: battle axes, swords, and morning stars, and then over on the far side of the room, a selection of Asian katanas, bo staffs, and throwing stars. I assume these are for decoration and not something we'll actually learn to use. But I can't be certain of anything at Kingmakers.

There are only four girls in the combat class, including me. The boys gaze hungrily at us in our shorts. We've only been out of civilization a couple of days, and already they've got the look of starving dogs.

I walk past Dean and Bram lounging on a pile of mats. Bram lets out a low wolf whistle, and Dean smirks. I'm sure he told Bram what happened.

Well, fuck them both.

Professor Howell joins us on the mats. He's medium height, trim and fit, dressed in an olive-green T-shirt and cargo pants. He faces us, hands clasped behind his back, smiling pleasantly.

"Good morning, students," he says. "In our combat cla
will be learning a variety of martial arts, self-defense, and wea
techniques. You'll have separate classes to learn artillery and ex
sives. This semester, we will be focusing on Krav Maga. As you
already know, it's a military self-defense and fighting system use
the Israel Defense Forces. It includes a combination of techni
drawn from aikido, boxing, wrestling, karate, and judo."

His keen dark eyes scan our group, looking over each stud
in turn.

"You." He points to the largest boy, a bull-like behemoth w
straw-colored hair and trunk-like thighs stretching the limits of
gym shorts. "Come up here."

The boy obliges, the gym mats indenting deeply under each
his steps.

"What's your name?" the professor asks him.

"Bodashka Kushnir." The boy smiles with an uneasy mixture
bravado and nerves.

"The primary tenet of Krav Maga is acting instinctively und
high-stress and unpredictable circumstances." The professor regar
the blond boy with a teasing glint in his eye. "How would y
describe your current level of combat skill, my friend?"

Bodashka considers. Goaded on by his friends watching, h
grins and says, "High."

"Excellent." The professor nods. "I thought so just by looking
you. Why don't we give a simple demonstration, then? Attack m
and if I'm able, I'll formulate a defense."

Bodashka seems to be gaining confidence by the moment. H
lifts his fists, facing the much smaller professor. The sense of antici
pation in the room is high. His Bratva pals cheer him on, while th
rest of us suspect what's about to happen.

The boy rushes the professor, throwing two jabs, a hard righ
cross, and then a surprisingly nimble kick to the face.

The professor barely has to shift his stance to block each one

ugh the blows are thrown with full strength, it's Bodashka
ces as the professor uses his elbows, forearms, and shoulder
t the strikes.

odashka throws his last desperate roundhouse kick at the
's head, Professor Howell ducks and neatly sweeps the boy's
rom under him, sending him crashing down on the mats.

gym echoes with the force of the boy hitting the ground,
nocked out of him despite the cushioning mats.

sure you've all heard the expression 'the bigger they are,
der they fall,'" the professor says dryly. "Beware a smaller
nt with a lower center of mass."

helps the chastened Bodashka up from the ground, then uses
demonstrate several basic blocks.

ce we all seem to understand the lesson, he splits us up into
practice.

u wanna have a go?" Leo asks.

not the first time we've fought. I've been wrestling and
Leo since we were old enough to stand.

rin at him. "Why not?"

e face off, waiting for the professor's signal to begin.

vait for Leo to make the first move.

e takes a playful jab at me, and I slip it easily, knowing that's
en close to his top speed. He's got those damn long arms, so I
o either dance way outside his reach or rush inside to hit him
e he can get me.

eo takes another playful swing, and as I try to duck it, he
for my leg exactly like the professor did. Even though I see it
ng, he's so damn fast that he still manages to knock my right leg
rom under me. I recover by rolling between his legs, jumping up
popping him in the kidney from behind.

"You little asshole," Leo says, seizing me by the wrist and twist-
my arm up behind my back.

I try to wrench my wrist out of his grasp before he can get me in a hold, but it's impossible. Faster than I can think, he's got my arm pinned behind my back and his other arm wrapped around my waist, the weight of his whole body bearing down.

"Submit," he growls in my ear.

"Fucking never," I hiss back at him.

"Don't make me break your arm on the first day of school." I can hear him grinning without seeing his face.

I stomp hard on his foot, forcing him to release me right as the professor calls time.

Leo backs off, chuckling. But someone is watching us.

Dean stares, his glinting eyes the only sign of life in his stiff, pale face.

Leo follows my gaze.

"See something you like?" he says aggressively.

"I already saw it this morning," Dean replies in his low, cold voice.

"What's that supposed to mean?"

"Oh, she didn't tell you?" Dean smirks. "Your girlfriend and I had an intimate encounter this morning."

"Oh yeah?" Leo laughs. "How early? Sounds like you were still asleep and dreaming in your bed."

But when he glances back at me, he can see my cheeks burning.

"What's he talking about?" Leo mutters, brows drawing together.

"Nothing." I shake my head.

"What did—"

We're interrupted by the professor asking for another volunteer. Scared off by the fate of the last volunteer, nobody raises their hand. Only Dean steps forward.

"I'll do it."

"Step on up." Professor Howell gestures to the empty space in front of him as if he were inviting Dean to take a comfortable seat on a sofa.

Dean approaches, his eyes fixed on the professor. He has neither the bravado nor the nervousness of the first volunteer. He radiates a cool confidence that has all of us watching intently, none more than Leo.

"A simultaneous block and strike can be highly effective," the professor says, demonstrating an outside block with his right arm and a counterstrike with the heel of his palm in the direction of Dean's face. "I'll attack. Let's see if our friend here can both defend and counterstrike."

Professor Howell comes at Dean without warning, firing two quick punches and an elbow to his face. Dean narrowly avoids all three, ducking and weaving in neat, tight movements.

As the professor aims a fourth punch at Dean's face, Dean knocks it aside and manages to tap the professor in the chest with a short, tight punch. As quick as the blow was, we all hear the impact. The professor is pushed back on his heels.

Dean's speed and precision are flawless. I can tell by Leo's silence that even he can't deny that Dean knows how to fight.

"Well done," Professor Howell says approvingly.

Dean nods, accepting the praise without comment. But I see a muscle jump in the corner of his jaw. He's pleased.

"Pair up to practice," the professor says.

This time, Leo isn't nearly as playful. We spar with each other, practicing counterstrikes. He's not really watching me. He keeps glancing across the room at Dean.

Because he's not paying attention, I hit him hard on the right cheekbone.

"Ow." He rubs the side of his face.

"Get it together," I say without sympathy.

He looks at me, his eyes searching my face. I've seen Leo's eyes up close enough times to have memorized their exact color. They're not brown, not really. Instead, there's a dark, smoky outer ring, almost as black as the pupil itself, then a bright amber iris that makes me think of an animal in the jungle—a tiger or a panther. A predator that can see in the dark.

Those eyes can be warm and laughing. Or they can be ferocious and feral, as they are right now. Studying me. Examining my every move.

"What was he talking about?" Leo demands.

"Who?"

"Dean," he says impatiently.

"Oh. It's nothing."

"It wasn't nothing. I saw your face. What was it?"

I sigh, rolling my eyes to buy time, because I really don't want to have to explain this.

"We bumped into each other this morning in the changing room. He's just trying to give me shit 'cause he saw me naked."

"He saw you naked?" Leo hisses.

"Yeah." I shrug. "But who cares? It doesn't—"

Leo isn't listening. He's glaring over at Dean again, fists clenched and jaw rigid. He's tense and coiled, like he wants to sprint over there and jump on Dean and beat the ever-loving shit out of him.

"Hey!" I say. "We're supposed to be—"

Leo rounds on me.

"Why didn't you tell me that this morning?"

"What are you talking about?"

"At breakfast. Why didn't you tell me that happened?"

He's glaring at me, cheeks flushed. He looks angry, but I know Leo well enough to see something else in his face. Something more like hurt or suspicion.

"I don't know," I stammer. "The whole thing was stupid."

"If he touches you again—" Leo growls.

"He's not going to touch me. Leo, you need to chill the fuck out—"

Before I can say anything else, the professor is calling the class to order again.

Leo is still simmering, his eyes returning to Dean on the other side of the room again and again.

And Dean looks back at us—not as often but with a cold fury that easily matches Leo's heat.

My stomach is churning. Classes have barely begun, and already Leo's getting into some kind of vendetta with Dean.

This isn't at all how I wanted to start at Kingmakers.

CHAPTER 7
LEO

After combat class, we break for lunch.

Anna's chatting with Ares about counterstrikes, but I'm still fixated on that fucking asshole Dean. Remembering the way his eyes ran over her body when he said, "I've already seen it." Like he owns her just because he saw her naked.

Just the fact that he saw her at all pisses me off. I don't believe it was an accident, not for a second. And I bet Uncle Mikolaj would be furious if he heard about it.

I'm supposed to be watching out for Anna, taking care of her. On the very first day here, some asshole is already trying to get his rocks off sneaking a look at her.

Not just any asshole.

Someone who wants to do us harm. Who's hated us our entire lives.

I'm scowling as we walk, barely listening to Anna's conversation with Ares.

Then I see the one thing that could possibly cheer me up.

A familiar figure slouches against the exterior wall of the armory, hands stuffed in his pockets. He's wearing the same clothes as everybody else, but somehow on him it doesn't look like a uniform.

Maybe it's because each piece fits him flawlessly, or because he's the only person I've seen who bought his trousers in sage green instead of in sober gray or black, and he's paired them with a set of limited-edition sneakers that I know sold out in about eight seconds when they hit the market. But of course, Miles has always been able to get what he wants.

He's got a shock of untidy dark curls that hang down over his face and a bored expression that shows that he's barely listening to the friend chattering away in his ear.

"Anna." I interrupt her conversation. "Look!"

Anna glances up. Her face breaks into one of her rare full smiles.

"Miles!" she cries, running over to him.

Miles is Anna's cousin by blood and mine too. His mom is my dad's sister, and his dad is Anna's mom's brother, if you can untangle that chain of connections.

He's a year older than us, so he's already in his second year at Kingmakers. That means we won't have any classes with him, but I was hoping we'd see him on campus pretty often.

The right side of his mouth quirks up in a slow, lazy smile.

"Hey, Tippy Toes," he says to Anna, allowing her to slip under his arm for a hug and even give him a quick kiss on the cheek. "Hey, All-Star." He gives me a nod and a fist bump.

I say, "I thought you'd be waiting up on the ramparts with a welcome banner for us."

Miles chuckles softly. "Sorry to disappoint."

If there's one thing I know about my cousin, it's that he does not give a fuck about disappointing people. In fact, I think his greatest pleasure in life is defying expectations. Or maybe it's getting in trouble and then slipping out of it again just as quick.

How Miles managed to graduate from Preston Heights without being expelled is beyond me. He hardly needs Kingmakers for an education in operating outside the bounds of the law. He ran a supply chain of ten different kinds of contraband out of our high school—everything from party drugs to cheat sheets—probably clearing seven figures of profit by the time he graduated.

Not that he needs the money. His father was mayor of Chicago for eight years, not to mention head of the entire Irish Mafia. The Griffins are rolling in cash, and Miles grew up in a lake house that looks like a transparent prism of glass perched up on stilts. No curtains—just trees all around, and then open water all along the lakeside. In certain rooms of the house, you can look down and see fish swimming under your feet.

"This is Ozzy," Miles says, introducing us to his friend.

Ozzy is on the shorter side, heavily tattooed and pierced through his nose, eyebrow, and every inch of his ears. He's wearing a sweater vest with no shirt underneath, so I can see the tattoos running down both arms, most of which look like they were done by amateurs at best and quite possibly by himself with his nondominant hand.

"The cousins." He grins, shaking our hands hard. "Why the fuck are you all so tall? What do they put in your milk in Chicago? It's bad enough standing next to Miles."

"Don't blame us for that one." Miles jerks his chin toward Ares. "He's independently overgrown."

"This is Ares," I introduce him. "He's from Syros."

"Where the fuck is Syros?" Ozzy inquires.

"It's a Greek island," Ares say, unoffended. "Close to Mykonos."

"That's alright." Ozzy gives a sympathetic nod. "I'm from Tasmania, and nobody gives a shit about that place either. Wouldn't know us at all if not for Looney Tunes."

"I don't know Looney Tunes," Ares admits.

"Well, shit." Ozzy laughs. "Never mind, then. Point is I'd rather nobody knows where I'm from than to have 'em make the same damn jokes over and over. It's all stereotypes! Thinkin' we say 'cunt' and 'mate' and 'how ya goin'."

"You say all those things," Miles points out.

"Not all the time, though!" Ozzy cries.

"Literally all the time," Miles says.

Ozzy ignores him, pressing on with his rant. "The fuckin'

number of times somebody says to me 'g'day mate.' I could tear my own arm off and beat 'em to death with it."

"You can do that while it's still attached, you know," Miles remarks.

"Wouldn't be as dramatic, though."

"I would never try to stop you being dramatic."

"You couldn't if you tried." Ozzy grins.

"Look out," Miles mutters under his breath, trying to step behind Ares so he can't be seen.

Too late. A furious voice cries out, "Nice try, Griffin. I see you over there, and I want my pen back immediately!"

A professor storms toward us, his big belly preceding the rest of his body and his face suffused with angry color. He's dressed in a tweed sport coat and highly polished brogues. Perched on the end of his nose is a pair of silver spectacles almost the exact same color as his beard. He looks like an intelligent man in the process of being driven mad, his hair standing up on end and his sport coat buttoned through the wrong hole.

Knowing my cousin, I can guess exactly what the impetus to insanity might be.

Miles steps out from behind Ares, hands still tucked in his pockets, his face the picture of confused innocence.

"Why would I have your pen, Professor? What good would it do me? You know I never take notes."

"Don't even try it," the professor hisses, pale eyes bulging behind his glasses. "Don't try to smooth-talk me. I've lost four pens since the semester started, four very expensive pens, every one gone missing while you were in my class."

"I don't think I'm the only one in that class," Miles says with calm reason.

"You're the only one with sticky fingers and the absolute fucking cheek to steal from me!" The professor stands with his nose only an inch from Miles's.

"Isn't your pen right there?" Miles nods toward the breast pocket of the professor's sport coat.

"That is a *different* pen," the professor says with barely concealed rage. "The last one remaining in my possession, in fact. This is a La Doña Menagerie fountain pen with a crocodile head design, individually numbered, one of only eight hundred and eighty-eight that were ever made!"

All of us gaze in wonder at the bit of the professor's pen protruding out of his pocket. I don't know shit about pens, but the silver filigree cap does look expensive, particularly if the tiny red stones studded all over it are genuine rubies.

"As you *very well know*," the professor hisses at Miles, "the pen you stole this morning was a Romain Jerome, made with reclaimed materials from the *Titanic*. Completely different in color and style."

"That does sound lovely," Miles says. "But unfortunately, I only use Montblancs. Romain Jerome is a little bougie for my tastes."

I think I'm about to watch the professor have an aneurysm on the spot. His face has gone way past red all the way to deep purple.

Unamused, he barks, "Turn out your pockets!"

"Don't you need a warrant for that?" Miles says in that dry tone that never betrays if he's joking.

"When you step foot on this campus, you sign your life over to me, boy," the professor hisses. "I could have you stripped and hung naked from the gatehouse if I cared to do it."

"Professor Graves," Miles says, one eyebrow raised. "I didn't know you thought about me that way."

The professor's hand twitches, and I'm pretty certain he wants to seize Miles by the throat and throttle him. I've wanted to do that a time or two myself, so I have a certain level of sympathy. But the bulk of my focus is on the impossible task of trying to smother the laugh threatening to bubble up inside me.

Professor Graves is clearly about to snap, and it would be just like Miles to wind him up to the breaking point, only to have the brunt of his fury pour out on me instead because I'm stupid enough to let out a snort.

"Turn. Out. Your. Pockets," the professor seethes.

"Alright." Miles pretends to be cowed into obedience.

He turns out the pockets of his trousers, revealing only a couple of coins, a lone stick of gum, a bent piece of wire that looks like rubbish though I have a sneaking suspicion could be used to pick a small and simple lock—like the sort that would keep a desk closed.

"Hmm." Miles shrugs. "No pen, I guess."

Professor Graves narrows his eyes, looking Miles over once more as if he might have said pen tucked behind his ear. I can tell he doesn't want to back down, but he can't think where else Miles might have hidden it. My cousin would never carry anything as plebeian as a book bag.

"This is your last warning," he says to Miles, in quiet fury.

"Professor..." Miles's face is fixed in such an expression of sincerity that even I almost believe it. "I know we got off to a rocky start last year, but this year, I'm determined to live up to your highest expectations of me. I really think you'll find that I surprise you."

"I doubt it," Graves says coldly. "Now clear out of here. This isn't a place to congregate."

"Yes, sir." Miles gives him a little salute.

The salute goes from his forehead straight out toward the professor. Graves is already turning away, so he doesn't see Miles's nimble fingertips making contact with the breast pocket of his jacket. Even I wouldn't have noticed the flash of silver in my cousin's hand if I weren't looking for it.

The professor stalks away.

Miles waits until he's fully gone before holding up Professor Graves's very last pen, turning the fine silver cap so it glistens in the sunlight.

"He's right," Miles says. "This really is an expensive pen."

"Going to add it to your collection?" I laugh.

"Oh, I didn't keep the others," Miles says carelessly. And with that, he chucks the pen in a clump of grass at the base of the armory.

Ares gives it a wistful look, like he might have wanted to use it, but he doesn't stoop to pick it up again. Ozzy has no such compunction—he grabs it and stuffs it in his pocket.

"Why do you come to school if you're determined to antagonize the teachers and never learn anything?" Anna asks Miles.

"Oh, I learn things," Miles replies. "Just not what they're teaching."

I ask him, "What does that professor teach?"

"Finance," Miles says. "You'll probably have him too. Luckily neither of you has the last name Griffin, so he won't hold it against you."

I'm not so sure about that. But on the other hand, I doubt Miles is the only student causing trouble at Kingmakers.

Speaking of which…

"I saw Dean Yenin," I tell Miles.

"Oh yeah?" he says without much interest.

"He's just as big an asshole as you'd expect."

Miles shrugs. "Assholes and psychopaths. That's half the kids at this place."

"The rest of them don't have a grudge against us."

"Don't be so sure about that," Miles says. "Anyway, I don't care about any grudge. So our grandfathers wanted to kill each other. Who gives a fuck? We never met either of them."

Actually, Miles is the only one of us who *did* meet Papa Enzo, even if he was just a baby at the time. Plus he still has his other grandfather, Fergus Griffin, while both of mine are dead. Maybe that's why he acts like it doesn't matter. Or maybe Miles truly doesn't give a fuck about anything.

I've never been quite as close to Miles as to Anna. Not only because he's a year older than us but because he's the only kid I know who slightly intimidates me. He's so fucking reckless. If there's a rule, he wants to break it deliberately, just to see what happens. There's no line for him. Nothing he won't do.

He reminds me of my uncle Nero, who can be pretty fucking scary.

Actually, most of my relatives are scary in one way or another. Uncle Dante is the size of a buffalo and could break your back with two fingers. I've heard rumors of what my own father had to do to secure his position as don. Even my aunt Aida—Miles's mom—has this streak of wildness you wouldn't expect from a politician's wife with three kids. On a trip to Hawaii, I saw her dive off a sixty-foot cliff into the ocean, laughing like a maniac, with no idea what was in the water below.

In a way it comforts me, knowing they all share that streak of madness that bubbles up in me sometimes.

But it scares me too, because it feels like we're race cars careening around on a track, barely clinging to our sense of control.

At Preston Heights, I was surrounded by a bunch of Camrys and Fiats. Now I'm at Kingmakers with a whole lot of other revved-up racers. And in the mass of Ferraris and Maseratis, it seems impossible that none of us will collide, bursting spectacularly into flame.

Miles and Ozzy join Anna, Ares, and me for lunch in the dining hall. The tables are packed with students.

Miles points out some of the kids from families we know—people I've met before or just heard of in passing.

"That's Calvin Caccia over there," Miles says, nodding in the direction of a surly-looking boy with a massive diamond stud in one ear, shoveling down a plate of fresh-made pasta as quickly as possible. "He's a junior, heir to one of the Five Families in New York."

Next to Calvin sits a reedy, bespectacled boy who's talking in his friend's ear a mile a minute.

"That's Damari Ragusa," Miles says. "He doesn't look like much, but he's got a half dozen siblings at this school, and they're all connected with the Italian families in Palermo and New York."

"I think I met his brother on the boat over," I say.

"Matteo?" Miles is already ahead of me. "Yeah, he's the baby of the family. Probably an Accountant like the rest of them."

"Who's that over there?" Ares asks, pointing to a table of well-groomed students. They've got uniforms on like the rest of us, but there's an undefinable air of style and wealth about them. It helps that half of them are blond and extremely good-looking.

"That's Jules and Claire Turgenev, Neve and Ilsa Markov, Louis Faucheux, and Coraline Paquet." Miles lists them off without hesitation. "The Markov sisters are from Moscow, and the Turgenevs are Paris Bratva."

"Siblings?" Ares asks.

Jules and Claire Turgenev certainly look alike—both have the same ash-blond hair and eyes of a peculiar smoky green. They look more like poets than mafiosi. Jules's hair is long and sun-streaked, and he wears a cross dangling from one ear. Claire has a dreamy expression and clear evidence of paint under her fingernails.

"Cousins," Miles corrects him. "Bit of a messy situation, actually. Claire's a year older, but Jules is the first male. Her mom and his dad are half siblings. They operate the Paris Bratva as a triumvirate, with Claire's dad as the third member. Not sure who's actually supposed to inherit or if they plan to keep that up. Both Jules and Claire are enrolled as Heirs."

"Jules is in my dorm," I say.

"He's a freshman." Miles nods. "Claire's a sophomore."

"There's Bram Van Der Berg." Anna glances toward the table where Bram sits with a half dozen friends—not Dean, though. "We met him in Dubrovnik. He was kind of an asshole."

"All the Penose are like that," Miles says carelessly.

Miles seems to know everyone, and everyone knows him. A dozen different people stop by our table to give him a quick fist bump or ask a question or shoot the shit. Even the juniors and seniors seem to respect him.

Twice I watch someone slip Miles cash while they shake his hand, and once I see him pass back a little packet in return. Looks like my cousin is up to his old tricks. I'm sure whatever he's supplying is all the more valuable in the isolated environment of the island.

"He's in our dorm too." I jerk my chin toward Hedeon Gray, who took a seat next to his roommate Kenzo but probably regrets it, since all Kenzo's friends are chatting away in Japanese.

Hedeon is handsome with a cleft chin, athletic build, and freshly cut dark hair styled in a fade. But he's got a permanent scowl and a defensive hunch to his shoulders that makes him look fundamentally unapproachable. He's attacking his lunch like he hates it.

"They made him the Heir, huh?" Miles raises an eyebrow.

"Why wouldn't he be?"

"He's adopted," Miles says. "He's not really a Gray. And he's not the only adopted son either. His brother's right over there."

Miles inclines his head in the direction of a table of Enforcers. I hope he's not talking about the guy who looks like he was carved out of granite with a dull chisel. He looks even grumpier than Hedeon, if such a thing is possible.

"That's his brother?"

"Silas Gray." Miles nods. "Now that's your classic psychopath. The Grays have spent more money paying off his victims than he'll ever earn for them. Probably why they gave the title to Hedeon."

I notice Hedeon didn't even consider sitting at his brother's table. There can't be much love lost between them if they won't even eat together.

"Where's the chancellor?" I ask Miles curiously. "I thought we'd meet him by now."

I remember the inky signature of Luther Hugo on my Kingmakers acceptance letter.

"Trust me, you're better off not seeing him," Miles says. "If you run into him, it means you've gotten yourself in pretty deep shit."

"Is he scary or something?"

"Yes," Miles bluntly states. "Anyway, you'll meet him once the Quartum Bellum starts."

"When will that be?" I try to keep the eagerness out of my voice.

"Couple of weeks," Miles says.

"Are you going to try to get the captainship?"

"Fuck no." Miles shakes his head. "I don't want that shit on my shoulders."

"I'd take it," Ozzy says. "Better to be the boss than have to listen to whatever other asshole gets it. It's like being president—if somebody actually wants the job, they're probably the worst person to do it."

"But you said *you* want it," Miles notes.

"Exactly." Ozzy grins. "And I'm the worst person to do it."

"What about you two?" I ask Anna and Ares.

"Maybe." Anna frowns. "I'd have to know more about it."

"Not me." Ares shakes his head. "I'm not interested in any of that."

I don't know if that's actually true or if Ares just thinks nobody would want to take orders from someone who's not exactly at the top of the social order here.

"I want it," I say firmly. "Because I want to win the whole damn thing."

Miles scoffs. "Freshmen never win."

"I will."

Miles just shakes his head at me, laughing silently. "Never change, coz."

That night, something happens to me that has never happened before.

I'm lying in bed in my dorm room, with Ares fast asleep on the other side of the room. He seems to have gone unconscious the second his head touched the pillow, but I'm still way too hyped up by the fact that I'm actually at Kingmakers, on an island in the middle of the Adriatic Sea.

My brain is swimming with the sights and sounds of the day, plus the wild fantasies I have for the upcoming year.

Fantasies are so much more than dreams—they're a vision of the path you need to take to get what you want.

Professional athletes know this. The visualization in your mind is as important as the physical practice in the gym.

So when I'm lying here like this, I'm not just reveling in pleasant dreams. I'm picturing my future.

I see myself becoming captain. I see myself becoming the first freshman to ever win the Quartum Bellum. And then I see myself taking over as don of Chicago. Becoming the most powerful Mafia boss on the East Coast. And then in all of America.

The fantasy builds and builds as I watch my future self achieve success after success.

But because I'm exhausted, after a time, I lose control of my brain and it starts to drift and float, spinning visions without conscious control. What I see becomes richer in detail, more real than the room around me or the sound of the ocean hitting the cliffs below.

I see the mansion I'll live in someday, even larger and grander than my parents' house. I see a yacht, a private jet, a bank account with an impossible number of zeroes.

And then I see something I've never seen before: two small children running around my house. Twins, of exactly the same height. They're turned away from me, so I can't see their faces, but I hear their little voices babbling, and I see their dark curls, just like mine at that age. I hear their little feet padding as they run away from me across a thick Persian rug.

I've never pictured having children before. I guess I always assumed I would, but I'm only eighteen. It's nothing I'm anxious to experience right now.

Still, it makes sense that a vision of my future would include the children who will continue the Gallo line. Why build an empire if there's nobody to receive it?

In that dreamlike state, I feel myself turn, looking for my wife.

Anna stands behind me, wearing an elegant black gown, her long sheaf of silver-blond hair lying over her shoulder.

I feel an immediate pang of guilt, because I'm not supposed to look at Anna like this.

Any idiot can see that she's beautiful, but I'm not supposed to notice that she's *sexy*.

I'm not supposed to imagine wrapping my hands around her tiny waist or pressing my lips against the silky smooth skin on the side of her swanlike neck.

I'm not supposed to imagine pulling the thin straps of that gown down her shoulders, baring those perfect breasts, and covering them with my hands.

I've been told that Anna is family all my life. I was raised to treat her like a sibling or a cousin.

Any time I noticed how good her hair smelled or how full her lips had become, I smothered that thought, if for no other reason than to keep Uncle Miko from murdering me. I told myself there were other beautiful girls, and I should pay attention to them.

I tried. I went on so many dates. But too often when I had the chance to take a girl out for a second or third time, something came up with Anna—she asked me to see a movie or come with her to some party. I always chose to spend time with her instead.

Now, in this dream state, Anna stands in front of me at her most stunning, her most sensual. Every line on her body is as flawless and mobile as a calligraphy stroke.

Her ice-blue eyes fix on mine, her pouting lips quirked up in that mocking smile I've never been able to resist…the smile that makes me want to do the most dangerous things, if only to impress her.

She trails her fingers down my chest, all the way from my breastbone to the waist of my jeans.

"Leo." She gazes up at me. "Is your cock as big as the rest of you?"

I swallow hard.

"Do you want to see?"

Anna nods, never taking her eyes off mine.

"You do it," I say. "Unzip my pants."

Her slim, pale hands fumble with the button of my jeans, succeeding on the second try. When she pulls the zipper down, my jeans slide right off me and disappear. Magically, my underwear does the same.

My cock springs up, harder than I've ever seen it. Throbbing, dying to be touched.

Anna looks at it, her eyes wide.

"Can I touch it?"

I'm supposed to say no. I'm supposed to stop.

But because this is a dream, I do what I want instead.

"Go ahead."

Anna kneels down in front of me. She parts those full, pink lips and takes the head of my cock in her mouth.

I feel one last stab of guilt, and then I stop thinking about that, because all I can feel is the exquisite sensation of Anna's mouth around my cock, Anna's tongue stroking the most sensitive spots, her soft lips sliding up and down on the shaft.

I've never felt anything so heavenly. I thrust into her mouth over and over until her low voice murmurs, "Go ahead. Come in my mouth."

Those words, in Anna's voice, do something diabolical to my brain.

I explode, so hard that hot cum pours out over the back of my hand like lava.

I jolt awake, realizing that it's my own hand gripped around my cock, not Anna's mouth. Anna isn't here at all. I'm alone in my bed, sweating and shaking in the aftermath of the hardest orgasm of my life.

The room is pitch-black. I have the feeling that I yelled out pretty loud. I wait in the silence, my heart pounding, cringing with embarrassment, praying that Ares didn't hear.

On the other side of the room, his breath remains slow and steady. His back is a solid lump under the blanket, unmoving.

Thank god.

My hand is a mess, and so are my sheets.

I can't believe I came all over myself like a fucking preteen.

I've never had such a vivid dream.

And I've *never* had a dream like that about Anna. My face burns in the dark.

I know it's wrong.

My family wouldn't like it.

Her family would *hate* it.

They'd think we were disgusting. They see us as cousins. I mean, we are cousins, just not biologically.

And most of all, Anna's my best friend. What would she think if she could see the dream I just had? Would she be furious that even I, of all people, can't resist objectifying and lusting after her?

I tell myself it can't happen again.

But my cock is still throbbing so hard I can barely tuck it back inside my pajamas.

CHAPTER 8
DEAN

THE FIRST FEW WEEKS OF CLASS ARE THE MOST DIFFICULT.

Just learning the sprawling layout of the castle is a challenge. The teachers have no patience for us showing up late and will lock the doors in our faces if we can't slip inside before the class time starts.

Slowly but surely, I'm learning which passageways will take you where you need to go and how to avoid the bright expanses of open courtyard on the hot, sunny days when I don't want to arrive at class sweating through my uniform.

The broiling days don't last for long. By the time October rolls around, there's a bite to the air in the morning, and the sea breeze shifts from refreshing to chilly. More students make use of the pullovers and academy jackets that came with our uniforms.

The curriculum is more rigorous than I expected. It's a good thing I like to read, because we're constantly being assigned projects that involve visiting the vast and cavernous library stuffed with dusty leather-bound books older than Charlemagne.

For those students who thought we'd only be learning how to count our money, the exacting research into poisons and explosives, psychological analysis, international finance, and the endless examination of legal loopholes is a bit of a nasty shock.

The students are divided into four divisions.

The Enforcers will work as soldiers and consiglieres. They take the most combat classes of anyone as well as learning the practical skills to be "fixers." Their curriculum includes negotiation and interrogation classes and also anatomy so they can learn to strike efficiently and how to dismember and dispose of a body if required.

The Accountants focus primarily on finance: investment, money laundering, asset diversification, and payment structures. That's what my father would have learned had he come to Kingmakers. Instead, he was trained by the bookkeeper who held the job before him.

The Spies are the smallest division and the least trusted. Every Mafia group needs Spies proficient in information systems, hacking, counterintelligence, liaisons, and security. But one of their primary purposes is to root out moles and traitors inside their own organization. For that reason, there's an inquisitorial tone to their studies.

The Heirs' curriculum is the most demanding of all. We're expected to learn leadership and control, but we also have to understand the responsibilities of everyone under our command.

The first few weeks among the Heirs are a scramble for power. We all want to be at the top, and none of us arc used to taking orders.

Even in my own damn dorm room, I butt heads with Bram, who's the leader of his wolf pack. I think he asked to room with me thinking he'd pull me into his group. Instead, slowly but surely, I've been bending him to my will.

The male hierarchy is a true meritocracy. To be the boss, you simply have to be the best.

And I am the best.

I'm the smartest, the strongest, and the most ruthless.

Bram is witty, and he knows how to fight. And he's got all the confidence of a leader. But he's buckling under the pressure of our classes. He'd be failing if I wasn't helping him out. And that means he owes me favors.

It starts subtly at first—Bram glancing over at me to see if I agree with his comments or if I laugh at his jokes. The other Penose notice. Soon they're looking to me for approval too.

Then there's our performance in our classes. The Heirs are constantly ranked against one another. It doesn't take long for everyone to see who's rising to the top of the lists in exams as well as in shooting, fighting, and infiltrating.

Soon it's me sitting at the center of our clique. Me deciding what we should do after class or on the weekend.

That's how subtly power shifts. Bram fights back at first. But eventually he caves, dubbing me his "best friend" and giving over final say in anything important.

Our group absorbs some of the Moscow Bratva, the Armenians, and a couple of Turkish Arifs. Soon I have a pack of a dozen of the toughest freshmen on campus.

Meanwhile, Leo Gallo builds his own group. He's more willing to take in the school misfits. That Ares kid, for instance—he's a fucking nobody. Poor as dirt, with no friends or allies to speak of. His parents are barely Mafia at all.

Then there's Leo's best friend, a fucking *girl.* You don't make a ballerina your right-hand man.

I'd guess the fact that Anna is undeniably beautiful (despite all the shit she smears on her face) has clouded his decision-making.

She's smart too, I'll admit it. We're battling for the top grade in our year. Leo might be up there too if he weren't equal parts lazy and arrogant.

Sometimes they're joined by Miles Griffin and that Australian punk he pals around with. But Miles isn't really part of their group.

I wouldn't call him part of any particular clique. He's a lone wolf, an agent of chaos. Useful, though—if there's contraband you want, he can get it. I've made use of his services myself, even though he's related to the murdering, backstabbing scum who killed my grandfather and burned my father alive.

I fucking hate the lot of them.

But I've got more important things to focus on.

I work my ass off studying during the week, and on the weekend the divisions throw secret parties that can be pretty fucking fun, sometimes on campus and sometimes in hidden nooks and crannies around the island.

I'm beginning to feel secure in this place. In fact, I'm actually starting to like it.

I never liked my father's house, and I fucking hated Moscow.

Visine Dvorca is beautiful. So is the castle. It's old but not filthy and musty like my father's house.

Here, it smells like stone and clean sea air and sometimes warm yeast from the bakehouse and the brewery. There's fresh oranges, warm bay leaves, wild mint, and sweet sorrel growing all over the grounds. The sun always comes back after cloudy days, and the castle is cool and damp, with no fucking snow, no slush or ice.

No father either.

I wondered if I would miss him. I used to see him every day after all. He's my only family.

But I haven't missed him at all.

I barely even think about him.

He sends a letter once a week. It's cold and formal, asking how my grades have been, telling me that he hopes I'm making a name for our family here.

I write back to him in the same way, listing off the exams where I took top marks, telling him in the blandest possible terms what we're learning.

The only time I don't feel entirely at ease is late at night when I can't sleep, when I'm lying on my bed with Bram snoring on the other side of the room and the waves hitting hard against the limestone cliffs.

Then I think of my mother.

I miss my mom. I fucking miss her. I know you're not supposed to admit that. You're not even supposed to feel it. I'm eighteen. I'm an adult now, a grown man. I shouldn't give a fuck about my mommy. Especially not a mother who's a drunk. Who left us.

But I miss her anyway.

And I hate that even worse.

It's been eight years since she packed a bag in secret and got on a plane. Five years since the last card she sent for my birthday.

I was only ten when she left. She could have taken me with her.

I know why she didn't. My father would have hunted us down. I'm his only child, his only son. His heir.

But she didn't even try. And I'm so fucking angry at her for that.

The birthday cards came from Barcelona, Lisbon, and London. Then they stopped.

My father never commented on the cards when they arrived or when they ceased. He's never spoken about her at all since she left.

I wonder if he knows where she is.

I wonder if he knows what happened to her.

As soon as the freshmen get into the rhythm of their new classes, the most popular topic of conversation switches from occasional mentions of the Quartum Bellum to a fixation on nothing else. Anticipation is high, as the new students allow their fantasies of glory to run wild.

It doesn't help that the upperclassmen relish in tormenting us with gruesome stories of competitions past. It's impossible to know which tales are accurate and which are embellished for the pleasure of seeing our faces go pale. What's certain is that every year at least one or two students suffer some grievous injury, and several have been killed.

"Why in the fuck are we competing in this thing?" I ask Bram.

He's been determined to become the freshman captain since day one, and he brings up the Quartum Bellum more than anyone.

"Because the winner is a fucking legend!" he says. "Nobody cares what your grades are, not really. This is the chance to prove your superiority over every other Mafia family—the only way to do it outside of an actual war."

He drags me over to the trophy hall in the annex of the armory.

"Look!" His eyes gleam with greed.

The hallway is lined with a double row of plaques, listing off the winning teams of years past. Each framed plaque includes a photo of the team captain, in crisp black and white, giving them an air of timeless grandeur.

Bram points to the most recent winner: a black-haired boy with a ferocious expression of triumph whose picture tops the last three years of winning teams.

"Adrik Petrov," Bram says in an awed tone. "He won the last three Quartum Bellums—every year but his freshman year. He's a fucking legend."

"Who is he?" I've never heard of this guy. "An Heir?"

Bram chuckles. "That's the best part. He's not an Heir at all. He was an Enforcer. He's one of the St. Petersburg Petrovs. But he's such a savage that he's practically taken over the city since he graduated."

Bram lowers his voice, even though there's no one else in the corridor with us, leaning over so his hot breath tickles my ear.

"Some people say he's going to take over from his uncle, in place of Ivan Petrov's actual son. That's the power of proving yourself here."

Interesting.

I don't have a place as boss assured in Moscow either. If winning the competition means something outside the walls of Kingmakers, it might be worth something to me.

And there's another reason I want it.

I've seen how badly Leo Gallo wants to win. He's an athlete, with all an athlete's idiotic obsession with hitting arbitrary goals.

He wants nothing in the world more than that stupid captainship. Which means I want nothing more than to take it away from him.

He thinks he's some kind of golden god. He walks around this campus like he owns it, and sure enough, the other students fawn over him until I could puke.

Even the teachers do it. They think he's so funny and charming. I think he's soft, like all Americans are soft. He was a big fish in a little pond. He'll find out soon enough what it's like to swim with actual sharks.

The most irritating insult of all is how Anna Wilk is always at his side.

There's a shortage of women on campus. Some are pretty, but none can match the ethereal beauty of Anna.

I've seen girls looking at me. Even some of the female students in the years above mine. But I'm not interested in any of them. I want the best or nothing at all. Anna is the best.

She's the smartest as well as the most beautiful. She's top of our class in grades—or she would be, if not for me. Our marks go back and forth, sometimes me on top, sometimes her.

The practical classes are different. There I'm vying with Leo Gallo all the way. Artillery, combat, reconnaissance, even scuba diving… If there's a physical element, then Leo shows a maddening talent that seems to come to him without effort or practice.

Each age group gets one captain: the freshmen, the sophomores, the juniors, and the seniors. Captainship will be determined by some arcane combination of scholastic performance, professor recommendations, and student vote.

We still don't have a clear picture of what the competition itself will look like—until we're called to assemble in the grand hall of the keep in the sixth week of school.

The grand hall is vast and dark, its towering archways like the rib bones of some ancient beast. If we're in the belly of a whale, then its heart would be the roaring fire in the cavernous grate at the far end of the hall.

The walls are hung with ancient banners of the ten founding families of Kingmakers. I don't know all their names, but I see their sigils clear enough on the dusty tapestries: a pair of crossed axes, a roaring bear, a mountain range with three peaks, a hawk on a field of stars, a golden skull with grimacing teeth, a sly red fox, a burning flame, a unicorn spearing a boar with its horn, a chalice of wine, and a griffin with its wings outstretched.

I wonder how many of those ten families still have descendants at this school. And how many even remember the mottos on their coat of arms.

I'm jealous of the students with a long family history. The only person in my family with any ambition, any honor, was my grandfather. Until he was murdered by Sebastian Gallo.

Sebastian tried to burn my father alive.

I look up at the banner directly over my head, with its deep red flame. If I were going to have a sigil, that would be mine.

The Gallos tried to destroy us with fire, but I became that fire instead. It burns inside me and will never go out.

The chatter in the hall dies down as an unseen figure enters the room. The students crane in their seats, wanting to get the first look at the man who strides in front of the hearth.

He's a little taller than average, powerfully built. His soot-dark hair hangs down to his shoulders, longer than his close-cropped beard. Threads of silver twine like wire through the black. His face is craggy and ravaged, much older than his body. His eyebrows are pointed at the outer corners, and his eyes peer out from under, glittering like two gems set in his ruined face.

When he speaks, his voice booms out, silencing the last whispers between students staring at him with awed faces.

"Welcome to Kingmakers. I hope by now you've all settled in. I don't think I need to go over the rules of this place—you read and signed them before you came. I don't think, either, I need to remind you that the reputations of your families rest on your performance here or that your destiny may well be shaped by what you learn within these walls. You are all adults, if only newly so."

He glares out over the crowd of students, who look less like adults than ever before in comparison to this man who appears as if he's lived a dozen lifetimes.

"My name is Luther Hugo. I'm the chancellor of this school...the last and final authority of all that goes on within these walls. My ancestor was Barnabus Hugo. He hung the very first banner in this hall."

Hugo points to the coat of arms depicting the golden skull.

"Of those first ten families, only seven now remain. Never forget that your survival is not secure. You could be the generation that squanders the legacy of your family. You could be the fool who terminates a line stretching back hundreds of years."

This isn't exactly the rousing speech the students were hoping to hear. Even Bram seems slightly unnerved. I doubt I'm as surprised as the others, since my family only just survived such an extinction event.

"Over the next several weeks, we will be evaluating your performance in your classes." Hugo stares us down in turn with those black flinty eyes. "Each year of students will cast a vote for their captain. The first challenge of the Quartum Bellum will take place the first week of November. That is all."

Abruptly, Hugo strides back the way he came, right hand tucked into the pocket of his formal double-breasted suit.

The students sit in silence for a moment, then break into excited chatter.

"I want my picture in that hall," Bram fiercely proclaims.

I don't respond, because I don't think there's a chance in hell of Bram getting the student vote, let alone the endorsement of the professors.

But I could.

CHAPTER 9
ANNA

I'M SETTLING INTO KINGMAKERS.

The most challenging part was finding somewhere I could practice dancing without unwanted interruptions. I tried several different places, including a disused classroom and the old wine cellar next to the dining hall. In the end, I settled on the abandoned cathedral on the far west side of campus. It's farther to walk than the other options, but no one comes in to disturb me.

Maybe at the time Kingmakers was built, our ancestral families still held some sort of religious sentiment. But it's been so long since the island had a chaplain that the cathedral has fallen into disrepair. Weeds grow up through cracks in the floor, and an entire pomegranate tree has sprouted in the middle of the chancel.

Some of the stained-glass windows have been broken by wind or birds, but most are still intact. Colored light speckles the floor. I hear the cooing of doves nesting up in the clerestory.

Dancing is the closest I get to a spiritual experience, so it seems fitting to practice here in the cool, airy silence. It's far enough away from everything else that I can play my music night or day without disturbing anyone.

The other minor annoyance is that I don't particularly like my roommate. There are only two other female Heirs in my year—Zoe Romero and Chay Wagner.

Zoe is Galician. She's tall, dark-haired, serious, and studious. I think we could have gotten along very nicely by sitting silently on opposite sides of our room doing our homework.

Unfortunately, Zoe got the one private room on our floor, which may be the size of a cupboard but at least belongs to her alone.

I have to share my nice big room with Chay Wagner, the Heir of the Berlin-based Night Wolves.

Chay is loud, confident, and unbearably cheerful. Couple that with a healthy dose of German bluntness, and I have to hear her opinion on virtually everything I do throughout the day.

Chay's petite, with strawberry-blond hair and full sleeves of tattoos on both arms. She tells me the tattoos were done by the best artists in Berlin as they passed through her father's shops. Each is in a different style, everything from pop art to ultrarealistic black-and-gray portraiture.

The Night Wolves are a fascinating Mafia group, a mixture of rock 'n' roll enthusiasts and bikers, from the era when both those things were illegal in Moscow. What began with underground concerts has grown into a string of tattoo shops and rock clubs across Europe, along with custom motorcycle shops and even their own racing team.

As heir to the Berlin chapter of the Night Wolves, Chay is something of a minor celebrity on campus, which is another reason our dorm room is never quiet. She says a German station tried to sign her up for a reality TV series, but her father flatly forbade it.

"I'm going to make my own clothing line after I graduate," she tells me. "Leather jackets, vests, biker gear, you know… I think Papa's wrong to avoid attention. Ninety percent of our revenue is mainstream anyway. I honestly think Papa only keeps up with the chop shops and the protection money 'cause he can't stand the idea of being fully law-abiding."

It's clear that Chay views Kingmakers as something to get

through to appease her father. She has almost no interest in our classes and barely bats an eye at her failing grades.

"Why do you study so hard?" she demands as I'm poring over an ancient leather-bound library book on contract law.

I shrug. "I like reading. I like learning things."

"You're competitive too," Chay says slyly.

"I don't think there's any point in doing something unless you're going to do it well."

"It's not just that. You want to be top of the class. I know you do."

I pause in my reading, wondering if she's right. Am I more like Leo than I realized?

"Maybe I'm just trying to prove that I'm good enough to do this job."

Chay laughs. "With all the idiots who manage to be bosses, I think you'll be fine."

The classes are challenging, but I really do like studying. It's a hundred times more interesting than the shit I had to learn in high school. Who gives a fuck about the order of the presidents or logarithms or the history of the fur trade? Everything I learn now I'll actually use someday when I take over my father's empire.

Leo and Ares are in most of my classes, which is nice. I hate the process of making new friends. I hate the part where you have to be polite and talk stupid nonsense to get to know each other. I already know everything about Leo, and Ares is so easygoing that he slipped right into our little group like he was always meant to be there.

On Wednesdays, Leo and I have a class called Environmental Adaptation. When I saw it on my schedule, I forgot for a minute what sort of school I was attending and wondered if it had something to do with going green.

Of course it has nothing to do with environmentalism. Instead, it's about acclimatizing to unexpected environments. In our first semester, this means learning to scuba dive.

Our instructor is a man named Archie Bruce, a Navy SEAL turned mercenary for hire. He's got a shaved head, pale blue eyes, and a giant beak of a nose that adds to his air of authority.

He teaches us in the underground pool beneath the armory.

The pool began as a natural sinkhole in the limestone, where seawater seeps. It's been dug out and enlarged, but the walls of the pool are still rough, pale stone, and the water is salty. It's much deeper than a normal Olympic swimming pool—even with the pot lights set into its walls, you can't see down to the bottom.

The underground cavern is vast and echoing. Professor Bruce barks at us to shut the fuck up, because he won't be repeating a single word of the lesson.

I watch closely as he shows us each piece of equipment we'll need and how to operate it.

I'm feeling anxious, because even though Leo and I have been swimming at Carlyle Lake since we were kids, I've never been entirely comfortable in the water.

The idea of breathing on the bottom of the pool, with the full weight of thousands of gallons of water on top of me, not to mention several million tons of mountain and castle overhead, is triggering a whole new level of claustrophobia.

"You okay?" Leo's golden-brown eyes search mine.

"Of course," I lie. "Why wouldn't I be?"

"No reason," he says with an easy shrug. But he grabs my hand and gives it a quick squeeze all the same.

Even after he lets go, the warmth of his hand seems to travel up my arm, spreading through my chest and slowing my heartbeat down just a little.

A dark-haired girl stands on the opposite side of the pool. We're taking this class with a bunch of Spies, and I assume she's one of them. Her black hair is almost blue in the reflected light of the pool. When I glance over at her, her eyes are fixed serenely on the professor. But I know she was watching us a minute earlier.

"Suit up!" Professor Bruce shouts. "I want you all in that pool in two minutes."

Leo and I don our equipment, which is cold and damp from the previous class. I'm wearing a thin, one-piece bathing suit, and I can feel my nipples poking through the material as I shiver.

Leo glances at my chest. I expect him to make a joke about it, but he looks away abruptly, tugging a little too hard on the strap of his face mask so the elastic snaps.

"Fuck," he mutters.

"Problem?" Professor Bruce says at once.

"I broke the band on my face mask."

"Figure it out," the professor says coldly. "The point of this class is to adapt and overcome."

"Swap with me," I murmur to Leo. "Your head's bigger than mine. I can just tie it in a knot."

"I have a big head?" Leo laughs, trading masks with me.

"You've got the biggest head I've ever encountered, in all ways," I tell him sweetly.

Leo chuckles and slips his mask into place. It's full-face and looks disturbingly like a gas mask, like we're in the middle of a war or a plague. I knot the back of mine and force it down over my head. It's too tight, but I can make it work.

Once we've got our flippers and tanks on, we drop down into the water.

Immediately, my heart begins to race. I haven't even put my face under yet. Sensing my stress, Leo sticks right beside me. Even though he's never done this before either, he already looks comfortable bobbing up and down in the water, as if his gear weighs nothing at all.

Professor Bruce gets into the pool with us. With his flippered feet and the powerful kicks of his legs keeping him buoyant, he looks like a burly frog.

He takes his respirator out so he can shout at us. "While we're on the surface, we'll practice hand signals, clearing our mask, and recovering our respirator. After that, we'll descend."

He teaches us the signals for *okay*, *stop*, *level off*, *ascend*, *descend*, and *follow me*. Then he goes over the mask and regulator techniques.

It all seems to fly by much too quickly, and I wish he'd run through it again. With each new instruction, the one before seems to dissolve in my brain. It doesn't help that I'm continually thinking of the hundred feet of empty water directly below.

"Do you understand it all?" Leo whispers to me.

"I…I think so."

"Just copy me," he says in his warm, reassuring tone. "I know what to do."

A lot of people think that Leo is overconfident. But when he says he can do something, he's almost always right. I'm keeping my heart rate under control because I trust him. I feel safe with him here beside me.

Too soon, it's time to descend. I fit my regulator in place and follow Leo as Professor Bruce takes us down to the bottom of the pool in measured stages. He uses our newly learned hand signals to tell us when to pause, when to pop our ears, and when to drop farther down.

Every few feet we descend adds an immense amount of pressure from the weight of the water overhead. I try not to think how far it is to the surface. I try not to consider how dependent I am on the little tank of air strapped to my back.

Leo stays right beside me. The release of bubbles out of the side of his mask seems slow and steady. I try to match it so I don't hyperventilate and use my oxygen too quickly.

We sink the final distance to the bottom of the pool and sit cross-legged in a big circle, with Professor Bruce at the center. The dark-haired girl and her redheaded friend are still directly across from Leo and me. It's hard to tell if they're smiling or not beneath their masks. Hard to tell if they're staring at us as much as it seems.

I try to feel the sense of calm weightlessness that's supposed to be pleasurable in this activity. Shouldn't diving be something like dancing? It doesn't feel like that to me. It feels like being encased in wet cement while breathing through a straw.

I'm relieved when Professor Bruce takes us back up to the surface.

That relief doesn't last long. He lifts his mask to say "This time, we're going to practice buddy breathing. If your regulator is broken or you've run out of air, you can make use of your partner's. This is the signal that means 'I have no air.'" He demonstrates the slashing movement of the hand across the throat. "We'll descend. Then I'll come around and take half the tanks."

My stomach lurches. I don't in any way feel ready to be down there without any air.

But there's nothing I can do except follow him back down under the water.

At least I've got Leo as my buddy. He isn't joking around like usual, probably because he knows I'm wound tighter than a guitar string. He sits right next to me on the rough and rocky bottom of the pool, waiting patiently for Professor Bruce to approach.

Leo is already undoing the straps of his tank, planning to offer it to the professor.

Our teacher senses weakness. He narrows his pale blue eyes behind his mask and shakes his head, pointing to me instead. With trembling hands, I unclasp my tank and hand it over.

The moment the respirator is out of my mouth, I start to panic. I look up at the distant, shining surface of the pool, impossibly far overhead. I couldn't swim all the way up there with the single breath captured in my lungs.

Leo removes his respirator and fits it in my mouth, resting his hands on my shoulders and looking into my eyes through our masks. He waits patiently while I take several breaths, watching my face.

I don't need him to speak to know what he wants to say to

me. With his dark eyes looking into mine, I can hear his voice in my head:

Relax, Anna. I'm right here. You've got this. I'm not gonna let you drown on the bottom of this pool. For one thing, your dad would kill me.

It almost makes me smile.

Only Leo's perfect calm allows me to maintain mine. If he had taken the air back too soon or even stared at me impatiently, I don't think I could have handled it.

I know what a good swimmer he is. I know how long he can hold his breath.

I take my time getting the oxygen I need, and then I pass the respirator back to Leo. He takes two quick breaths and gives it to me again, watching me closely through his mask. I can see his concern. I know he'd never leave me without air.

Professor Bruce makes us sit down there for over twenty minutes, sharing respirators.

Two of the sets of students can't handle it. One of the Spies starts squabbling and nearly pulls the hose right out of the tank before the professor intervenes. On the opposite side of the circle, an Albanian Heir named Valon Hoxha loses his nerve completely and goes kicking off the bottom without any tank, trying to swim for the surface.

He only makes it halfway before he takes an involuntary gulp of water and starts to drown.

Lucky for him, the professor is right behind him. He puts the thrashing Hoxha into a headlock and forces the respirator into his mouth. Still thrashing and fighting, Hoxha is dragged up to the surface and tossed out of the pool by the irritated professor.

Professor Bruce finally returns alone, signaling for us to follow him up.

I still don't have an oxygen tank.

Leo grabs my hand and starts swimming slowly upward. He pauses frequently so we can control our rate of ascent, passing the respirator back and forth.

Even with all his help, I'm wildly relieved when my head breaks the surface again and I can take full, unobstructed gulps of air.

Leo pushes his mask up on his head, grinning at me. "You did it!"

"Only because of you," I say honestly.

He shrugs. "I'm only passing history because of you. But don't tell Ares that, 'cause he's under the impression that I've been studying on my own."

I snort. "Who told him that?"

Leo grins. "Somebody who didn't want to accept another invitation to the library."

I strip off the wet, chilly scuba equipment.

All around me, my fellow students are doing the same.

I notice that Hedeon Gray wore a T-shirt down into the water, even though he's in good shape and has nothing to hide.

As he pulls off his tank, his shirt rides up, and I get a look at his bare back.

He's covered in scars, layer upon layer of them. Thick, twisting, overlapping bands running in all directions.

I don't mean to stare, but I'm frozen in place, never having seen anything so brutal.

Hedeon jerks his shirt back down, glowering at me.

I whip around quickly, trying to pretend like I didn't see, though we both know I did.

"What?" Leo says.

"Nothing." I shake my head.

My stomach is churning. Those aren't the scars of an accident or injury.

Someone did that to him.

Even though Leo's in most of my classes, our schedules don't entirely align.

On Tuesdays and Thursdays, I have International Banking while Leo and Ares take Torture Techniques. Most of the rest of the students in my banking class are Accountants.

I don't mind. I like the Accountants. They're focused and methodical. Not a bunch of aggressive meatheads like the Enforcers or sneaky and suspicious like the Spies.

The class is competitive, though. Some of the most brilliant kids in our year are Accountants. It's been a struggle to even stay in the top twenty percent.

If I want the head spot, I'll have to beat out Dean Yenin. He's in this class too, though thankfully not with his henchman Bram. He sits two rows behind me, where I can feel his eyes boring into my back, especially if I've just answered a question correctly.

I've tried to avoid speaking to him since the changing room incident. He seems perfectly content to avoid me too, though I've caught him glaring at me more than once.

I don't know if he hates me because I'm best friends with Leo or if he knows that my father helped Sebastian Gallo secure his hold on the Chicago territory contested by the Bratva.

My dad wasn't directly involved in the killing of Dean's grandfather or the mutilation of his father, but he did murder some of the Yenins' men, and there's plenty of bad blood to go around.

I wish we could put the whole thing behind us. It's a twenty-year-old feud, and no one has clean hands.

Leo enjoys conflict and competition. I just want to be left alone to get my work done in peace.

I'm not sure what Dean wants. I haven't seen him picking fights and causing trouble as much as his roommate, but he certainly surrounds himself with bullies and assholes. And I don't think he's smiled once since we got here.

Not that I'd usually judge someone for that. I'm not too free with smiles either.

Today we're learning about offshore accounts.

Professor Graves is up at the blackboard going on about shell corporations. He's the same professor who was hollering at Miles on the first day of classes (rightfully so), but luckily he hasn't seemed to remember that I was present for the theft of his very last pen. Or at least he hasn't been any ruder to me than to anyone else in our class.

I'm taking notes by hand, filling my fourth notebook of the semester. I write down most of what the professor says, but I also like to draw. Right now, I'm making a diagram of tax havens, shaped like Russian nesting dolls. Even though it's not really necessary, I'm decorating each of the dolls with a little headscarf and a floral-patterned apron.

"Nonprofit entities can be useful as an extra layer of insulation," the professor says. "A private foundation can then own a corporation, adding another diversion to your tax-evasion schematic."

We're up on the third floor of the keep, which means the sky outside the window is full of large, heavy clouds steering through the wind like barges on water. No sunshine today—just a slate-gray sky and those clouds, dark on their underbellies with unshed rain. The air is fresh with geosmin.

I draw rain clouds over my nesting dolls.

"For this assignment, I'll be splitting you into pairs," the professor says.

I look up sharply. I wasn't paying attention to the details of the assignment, and he hasn't written them on the blackboard.

"Wilson and Paulie," the professor says, looking around the room. "Kyrie and Nelson. Anna and Dean."

My stomach clenches up. I throw an involuntary glance in Dean's direction.

He looks just as annoyed as I am. But he doesn't hesitate in scooping up his books and coming to join me at my table.

"Which part of the assignment do you want to do?" he demands as soon as he sits down.

"Well… I…"

I haven't thought it over, because I wasn't listening.

Dean looks at my open notebook, at the nesting dolls and the rain clouds. He scowls.

"Do you even know what we're doing?"

"Yes," I lie. "Don't forget, I've got the best grade in this class."

Only as of last week, because I beat Dean on our most recent exam by a measly two points.

I can almost hear Dean's teeth grinding together behind his full bottom lip.

The softness of Dean's features does not at all match his personality. His white-blond hair, porcelain skin, long lashes, and pouting mouth are completely at odds with his constant sneer and a body carved out of marble.

I bet he hates being pretty.

I can sort of identify with that. I don't look on the outside how I feel on the inside.

I look like I should be sweet and delicate. But I could slit a throat without flinching.

For that reason, I would never underestimate Dean.

He spits, "You won't beat me at anything by end of term."

I shrug. "I guess we'll see. We'll both be getting the same grade on this project, so you might as well tell me how you want to divvy it up."

Dean lets out a slow exhalation of annoyance, then explains the assignment to me over again, each of us marking down the parts we intend to handle.

"It's an analysis of Caribbean versus Swiss banks," he says. "We'll have to present together, so we can't do all the work separately."

"That's fine." *Not fine, but I can make it work.* "We can get the books from the library after class."

It's strange sitting side by side with Dean as the professor finishes the lecture. I haven't been this close to him since we collided in the changing room.

He smells clean like he did then, like soap and fresh shampoo, even though he hadn't showered yet. It brings back our first meeting vividly.

I keep my eyes rigidly fixed on the blackboard, hoping he doesn't notice the color in my cheeks. I don't know why I still feel embarrassed about that. It's not like me to hold on to some silly, insignificant mistake.

When the professor dismisses us, Dean snatches up his books again and starts walking in the direction of the library without checking to see if I'm following him.

I sling my bag over my shoulder, taking long strides to catch up with him.

Dean hears my boots hitting the flagstone floor and glances down at my feet.

"Did you draw all that too?"

I doodled all over my Docs with white pen. Moons, stars, dragons, vines, rivers, flowers, and birds.

"Yup."

"Drawing and dancing," Dean says. "Maybe you should have gone to art school."

"I'm right where I want to be," I tell him coldly. "I'm an Heir. Isn't your father a bookkeeper?"

If looks could kill, I'd shrivel and die on the spot from the glare Dean throws at me.

"It doesn't matter what my *father* is," he spits back at me. "I'll be *pakhan* because I'll earn it myself."

Ha. Nice to know I can get under Dean's skin when I want to.

It's a long walk to the library, located in the tallest tower on the northwest corner of campus. The bookshelves form a vast upward spiral, like in the lighthouse of Alexandria. The books are mostly organized by topic, but when you can't find something, you can always ask Ms. Robin.

The librarian is shy and quiet, but quite beautiful behind her thick glasses. She's got auburn hair and hazel eyes, and she's probably in her forties, though she dresses like an old cat lady.

I'm curious how she came to work at Kingmakers. Virtually all the professors were mafiosi themselves, but she obviously wasn't. She's so timid that she almost jumps out of her skin if you close a book too hard. She must be somebody's daughter or niece.

She probably likes working here, because Kingmakers is so isolated, and the library is quiet and peaceful. Besides, it's a dream for anyone who likes reading, which Ms. Robin clearly does. Every time I come here, she has her nose buried in a book or a bunch of papers and charts spread out at her desk.

I don't have to ask her where the banking section is, since I've come looking for materials for this class plenty of times before. Dean and I scour the shelves, finding a half dozen books that should help us.

Dean hauls them down—a mix of modern publications and a few old tomes thicker than a phone book.

He gets distracted when he spots an old copy of *Blood Meridian* already lying butterflied on our reading table.

He picks up the book, turning through the first few pages, his eyes betraying his interest as they flick back and forth.

"Have you read that one before?"

Dean startles, like he forgot I was standing there. He drops the novel back down on the table like I caught him looking at porn.

"Yeah," he admits. "I've read it."

Interesting.

I suppose I shouldn't be surprised. After all, Dean is one of the top students in our year. He obviously isn't stupid. I just didn't picture him as someone who read novels for fun.

"Was it for school?"

He frowns at me. "No. It wasn't for school."

"Just curious," I say. "Cormac McCarthy is one of my favorite authors."

His lips tighten, and for a moment I think he's going to say something rude. Or at the very least tell me we should focus on our project. Instead, he says, "I liked *No Country for Old Men* better."

"Have you seen the movie? It's one of the best adaptations I've seen—maybe even better than the book."

"The movie's never better than the book," Dean scoffs.

"It can be," I counter, listing off the best examples on my fingers. "*Fight Club*, *Gone Girl*, *The Silence of the Lambs*, *Jaws*..."

Dean stares at me. It's odd looking at his face this close. His eyes are the exact same color as Aunt Yelena's. It's a shade of blue I've never seen on anyone else, like the irises that grow in the walled garden at my parents' house.

"Maybe you're right," Dean says unexpectedly.

My mouth falls open. Of course I thought I was right all along. But I didn't expect him to admit it.

We sit down next to each other at the ancient, heavily scarred library table. It might be strange for some of the students to live in a place where every stone, every sconce, every piece of furniture is centuries older than they are. For me, it just reminds me of home.

I like objects with history. I like to think about who sat at this table before me and who might sit here in ten or twenty or a hundred years. This library is full of the discoveries of thousands of people. That's the strength of humans. We can collaborate. We can share. A thousand of us together are infinitely stronger than any one person can be.

Assuming we can get along.

Dean opens up his notebook and starts telling me what we're going to do for the assignment.

"Hey," I interrupt. "You're not in charge."

His lip curls. "And you think you are?"

"It's a partnership," I say. "Ever heard of it?"

"No," Dean says seriously. "I've always found that there has to be a leader. One person at the top. It's usually best if that person is me."

"Well, in case you haven't noticed, all the Heirs feel that way."

Dean raises an eyebrow. "There's wanting to be the man, and then there's actually being the fuckin' man."

"I prefer to be the fuckin' woman."

Dean laughs. It's not a mocking laugh. Actually, it's pretty genuine. "Oh yeah?"

"Yes."

"Maybe I would too. If I looked like you."

He's already turned back to the stack of books in front of him, but I'm still examining that particular comment in my brain.

Was that a compliment?

Impossible to say, because Dean goes right back to being cold, stiff, and businesslike as we work our way through the reading materials for the next hour, muddling through comparisons of banking systems, taking plenty of notes by hand.

Contrary to what he said, Dean actually does cooperate pretty well once we're in the swing of it. He's clever, detail-oriented, and organized. We only argue once over whether we should weigh the historical benefits of each banking system or focus on their current strengths and weaknesses.

By dinnertime, the frosty tension between us has melted enough that Dean says, "Can I ask you something?"

I'm wary as I give him a slight nod. "Go ahead."

"Why do you paint your face like that?"

It's a question I hate, and it immediately makes me lose whatever charitable feelings I was developing over our successful cooperation.

I scowl at him. "Because I like it."

"What does it mean, though?"

He's looking at me, genuinely curious. Not trying to give me shit or preparing to make some dumb fucking joke about it.

"You want the real answer?"

"Yes," Dean says. "Or I wouldn't ask."

"Clothes, hair, makeup…it's all part of your personal brand. What represents you. How you want other people to perceive you."

"So you want to be perceived as…dark and scary?" Dean says.

"No. It's more about how I *don't* want to be perceived. I don't want people to see me as someone who seeks approval or belonging. I don't want to be a part of trends or styles. And I don't want to look like I'm trying to attract anyone."

"You don't want to attract anyone?" Dean says, disbelieving.

"No. I don't."

"Why not?"

"There's no one I want to attract. I don't like dating."

Dean gives me an inscrutable look. I expect him to ask if Leo and I are dating. Or maybe to ask if I like hooking up. That's usually the next line of questioning—*If you don't want to date, do you at least want to fuck?*

Instead, he says, "I know what you do like."

"Oh yeah? What's that?"

"You like dancing."

"No big mystery. You saw me practicing."

"I know you practice every day. In the cathedral."

I can feel my cheeks getting hot. I wish they didn't do that. I can keep the rest of my face still and expressionless when I want to, but I can never stop that damn pink flush spreading across my face.

"How do you know that?" I say stiffly.

"You're not the only one who can't sleep. I wander all over this place."

It makes me feel strange knowing that Dean is walking around the grounds in the middle of the night just like I am, when most everyone else is asleep.

To change the subject, I say, "My mother's a dancer."

"She taught you?"

"Yes."

"You must be close," Dean says.

Now I notice something in his face that I don't think he would want me to see. Pain. And envy.

"She loves me," I say. "But we're not close. Not as close as we should be. I'm not like her. I couldn't be, even if I wanted."

I don't know why I told him that. Habits of honesty, I guess. I'm too used to spending time with Leo, where I say exactly what I think and feel all the time, never holding back. Well, almost everything.

"Why would you want to be like your parents?" Dean says, his face darkening. "I hate when I—"

He breaks off abruptly, biting back the rest of his words.

I wish he would finish. I very much want to know what the end of that sentence would have been.

Instead, he shoves back from the table, closing his notebook and stuffing it back in his bag.

"I'm hungry," he says. "That's enough for today."

Without waiting for me to respond, he swings his bag over his shoulder and stalks out of the library.

I stay exactly where I am, thinking over the dozen different things he might have been about to say.

I don't think Dean stopped talking because he didn't want me to hear it. I think he stopped because he surprised himself with what almost came out of his mouth.

I can't be sure, but it seems most likely that he was about to say *I hate when I'm like my father.*

CHAPTER 10
LEO

ANNA AND I ARE HIKING ON THE EAST SIDE OF THE ISLAND. IT'S Saturday, which means we have no classes and plenty of time to explore. On the weekends, everyone takes the chance to get off campus, to go visit the little village down by the harbor or wander around the fields, farms, vineyards, and beaches.

The village doesn't offer much of interest—or at least it wouldn't if there were other options for entertainment. But any change of place seems exciting on the island. So Anna, Ares, and I often walk down to have coffee and scones in the little café on the harbor's edge or to eat freshly battered fish and chips at the even smaller restaurant that serves only the one dish.

I'll admit, it's the best damn fish and chips I've ever eaten, with bass caught the same morning, still cold from the ocean when they throw it in the fryer. That's the only way I enjoy seafood: battered, fried, and disguised.

I'm thinking we should get some as soon as we're done hiking. It takes a lot of calories to move this giant body around, and I'm fucking starving.

Anna likes to hike the cliffs right above the bay. They're not quite as steep as the cliffs directly below Kingmakers, but there are plenty of parts on the trail where the path becomes so sheer that you have to climb up the rock hand over hand.

I can see Anna ten feet above me, hauling herself up the white rock, nimble as a mountain goat. She always hikes like she's in a race, trying to power through it as quickly as she can. I'm faster than Anna and stronger, but she's got an engine. She never seems to tire, or at least she'd never let me see it.

I'm grinning as I climb a little faster, trying to catch up with her.

We wore hoodies when we left early this morning, because the sky was overcast and the wind was chilly. Now that the sun has come out, I'm sweating.

As I get closer to Anna, her foot slips out from under her. I catch her heel neatly in my hand, pushing her sneaker up again so she can regain her position.

"Saved you," I say.

Anna looks down at me, tossing her long blond ponytail back over her shoulder.

"I wasn't going to fall," she says scornfully.

"Of course not. 'Cause I was right here to save you."

She makes a disdainful sound and climbs even faster. She's smiling, though. I can always make Anna smile whether she wants to or not.

When we reach the very top of the cliff, Anna sits down on the shelf of rock overhanging the ocean. This is the goal, the reward for the climb. One of the prettiest views on the island.

You can see the fishing boats out on the water and the waves hitting the rock at the base of the cliff, churning up thick white foam. Down to our left, the half-moon-shaped village clusters around the harbor, each of the buildings perfect and uniform in miniature, like a model set.

Anna looks out over the water, her pale blue eyes keen and intent. I want to know what she's thinking. I always want to know all the thoughts whirring away inside her head.

I know there's something fascinating on her mind—she's never just spacing out, dreaming of nothing. Anna is brilliant. One of the few people who continually says things I've never even considered before.

Before I can ask her what's on her mind, she pulls her sweater over her head so she can cool off in the sea breeze. She's wearing a leotard underneath—dark gray, backless, with a mesh of fine straps crisscrossing over her spine.

Anna has the clearest skin I've ever seen. It's smooth and flawless all across her shoulders and back, luminescent in the sun. The only marks on her flesh are the finely drawn tattoos that represent all the people she loves: her mother, her father, her sister, and her brother. None for me, though. I wonder if she'd get one with me if I asked.

I have the urge to run my finger down the script written along the back of her arm, an urge so strong that my hand is already moving before I realize that's weird, and I clench my fist in my lap instead.

"What's up with you?" Anna says.

"Nothing," I say. "Cramp."

Anna takes my hand in hers and massages my palm with her fingers. She presses her thumbs firmly into my flesh, finding all the tired muscles, bringing them back to life.

It feels good. Really good. Her hands are soft and strong at the same time.

"I never think of you as a girl," I blurt out.

"What do you mean?" Anna falters in the massage.

"You know how some people are sort of a cliché of themselves? I never think of you as a girl or a ballerina or whatever category. You're just...yourself. Your own combination."

"Thanks, I guess," Anna says.

She's not meeting my eye. I think I insulted her accidentally.

"There's nothing wrong with being a girl," I say, wishing I could explain better what I mean.

"I know," Anna says.

"I only meant—"

"It's fine, Leo. I understand you."

She always does. But she looks troubled. Not entirely happy all of a sudden.

"How's your banking class going?" I ask her. It's one of the classes we don't share.

"Fine."

"Pretty dull with all those Accountants?"

"No. It's not dull. I've always liked numbers."

There's silence for a moment while I try to stop myself from asking what I really want to ask. Anna is stiff, anticipating it.

At last I say, trying to sound casual, "I hope Dean's not giving you any shit."

I don't like that they have that class together without me there.

It shouldn't matter, but it irritates me, like something caught in my teeth.

When Anna's in that class and I'm in Torture Techniques, I can't stop thinking about her and that asshole trapped in the same room together.

I've seen how he looks at her. Like she's a piece of meat and he's starving.

Knowing he's leering at her all hour long is almost worse than the actual torture techniques that our professor occasionally demonstrates on an unwilling volunteer.

"He isn't bothering me," Anna says.

I see her cheeks flushing pink, and I know there's something else to be said but she doesn't want to tell me.

"What is it?" I say.

"I... We're working on a project together." Anna hurries to add, "The professor assigned the groups."

"Just the two of you?" It comes out harsh. I don't know why my heart is beating so fast. It's just a school project.

"Yeah," Anna says, feigning casualness.

I try to sound even more casual. Like I don't care at all.

"How's that been?"

"Surprisingly good."

My stomach gives a hard twist. It's stupid—I don't want Dean to be an ass to her. I don't want her assignment fucked up. Anna's grades are important to her. But somehow the fact that it's going well makes me feel even more shitty and anxious.

"Well, he's...smart," I say grudgingly.

"Yeah, he is," Anna agrees.

She agrees too easily. Too enthusiastically. My stomach clenches up even harder. My face is hot, and the sun feels too bright. I pull my own sweater off with unnecessary aggression.

"The weather's all over the fucking place here," I grumble. "One minute you're freezing, and the next you're sweating your balls off."

"Not me," Anna says, a strange edge to her voice. "'Cause I don't have balls. 'Cause I am, in fact, a girl."

"I know that."

"Come on," she says, standing abruptly. "Let's walk down the long way so we can go into town. I want to get more stamps."

She's always writing to her little brother and sister. Probably her parents too.

My mom expects me to call every week, and my dad gets on the line for at least part of the time. He's genuinely curious about Kingmakers. My mom's questions are mostly intended to reassure herself that nothing horrible is about to happen to me here.

As Anna and I walk down the gentler slope toward the town, I find myself following along behind her again so I can watch her without her knowing.

I watch her smooth gait, her long legs striding down the hill. Her sheaf of silver-blond hair swinging back and forth like a pendulum. The edge of her face in profile as she glances back at me.

For one brief moment, I remember the dream I had about Anna during our first week at school. And then I stuff that memory back down inside me, like I've tried to do every time it pops up in my brain.

We've barely stepped foot on the main street of the village when we bump into Ares coming out of the post office. He's got a couple of letters in his hand. When he sees us, he stuffs them into his pocket, not caring if they get crumpled.

"Hey!" I say. "I thought you were studying this morning."

"I finished."

"I think you were just trying to get out of hiking. I don't blame you. Chasing Anna up the cliff is brutal. Not everything has to be cardio, you know, Anna."

"Everything should be, though," she says, smiling.

"You're a masochist."

"What does that make *you*?" Ares says.

"A hedonist." I grin. "I've been dreaming about fish and chips all the way down the hill. You want to come?"

"I just ate breakfast," Ares muses. "But hell yes, I want chips."

We wait while Anna buys her stamps, then head over to the tiny restaurant that barely looks bigger than a phone booth from the outside. There are no tables or chairs to sit down at once you've got your order. You just take your hot, greasy packet, wrapped up in newspaper, and it's up to you to find a comfortable rock or curb so you can attack the food.

We order from the local who always scowls at us like he's in a terrible mood but still gets our order out in less than five minutes, in hot, crispy perfection every time.

"He doesn't look like a magician." I bite into a golden-brown chunk of bass. "But he's doing some kind of sorcery back there."

"His apron's always clean," Anna says. "And so are his hands. I bet his kitchen is perfectly organized."

"Do you think the locals hate us?" Ares asks in an undertone. "Sometimes I feel like they're glaring at us."

"The village couldn't exist without Kingmakers." Anna shrugs. "Most of the people on the island work for the school in one way or another."

"Who cares?" I say. "As long as they keep cooking for us."

Ares attacks his fish and chips like he hasn't had breakfast in months, let alone an hour ago. He's filled out a little since we've been at school, but he's still lean. Apparently he'd need an IV drip of pure butter to actually get chubby.

Anna douses her chips in malt vinegar until my eyes are watering.

"What's wrong with ketchup?" I ask her.

She says, "I like 'em this way."

"It's the European way," Ares informs me. "Vinegar is better than ketchup."

"Oh yeah?" I say. "What about fry sauce?"

"What's fry sauce?" Ares looks concerned.

"Mayo and ketchup mixed together."

"No." He rejects that at once. "Only Germans put mayonnaise on fries."

I'm starting to cheer up a little, sitting in the warm sun with two of my favorite people. Both Ares and Anna are supremely relaxing company. Ares is so laid-back that I think he'd stay calm even if he woke up with his room on fire. And Anna is just...someone I could be around forever.

As we're eating, two girls from the school come strolling by, each carrying a little bag from the tea shop.

"Morning," the girl nearest to me says as she passes. She's got blue-black hair and straight brows that go up at the outer edges like a Vulcan. She's in our Environmental Adaptation class. I think her name is Gemma.

"What's in the bag?" I ask her.

"Crystals." She stops to show me. She pulls out several small crystals, wrapped individually in tissue. One looks like rose quartz, one might be amethyst, and I don't know the others.

"Pretty," I say.

"Thanks." She smiles at me like I complimented her personally, not just the crystals.

"What are they for?" Ares asks.

"They have healing powers."

I hear Anna let out a little puff of air next to me, which I know was a very quiet snort. Anna doesn't think much of mysticism.

As quiet as she was, Gemma zeroes in, her dark eyes narrowing. "Not a believer?"

"No," Anna says coolly.

"That's fine." Gemma tosses her head. "Most people don't understand it."

"It's hard to understand things that are made up," Anna agrees with maddening calm.

Gemma's redheaded friend quickly interjects, "Are you all coming to the party tonight?"

"What party?" Ares asks.

"A bunch of us are going down to Moon Beach once it gets dark."

"You should come," Gemma says, her eyes focused intently on me alone.

"Maybe we will," I say.

"See you tonight, then." Gemma wiggles her fingers at me.

"Bye." Her friend waves to Ares.

Anna crumples up the newspaper containing her last few fries.

"You're coming too," I inform her.

"I don't think so."

"What's wrong? You don't like those girls?"

"I like Shannon. She's in my contracts class."

I notice she's avoiding mention of Gemma.

"Come on," I coax. "You love parties."

Anna looks at me, her blue eyes clear and steady. Quietly, she says, "Do you want me to come?"

"Of course I do."

She's silent for a moment. Then she says, "I'll come."

"Good." I grin. "I know *Ares* will be there. That Irish girl invited you particularly."

He smiles, shaking his head. "She was just being friendly."

"Oh yeah." I snort. "I think she wants to be *very* friendly with you."

Anna's quiet on the walk back up to the school. Ares is talking about our upcoming Security Systems exam.

"I thought it was going to be security in general, but it's almost all electronics and computer systems," he says glumly.

"You'll pass," I say. "You're in the library more than both of us combined."

"Because I have to be." Ares sighs. "I don't just read something once and remember it forever like you two."

"Just Leo," Anna says. "I actually study."

"I study too." I'm wounded.

Anna snorts. "For five minutes before the test."

"That counts."

As we head through the heavy stone gates onto campus, I hear students congregating in the commons—excited whispers and groans of irritation.

Before I can even get close to the message board to see what's been posted, a heavy hand claps me on the shoulder.

"Congratulations." Hedeon Gray grimaces like it hurts him to say it.

"For what?"

"They posted the captains."

I rush forward, needing to see with my own eyes if Hedeon told the truth. Sure enough, a paper has been pinned to the board, bearing four names in fresh blue ink.

Team Captains:

Freshmen: Leo Gallo

Sophomores: Kasper Markaj
Juniors: Calvin Caccia
Seniors: Pippa Portnoy

"You got it," Anna says with real pleasure.

I pretend nonchalance. "Of course I did."

In truth, I wasn't that certain, and seeing my name written down sets me on fire.

I wanted that captainship. I really fucking wanted it.

And obviously I thought I was the one for the job, but there was pretty tough competition. I didn't have the highest grades in our year, so it must have come down to practical performance or the student vote.

"Nice." Ares bumps my fist. "I really didn't want it to be some asshole like Bram."

I just didn't want it to be Dean. He was my biggest competition.

I look around gleefully, wanting to see the rage in his face when he reads the list. Unfortunately, he's not around.

That's fine. I'll rub it in soon enough.

I wish the competition started today. I'm so fucking ready. I'm gonna be the first ever freshman to win this thing.

"Looks like most of the team captains are Heirs," Anna muses, reading the rest of the list.

I'd barely even glanced at the other names. Now I read them more carefully, considering who I'm up against.

I know who Pippa Portnoy is, because she was Anna's guide on the first day of school. She's the least physically intimidating of the captains, only five feet tall and pixyish. But that doesn't fool me. Anna told me Pippa's top of the senior class in grades and sly as well as smart. She's always surrounded by friends, who pay her obvious respect despite her tiny frame.

"Where's Pippa from anyway?" I ask Anna, thinking I'd better do a little research on my competitors.

"She's the heir to the Liverpudlian Mafia," Anna says. "And she's betrothed to the heir to the Real IRA, Liam Murphy. Her family specializes in drug trafficking and contract kills, so don't think she's a sweetheart just because she looks like Audrey Hepburn."

I assure her, "'Sweetheart' is not an assumption I make around here."

"Calvin Caccia's the one Miles pointed out to us in the dining hall," Ares says.

"Right." I nod. "From New York. What about the other one? Kasper Markaj. Anybody know him?"

"He's the only one who isn't an Heir," Anna tells me. "He's an Enforcer for the Albanians. Big dude, longish hair—the one always playing soccer outside the walls."

The competition seems a lot more real all of a sudden. Particularly with the other freshmen eyeing me, sizing me up. Hoping that they picked the right person to lead us. Plus a few resentful side-eyes from those who wanted the captainship themselves.

I'll have to get them all behind me, one way or another. Or we don't have a hope of winning.

I look across the commons at Bram Van Der Berg, who's glaring at me with pure loathing, arms folded stubbornly across his chest.

I need every last soldier. Even the ones who hate me.

CHAPTER 11
DEAN

I'm lying on my bed reading a book when Bram comes storming in. Bram is moody as fuck, and he's always getting riled up about something. They probably ran out of the bread he likes down in the dining hall.

"Fucking bullshit!" he cries, throwing himself down on his own bed. His mass makes the springs creak alarmingly, and he doesn't seem to care that he's getting his dirty boots on his blanket. He also appears to have a fresh bandage wrapped around his forearm.

"Problem?" I say, turning the page of my book.

Bram glares at me.

"Why are you *reading*? I thought you finished that project with Wednesday Addams."

Bram thinks he's funny. Calling Anna "Wednesday Addams" is low-hanging fruit.

It doesn't suit her anyway. She's not gloomy and sarcastic. If I were going to liken her to someone from a movie or TV show, it would be…Dark Phoenix from *X-Men*. Powerful and otherworldly.

Of course I'm not going to say that to Bram.

I'm not going to say anything to him about Anna.

He's right that our project is finished. We got a perfect score, including bonus credit for the illustrated chart Anna made to accompany our oral presentation.

I'll fucking choke if I have to watch that all night.

"I don't know if I feel like going out."

"Suit yourself," Bram says, rolling off the bed and pulling his shirt over his head. Bram's back is thick with muscle and several nasty scars to go along with the one on his face. I've heard him tell a lot of stories about how he got his scars, but none of them match up, so I doubt he's ever told the truth.

He leaves after changing his clothes. I read for another hour or two, then head down to the dining hall when I can't ignore my stomach rumbling any longer.

They're serving roasted chickens, each one split in half and stuffed with rosemary and thyme out of the castle gardens. Next to that, potatoes so crispy and brown that they're bursting out of their skins.

I haven't had food this good in...almost ever. I miss the odd thing I used to eat in Moscow. I love a good borscht. But in general, the food at Kingmakers is much better than anything I bought from corner stores and diners.

I sit with Bodashka and Valon, who are debating the merits of their favorite football teams—a foolish endeavor since none of us have seen a game in two months. I'm trying not to listen to them, which is why I can easily hear the conversation of the two girls at the table behind mine.

"Can I borrow your silky top—the one that looks like lingerie?"

"If you want."

"It looks sexy on me, don't you think?"

"Yeah...but I don't know if it will matter."

"Why?"

"Well...he's bringing *her*, isn't he?"

"Just because she's coming doesn't mean he's bringing her like a date. They're not dating."

"How do you know?"

"They're cousins."

That makes my ears prick up. They're talking about Leo and Anna, I know it. There's not that many cousins at Kingmakers. Not many worth talking about anyway.

I glance back over my shoulder, subtle so that the girls won't notice. I see a raven-haired one and a redhead speaking with their heads close together.

The dark-haired girl is Gemma Rossi. She may look like a princess with her perfectly pressed blouse and her Alice band, but Valon has an Artillery and Marksmanship class with her and he said she's a damn good shot.

I don't know the other girl. She sounds Irish.

Gemma looks intense and determined. The redhead wrinkles her nose, making a face like she knows her friend won't like what she's about to say.

"I mean...it's pretty obvious he likes her. Are they even actually cousins? Marina Voss told me—"

"They're not dating!" Gemma interrupts. "I've never seen them hold hands or anything. He likes me, I know he does. He said he'd come tonight as soon as I asked him."

I turn back to my chicken, taking a huge bite out of the thigh to stop myself telling Gemma that she's fucking delusional. I don't know what the deal is with Leo and Anna, but I know for sure that no guy with two eyes in his head would pick Gemma Rossi when he can see Anna Wilk standing right there.

Still...knowing that Anna's going to the party has an effect on me. It makes me want to go too, even if it means seeing Leo smirking and accepting a hundred slaps on the back.

Anna will dress up in her street clothes and probably wear her hair down and paint her face like the queen of the undead. And that's something I want to see, even if it's from a hundred feet away.

Making a decision, I shove my plate away and stand up, startling Bodashka and Valon midsentence.

"Where you going?" Valon asks.

"I'm gonna take a shower."

The party is way down on Moon Beach, one of the only parts of the island that has a white-sand beach. The beach is tiny and shaped like a crescent moon, and you can't actually swim there—not unless you want to be dragged away and drowned by the intense riptides only a dozen yards out in the water. But it's a popular place for students to walk or lie out and tan when the weather is nice.

To combat the night chill, some of the kids have built a bonfire that fills the air with sparks, bathing the sand in shifting, orange-tinged light.

I walked down here with Bram. He's recovered his spirits enough that he immediately seizes a dusty bottle of wine from one of his Penose and chugs half of it down.

"Where's the fucking music?" he shouts.

"I've got a speaker," Chay Wagner says.

I already knew of her before I ever came to campus—the Night Wolves have a sort of celebrity cachet. But I'd know exactly who she was either way because she rooms with Anna. She's a pretty girl, petite but strong, dressed like a rock star in tight leather pants and an artfully slashed Guns N' Roses T-shirt.

The speaker she sets up atop a pile of driftwood is the same one that Anna uses when she practices dancing.

The music pours out, boisterous and loud, echoing off the limestone cliffs: "Daisy" by Ashnikko.

I forgot how long it's been since I watched a movie or a TV show or listened to music on earbuds. Kingmakers is a castle frozen in time. With everyone wearing uniforms and spending all their time studying or punishing their bodies in the gym, it might be today or twenty years ago or a hundred.

Anna's roommate is here with her speaker, but not Anna herself. I hadn't planned to drink, but as an hour passes with only the same classmates I talk to every day and not the one person I actually wanted to see, I become irritated and angry, and I take the remaining half bottle of wine from Bram and chug it down.

"There you go," he says approvingly.

I don't usually drink with him. I don't drink much at all or use drugs. I have a hard enough time controlling myself without taking the governor off. Who knows what I might do if I were completely uninhibited?

"Do you want to dance?" a curly-haired girl asks me nervously. I think she's in my combat class.

"No."

I don't dance. I'd feel like a fool doing that publicly.

"Okay. Sorry," she mumbles, hurrying away with her face flaming.

"What's your problem?" Bram says. "She's not bad looking."

"You fuck her, then."

"I will if I can." Bram grins. But he stays where he is, sipping a mixed drink out of a plastic cup. His wolflike eyes are roaming the fifty or so students scattered around the fire. Like me, he doesn't want just any girl. He wants the best he can get.

Finally, I see what I was waiting for all this time: Anna Wilk.

She strides across the sand, graceful as ever, while everyone else slips and stumbles on the uneven ground. Her long, silvery hair is loose, just like I hoped. It falls all the way down to her waist when she doesn't have it twisted up in a bun or a ponytail.

We're not supposed to wear our normal clothes even on the weekend, but everybody does when they leave campus.

Anna is wearing jeans that are more holes than material, her pale skin showing through the slashes, gleaming gold in the firelight. Her top is likewise a complicated assortment of straps and buckles. All I care about is how painfully tight it looks—how it shoves up her small, round breasts and emphasizes the impossible circumference of her tiny waist.

My cock is rock-hard in my jeans, and she's only taken five steps across the sand.

Bram follows my gaze. He lets out a low chuckle.

"Ohhh...that's what you were waiting for."

I don't answer him. Right behind Anna, following her as if they're bound together by an invisible cord, is Leo fucking Gallo. He strides along behind her, tall like her, fit like her, glowing in the firelight like a golden lion.

But he's not made for her.

I am.

If Leo is the sun, then I'm the whole expanse of the night sky. And that's where Anna belongs—wrapped up in my arms like the moon goddess she is.

My need for her is so sharp and intense that I can taste it in my mouth like acid.

Just as I expected, Leo's lapdogs flock around him, alive with conversation about the upcoming challenges. They surround him, demanding his attention, distracting him from Anna.

Anna doesn't mind. She steps aside to let them speak to Leo. Spotting Chay by the fire, she joins her roommate instead, and the two girls talk, giggling together about something I can't hear. Chay picks up the speaker, and Anna fiddles with it for a moment, turning up the volume and also changing to a different playlist.

"Daisy" disappears, and Anna's favorite song starts to play instead. I know it's her favorite because she plays it over and over when she's practicing in the empty cathedral.

She doesn't know how many times I've crept into the church to listen. I don't watch her for long—I wouldn't risk her catching me. But I always peek around the corner at her at least for a moment so I'll get an image of her burned in my brain, poised on tiptoe in the beams of multicolored light, mid-pirouette or mid-leap, her long legs stretched out at the most outrageous angle.

"Love Chained"—Cannons

This song plays over and over in my head. It means Anna to me.

I'm watching her talk to Chay. I'm tracing the emotions that pass over her face, subtle and fleeting like shadows on water. Anna is a mystery. I've only scratched the surface of what she keeps locked up inside her.

She glances up, and our eyes meet.

There's no hiding the fact that I was watching her. I don't want to hide it.

I leave Bram standing alone, and I stride over to her, shouldering my way through anyone that stands between us.

"Hello," she says cautiously.

I say, "I was waiting for you."

Her face colors, and she shoots a glance at Chay, who stands watching us, wide-eyed.

I don't give a fuck about her roommate.

I say to Anna, "Dance with me."

I never dance. But that's what comes out of my mouth, and I don't take it back.

Now it's Leo she glances at—Leo talking and laughing with a dozen different friends. He doesn't care that she's over here. But she checks in with him anyway.

"I don't think that's a good idea," Anna says quietly.

"Why not?" I demand.

Her blue eyes meet mine, clear and blunt. "You know why."

I sneer, "Because of *him*?"

"I don't want any trouble between you two."

"He has nothing to do with this." My hand closes around her wrist.

It's the first time I've touched her since we collided in the changing room. Her skin is burning hot from her proximity to the fire.

Anna hesitates. Then she twists her wrist quickly, slipping

it from my grasp before my fingers have even finished closing around it.

"No," she says.

She turns and walks away from me, back toward Leo.

My teeth grind together so hard I think they might break.

The rage I feel toward Leo Gallo is a hundred times hotter than this fire. I could set him aflame if he so much as looked at me.

Chay regards me with open curiosity, hands stuffed in the pockets of her leather pants.

She says, "You're full of surprises."

Biting back what I'd like to reply, I skulk back over to Bram instead.

"No luck, huh?" he says, with an infuriating mixture of pity and smugness.

My fists clench. I'm so angry I could hit him right in the face.

Before I can do anything, he says, "Here," and presses something into my palm.

It's small and hard. A pill—round, yellow, smaller than my pinky nail.

"There's other ways," Bram says, his eyes gleaming in the firelight.

"What the fuck is this?"

"Drop it in her drink. She won't turn you down after that."

A fucking roofie.

I don't want Anna passed out and helpless. I want her riding on top of me, her long hair a curtain around us, her gorgeous face wild with the sensation of my cock sliding in and out of her.

I'm about to drop the pill in the sand.

Then I look over at Leo and Anna, and a different idea strikes me.

"Thanks," I say to Bram.

I find the makeshift drink station on the edge of the sand, and I mix up a cocktail—light on liquor, heavy on fruit punch. I drop the pill inside and swirl the cup to help it dissolve.

Then I look for my quarry.

I see her standing next to her redheaded friend, wearing a silky camisole top, her hair and makeup done with a pathetic level of care. All for nothing. I doubt Leo has glanced over at her once.

I sidle up to them, holding the drink casually as if it's mine.

"Enjoying the party?"

Gemma looks surprised that I'm talking to her. "I guess," she hesitantly says.

"How about you?" I say to her friend.

"Aye." The redhead has a little more enthusiasm.

"Hey, didn't you ace the last shooting match?" I say to Gemma.

"Yes." She frowns. "But how did you—"

"Leo mentioned it." A lie—it was Valon who told me. But she's too stupid to realize that Leo and I don't talk about anything, let alone about her.

"Oh!" she says, almost clapping her hands together with happiness. "He did?"

Gemma throws a triumphant look at her friend. The redhead is frowning slightly but doesn't say anything.

"Speaking of Leo," I say to Gemma, "have you congratulated him yet?"

"No."

"You should." I thrust the drink into her hand. "Give him that—it's his favorite. See if he wants to toast with you."

Now she's eager. "Okay!"

She hurries off across the sand, carrying her drink and the one I laced. I watch closely to make sure she gives Leo the right one.

She puts it right in his hand, babbling something up at him. Leo listens with a bemused expression, then grins and shrugs and holds the drink aloft for a toast. His tight little group of friends cheers him, and then they all raise their glasses to their lips. Leo swallows his drink down in one draft.

The redhead watches all this just like I do. Then she turns

to me, her pale green eyes fixed on my face and her scowl deeper than ever.

She says, "Leo didn't tell you that."

I give her a cold look. "How would you know?" And I walk away from her.

As I pass Anna's speaker, I knock it with my elbow as if by accident, and I kick a little sand over it with my heel as I keep on walking.

CHAPTER 12
ANNA

"You want to go to the party together?" Chay asks me.

She's already dressed in tight leather pants and a half dozen layered necklaces. She looks antsy and excited. I know she's got a crush on some beefy British Enforcer, and she's hoping to make a move on him tonight.

"You go ahead," I say. "I'm not even close to ready."

The real reason is that I want to walk down with Leo, just the two of us. But I don't want to say that to Chay.

"You mind if I borrow your speaker?" she asks. "We wanna have music."

"Help yourself."

"I should have snuck one in too," she grumbles. "I was scared to break the rules. The acceptance letter was so terrifying. I wish I'd brought more clothes too."

"You only were allowed one bag. Where would you have put them?"

Chay already brought twice the amount of clothes of anyone else. Her suitcase was bursting at the seams. She didn't bring a single pair of pajamas in favor of stuffing dozens of vintage band tees into her bag, plus eight different pairs of heels. She wears stilettos to class every day, along with an assortment of studded bracelets and chain belts that clink when she walks.

"I could have worn at least five more outfits if I layered," Chay says mournfully. "I could have gotten on that boat wrapped up like an onion."

"You would have died of heatstroke," I remind her. "It was boiling that first day."

"Worth it!" Chay is vehement. "Anyway, I'll take this down now, if you don't mind."

"Go ahead."

She grabs the speaker, and I head down to the showers.

I spend a lot more time than usual getting ready for the party.

I wash and dry my hair, which takes fucking forever. It's three feet long, poker straight, and fine as spider silk. But the work is worth it, because when it's clean and loose, it glides across my skin and glimmers like metal where the light hits it.

I put a sheer smoky shadow around my eyes that makes my irises look more gray than blue. Then I turn my brows into dark slashes, line my eyes with a catlike wing, and lift my black lipstick to my lips.

I hesitate.

Without acknowledging the reason why, I put the lipstick back in my bag, leaving my mouth bare.

Then I spritz myself with perfume and put on my favorite necklace.

Leo gave it to me when we were only eight years old. The chain is so fine you can barely see it on my skin. The pendant is a tiny crescent moon.

He only wears one piece of jewelry himself: a gold St. Eustachius medallion from his father.

When I'm finally ready, I head down to the gnarled olive tree at the northwest corner of the keep. That's where Leo and I always meet, because it's exactly halfway between our dorms.

He's already standing there, chatting with Miles and Ozzy. His face is glowing with pleasure, and I'm sure he's telling Miles that he was picked as captain. Not that it'll be news to Miles—he's always first to know anything that happens on campus. He probably knew Leo got it before it was even posted.

"Hey, Black Swan," Miles says, slipping something into my palm. I look down, seeing my favorite chocolate bar—Dairy Milk Marvelous Creations. It's the weirdest candy ever created—pop rocks and jelly beans mixed with chocolate. I'm obsessed with it.

"What the hell, Miles?" I laugh. "I can't even find these in America."

"You don't want to know what I had to do to get that," Miles says darkly.

"If you murdered fewer than three people, it was worth it." I rip it open immediately and take a huge bite. "Oh my god," I moan. "I've missed you so much."

Leo shakes his head with a revolted expression. "That candy is a war crime. Worst thing Britain ever did to us."

"Maybe you'll like it now." I shake it in his face teasingly. "You're not as picky as you used to be. I actually saw you eating salmon this week."

"I was desperate," he says with a long-suffering expression. "But I'll never be desperate enough to eat exploding chocolate."

"Can I try it?" Ozzy is wildly curious.

"Of course." I hand it over.

He takes a bite, chewing cautiously. After a moment, as the chocolate melts on his tongue and the pop rocks begin to erupt, he shivers like an electric current ran up his spine. "God no!" he shouts, handing me back the rest of the bar.

"It's great, right?"

"I hate it...and I love it." He gives a ghoulish grin, eyes rolling back.

"You coming down to the beach with us?" Leo says to Miles.

"Maybe later," Miles says. "Got some stuff to do first."

Leo doesn't bother to ask what kind of stuff. Miles delights in being elusive.

"See you later then maybe," Leo says.

"What about Ares?" I ask Leo.

"He didn't want to come. Said he was studying."

"You think that's what he's actually doing?"

"I dunno." Leo shrugs. "He might just want to be alone in the room for once. Kingmakers isn't the easiest place for an introvert."

"Tell me about it," I say, thinking of Chay's incessant commentary. I've come to like her more the longer we've been roommates. She's blunt and funny and doesn't hold a grudge about anything. But I do wish she didn't feel the need to tell me every single thing that happens to her over the course of the day.

I can't say I'm sorry that it's just Leo and me walking down to Moon Beach.

It's been a while since Leo saw me in anything besides our school uniform. As we slip between the twin figures guarding the stone gates of campus, I catch his eye drifting down to the exposed flesh not covered by my corset top.

He pulls his gaze quickly back to the rocky path in front of us, but I know he was looking at me in a way he never used to do back in Chicago.

Neither of us is speaking. There's a strange tension in the air—like a breeze you can hear but not quite feel on your skin, not just yet.

Something is going to happen tonight. I'm sure of it.

I don't have any reason to believe it, but my heart is racing all the same. Leo looks lean and powerful, stalking down the path in the moonlight. He's almost vibrating with energy.

You would think I'd be used to his beauty, having known him all my life. But instead, it's the opposite—he's my standard of what a man should be. Tall, muscular, walking with the rangy grace of a lion. His amber-colored eyes and his deeply tanned skin make him look exotic, like he could be from anywhere. His skin and hair glow with health and vitality. His teeth gleam every time his full lips part in a smile.

"What are you staring at?" he asks.

"I'm looking at you," I say honestly.

"How come?"

I take a deep breath, trying to make myself brave enough to say what I want to say.

"I feel like things have been different since we came to Kingmakers."

Leo looks at me, serious for once. "Different between you and me?"

"Yes."

There's a long silence in which my heart beats so hard against my ribs I think I'll have a bruise inside.

"I think you're right," Leo says softly.

We've stopped walking, and we're standing in the middle of the path, facing each other. There's only a foot or two of space between us. The night feels suddenly twenty degrees warmer. Enough that my skin starts to sweat ever so slightly.

I've never seen Leo look at me this way. He looks…almost scared. Leo's never scared.

His tongue moistens his bottom lip, and he opens his mouth, about to say something. Then someone hollers, "Leo!"

Matteo Ragusa and Emile Girard come jogging down the path, followed close behind by a couple of girls from our year.

"Did you see Bram pitch a fit that he didn't get captain?" Matteo says gleefully. "He punched a hole through a window and cut his arm open, the dumb shit. Had to go to the infirmary and get stitches."

Leo pulls me close for a moment, murmuring in my ear, "I want to finish our conversation later."

Then he releases me, laughing loudly and saying, "God, what I'd pay to have that on video."

"Not like he was gonna get it anyway," Matteo says. "His grades are shit."

"He's a good shot, and he did well in our scuba classes," Emile says.

"Not well enough, obviously." Matteo laughs.

We continue on down the path as a group, Matteo and Emile flanking Leo, and me trailing along behind between the boys and the girls. Leo glances back at me several times, but Matteo and Emile are both yammering away at him from either side.

I'm half-disappointed and half-relieved. My nerves were so acute that I almost felt like I was going to puke. It might be better to get a drink in me before we try talking again.

It takes the better part of a half hour to walk down to the beach. We have to cut across a vineyard, then scramble down a steep slope to find the path. There's no streetlights anywhere on the island, so all this is done in the dark, all of us tripping over unseen rocks and clumps of grass along the way.

We can hear music playing long before we arrive. Chay is making use of my speaker, running through one of my playlists. I can hear the crackling of a bonfire and the steady wash of waves on the shore. Some of the kids are already shouting and laughing, sounding tipsy though the party's only just begun.

As soon as we step foot on the sand, several people shout Leo's name and rush over to talk about the upcoming competition. The freshmen are excited—if anyone can make us win, it's Leo. The sophomores and juniors at the party openly laugh at our hopes.

"You're gonna get fucking slaughtered," Matteo's brother Damari informs us.

"Maybe." Leo grins. "But I like my chances better than yours."

Calvin Caccia crosses his arms over his chest, frowning. He was chosen as captain for the juniors. And he probably feels some extra rivalry with Leo since he's in line to become an Italian don himself, in New York instead of Chicago. The Gallos and the Caccias have done business together in the past. Calvin and Leo will likely have to contend with one another outside Kingmakers. How they fare against each other in the Quartum Bellum may set the tone for those encounters.

"Why is that exactly?" Calvin says in his gravelly voice.

Leo shrugs, smiling easily. "I always bet on myself."

"Would you like to place a bet on the first event?" Calvin says. His blocky face is stern and unsmiling.

Leo grins back at him, totally undeterred. "What kind of bet?" he says.

"My team places higher than yours in the first competition," Calvin says. "Loser comes to breakfast naked the next day."

Leo laughs. "That's a win-win for you, Calvin. Either you beat me, or you get to see me naked."

The corner of Calvin's mouth quirks up in the ghost of a smile, and he holds out his large, callused hand to shake. Leo returns his grip just as hard.

"As if you needed any more pressure on you," I say to Leo after Calvin has ambled off to refill his drink.

"I like to keep things interesting." Leo opens his mouth to say something else, but he's immediately interrupted by several fresh classmates who want to speculate on the upcoming events.

Leaving them to it, I head over to the bonfire to get a drink. Chay is messing with my speaker, trying to change the playlist.

"It's repeating the same six songs," she says. "How do I get it to—"

"You're not on the full list. You're just doing most frequently played. Here, let me—"

The system is ancient. It was almost impossible to find a stereo that ran off batteries. Kingmakers has a huge generator that operates the electric lights and other systems that need power, but there's almost no outlets anywhere on campus. That's to help discourage students smuggling in phones, tablets, and so forth. We have to write all our assignments by hand, and the only news we get is via phone calls and letters from home. Even the phones are a single bank of repurposed booths that can only be used to call out on Saturdays and Sundays. No calls can come in except through the main office.

"There," I say once I've switched over the playlist.

Immediately, my favorite song begins to play. I've heard it a thousand times, but I never get tired of it.

"Thanks!" Chay says.

"No problem. You been down here long?"

"About an hour. Sam isn't here yet." Chay pouts.

"Did he say he was coming?"

"Yeah. He comes to all the parties. He was the one who threw the rager in the gatehouse last week."

"Nice," I say, trying to be polite. I don't get the appeal of Sam Underhill. He's your typical class clown personality, always willing to make a fool of himself for a laugh. Chay seems to love it, though, so I guess it works.

I can feel eyes on me, and I glance up, thinking it's Leo.

Instead, I see Dean Yenin standing on the other side of the fire staring at me. The moment he catches my eye, he starts walking over to me. I have an impulse to flee, but I hold my ground.

Dean doesn't stop until he's right in front of me, his chest only inches from mine, so I have to tilt my head back to look up into his face. When Dean isn't smiling, he looks furious, and I can feel Chay watching us curiously, unsure if Dean wants to hit on me or fight me.

"I was waiting for you," he says in his blunt way.

I can feel myself blushing, hard as I try to fight it. I hate that he can embarrass me like this. I usually have such good control of my reactions.

"Dance with me," he demands.

"I'm not going to do that."

"Why not?"

"You know why."

We can both see Leo off to our right, still surrounded by friends, laughing and joking. He won't stay distracted for long if Dean tries to waltz me around in front of him. I know Dean hates Leo. I'm not going to let him use me to start some kind of a fight.

"He has nothing to do with this."

Dean's hand snakes out and grabs my wrist with that alarming speed he seems to possess. I have to twist my wrist hard to break free of his grip, and the moment I do I hurry away from him before he grabs me again, before he can make a scene in front of all these people.

My face is flaming, and I don't understand what the fuck he thinks he's doing. I thought Dean and I had reached a kind of reasonable equilibrium. We finished our banking project with minimal conflict. In fact, we got a perfect score. I thought that was proof that if we couldn't be friends, we at least didn't have to be enemies.

But now he's trying to stir up some kind of shit with Leo again.

Then I remember why.

The captainship. It was announced today. Dean must be pissed that Leo got it instead of him. Makes sense. I can't imagine Dean is going to enjoy taking orders from Leo. Same with Bram.

Leo's going to have a tough time winning when half his team is in mutiny.

I want to talk to Leo about that—about a lot of things, actually—but there's so damn many people crowded around him, I can't do more than catch his eye, for which he gives me a warm and apologetic smile.

Usually I don't mind that Leo is so popular. I want him to get all the love and attention in the world. But right now I feel anxious, our unspoken and unfinished moment gnawing at me.

"It's all war games!" Matteo is saying, swinging his arms around so wildly that his drink sloshes out of his cup, dousing his sleeve. "The upperclassmen will have more experience, obviously, but if we can—"

I never hear Matteo's brilliant plan, because Gemma Rossi pushes her way into the center of the group, clutching two red plastic cups in her hands.

"Leo!" she says. "I heard you made captain! Congratulations! Guaranteed we'll win with you leading us!"

She looks up at him, batting both eyelids as hard as she can. She stepped on my foot on her way by, and I'm seriously regretting not tripping her as I'd considered doing. With her hands full, she would have fallen flat on her face.

"Let's all toast Leo!" she chirps, thrusting one of the drinks into Leo's hand.

Leo shoots me a look, knowing that I've got a massive eye roll just waiting to be deployed. But I don't let it loose. I don't feel sarcastic or amused at the moment. I just feel…anxious.

Everyone holds their makeshift drinks aloft—the dusty bottles of homemade beer brewed at the castle that are supposed to be for teachers but are frequently stolen by students. The wine made at the vineyard south of campus, the bottles stamped with the Visine Dvorca label. And the cocktails mixed with smuggled liquor that students snuck in their suitcases or bought at outrageous prices from the fishermen who go back and forth with supplies for the island.

I don't have a drink. Leo holds out his cup to me, but I shake my head. So he toasts himself along with everyone else, drinking down whatever Gemma brought him, grinning as everyone cheers for him.

Leo lowers his cup, licking his lips with relish.

"I'm telling you, it all comes down to game theory," Matteo says.

"No, it's pure fitness," his friend argues.

At that moment, the music cuts out abruptly. It resumes a moment later, but it sounds garbled and dull.

I look around to see if Chay is fucking with the speaker again. Or maybe it's the long-awaited Sam, who has arrived at last and is chucking a football back and forth across the sand with Kasper Markaj with no regard for who or what lies between them.

Chay is nowhere to be seen, and neither is the stereo. The pile of driftwood that held it aloft now holds nothing at all.

Swearing under my breath, I stalk over to the fire so I can see what the hell happened.

Following the sputtering sound, I find my speaker half-buried in sand. Some idiot must have knocked it over—definitely Sam, I bet.

I pick up the speaker, stopping the music so I can remove the outer shell, take the batteries out, and clean all the sand out of it. I should never have lent it to Chay in the first place. If it gets broken, how the hell am I going to practice in the mornings?

After twenty minutes of painstaking cleaning, I'm pretty sure I got every last grain of sand. I use my fingernail to screw the case together again, then I check to make sure it's still working.

The playlist resumes at exactly the same spot, thank god. The one good thing about old electronics is they're built like tanks. Made to be bashed around without consequence.

I stand up triumphantly, brushing off my hands.

A lot more kids have streamed into the party, and the little beach is packed with people now. Everybody is drunk enough to think they know how to dance, and they hoot and whistle as the music resumes.

Couples are sneaking off into the scrubby stands of trees around the beach, dragging blankets along with them so they can lie down on the sand and remove as much clothing as they like.

Some of these couples aren't couples at all but rather two boys paired up with one extremely tipsy girl. It's a sight I've gotten used to seeing at Kingmakers, where the gender balance is so far out of whack.

We're not supposed to be fucking each other at all. Some of these girls are already locked into marriage contracts with other Mafia families. Some of the boys too. But with no one here to stop them, they've obviously decided to take their chances.

The days when you were expected to show up on your wedding day a virgin are far behind us. In my parents' time, some of the old-school families still expected a medical examination to prove you were "intact." Now all you have to pass is a pregnancy test. The only thing the families truly care about is that their heirs are actual blood relations.

Even my uncle Callum had an arranged marriage with Aunt Aida. You'd never guess it now from how obsessed they are with each other.

I have a lot of examples of marital bliss to draw from. Like Aunt Riona and Uncle Raylan out in Tennessee with all their boys. They seem like a funny match; she's a ball-busting lawyer, and he's pure Southern charm. Yet it's clear they adore each other.

Not to mention my parents, who are more in love than any two people I've seen.

Maybe my standards are too high. If I ever get married, I expect nothing less than perfect devotion from my future partner. Who could live up to that?

There's only one person in my life who's never let me down.

I search the crowded beach for Leo, but he seems to have disappeared.

Leo and I were raised like blood cousins, even though we're not. Our parents saw us as family. It was assumed we'd see each other the same way.

I've known him since birth. We really did grow up next to each other. I should see him as a brother…

But I don't.

That's becoming clearer to me every day.

These feelings I have…these urges…they're not going away.

The harder I fight to crush them down, the stronger they arise, over and over again, like a hydra with a hundred heads. I cut one off, and two more come roaring back.

I think Leo feels it too. At first, I thought he didn't. But he gave up his scholarship to come to Kingmakers with me, even though his mother hated the idea. And ever since we got here, things have been different between us. I've seen him looking at me. I see how jealous he gets when Dean talks to me.

I felt something between us tonight. I know he felt it too.

I want to finish our conversation. I look around everywhere, wondering where he disappeared to so quickly. I walk down to the water, but nobody is stupid enough to try to swim here, not even when they're drunk.

I head back up to the cliffs, checking the steep pathway to see if he went back that way for some reason.

I walk all the way around the bonfire, wondering if I could have somehow missed him in the crowd of students. It's hard to push my way through the crush of people, especially when Chay is trying to pull me into dancing with her and Matteo is trying to ask me some asinine question about an upcoming history exam.

The only place I haven't checked is the little stands of trees on either side of the beach.

My boots are filling up with sand. I take them off, pouring them out and slinging them over my shoulder by their strings. I pad across the ground in sock feet, peeking into the scrubby woods to see if Leo came this way.

All I see are couples writhing around on blankets or making out pressed up against trees.

I'm about to turn back when I hear a moan that sends a shiver down my spine.

I've never heard him make quite that sound before. But I'd know Leo's voice anywhere.

I turn and peer through the darkness at a particularly dense stand of trees.

There's Leo, slumped against the trunk of an almond tree, his head leaned back and his eyes half-focused on the leaves above.

Gemma is on her knees in front of him, hard at work on his cock. I can hear the wet sounds of her mouth, and I see her dark hair swinging as her head bobs up and down.

My stomach clenches so hard that I almost vomit right there on the sand. It takes all my strength to swallow it down, everything I have to choke back the sob that wants to burst out of me.

The only thing I can think is *He can't see me. Can't hear me.*

So everything I feel, a pain so heavy, so dense, so cold, so poisoned, has to be swallowed down inside me where it bleeds through every part of me and spreads through every cell.

I've never been so disappointed.

Every step along the long, dark route to the castle, I fight not to cry.

CHAPTER 13
LEO

I'M HAVING THE MOST INCREDIBLE DREAM.

I won the final challenge in the Quartum Bellum. The whole school is swarming me, lifting me up on their shoulders, chanting my name.

I look out over the sea of people, and I see Anna standing there, looking up at me. Her blue eyes glimmer like stars. She's smiling at me; she's so fucking proud of me.

I push through the crowd to get to her, and I lift her up and spin her around. Her long hair swirls around her just like it does when she's dancing.

I set her down, and she looks up at me the way she did when we were standing on the dark path on the way to the party. She has the same expression on her face—frightened but hopeful. I can see that she loves me. I always knew she loved me. But this is something else—not the love of a cousin or a friend. This is the love of a soulmate. Of a woman who wants me as badly as I want her.

I kiss her, just as I imagined doing earlier in the night. I touch those soft, warm lips with mine, and I taste her sweetness.

I slide my hand down the small of her back. I wrap my arms around her.

And then everyone around us disappears, because Anna is pulling me away. She's leading me by the hand, pulling me into the woods. Her fingertips trail down my chest, down my stomach, lightly touching the button of my jeans. She's doing what I fantasized that night in my bed. This time, I don't have to feel shame and guilt, because I'm aware it's only a dream, even though it feels so real.

She pushes me up against the tree, then drops to her knees in front of me. I feel her soft hands fumbling with the button of my jeans, and she pulls down the zipper to let my cock spring free. She's closing that warm, wet mouth around my cock...

I'm looking up at a lattice of leaves and branches, with pinprick stars beyond. But the stars aren't stationary. They're spinning around and around my head, which is making me feel dizzy and sick.

Anna's mouth feels good on my cock, but the rest of me doesn't feel good at all. My head is heavy, and my stomach is churning. I don't seem to have control over my arms and legs. My hands are hanging loose at my sides, and my head flops against my shoulder.

I hear a wet, repetitive sound like a dog licking me.

My cock isn't hard anymore. I feel too sick.

"Is something wrong?" a voice says.

I flop my head forward so I can look down.

A strange face is peering up at me. Not Anna's face. This girl has black hair, not blond, and her eyes are darker than Anna's. They're flat and glittering in the near darkness. She looks spooky, crouched down there looking up at me with her face all wet and her makeup all messy.

"What are you doing?" I mumble.

"What do you mean what am I doing?" The girl giggles. "What do you think I'm doing?"

She grabs my limp cock and puts it back in her mouth. She's sucking and slurping on it, trying to bring it back to life. It feels like I'm being eaten alive.

"Knock it off." I try to push her away.

My hand is like an empty glove on the end of a noodle. I've got no control over it.

And my voice is mushy. "Knock it off" sounds more like "Knog id dov."

The girl doesn't seem to hear me. She keeps going. The bobbing of her head is making my body rock, which is making me seasick.

"Stop," I say, even more weakly.

This time she does understand, at least enough to sit back on her heels again.

"What's your problem?" she says.

Given the chance to move, I heave myself away from the tree. But I underestimated how much I needed the support. I tumble forward on my knees, then drop down on all fours. This is way too much motion for my stomach to handle. I start puking all over the ground.

"How much did you drink?" the girl says, part disgusted and part concerned.

I don't know how much I drank. I can't remember.

The beginning of the night seems to be dissolving away. I don't know how I got here or what's happening.

If I focus hard, I can sort of remember that the girl's name is Gemma and we have that scuba class together. But everything right before this moment is a throbbing dark haze.

"I need to leave," I tell her.

"I don't think you're going to make it very far," Gemma says.

I open my mouth to reply, but all that comes out is more vomit.

CHAPTER 14
DEAN

I FOLLOW ANNA BACK TO KINGMAKERS.

I keep a long space between us so she won't hear me.

Honestly, I don't think she'd hear a brass band behind her. She's stumbling along with none of her usual grace.

I don't like seeing her like this. It pains me to hurt her. But it pains me more to think that she's upset over that fucking asshole Leo Gallo. He doesn't deserve her devotion. It took him all of thirty minutes to stumble off in the woods with Gemma Rossi. There's no drug on earth that could distract me from Anna.

I watch her every moment from the beach to the castle. She's fleeing across the ground like a white bird, her hair streaming behind her. And I'm chasing after her like a hunter with an arrow at the ready.

When she passes through the gates into Kingmakers, I watch to see which direction she turns.

Just as I expected, she veers left, away from her dorm. I know exactly where she's going.

She passes between the gatehouse and the greenhouses, then shoots the gap between the dining hall and the brewery. She takes a hard left, passing the library tower, hurrying on toward the cathedral on the far west side of campus.

The cathedral looks skeletal and spooky in the moonlight.

The large rose window above the double doors peers at us like a baleful eye.

Anna doesn't have her speaker—she forgot it at the party. But she came here anyway because this is her sanctuary.

She's already inside before I reach the doors. As I slip through, I expect to hear her sobbing echoing around the stone walls.

Instead, there's nothing but silence.

I walk quietly up the nave, my eyes sweeping the shadowy spaces for any sign of Anna. All the furniture has long since been removed from the cathedral—no pews, no altars, no shrines. Even the doves are quiet, asleep up in the rafters.

At last I see Anna, sitting on the stone floor of the chancel with her knees tucked up against her chest, her arms wrapped around her shins, her silvery hair a shroud around her.

"Anna," I say.

My voice echoes in the empty space even though I spoke quietly.

Her eyes fly up to meet mine, and even then I can tell she's looking for Leo. She thought he came after her. Painful disappointment flashes across her face when she sees it's me instead.

She jumps to her feet, tossing her hair back over her shoulder, trying to maintain her composure even now.

I feel wild admiration for this girl who refuses to show a single crack in her armor, even when I know she's about to break apart.

"What are you doing here?" she demands.

I hear it, though she tries so hard to hide it...a quaver in her voice.

I cross the room in three steps and wrap my arms around her.

I pull her close against my chest, cradling her head in my hand, pressing her cheek against my heart. She tries to pull away, but I keep her pinned in place, my other arm wrapped tight around her body.

I force her to take comfort from me.

She fights me, but not hard. She's too beaten down by what happened. The strength has gone out of her.

After a moment, she submits.

She stops struggling, and she lets me hold her.

I inhale the scent of her hair—smoky from the fire but still fresh and clean underneath.

I hold her tight, making her feel the warmth of my body, the strength of my arms, the tremor of muscle that betrays how long and how intensely I've wanted this.

And then some magic happens, something I couldn't predict: Anna starts to cry.

She cries like her heart is breaking. Her tears soak the front of my shirt, and her whole body shakes. When she looks up at me, her eyes are bright and wet, and her lips are trembling.

I see the moment, and I seize it without hesitation.

I kiss those soft and devastated lips.

CHAPTER 15
ANNA

THE NEXT MORNING, I SKIP BREAKFAST, BECAUSE I DON'T WANT TO see anyone.

It doesn't work. Leo immediately corners me outside my dorm tower as if he's been waiting down there for hours.

He looks awful. His hair is a mess, and he has dark circles under his eyes. As soon as he sees me, he runs over and practically pins me against the wall with his bulk so I can't escape.

I try to slip past him, saying, "I can't talk right now. I have to get to the library." It's a transparent ruse. Leo doesn't buy it for a second.

"Anna, please," he begs. "I don't know what happened last night."

"I do."

I didn't want to have this conversation, but now that he's forcing me into it, the memory of the night before comes flooding back into my brain, more painful than ever. I can see him leaned up against that tree, his head tilted back in pleasure, and I can hear—as if it's right in my ears in this moment—Gemma's slurping mouth.

Last night, all I felt was hurt. But this morning, that hurt is turning into bitterness.

I know that Leo and I aren't dating. I know we didn't say anything explicit to each other. But just as clearly, I know there was something between us—an understanding, an intention. It wasn't all in my head.

Leo didn't give a fuck about that. The moment he had a chance to go off in the woods with Gemma, he took it. He didn't think about me at all.

"I saw you," I tell him, my eyes burning into his. "I saw you letting that little whore suck your cock."

I don't actually feel great about calling Gemma a whore. After all, it's not like she knew the fantasy I had in my head about how my night was supposed to go. It's not like she had some responsibility toward me. We're not even friends.

It's Leo who hurt me, not her. But in my fury, I use the most vicious words that come into my head, and I apply them mentally to Leo as well as to her.

Leo is a whore. He loves attention wherever he can get it. He doesn't understand the first thing about fidelity or love.

He's stammering and stumbling, nowhere near his usual smooth self.

"I was really drunk," he says. "I swear, I didn't mean to do it. I don't have a clue how it happened."

I stare at him like I don't even know him. "That's a pathetic excuse."

"I know!" he cries. "I know it is! I've never lost control like that. I don't understand it."

Leo's attempt to explain himself is just making me angrier.

"I don't want to hear it," I seethe at him. "You can fuck whoever you want. Just leave me out of it."

"Anna... I know... I wanted..."

He's stammering at me helplessly, unable to say what he wants to say. I already know what he's trying to tell me. He regrets being so careless. He didn't realize how much it would hurt me.

But that's Leo's problem—he's fucking thoughtless.

I try to push past him again, and in desperation he cries, "Where did you go last night?"

"I left."

"You came back here all alone?"

I'm impatient with this line of questioning. I don't appreciate Leo acting protective after he ripped my heart out.

Also a small, ugly part of me wants to hurt him back.

So I say, "No. I wasn't alone."

Leo can hear the menace in my voice. His eyebrows draw together.

"Who was with you?"

He doesn't really want to know the answer.

I look at his handsome face. The face that I've loved all my life. The face that I've never tried to drag down from happiness to sorrow, not once.

I know that I should take a day or two to cool off. That's why I didn't go down to breakfast—I wanted to avoid this exact conversation until I was in a more rational state of mind.

But the other part of me—the part of me that called Gemma a whore, the part of me that's angry and vengeful and self-destructive—that part answers Leo, the words leaving my lips before they've even formed in my brain.

"I was with Dean Yenin."

Leo stares at me.

I regret it already. I regret saying it. I regret doing it. I regret everything that's happening.

Too late.

Comprehension sweeps his face like a dark cloud passing over the sun.

"Dean…"

He says it low and guttural, a sound too much like the noise he made last night when he was with Gemma. When my head turned toward him in the dark, knowing the sound of Leo anywhere.

Anger, fear, sadness, regret. They cycle through me over and over until I have no idea what I want or what I feel.

Regret, sadness, fear…anger.

Wildly, defiantly, I lift my chin. "That's right."

"What do you mean you were *with* him?"

"What do you think I mean?" The words spill out of me. "I can do whatever I want. I'm a free agent, the same as you. Isn't that right, Leo? After all, we're just *cousins*."

I spit out that word like I hate it.

Maybe I do.

I wanted to take a little cut at Leo, in revenge for how he made me feel. But I seriously underestimated how furious this would make him. His eyes blaze like yellow fire, and now he is truly pressing me up against the stone wall at the base of the staircase, his fists clenched at his sides and his long frame trembling from head to toe.

"Are you insane?" he hisses at me. "You're not dating Dean Yenin."

"It's none of your business who I date," I inform him. "You're not the boss of me."

Leo is pressed closer against me than we've ever been in our lives. His chest crushes me, and his thigh pins my hip to the wall. His hand twitches, and I think he's almost angry enough to grab me by the throat. He's desperate, and he's cracking. Neither one of us is ourselves, let alone the person we usually are to each other.

Leo's shouting right at me, our faces inches apart.

"He's our *enemy*! And he's just using you to try to get back at me!"

I laugh in his face.

"You really do think the whole world revolves around you, don't you? Is it so impossible for you to believe that someone could like me?"

"Don't be ridiculous!" Leo says "It's got nothing to do with that. It's Dean. He's a slimy, manipulative, conniving—"

I cut him off. "I don't want to hear it. I'm sick of your stupid rivalry. And I'm sick of you thinking you can control me while you run around doing whatever you feel like."

I try to duck under Leo's arm, and he tries to grab me, holding me back.

This time I shove him, harder than I've ever shoved him before. This isn't play fighting; this is me telling him that if he doesn't keep his fucking hands to himself, I'll break his wrist.

We're both breathing hard, and Leo's expression is like nothing I've seen before. He's a stranger to me. I don't know him, and he doesn't know me.

"Just *stop*," I hiss at him.

He hesitates. For once in his life.

In that moment, he looks like a confused little boy.

I walk away from him, and this time he doesn't try to stop me.

That Sunday afternoon is long and lonely. Usually Leo, Ares, and I would do schoolwork in the library or walk down to the village together. Or we might play cards with Miles and Ozzy or steal raspberries out of the greenhouse.

Today, I don't feel like doing any of that. I can't even practice dancing because I forgot my speaker in the dorm room, and Chay has been sleeping all damn day after stumbling home at 5:00 in the morning. She had sand in her hair and her top was on backward, so I'm assuming Sam stopped playing football long enough to notice her, or Chay homed in on someone else equally interesting.

I make sure to visit the dining hall as soon as dinner service starts, before anyone else is there. I grab a fresh-baked roll and two apples so I can eat somewhere else. It's not only Leo I'm avoiding—I can't face the thought of seeing Dean either.

I don't believe for a second what Leo said about Dean using me to get close to him. Dean hasn't asked me about Leo one time or about any family members we might have in common. If anything, he's avoided the topic. And I've caught Dean looking at me enough times to know that he's been interested in me for a while.

No, if anything, it's me who used him to feel better last night.

And me who used him to make Leo jealous this morning. I feel guilty about that, and I don't know how to tell Dean that it was only a moment of weakness, that he and I won't be dating. If that's even what he wants.

I eat the roll and one of the apples while walking over to the library tower.

I don't even have to walk through the doors to know that the library will be empty. The weather outside is warm and balmy, and all the other students are taking the opportunity to play in the sunshine or recover from their hangover in the sea breeze.

As I ascend the spiral stairs leading up the interior of the tower, I can almost feel the weight of ten thousand books creaking and groaning over my head on their ancient shelves. The air feels thick with the thoughts of so many people long dead, their words whispering out of the pages.

I pad across the oriental rug, spotting Ms. Robin in her usual position behind the main desk, her head bent over a half dozen unfurled architecture schematics, the ink so faded that it might as well have been written in spilled tea.

She squints down at the yellowed paper, her nose barely an inch from the page, one long, slim finger trailing under a bit of script as she tries to read a minuscule annotation.

I clear my throat so I won't startle her.

She jumps anyway, her thick glasses sliding down her nose.

"Anna!" she squeaks. "I didn't hear you coming up."

"What are you working on?"

"Oh, it's nothing." She rolls up the long scroll. "Nothing interesting."

"You're always working on something."

"Well…" Ms. Robin hesitates, as if embarrassed to say. "I'm doing a dissertation on the floor plans of ancient monasteries. I have a theory about the aqueduct systems built on the Roman model."

"Is that why you came to work at Kingmakers?"

"Yes," she says. "The archives here contain maps and documents you can't find anywhere else in the world. And they're almost totally unstudied by mainstream academia. It's quite tragic, actually. The wealth of knowledge here is secret, for obvious reasons. And what I'll be allowed to publish is limited. But I'm extremely lucky to have been provided this access. It's not easy to secure a position here. The previous librarian held this job for thirty-seven years! I don't know if I'll be here that long, but who knows? It is incredibly peaceful. I've never gotten so much work done."

She smiles, showing a row of very pretty white teeth. I haven't been this close to Ms. Robin before, and I see that what I suspected is accurate. Beneath the straggly red hair and the thick glasses and the cardigan that looks as if it were knitted by a novice, she's quite beautiful.

"Is this your first year here, then?" I ask her.

"Yes. I started this fall, the same as you."

"Is your family connected to Kingmakers?"

"Luther Hugo is my uncle," she says. "He's the one who got me the job. Only he didn't exactly tell me what sort of school it was. I feel stupid now, not realizing. I guess I'm not very good at picking up on hints."

She pushes the heavy glasses up on the bridge of her nose, shaking her head at herself.

"Don't feel bad," I tell her. "A lot of the kids here were raised without a real idea of what their families did. Not me, but plenty of the others."

"You always knew?" She peers at me with her head slightly tilted.

"Yes. But my mother didn't. She thought her father was a businessman and her brother was a politician, mostly."

"It's the *mostly* that gets us." Ms. Robin laughs.

She has a soft, mellow laugh. Ms. Robin has a strange charisma—you don't see it at first. But the closer you get to her, the more it pulls you in.

"Anyway," she says, "I'm sure you didn't come here on a Sunday afternoon to hear all about me. What can I help you with?"

I tell her the book I need for my Contracts and Negotiations class, and she helps me locate it, way at the top of the tower, on one of the shelves that requires a rolling ladder to reach.

I say, "I'm surprised you know where everything is already."

"Well..." She smiles. "I literally live here. Up there."

She points to the ceiling. I see a trapdoor in the roof that appears to lead to an attic space nestled under the pointed peak of the tower.

"You sleep up there?"

"Best view on the island."

"Lonely, though," I say without thinking. I only meant that it was the most distant and isolated part of the castle. But I regret my thoughtless comment when I see the flash of pain on Ms. Robin's face.

"Yes," she says quietly. "It can be."

I return to my dorm with my arms full of books, not bothering to be quiet since Chay must be awake by now. As I push my way through the door, I see the silhouette of someone standing by the window.

I drop my books down on the bed, saying, "Thanks for remembering to bring my speaker back, despite being maybe twenty percent conscious."

"Chay's not here."

I spin around at the masculine voice. Dean is right behind me—freshly showered and shaved, wearing an immaculately pressed dress shirt and trousers. He's got his hands tucked in his pockets, and his pale blond hair falls down over his left eye as he looks at me sheepishly.

"It's me," he says unnecessarily.

"Right." I wish I still had my books to hold as a barrier between us. "I can see that now."

"I was looking for you all day," he says. "I figured you'd have to come back here eventually."

"You're not supposed to be in the girls' dorms," I remind him. "You'll get yourself in trouble."

"I think I'm already in trouble," Dean says in his low voice.

That voice sends a shiver up my spine—half-intriguing, half-terrifying.

"Dean—"

"I know what you're going to say," he says, interrupting me.

"What am I going to say?"

"You're going to tell me that last night was a mistake. That it only happened because you were upset with Leo."

I look at him, lips parted, tongue still. I didn't think he already knew that.

"I don't care," he says. "I want you anyway."

I swallow hard. "Leo thinks you're only interested in me because you want revenge on him."

Dean gives me an intense look. "Leo's a fucking idiot. He had you right next to him all those years, and he didn't do a damn thing about it."

After the beating my ego took last night, Dean's words mean something to me. But I can't eat it up just because it feels good. I have to be honest with him.

"Dean," I say softly, "what I feel about Leo…it's not a crush. It's not something I can turn off. Even when I'm fucking pissed at him."

"I don't care," he says again.

And now he crosses the space between us, covering the ground before I can blink, picking up my hand and holding it cradled in both of his in front of his chest. I can feel the calluses on his palms from his endless hours of jump rope down in the gym. I see his knuckles, bruised and swollen from hitting the heavy bag with the cold, silent fire that lives inside him.

"Just give me a chance," he says. "One date, that's all I'm asking.

If you don't want to be with me, I can't make you. But give me a chance at least."

He looks at me with those eyes that are more purple than blue. His face is both stern and vulnerable. It's a painful combination, one that's hard to look at without dropping my gaze.

I say, "This thing with you and Leo…"

"I'm not going to pretend that I'm fine with what his parents did to my family," Dean says. "But that's got nothing to do with you and me."

"I don't want any fighting."

His lips press together in a thin line. He's silent for a moment, thinking. Then at last he says, "Fine. As long as I'm with you, I won't do anything to Leo."

"We're not together, though," I tell him. "It's just one date."

Dean lifts my hand and presses it to his lips.

He looks in my eyes, fierce and intent.

"It will be more than one date."

CHAPTER 16
LEO

IMAGINE THAT YOU'RE STANDING ON A CLIFF, AND YOU DON'T realize it's a cliff. You think you're on solid ground. Until your feet slip out from under you. You begin to fall. After that first terrifying lurch, you pinwheel your arms, trying to catch your balance. But you keep falling and falling. You think to yourself *I'm gonna smash on the ground any second now. I'm not gonna survive this.* Yet you fall and fall and fall. And eventually you realize there is no bottom—you're plunging down into hell.

That's what it was like losing Anna.

There is no bottom.

I'm still falling.

Every day that passes is worse than the day before.

If only I hadn't been so fucking stupid the day after the party. If only I'd begged and groveled and apologized.

But I woke up with my head still fuzzy and throbbing. I rolled out of bed, not even sure how I got there in the first place. I had a vague memory of a girl looking up at me from her knees—a girl with dark eyes and hair, a girl who definitely wasn't Anna.

I knew I'd fucked up somehow. But I didn't really feel like it was my fault. It all seemed like a dream, like it had happened to somebody else.

So I waited outside her dorm to apologize, but it was only a half apology. My head was throbbing, and my stomach was churning. I thought Anna would see as clearly as I did that the night before was just a stupid mess, that it didn't mean anything. I thought she knew how I felt about her.

I was wrong.

I should have seen how much I'd hurt her.

The pain was clear on her face. If my own head wasn't pounding like a drum, I would have recognized it.

Instead, I lost my temper.

She told me she walked home with Dean, and I felt this overwhelming wave of jealousy and rage. I didn't know if she had kissed him or fucked him or just walked next to him, and I didn't care. I felt that she belonged to me and that Dean had tried to steal my property.

Looking back on it now, I could punch myself in the face.

I hadn't done anything to make sure that Anna was mine. I just assumed that I owned her and I always would. I thought I possessed her without actually earning it first.

So I shouted at her. Insulted her. And drove her away, at the one and only moment when I might have been able to convince her to stay.

And now she's with Dean instead. And I fucking hate him.

But not nearly as much as I hate myself.

I lost the one person in the world who mattered most to me.

And here's the most ironic part of all. Yes, it makes me fucking burn with jealousy to see the two of them together. To see them walk hand in hand across the commons. To see him put his palm on the small of her back or trail the back of his fingers down her cheek. And when he kisses her...I've never been closer to murder.

But the thing I miss most of all is my best friend.

I never realized how much of every day centered around Anna. She was the first one I told my news to, the person I most wanted to impress. When I'd tell a joke, I'd look at her to see if she laughed.

If I wanted to go for a run, get something to eat, or go exploring, I always had her by my side. If I needed advice or comfort, she was the only one I'd trust to give it. She knew me. She knew my whole history and exactly who I was. She can't be replaced.

I spend most of my time with Ares now. And he's a good friend, don't get me wrong. But he's not Anna.

I never realized how lonely a day can be. I'm surrounded by friends and classmates, but that's all they are. Nothing more.

Anna sits by Dean now or with the two other female freshman Heirs, Chay and Zoe. She eats lunch and dinner with them.

We're not enemies—she's polite to Ares and me when she sees us. But polite is almost worse than hateful. Because there's no passion in it. No sense of care. There's a barrier between us now. I can see her but not feel her. It hurts so fucking bad to be this close to her and yet so far away.

My parents can tell something's wrong. When I call them on the weekend, they can hear that all the joy has gone out of my voice.

This last Sunday, my dad left the call to answer the doorbell when it rang, and my mom said, "Leo, *milyy*, tell me what's wrong."

"Nothing's wrong, Mom," I said. "I'm doing well in school. My grades are picking up. I've gotten back to lifting most mornings. I've even been eating salads. You'd be proud of me."

"I am *always* proud of you, my love," my mother said. "But I know you, Leo. I know when you're hiding something from me."

"There's nothing," I lied. I couldn't tell her what I'd done.

My mom is clever, though. Maybe even more clever than my dad.

"Has something happened with Anna?" she asked shrewdly.

Even just hearing Anna's name created a lump in my throat that almost suffocated me.

"No," I lied again. "I've got to go, Mom. There's other people waiting for the phones."

I hung up before she could answer, vowing to wait at least

two weeks to call her back again. Hoping she'll have dropped it by then.

The first competition takes place at the beginning of November.

I face it with dread. I seem to have lost that burning confidence that's always been inside me like a pilot light, never going out, always ready to flame into a raging bonfire whenever I need it.

The concept is simple: a modified version of capture the flag. Each team gets their own base on their own area of the island. And we each have a flag to protect: white for the freshmen, silver for the sophomores, green for the juniors, and black for the seniors.

"Why's ours the easiest to see?" Bram grumbles.

"Who cares?" Dean replies coolly. He looks calm and alert, standing in our makeshift base that's actually an empty sheep pen on the east side of the island.

I hate the look of smug satisfaction on his face. It torments me almost more than the presence of Anna herself.

Anna is leaning up against the fence, arms crossed over her chest, face somber and unsmiling. We made eye contact briefly as our team assembled, but it's been several weeks since we've had an actual conversation with each other, and it's clear to me that she's dating Dean, even if they aren't doing anything as obvious as holding hands at the moment.

I know there's no way Dean could sit here so cheerfully, listening to me lay out the plan, if he didn't feel like the captainship barely mattered anymore, that he already has something better.

I look at Anna, wondering if she's missing me the way I'm missing her. Or if she only feels pity for me, because she can tell that I'm hurting.

Not having Anna as my best friend anymore is like having empty sockets where my teeth used to be or a stump instead of a hand. A hundred times a day, I think of something funny to tell her or a question I want to ask her. And then I remember that we're barely on speaking terms.

For the first time in my life, I can't eat. My shorts feel looser than normal around my hips, and it pisses me off to see Dean looking healthier, his hair sleek, his skin as clear as Anna's. I hate that they look good next to each other, that he matches Anna better than I do, both blond and fair. I feel like he's sucking the life out of me. As I get weaker, he gets stronger. Anna was my life force, and he stole her from me.

We're all dressed in our gym attire—gray pullovers as well as shorts, since it's windy and sunless. The seabirds make harsh cawing sounds as they're buffeted side to side while trying to take off from the rocky cliffs.

I have the seventy freshmen spread out around me, like a general marshaling his troops. I know I have to speak confidently and clearly. It's my first time leading them. Everything hinges on my ability to convince them to follow me without question and without hesitation.

Obviously, I can't expect that from Dean. The most I can hope is that he'll refrain from outright sabotage.

In that case, I guess I should be grateful that he has Anna to distract him. He doesn't seem to give a shit that Bram is in a foul mood. He doesn't seem concerned about anything.

I, on the other hand, have the weight of the world on my shoulders.

We each have a white tail tucked in the waistband of our shorts. Like flag football, anyone from the opposing team can steal your tail. Then you go directly to jail. You can break your teammates out of jail, but you risk losing more men to do it. At the same time, we have to protect our own flag while attempting to steal the flags from the other teams.

Our flag is attached at the top of a ten-foot pole. We can move the flag but not conceal it entirely. It has to stay on the pole.

"We should take the flag to the farthest corner of our territory so they have to advance across the most ground to attack us," Jules Turgenev says in an imperious way.

The other freshmen Heirs aren't taking too kindly to me being in charge. Jules is in my same dorm, and we haven't had any conflict up to this point. He mostly keeps to the other Frenchies, be it his roommate Emile or the Paris Bratva. But like most of the Heirs, he's fit, good-looking, haughty, and used to telling people what to do.

"No." I try to sound calm but authoritative. "We're taking it up on the hill. It'll be visible, but no one will be able to sneak up on us."

Jules exchanges a dubious look with Hedeon Gray. I ignore them both. I'm in charge. As long as my orders make sense, nobody will challenge me directly.

Quickly, before anybody else can pipe up with their strategy, I divide the freshmen into groups. We need jailers, guards to keep the flag safe, and attack squads to go after other flags.

I'm torn because I know how fucking fast Dean is, but I'm not sure if I can trust him to go after a flag. It might be safest to appoint him jailer where the worst damage he can do will be to let his prisoners go too easy, which I think his pride will prevent.

In the end, my need to win overrides my caution. I task Dean, Bram, Valon Hoxha, and three more of their crew with capturing the sophomore flag.

Gritting my teeth, I assign Anna to their team as well. The last thing I want to do is push Anna into Dean's arms, but I know how badly he wants to impress her. He won't fuck up if she's watching.

My other dilemma is whether to focus on attacking one particular team or try to steal multiple flags at once.

We know the territories of the other teams but not precisely where they'll be keeping their flags. The juniors are north, closest to the school, in a rocky area full of boulders, crevices, and scrubby olive trees. The sophomores are west of us in the vineyards. And the seniors have the most defensible area of all: the river bottom.

I decide to send out a second unit against the juniors but to leave the seniors alone, at least at the beginning. Maybe it's cowardly, but something tells me that stealing Pippa Portnoy's flag isn't going to be easy.

Professor Howell is running the challenge. He starts us off by sounding a klaxon that you can hear clear across the island. It blares out, probably startling every last sheep and goat for miles around.

My first two attack teams sprint off north and west in the direction of the junior and sophomore teams. Dean stays put, watching me out of the corner of his eye.

I'm reserving Dean's team. I haven't told the first two teams, but they're the pawns, so to speak. I don't want to risk my fastest runners first, so I sent out the B-teams, knowing they might be caught. Meanwhile, I set up my defensive players in a perimeter with several perched up in hidden vantage points so they can call out warnings to the players below.

So begins a six-hour sweaty, bloody battle that drags on and on. The territory we have to cover is huge, and it soon becomes clear that this is a battle of endurance and attrition as much as of bold attacks.

Twice our attack squads are captured, once by Kasper Markaj, who put the majority of his players on defense and who is resolutely hunting down the opposing players and locking them up in his near-impregnable jail, and once by Pippa Portnoy, whose senior players seemed to melt out of the shadows and creep up out of the field grass with supernatural speed.

I soon realize how much more experienced the upperclassmen really are. We almost lose our flag in the first twenty minutes when Calvin Caccia's junior team launches a blitzkrieg up our hill. If I hadn't personally snatched six or seven tails off his attackers, splitting his group in half, we wouldn't have been able to hold them off.

I have to be in a hundred places at once, sweat running down my face and stinging my eyes as I try to coordinate a dozen different groups, shifting and moving them like pieces on a chessboard, altering my strategy with each new wave of attacks from our enemies.

And all the time, I can't stop watching Anna. She's following my instructions perfectly, but I can't help feeling that we aren't working together like we used to. She isn't fighting me, but she isn't giving me advice either—she's just obeying. There's nothing satisfying in that. It feels hollow.

I think she could help me more if she wanted to.

At least she's accomplishing her purpose in spurring Dean to his best efforts. He comes back twice from Markaj's territory, filthy and drenched in sweat, his team decimated to him and Valon alone. The third time, he recovered Anna and the rest of his men, having successfully broken them out of jail. I wish he'd have brought the flag back instead, but it's better than nothing.

I hear Professor Howell's klaxon sound again, and a puff of silver smoke goes up in the sky from the direction of the seniors' territory. That means they captured the sophomore's flag. Kasper Markaj's team is out of the competition.

I'm glad it's not us, but I feel bad for him all the same. He's a decent dude, and quite honestly, I'd rather face off against him in the subsequent challenges instead of the more aggressive Calvin Caccia or the more devious Pippa Portnoy.

A skinny spy called Casey Pope groans from inside our jail. "What?" he cries. "First out? No fucking way. Not possible."

"Unless I'm colorblind, that's definitely our shade of gray." Ozzy laughs. He's sitting in jail right next to Casey, but he doesn't seem too upset about it. I got the impression that he and Miles were giving the game about the same level of seriousness they would apply to a rousing round of Monopoly.

Hedeon Gray, by contrast, is treating it like the Battle of Stalingrad. He's shaping up to be an excellent second-in-command, having shaken off the disappointment of not being captain himself.

"I don't care if you're tired!" he bellows at a couple of freshman Accountants. "Get the fuck back out there and guard that flag!"

It's good to have him supervising the defense, because as the game is wearing on, the juniors are getting increasingly nasty in their attacks. There's no need for violence—all you've got to do is snag someone's tail and they're off to jail. But the juniors are deliberately hitting us with tackles and elbows to the face in an attempt to intimidate and demoralize.

Hedeon and his brother Silas, without actually speaking to each other, are ramping up our defenses in response. Hedeon's organizing groups of freshmen to hide and attack from the side as the juniors rush our flag, and Silas jumps into an all-out brawl with two of the most violent juniors.

I've got to keep an eye on Silas because he's brutal, without thought or strategy. He bowled over one of our own teammates while attacking one of Pippa's seniors, spraining the kid's ankle so bad that he had to hobble off to the infirmary.

His face is expressionless as he watches our injured player depart the field.

Hedeon locks eyes with me and gives one slow shake of his head before returning to the task at hand.

I sent Ares out with my best attack squad to steal the flag from the sophomores, but now that I've seen the silver smoke, I know that won't do any good—their flag has already been captured. Hopefully Ares saw it as well, and he's turned his efforts to some other purpose.

If the sophomores are out, technically we've already secured our position in the next round. We're just battling for bragging rights. But there's also the little matter of my bet with Calvin Caccia. I don't fancy coming down to breakfast naked tomorrow.

I've got to get that fucking flag—either the juniors' or the seniors'.

"You got this covered?" I say to Hedeon.

"Yeah." He nods. "Nobody's laying a hand on our flag."

I look around at my remaining freshmen. My army is getting thin. Too many have been captured, and we haven't managed to break them out again.

My options are limited. I consider Matteo Ragusa, then discard that idea—he's clumsy as fuck and more likely to trip me than help me. Then I see Jules Turgenev, bleeding heavily from the nose thanks to one of Calvin's goons.

"Jules," I shout. "You're with me."

Jules falls into place next to me, running easily over the uneven ground. He's filthy with dirt and blood, but that hasn't wiped the haughty expression off his face, like he's a prince forced to consort with commoners.

"Where are we going?" he demands.

I hesitate.

The juniors are the obvious target. I know exactly where their flag is located—on top of a rocky outcropping, as far back in their territory as possible.

By contrast, Pippa has been moving her flag around continuously. She never keeps it in the same spot for more than ten or twenty minutes, which means it isn't always fully protected, but it's difficult to plan an attack ahead of time without knowing where it will be.

The juniors' flag is heavily protected. I only have Jules with me. We're unlikely to make it through alone. Plus, Ares probably switched his strategy to attack the juniors once he saw that the sophomores weren't an option anymore.

"We're going to the river bottom," I tell Jules.

He raises an eyebrow but doesn't say anything.

The seniors got the best territory—the area surrounding the one and only river on the island, which cuts through one of the most heavily forested areas. It suits Pippa's strategy of stealth and mobility.

"How do you expect to find the flag?" Jules asks me.

"By getting a better vantage point." I nod toward a wind-blasted pine.

Reluctantly, Jules follows after me as I hoist myself up into the tree. We climb higher and higher, the trunk swaying alarmingly under our combined weight. Once we're as far up as we can go without risking the increasingly thin branches breaking away beneath us, I wedge myself against the trunk and peer around, looking for signs of movement.

Jules seats himself likewise, shaking his shaggy blond hair out of his face and pulling a pack of cigarettes from his pocket.

"At least there's time for a smoke." He extracts one long cigarette from the pack and holds it to his lips in the European way, pinched between thumb and forefinger.

I pluck it out of his hand before he can light it.

"Someone will see the smoke."

Irritated, Jules flicks his Zippo closed.

That gives me an idea. I doubt Jules is the only student who smokes. It's been six hours. As scared as they must be of Pippa, I bet her soldiers are getting pretty bored of hiding with that flag.

Instead of scanning for a scrap of black fabric, I start looking for a faint gray haze down among the trees. And then I spot it, half a mile to the west of us.

"There they are," I breathe.

Jules peers in the direction of my pointing finger.

"There's six of them," he says. "And only two of us."

I grin. "But we have the element of surprise."

Quickly and quietly, Jules and I descend from our position. We creep up on the seniors, two of whom are sharing a quick cigarette while a third checks his watch.

"We've got to move again in four minutes," he warns them.

Barely whispering, I say to Jules, "Attack from behind. Grab as many tails as you can as fast as you can."

He nods. Jules is quick. That's why I brought him.

He circles around to get behind the seniors. Then he bursts out from cover, snatching off two tails before the seniors can even turn around. The senior with the watch tries to grab him, but Jules slips his grasp.

That's my moment, the second of distraction before they realize that Jules can't possibly have come alone. Already two of the seniors are catching on, about to turn and look for the rest of the attackers. Before they can do it, I'm already running full tilt toward them.

The senior with the watch dives for Jules, just missing him and falling on his hands and knees. I plant my foot in the middle of his back, launching myself off him like a step stool so I can leap up and rip their flag off the pole midair.

I'm sprinting before I even hit the ground, running away as fast as I can without looking back to see what happened to Jules. He'll understand—the flag is the goal, no matter the casualties.

The seniors are chasing after me, howling with rage. I've got long legs and a clear shot ahead. That's the weakness of Pippa's strategy—her defenders are out in the middle of nowhere, and now they're all behind me.

It's almost three miles back to my own base. I run the entire way, leaving no chance for recapture.

Jules never rejoins me. I hope the seniors didn't rough him up too bad out of anger.

As I near our home base, I see a horrible sight: no white flag on top of our pole.

Hedeon is pacing around at the base of our empty pole, unsure whether to pursue the flag or wait for me to return. His face switches from guilt to disbelief as he sees me running up with the black flag in hand.

"Run!" he bellows. "Fucking run!"

He doesn't have to tell me twice. Even though I've got a killer stitch in my side and sweat streaming down my face, I double my speed, trying to get the flag back to base so I can set off our black smoke bomb.

Too late…

With a boom, the juniors detonate their white smoke. They stole our flag and beat me back to base with less than thirty seconds to spare.

I have to drop the black flag where I stand, grimacing in disgust. One of Pippa's soldiers comes to retrieve it, and twenty minutes later, I see a puff of green smoke from the river bottom. They got the juniors' flag too.

Ares comes jogging back shortly after, a nasty gash on his cheek and his hands empty. Dean and Anna are close behind him.

"Liam Murphy stole the flag ten seconds before we got there," Ares says furiously. "We were so fucking close."

Dean stuffs his hands in his pockets, an inscrutable expression on his face. I can't tell if he's irritated that Pippa's attack dog beat them out or if he might possibly be trying to hold back a smile.

CHAPTER 17
DEAN

Anna is proving hard to crack.

After my early success in throwing a roofie grenade between Leo and Anna, blasting their friendship apart, then capitalizing on Anna's moment of weakness to kiss her, I thought it would be cake. But her attachment to Leo is more deeply rooted than I realized.

She tries to hide how much she's hurting, but it's obvious. It drives me insane how she still looks for him in every room, how her head lifts every time he speaks.

I need to seal the deal with our date.

I'll go all out. Orchestrate a fucking symphony of romance.

It won't take long for Leo to realize what a fool he's been to let her go. I have to act fast, before he worms his way back into her good graces.

I spend a week planning it. I study everything I can about Anna, quizzing her roommate and her classmates, racking my brain for every last bit of information she's ever let slip, trying to figure out what would be the perfect date.

Her roommate, Chay, isn't helpful. She already doesn't like me, so she flatly refuses to talk about Anna behind her back. Our classmates are even more useless. They don't know Anna any better than I do.

The only people at Kingmakers who could have given me tips

are Leo Gallo, who'd rather cut my throat than help me, or maybe Miles Griffin, whose cousins are the only thing he won't sell for cold hard cash.

In the end, I do something kind of fucked up.

I break into her room again and read all her letters from her sister.

I skip combat class to do it, knowing that Anna will be occupied. I sneak into her room and read all fourteen letters, one for each week we've been at school.

The letters are a treasure trove of information. I only wish I could see the ones Anna wrote back.

She told me that she's closer to her little sister than to almost anyone and that her sister likes to write. That much is obvious from the letters—they're half essay, half diary, long and full of ruminations, descriptions, and reminiscences.

The latter is the most useful part—Cara recalling shared experiences with Anna that I can use to my advantage.

I devour the letters. It's like watching scenes from Anna's childhood through her sister's eyes.

> *Do you remember when we floated through those caves in Belize? I was claustrophobic and it scared me, floating on the water in the dark. You told me to close my eyes. You said I'd see better that way, using my ears instead. You said we were in the heart of the earth and there was no safer place to be...*
>
> *I'm scared of everything, and you never seem afraid of anything. Heights, dogs, cemeteries, blood...*
>
> *Watching you be brave makes me feel more brave.*
>
> *I miss you. Mama and Papa miss you. Even Whelan, though he wouldn't admit it.*
>
> *Did I tell you he's been sneaking into your room just to sit in there? Not even to fuck up your stuff.*

I guess he does have a heart after all under all that demon-energy.

Don't worry. He hasn't been touching your birds. I've been taking care of them, and I don't let him in the aviary.

Too bad Mama's allergic so we could never have a dog or cat. I'll get a puppy someday. I'll bet you'd rather have a cat. Haha no that's too tame—maybe a snow leopard.

I think Papa had trouble at work this week. He was out all night on Thursday and Friday. Mama waited up for him, and you know she only does that when there's a problem.

How are your classes? Are you still learning to scuba dive?

Two hours go by in the blink of an eye. I totally lose track of time, only realizing when I hear girls' voices right outside the door.

I freeze, knowing I'm completely and totally fucked.

Thank god it's only the Galician Heir talking to Pippa Portnoy. I wait until they pass the door, then hurry out before Anna comes back for real.

It's addictive, learning things about Anna that she had never told me. Things that might take months or years for her to say.

I use the information to plan our date. It can't be anything as prosaic as a walk around the island or going to the café in the village.

I have to impress her. I have to make her feel something—something that will cut through the morass of her attachment to Leo Gallo.

I wait for her outside her dorm. She comes down a few minutes late, looking hesitant, like she considered not coming down at all. I can tell she took care getting ready, though, and that's all the encouragement I need.

I no longer dislike Anna's odd way of dressing. Instead, it's having a Pavlovian effect on me. The moment I see her torn tights or her thick black eyeliner, my cock stiffens and my heart races. I want to tear those tights right off her. I want to see her makeup run down her face with those full, pouting lips wrapped around my cock.

But not yet…

I have to be patient.

I take her off campus, because I know she'll never be comfortable inside the walls of Kingmakers where Leo might see us together.

"Where are we going?" Anna asks me.

"You'll see."

We head down the winding main road of the island that leads from the school down to the harbor. I walk slowly, wanting to have plenty of time to loosen Anna up with conversation about her favorite books. I already know from one of her sister's letters that Anna loves Jane Austen novels, and I read one on purpose earlier in the week, sitting in one of the overstuffed armchairs in the library.

I mention it casually and watch Anna's face light up as she says, "I love *Persuasion*! Everybody thinks *Pride and Prejudice* is her best one, but *Persuasion* has such a beautiful arc from melancholy to happy."

I don't see it as deceiving her. I see it as evidence of what I'll do to make her happy. What I'll do to give her the conversation she deserves—centered around her likes and interests instead of around whatever bullshit Leo Gallo would have talked to her about. He wouldn't have read a book just to discuss it with her. He wouldn't have spent all week planning a date.

When we get to the sheep farm, I take Anna right into the little stable I staked out earlier in the week.

"What are we—" she asks again. Then she breaks off, seeing what I brought her to see.

Three little lambs curled in a pile, two white and one black.

Their mother stands nearby, looking exhausted.

"What are they doing here?" Anna asks in amazement.

"Sometimes they come early in the winter," I say. "This ewe had three, so the farmer's been bottle-feeding them. He said we could help if we wanted."

Actually, I bribed him with a substantial wad of cash so I could bring Anna here on this little excursion. I figured from her sister's letter that she must love animals.

Sure enough, she gladly takes the bottle of warm milk I fetch from the farmhouse and kneels down in the straw so she can give it to the greedy lambs. The ewe doesn't care—she seems relieved that we're here to share the workload.

The lambs are only three days old. Their knees are still knobby and uncertain, their coats puffy and clean. They tumble over each other, fighting for the bottle. Anna laughs with delight, pulling them onto her lap and feeding them in turn.

The little black lamb nibbles at her fingers, and one of the white lambs tries to sample her hair. Anna presses her nose between their ears and inhales the clean scent of their wool.

I don't give a fuck about the lambs. I'm watching Anna—watching her face soften, her lips part, her defenses drop.

At Kingmakers, she's always so intent on showing that she's tough and emotionless. Here, just a couple of miles away, just us and the animals with no one else to see, I catch a glimpse of the real Anna. The same one I saw the night of the party. The one with a vulnerable heart.

"Do you want to feed them?" Anna asks, looking up at me.

"Sure," I say, just for an excuse to sit down beside her in the hay.

I grab one of the white lambs and stuff the bottle in its mouth. It snuggles up against me, its rapid little heart beating against my hand. I'm surprised how soft its wool feels and how comforting its warmth and weight seems, despite its tiny size.

"I'm not a vegetarian," Anna says. "But I could never stand to eat lamb. They should have some time to live, even if they're slaughtered in the end."

"I think they just use these sheep for wool."

"Have you ever seen pictures of that sheep that ran away and hid in a cave for six years?" Anna laughs. "When they finally caught him, his coat had grown so big that they shaved sixty pounds of wool off him."

"Sixty pounds?" I wrinkle my nose in disbelief.

"Yeah! He became a celebrity in New Zealand."

"You're making this up."

"No, I'm not! He was on TV. They wrote children's books about him. He visited the prime minister."

I want to kiss her again right there, with her defenses low and her oxytocin high from contact with the lambs.

But I wait. Patiently and strategically.

We walk down to the beach next. Not Moon Beach, because I don't want her thinking about Leo when I need all her attention focused on me.

Instead, I take her down to the east side of the island where the waves have hollowed out caverns in the limestone. We walk through the caves, stalactites hanging down like pale stone icicles and seawater seeping into pale green pools in the rock.

I brought a backpack full of food stolen from the kitchen: oranges, bread, cheese, and two bottles of the local beer. I knock the caps off the beer, handing one to Anna.

She takes it from me. I peel an orange and hand that to her as well.

"Dean," she says, and I know immediately from the tone of her voice that she's going to say something about Leo. "This has been really nice, but I—"

I interrupt her. "I know you like spending time with me."

"I do," she admits.

"And I know you have feelings for Leo."

She doesn't reply to that but sits quietly in the dim green light of the cave that makes her eyes look blue-green too, like arctic seawater.

"He had his whole life to love you, Anna," I say fiercely. "He never did anything about it. I wanted you the moment I laid eyes on you."

Anna is silent, biting the corner of her lip. She holds the peeled orange in her hand, untouched.

"I can't stop how I feel about him," she says quietly. "I've tried."

"I'm not trying to stop you."

That's a lie. I plan to slice through every tie that binds her and Leo together, one by one. But I have time to do it. For now, all I need is for Anna to let me in, just a little.

"All I want is a chance. To see if you could maybe feel something for me too."

She presses her lips together, and I think she might be about to shake her head, so I grab her by the hand and pull her up from where she's sitting on the soft, chalky limestone.

"Here," I say. "Come look at this."

I pull her deeper into the cavern, to the place where the seawater pours in from the ocean as the tide comes in. It's dark here, almost fully dark. Unconsciously, Anna's fingers interlock with mine.

"What are you showing me?"

"Just wait."

The water pours in with each set of waves, cold and dark.

And then, as the incoming waves churn against one another in the dark recesses of the cavern, the pools begin to glow. The light is faint at first, just threads of turquoise in the black water. Then the color spreads, until the entire pool is illuminated with vibrant, shifting, moving light, organic and surreal. The light reflects off the cavern walls and glimmers on Anna's smooth skin.

She stares at me wide-eyed. "What is that?"

"Dinoflagellates. They're bioluminescent."

It's like a million tiny fireflies underwater. Each fresh wave from the ocean increases their supply and their agitation. Soon the whole cavern is glowing, and Anna's mouth is open in awe.

That's when I kiss her again. Her lips are already parted, and I slip my tongue into her mouth, tasting the warm remnants of the beer and the sweetness of Anna herself.

I pull her hard against me. I was trying to restrain myself, but it's impossible when the taste of her makes me starve for more, and the feel of her lean, tight body against mine makes me want to rip every scrap of clothing off her so I can see that naked flesh I've been obsessing over since the very first day of school.

My hand cradles the side of her throat. I let my fingers slide down to her collarbone and then the top of her breast. I dip my fingers under the tight material of her top, down the warm swell of her breast, my ring finger just grazing her stiff nipple before Anna puts her own hand over mine to stop me.

"Wait," she says.

I stay still, though I don't want to. I still have one hand gripping her hip and the other resting on that perfect breast. I want to pull her back into me, yank her top down entirely, and take that hard nipple in my mouth.

"I'm not…very experienced," Anna stammers. "You'll have to go slow."

It's in that moment that I realize that Anna is a virgin. Never in my wildest dreams had I thought a girl that gorgeous could come to college still a virgin. Bare minimum, I'd assumed that she and Leo must have fooled around at some point in their past. I can't imagine how he had that cherry in the palm of his hand without popping it.

If I thought I was infatuated with Anna before, it's nothing compared to the obsession that seizes me now.

I silently swear that I'll take Anna's virginity or die trying. I'll be her first lover. And that's what will bind her to me, no matter what Leo tries to do after.

I literally salivate at the thought. I have to swallow hard before I can reply, "That's alright. I understand."

If Anna says I have to "go slow," that means she's going to let me try. She's going to keep seeing me. Which means I have to be careful not to fuck it up, not to scare her off. Even if it seems impossible. Even if it's torture trying to keep my hands off her.

So that's what I do. I kiss her again, slowly and gently. And then I take her back up to Kingmakers, back to her dorm. I don't try to push it any further, so she'll believe I'm respectful. So she'll come out with me again.

And all the while, I'm plotting how I'll be the first person on this planet to fuck Anna Wilk, so I'll have that piece of her always. So she'll belong to me.

In the weeks that follow, I pursue Anna relentlessly. I take every possible opportunity to keep her away from Leo, inviting her to sit with me in our shared classes and during meals, constantly trying to tie up her time with dates and activities that don't involve him.

The first challenge of the Quartum Bellum is the best part of all, because Leo himself is forced to pair Anna and me together so I'll have a babysitter. Granted, it does prevent me from sabotaging, but it also gives me plenty of opportunities to remind Anna what a great team we make together and to dramatically rescue her from jail.

I'm irritated when Kasper Markaj gets himself kicked out of the competition so easily, but at least the freshmen place last of the three winning teams. Best of all, Leo loses his stupid bet with Calvin Caccia.

He has to come down to breakfast the next morning stark naked.

I expect him to back out of the bet or at bare minimum to slink through the dining hall with an appropriate level of embarrassment.

Everyone in school has heard about the terms of the bet, and every single seat is packed with students waiting to laugh and jeer at the sight of the cocky freshman literally stripped bare.

Instead, Leo strolls into the dining hall at the stroke of eight, naked as the day he was born. He's grinning and waving at his friends, freshly showered and wearing only a pair of flip-flops.

He takes his time selecting his bacon and eggs from the chafing dishes, then chooses a seat right in the middle of the hall, attacking his breakfast with apparent enjoyment.

While some of the juniors and seniors continue shouting and jeering at him, it's impossible to come up with much in the way of insults when Leo is such an undeniable physical specimen.

I fucking hate his guts, and even I have to admit that his height, his tan, and his physique leave little to scoff at. In fact, I think it's making him more popular than ever, especially when the girls get a good look at the package swinging between his legs.

Gemma Rossi leans forward in her seat, openly staring at his cock, practically salivating—something that doesn't go unnoticed by Anna.

I expected to enjoy Leo's humiliation, and instead I'm seething with irritation long before he even sits down.

It doesn't help that I can see Anna's eyes irresistibly drawn toward Leo again and again while she tries to ignore him, eating her breakfast next to Chay.

Before Leo even finishes his food, the jeers turn into a chant, led by the freshmen and a substantial number of sophomores who don't seem to give a fuck that they lost their place in the competition.

"Leo! Leo! Leo! Leo!"

Their voices echo around the dining hall and the plates rattle as they pound the tables with their fists.

I'm gripping my fork so hard that I've almost bent it in half.

How in the *fuck* does everything Leo touches turn from shit into gold?

"Leo! Leo! Leo!"

He stands up from his seat, giving the crowd a little salute. Then he sinks into a deep bow with his naked ass pointed in the direction of Calvin Caccia's table. The dining hall erupts in howls of laughter, while Calvin's face turns an ugly shade of puce.

I shove my plate away from me, furious and disgusted.

I can't help looking over at Anna again. She's watching Leo, the tiniest hint of a smile tugging up the corner of her mouth.

Somehow, I'm burning with envy. Leo is naked, disgraced, and publicly shamed. And I'm sitting here jealous of him yet again.

CHAPTER 18
ANNA

Christmas at Kingmakers is depressing. We aren't allowed to go home to see our families. We can't send them gifts either, though they're permitted to send one package to us.

I receive mine the week before the holidays. It contains four new novels that I'm sure my mother picked out because they're all beautiful hardcovers with gold leaf and illustrations.

My father sent me a new charm for the bracelet he gave me six years ago. It's a tiny golden compass that actually opens and shuts on its minuscule hinge. I wonder if it's meant to symbolize me finding my way home again eventually or if it's supposed to point me in the direction I should go next.

Cara sent me a packet of pretty stationery so I can keep writing to her, and Whelan drew me a picture of him riding on the back of a dragon, gleefully torching a village below. I hang it up over my bed.

Classes go on as usual, but in an effort to make the holiday festive, the teachers are throwing a party on Christmas Eve—the first *official* party of the school year.

We're supposed to dress up. I tell Dean that I don't want to go together, not as a couple, but I do agree to dance with him.

Zoe Romero promises to attend with us as well. She doesn't come to the off-the-books student parties for fear that someone will rat her out to her heavy-handed parents.

Zoe is the third freshman Heir in our dorm. I've been spending more time with her since Leo and I haven't been on the best terms.

Zoe, Chay, and I have formed an unlikely trio. Chay didn't like Zoe at first because she thought she was too serious and stuck-up, and Zoe I'm sure was annoyed by the constant parade of friends Chay invites to come hang out in the common room right outside Zoe's door.

Zoe spends most of her time studying because her parents are strict and demanding, expecting a constant accounting of her grades and requesting that her cousins at the school keep a close eye on her in case she dares to transgress the bounds of the restrictive marriage pact they signed when Zoe was only twelve years old.

Zoe is engaged to one of the sophomore, a German Heir named Rocco Prince. Chay already knew him because they attended boarding school together. That's how she and Zoe finally bonded—over their mutual hatred of Rocco.

"He cut off a little kid's ear in the village outside our school for no fucking reason at all," Chay says. "Even the teachers were scared of him."

"I loathe him," Zoe says quietly.

Her family didn't want her to attend Kingmakers at all. They only agreed to it because Zoe said she wouldn't go through with the marriage otherwise. The wedding date is already set for a week after graduation.

Chay and I learn all this when Miles gives me a bottle of Ballantine's smuggled in from the mainland, and I invite Zoe to drink it with us. She's safe taking a drink in our room where no one can see her, and she obviously needs it—she's been looking pale and somber all week.

"Is Rocco ever halfway decent?" I ask Zoe.

"Never," Zoe says with a shudder. "He's too smart to do anything out in the open—at least anything that our families would view as crossing the line. But the things I've heard...the rumors... He makes me sick. He's been staring at me like he wants to peel my skin off since I was a little girl. And he has no sense of humor whatsoever. I've never heard him laugh."

Since Zoe is one of the most serious people I've ever met, I can hardly picture someone even more humorless.

"Why are you going through with it, then?" Chay asks. "You're the Heir, aren't you? You've got other options."

Zoe says, "My father would kill me if I didn't. He already hates me for being born a girl. Every time he sets some impossible standard for me, I meet it thinking I'll win him over eventually. He only despises me more. Well, he finally thought of a way to make me what he wants—powerless and miserable."

I ask, "What if you ran away?"

It's not a brilliant plan, just the first that occurs to my tipsy brain. It's hard to hide in the underworld. Mafia families are much too practiced in tracking down traitors, thieves, and witnesses.

Zoe shakes her head for a different reason. "I have a sister. Catalina is only a year younger than me. Even if I could do it, my parents might scratch my name off the marriage contract and write hers instead. I'd only be dropping my burden onto her shoulders."

She's quite drunk by this point, though you wouldn't guess it. She's still sitting upright in her chair, her voice measured and clipped, with no hint of slurring. I only know she must be intoxicated because I watched her down ten shots with my own eyes. That and the fact that I'm learning more about Zoe in one hour than I've discovered all semester.

"That's crazy!" Chay cries. She's much more obviously drunk, her cheeks flushed and a button torn off the front of her school blouse from when she gestured a little too wildly telling us a story about her very first motorcycle. "What are you gonna do? You can't just marry this guy and be fucking miserable."

"I don't know," Zoe says quietly. "Maybe I'll turn into a bird and fly away."

A tear slips down her cheek, unnoticed by Zoe as she looks out the window to the stormy sea beyond. Maybe she's picturing soaring away across the water. Or maybe she's imagining leaping from those cliffs, whether she can fly or not.

I put my hand over hers, unable to think of anything useful to say.

The next morning, we all wake up with raging headaches after falling asleep in highly uncomfortable positions. I slept in the middle of the floor with a shoe for a pillow.

I think Zoe hopes we were drunk enough to forget what she said.

But I watch how she cringes every time Rocco corners her in the hallways, leaning close to whisper god knows what in her ear.

I see how she stands still as stone while he trails his finger down her cheek, seeming to enjoy his fiancée's obvious distaste for him.

Soon, I begin to despise Rocco just as much as Zoe and Shay.

The night of the Christmas dance, Chay, Zoe, and I all get dressed together in Chay's and my shared room.

Our dorm is the smallest but arguably the prettiest on campus. It used to be the solar, which was the private quarters of the lord and his family. For that reason, Chay's and my room is much larger than normal, with an actual working fireplace and a large picture window that looks out over the cliffs.

Pippa Portnoy's room probably belonged to the lord himself—it's the largest and grandest of all, though I prefer ours since she only faces the armory. Pippa doesn't share with anyone, having successfully bullied the other female Heir in her year into taking a far inferior room. Claire Turgenev and Neve Markov, the sophomore Heirs, room together on the next floor down.

Our room is looking a lot more homey than when we first

arrived. Chay and I have hung up dozens of our sketches on the walls. Mine are mostly botanicals and landscapes—bits of the island I've seen while exploring. Chay's are almost all tattoo designs that she intends to put on herself, though I'm not quite sure where she's going to find the space.

Chay's mother sent her a hand-knitted blanket as her Christmas package, so her bed is covered in sea green and blue instead of the usual plain gray. Even my ballet shoes hanging by their ribbons from the armoire add a certain personal touch to the space.

Chay is rooting through her clothes, trying to decide what to wear.

She throws a dark ombré dress down on my bed.

"That would suit you."

I didn't think to bring any formal gowns in my suitcase, and I wouldn't have had room anyway. I like the one Chay is offering. It looks black up on the shoulders and bust, shading down to emerald by the hem.

"Will you do my makeup too?" I ask her.

"Of course!" She loves when Zoe and I consent to be her Barbie dolls.

Chay gives me a kind of glittery, smoky mermaid eye, and I wear my hair down, tied back at the temples with a black velvet ribbon.

She goes lighter on Zoe because she knows Zoe doesn't like wearing too much makeup. She doesn't need it anyway—her skin is clear and glowing, and her thick black lashes and brows look painted on in ink.

Chay is stunning in a flame-red dress with a dramatic slit up the side. She has on a pair of bracelets that looked like steel manacles and heels that could kill a man. She isn't dating that idiot Sam anymore, and it's clear she's on the hunt for a new paramour.

Zoe looks the loveliest of all in a stark navy dress that covers her from throat to wrist to ankle but can't conceal the stunning figure underneath. With her long, dark hair pinned up on her head like a crown, she looks like a queen. If she were allowed to dance with anyone she liked at the party, she'd have an endless supply of eager boys lining up.

The grand hall on the ground floor of the keep has been decorated for the party. Strings of golden lights run across the room, forming a kind of canopy overhead like a luminescent tent. A huge table along the wall groans with food, and champagne and wine are on offer, since apparently Kingmakers is honoring the European standards for drinking and not giving a damn that most of us are underage in American terms.

Bram intercepts us as soon as we walk through the door. He gives me a nod that is, for him, friendly. He's been much more polite since I started dating Dean, which I'm not sure is an improvement.

I have to admit, Bram looks almost handsome in his black tux, with his long hair combed back and his face properly shaved.

He wastes no time in spoiling the effect by slinging his arm over Chay's shoulder, leaning on her heavily and trying to peer down the front of her dress while he drawls, "Save your first dance for me, princess."

"You surprise me, Bram," Chay says cheerfully. "I've never seen a pig that could dance!"

Bram's burly arm tightens painfully around her shoulders, but Chay refuses to flinch. He pinches her chin in the claw of his hand and forces her to look up into his face until their noses are almost touching.

"That big mouth is going to get you into trouble someday," he snarls at her. "Unless you learn how to use it for its intended purpose."

"Are you talking about sucking cock?" Chay says calmly. "I'm sure you could give me some tips. Seeing as you've always got your mouth latched firmly around Dean's—"

Before she can finish that sentence and send Bram into a complete rage, Dean says, "Who's talking about me?"

He came up behind me, silently laying his palm on my lower back so a shiver runs down the length of my spine.

"Nobody," I say. "Bram was just leaving."

Bram turns his scowl on me but doesn't dare say anything with Dean standing right there. He lets go of Chay's face and stomps off, leaving a wake of fury behind him.

"What's his problem?" Dean says.

"Nursed too long or not long enough," Zoe says dryly.

Dean gives a little snort. "Is that what causes it?"

He's in an abnormally good mood, and he looks abnormally handsome too. He's wearing a white dinner jacket with a single pale purple bloom on the lapel. I wonder where he got it. Probably out of one of the castle greenhouses.

Seeing my eye land on the flower, he says, "Don't worry. I got you one too," and he tucks a matching bloom into the velvet band holding back my hair.

As he does so, I glance across the room and see Leo watching us.

If Dean looks better groomed and better rested than ever, Leo is the opposite. I've never seen him such a mess. He hasn't cut his hair in weeks, and the dark curls look wild. He likewise hasn't shaved or dressed properly for the dance. He's just wearing his normal school trousers and a button-up shirt, neither properly pressed.

But it's his face that haunts me. He's lost weight, enough that his cheeks look hollow and his whole frame is slightly diminished. Maybe it's just the slump in his shoulders. Leo had always been illuminated by a light so bright it could blind you. Now it's gone. He looks miserable, exhausted, and just…so fucking sad.

It's killing me seeing him like that.

It must be the stress of the Quartum Bellum. We made it through the first challenge, but only just barely. I know that won't be good enough for Leo. It's all or nothing for him. Win or kill yourself trying.

Leo and I have barely spoken since then. I know he hates that I'm dating Dean.

Maybe he misses me. I know I miss him—horribly and constantly.

But I don't kid myself that's the reason he looks so distraught. Dean was right about one thing: Leo had his whole life to make a move on me if that's what he wanted. He never did. And when I tried to make something happen, he took the first opportunity to blow it up in my face.

That's what I've decided since that night—whether Leo consciously meant to hurt me or not, he sabotaged any chance of us being together. He wasn't ready, or he didn't want it.

Either way, I'm not going to chase after him. I already opened myself up, made myself vulnerable, and look what it got me: the worst night of my life. I never want to feel pain like that again.

So I look at Leo from across the room, and I raise my hand in a silent wave. Letting him know that there are no hard feelings. That we can still be friends. But it's better to be friends from a distance for now. Until I can kill the part of me that still longs to run over there and feel his arms wrapped around me.

When I turn my head straight again, Dean is silently watching me. I know he saw me wave to Leo.

"Do you want to go over there?" Dean's face is stiff and pale, like it always is when Leo comes up between us.

"No." I shake my head.

Part of me desperately wants to go over to Leo, to try to heal this rift torn between us. To do whatever it takes to make things right so we can talk and laugh and be comfortable together like we used to.

The other part of me knows that's impossible.

Things could never go back to the way they were, so it's pointless to try.

This is the new reality. Leo over there. Me over here. The Grand Canyon between us.

I grab a glass of champagne off the closest table and gulp it down, trying to convince myself that I'm having fun. I agree to dance with Dean, and I let him waltz me around the floor, forcing myself not to look to see whether Leo is still watching.

Dean smells clean and fresh like always, and he moves with smooth confidence. His hand is strong on the small of my back.

I drink more champagne, then a glass of wine. Dean offers to get me a plate from the buffet, but I shake my head. My stomach is churning too much to eat.

Chay is dancing with Thomas York. He looks dumbfounded, like he can't believe his luck. She's danced with half the boys at the party and shows no signs of slowing down.

Zoe hasn't danced with anyone.

"I'll probably head back soon," she says, stifling a yawn behind her hand.

She stiffens as Rocco Prince approaches, his slicked-back hair giving his face a hollow, cadaverous look. His lips are liverish in the dim light.

Zoe stands up to meet him—not out of excitement, I don't think. More likely because she doesn't want to be in a vulnerable seated position.

"I didn't know you were coming," she says nervously.

"Didn't know or hoped I wasn't?" Rocco says in his low, soft voice. There's an uncomfortable hissing sound in the way he forms his *s*.

Zoe stays silent, too honest to lie.

"Come." Rocco takes Zoe's arm. It isn't a request. He steers her onto the dance floor, his hand tightly pinching her bicep. Then he forces her through the steps like he's a puppeteer and she's the marionette.

"He disgusts me," I say to Dean, watching them.

"You shouldn't say that so loud," Dean replies. "The Princes are powerful. It's a good match for her."

"You can practically see her skin crawling."

Dean shrugs. "Not every alliance is a love match."

I narrow my eyes at him, annoyed by his complacency. "Your mom was a nurse, not a mafiosa. Your dad married her because he loved her."

"That's right," Dean says coldly. "And look where that got them."

I take another glass of champagne and swallow it down.

As the night wears on, the music becomes less formal. The playlist shifts from classical to pop, and students crowd onto the makeshift dance floor as waltzing turns into grinding.

Even some of the professors are dancing. I see Professor Thorn looking much less buttoned-up than usual, dressed in a glittering black gown with her dark hair down from its tight bun. She's being spun around by Professor Howell—no mean feat considering she's a head taller than him.

Professor Bruce looks like he wants to dance, but Professor Graves is talking away in his ear, his face flushed from what must be his third or fourth glass of wine. I check the breast pocket of Graves's jacket and can't help giggling to myself when I see only a sad-looking Bic poking out.

Even Chancellor Luther Hugo makes a brief appearance, sitting down with the ghoulish Professor Penmark, who teaches Torture Techniques, drinking a single glass of port in the overstuffed chairs set in front of the roaring fire, before sweeping out of the room again as quickly as he came.

I rarely see the chancellor on campus. I don't even know if he stays at Kingmakers full-time. It's possible he avoids us students to maintain his aura of authority and danger. Or alternatively, he might simply be busy with administrative tasks.

The only staff member I don't see is Ms. Robin. That doesn't surprise me—she's painfully shy, and a party is the last place I'd expect her to be. She rarely even eats in the dining hall, though plenty of the other professors take their meals along with the students.

I wish she had come. Even though she's not actually a teacher, she's my favorite staff member. I bet she'd look pretty all dressed up.

The music switches to a remix of "Candy Shop," an old favorite that Miles, Leo, and I used to play.

Unable to help myself, I look for Leo again, thinking he won't miss a chance to dance.

Everyone in our family loves dancing. Miles is right in the thick of it, with a small halo of space around him because he's really fucking talented and plenty of people just want to watch him.

Leo isn't next to Miles, however. I spot him sitting at a side table, surrounded by Ares, Matteo, Hedeon, and a few other friends but not talking to any of them.

Trying to cheer myself up, I join Miles and start doing this silly routine we created when we were about ten years old. It's old-school hip-hop—a whole lot of bust downs and body rolls and figure-eight sways. Miles jumps right in on it, and for a second I'm happy again and almost laughing, because Miles is smooth as fuck, he's got swagger and style, and there's nobody more fun to dance with.

Ozzy is whooping and laughing, trying to copy us, and soon we have a dozen kids trying to learn the routine.

I'm getting pleasantly sweaty, finally feeling that sense of buoyancy again, like everything might work out someway or somehow.

I look up, thinking maybe Leo will join us. He knows the dance as well as I do. But he isn't sitting at the table anymore. I look around, trying to peer through the press of bodies. I can't see him anywhere. He's completely disappeared.

I'm disappointed and almost angry. I don't know why I'm angry. Maybe because that bubble of happiness popped as quickly as it came.

I stop dancing after that, but I don't stop drinking. I lose count of the flutes of champagne I down in a gulp. Dean practically has to carry me back to my dorm an hour later.

He pins me against my door, attacking me with his lips, thrusting his tongue in my mouth, biting and sucking on my neck.

My head is spinning, and I can barely stand up. I don't know why I feel so miserable and so confused. Nothing went wrong at the dance. It should have been a festive night.

I'm trying to tell Dean to stop, to let me go to bed. I drank too much, and I'm afraid I might throw up from the aggressive kissing.

Before I can get the words out, he shoves my legs apart with his thigh and shoves his hand up under my skirt. He pushes his fingers under the elastic of my underwear and starts rubbing my pussy.

I'm leaning hard on his shoulder, unable to hold myself up. If he wasn't pinning me to the wall with his weight, I'd fall over. I feel limp and out of control, unable to close my legs with his knee pressing my thigh against the wall and my arms trapped between us.

"Dean, don't—" I try to say, but he silences me with his mouth on mine. Meanwhile, his fingers are stroking up and down my pussy lips, his middle finger grazing over my clit with each pass.

His fingers are getting wetter and wetter, and I know he can feel that as easily as I can. With each stroke of his hand, my clit becomes more sensitive, and the warm throbbing spreads down my thighs and up into my belly.

Now his fingers are parting my pussy lips, and I know he's feeling for my entrance, wanting to slip his fingers all the way inside.

I try to turn my head to the side, but he keeps his lips locked on mine, his tongue shoved into my mouth so I can't speak.

He pushes one finger inside me, then two. Meanwhile, his thumb rubs back and forth across my clit, and my pussy clenches helplessly around his fingers.

I can feel his erection through his pants, grinding hard against my hip. I can feel his hunger too—his hot breath and his rabid desire for me. I'm aroused whether I want to be or not. It's an uneasy mixture of guilt, fear, and desire.

Dean releases my mouth at last and starts sucking hard on the side of my neck while he fingers me roughly.

I can't stop it. I can't hold back. I start to come around his fingers. As I shiver and clench, Dean whispers in my ear, "You're going to give me what I want, Anna. Sooner or later."

January arrives cold and gray. For the first time, I'm truly feeling how lonely and isolated Kingmakers is out in the middle of the ocean. The wind howls at night like it's trying to tear the castle right off the cliff, and the sea spray freezes into thick black ice along the balustrades.

Now we're all making use of the blazers and pullovers that came with our uniforms. The girls are complaining about their skirts, and it's become a trend to borrow an oversize sweater from the boy you like because their pullovers are thicker, and if the boy in question is big enough, the sweater will cover your hands and come almost down to your knees.

Dean freely offers his sweater to me, but I don't take it. I'm annoyed with him. He asked me to eat lunch with him, only to have Bram Van Der Berg and several others of their gang sit down all around us five minutes later.

I don't like Bram, and I don't particularly like how Dean behaves when Bram's around. It brings out the side of Dean that's callous and even a little cruel.

Bram apparently isn't enjoying his ham and peas. He's flicking the unwanted peas in the direction of Matteo Ragusa and Paulie White. Paulie is pretending not to notice the peas hitting his arm, but I can see his thin freckled cheeks turning pink.

I know Dean can see what's happening just as clearly as I can, but he's ignoring it entirely, talking to me about our Contracts and Negotiations class that morning. He doesn't give a fuck about Matteo, who's a known friend of Leo's, or Paulie, who's nerdy and awkward and only an Accountant from a minor Mafia family.

Bram launches his next pea particularly hard, hitting Paulie on the ear.

"Could you stop it?" I snap at Bram, interrupting Dean midsentence.

"Why should I?" Bram says lazily, setting another pea in his spoon and preparing to launch it over to the next table.

"Because you're acting like a fucking child."

"Control your girlfriend," Bram says to Dean.

Before Dean can say anything to either of us, I whip out my hand and overturn Bram's plate, sending the remains of his ham, gravy, and peas flopping directly onto his lap.

Bram leaps up from the table, the crotch of his trousers stained with grease and his fists balled at his sides.

Dean and I jump up too, Dean wedging himself in the middle, facing Bram and simultaneously pushing me back behind him.

"Don't even think about it," Dean says to Bram.

"She's making you soft," Bram hisses back. "Be careful, or you'll end up like your father."

Dean seizes Bram by the front of his shirt, and for a second I think they are going to start swinging at each other. But one of the Penose gives a soft whistle, jerking his head toward the doorway where several of the burly kitchen staff are standing watching. The dining hall is not a good place for a fight.

Reluctantly, Dean lets go of Bram. They're both breathing hard and glaring at each other. Bram steps back slowly, then nods to his Penose. They stride out of the dining hall, leaving only Dean's Bratva sitting at our table still.

Dean expects me to sit down again too, but I've lost my appetite.

"Where are you going?" he demands.

"To my next class."

He follows right after me and tries to take my arm in the hall. I pull it away from him.

"I don't need you to escort me."

"I'm just walking with you," Dean says, grabbing my arm harder and forcing me to stop. "What's your problem? I stood up for you with Bram."

"You didn't say anything about him being a fucking asshole to Matteo and Paulie, though."

"Why should I care what he does to them?" Dean scans my face with his purplish eyes, genuinely confused.

"Because he's a bully."

"So what? This isn't an ice cream social. It's Kingmakers. Bram's an Heir. They're nobodies."

"That doesn't mean he has to be a dick for no reason."

I try to keep walking, and again Dean stops me, backing me up against the wall. Now he's really starting to piss me off.

"You're an Heir too," Dean says, his eyes fixed on mine. "You're going to have to command men like Bram. You won't win their respect being sweet and sentimental."

"I'm not fucking *sweet*," I snarl at Dean. "And I don't need you to tell me how to be a leader. I'll control my Braterstwo because they *will* respect me. Because I'll have honor and discipline, and I'll demand the same from them. I'll cut a man's throat if I have to, but I won't torment him for fun."

With that, I push past him and stomp off to my next class.

I'm angry with Dean for being patronizing but also because I'm afraid that he might be right. My men will always be looking for signs of weakness in me. I'll have to be more ruthless than any of them to show that I'm strong, that I have what it takes to be a boss.

CHAPTER 19
LEO

THE WEEKS AFTER THE FIRST CHALLENGE ARE A STRANGE MIXTURE of accolades from my fellow freshmen and thinly veiled hostility from the upperclassmen.

Surprisingly, Kasper Markaj is the only person not holding a grudge. He came up to me right after the challenge and clapped me on the back, saying, "You did well. Your team trusts you."

I said, "It was bad luck that you were first out."

He shook his head, his broad, friendly face resigned. "There's no luck in competition. Only good and better strategies."

We only placed third in the challenge, but we managed to steal Pippa Portnoy's flag, an affront that didn't go unnoticed.

I often find her watching me now, sly and silent, her lips quirked up in a perpetual smirk. When she's not actually around, it's almost worse, like when you lose sight of the spider in your room. I'd rather have her in plain view where at least I can see what she's up to.

I'm drawing glares and mutters everywhere I go on campus, and a couple of not-so-joking threats.

Miles seems to find it all hilarious. He couldn't care less that his own sophomore team is out of the challenge.

"They don't know what a desperate little psycho you are," he tells me cheerfully. "They don't know you'd literally rather die than lose."

"Right," I say dully.

Winning has always been the most important thing in the world to me. When we arrived at Kingmakers, there was nothing I wanted more than to get the captainship and be the first freshman to ever win the Quartum Bellum.

But with each week that passes, I struggle to feel even basic enthusiasm about the next challenge.

My competitors don't share my ennui.

Calvin Caccia has gone from friendly rival to all-out enemy. He didn't appreciate my stunt in the dining hall, which fulfilled the terms of our bet but not quite the spirit.

For me, that was the last day I felt anything approaching happiness. The cheers and backslapping from my fellow freshmen gave me a burst of triumph. But it faded away almost immediately, and I sank back into the gloom that's been suffocating me for the last two months.

I feel dull and drained, and I'm finding it hard to care about what I'll be facing next.

"The first one was sort of a warm-up," Matteo says, "but they won't go so easy on us next time."

"You thought that was easy?" Ares cries. "We almost lost."

"Yeah, well, it's gonna get a lot worse," Matteo says darkly. "Last year in the second challenge, one of my brothers broke his leg so bad they almost had to amputate it."

"Why in the fuck are we even doing this?" Ares shakes his head in wonder.

"Why did we come to Kingmakers at all?" Matteo grins. "To live a life less ordinary."

"Ordinary life was nice," Ares says wistfully.

Since I've been in such a low mood myself, I'm becoming more cognizant of the fact that Ares isn't always as cheerful as I thought. What I'd first taken for a laid-back attitude, I'm now realizing might actually be a carefully cultivated sense of calm to conceal the more turbulent emotions underneath.

I thought that Ares disappears into our room or the library because he gets tired of the constant socialization required to live, eat, sleep, and study on campus. But now I think it might be something else. I think he might be depressed. When I come across him unexpectedly, when he doesn't know anyone is watching, he sometimes looks discouraged or even upset.

When I try to talk to him about it, he brushes me off, smiling and telling me I'm imagining things.

"I'm just tired," he says, pushing his hair back out of his eyes with a sweep of his hand. "It's all this homework. I never did that great in school. Probably never wrote so many words in my life as I did last semester."

I can tell that Ares isn't going to open up to me. He doesn't want to confide in me. And that makes me realize I'm not as good a friend to him as I thought.

Maybe I'm not that great a friend to anybody.

I was blazing through life with me at the center of my own universe and everybody else in orbit around me. I took for granted that they were all as happy and content as they seemed. I never bothered to look that deep below the surface.

I thought of myself as the star of the show, and honestly, Ares was a sidekick. I hadn't really considered him as a person with struggles as acute or complex as my own.

The same was true with Anna. I made assumptions about her feelings and her goals. I wasn't careful to find out what she really wanted. I took her for granted.

I don't think I can win her back, but at least I can treat Ares better. I try my best to help him with his schoolwork, introduce him to pretty girls, and ask him a hundred questions about his family and his home, hoping I can figure out what's bothering him.

It's probably too much, because after a week or two of this Ares says, "Do you need a kidney or something? You're being too nice, and it's freaking me out."

"No," I say, embarrassed. "Sorry. I'm just trying to…you know. Be a good friend."

Ares laughs softly, shaking his head at me. "You're the best friend I've got here."

"Yeah?" I smile. "Alright. I'll take it down a notch, then."

I try to buckle down and apply myself to my classwork instead. It's the only way not to constantly be staring at Anna, who likewise attends most of my classes, usually sitting only a few desks away from me.

Every time she speaks or laughs with any of her other friends—even her female friends like Chay and Zoe—I burn with envy. And when she talks to Dean, I want to set the whole school on fire.

Dean is some kind of dark doppelgänger who managed to switch places with me. Now I know exactly how he felt the first few months of school when it was Anna and me sitting together, Anna and me exchanging glances when the teacher said something amusing, Anna and me casually leaning against each other as we walked across the commons.

He took my place, and now he's basking in the light of the most beautiful girl in school and I'm the one locked outside, jealously looking in with my face pressed up against the glass.

On January 17, I call my parents like I do every weekend. My mother picks up the phone on the first ring, sounding uncharacteristically excited.

"Leo!" she says. "How are you?"

"Decent. You know…tired, but doing alright."

"We've got something to tell you," my dad says, his voice tight with anticipation.

"What is it?" My stomach clenches. I'm not really in the mood for a surprise at the moment.

"We're going to have a baby!" my mom says in a rush. "You're going to have a sibling!"

"I—how?" I stammer out.

My parents tried for years to have another kid. It never worked. My mom never even got pregnant, let alone carried a baby all the way through.

Now that she's forty-three, I thought they were long past trying.

"It happened in the usual way," my dad says and laughs.

I can tell he's over the moon, but it's my mom I'm listening to—her shaky breath, the way she's trying to hold back tears. She's wanted this so badly for so long.

And she deserves it. She was the best mother in the world to me. I don't have the heart to be anything but happy for them. Having recently tasted disappointment myself, I won't say anything to puncture their excitement.

"Congratulations, Mom. This is such good news."

"You're happy, Leo?" she asks me.

"Yes," I insist. "I can't wait to meet him."

That's not a hundred percent true. I've been an only child my whole life; the idea of a sibling at this late date is more bizarre than enticing. Also, having just been cut out of Anna's life and replaced with Dean, I can't say it's pleasant to picture my parents centering their whole lives around some bouncing new baby.

But it's not my choice. None of these things are my choice.

I'm trying not to be selfish and immature anymore.

I'm going to support my parents and see if I can be a better friend to this kid than I was to Anna.

Three days later is Anna's birthday. I didn't think to bring a gift to Kingmakers, so I pay the gardener an outrageous sum for a potted orchid and leave it outside her door. I know she'll know it's from me even without a card, because orchids are her favorite.

I wouldn't know what to write in a card. I wouldn't even know how to sign it. "Love, Leo" doesn't seem right anymore.

When I see her in chemistry class that afternoon, she gives me a small smile but doesn't mention the gift.

I don't bring it up either.

The last week of January is the coldest yet. The air is full of sleet, and the grass is frozen solid on the ground.

Regardless of this, Professor Knox demands that we go outside for target practice.

"How are we supposed to shoot if our fingers are frozen solid?" Hedeon moans.

"Not all battles take place in perfect weather," Professor Knox says mercilessly.

We all troop out to the shooting range south of campus. It's a miserable walk over and even worse when we have to lie down on the frozen earth to set up our sniper rifles.

The shooting range is just a field, at the end of which you can see a row of metal targets in human shape. Or at least once you've put your eye to the scope you can see them. They're nothing but faint silver gleams to the naked eye.

Ares is acting as my spotter for the first round, and then we'll switch positions. Anna is off to my right, spotting for Chay. Dean isn't in this class, thank god.

I feel bad for the girls lying on the cold ground in their short plaid skirts and bare knees. Anna is wearing tights instead of socks, but she's still shivering with her arms wrapped around herself.

"Wind speed eight to twelve," Ares tells me, checking the anemometer.

I make the necessary adjustments, then gently squeeze the

trigger, keeping my eyes open the whole time. I see a spark as my bullet grazes the edge of the target.

"A little to the left," Ares says unnecessarily.

"I know," I grumble.

Next to me, Chay gives a little whoop of triumph as she hits her target dead center.

Once I've hit the target four times, Ares and I switch positions. I stand up, shaking out my cramped legs.

Anna is still waiting her turn, hopping in place to try to stay warm. Her lips are turning blue. Without thinking, I strip off my sweatshirt and thrust it into her hands.

"Don't be silly," she says, teeth chattering. "You'll freeze in a T-shirt. I've got my blazer on."

"Your blazer isn't doing shit," I tell her gruffly.

She looks up at me—the first time we've made eye contact in several days. It's the first time we've stood this close in weeks. I see a familiar glint of gold on her neck—the superfine chain with the tiny moon pendant I gave her so long ago when we were only kids. She's still wearing it.

"Are you sure you won't be cold?" she says in her low, clear voice.

In that moment, with Anna standing only inches in front of me, her blue eyes fixed on my face, I don't feel cold in the slightest. Actually, I'm flooded with warmth. The wind feels like nothing anymore.

"I'm sure."

"Well…thanks, then." She smiles at me for the first time in a long time, then pulls the sweater over her head. It's so big on her that she looks like a little kid with her clunky boots and her wind-blown hair and her big blue eyes looking up at me. It's incredibly endearing.

I have to turn away abruptly before I say something that will only humiliate me.

"You okay?" Ares says as I resume my position next to him.

"Of course." I grit my teeth against the cold.

The warmth of Anna has already faded away, and I can tell it's going to be a miserable thirty minutes to finish this class.

"You want *my* sweater?" Ares says, trying not to grin.

"No," I say. "And shut the fuck up."

Ares chuckles as he presses his eye against the scope. "There's the Leo I know and love."

CHAPTER 20
DEAN

I THOUGHT I'D SNARED ANNA AND IT WOULD BE A SMOOTH progression from our first date to me taking full possession of her.

Instead, a most unwelcome and perverse thing begins to happen.

The more I tighten my grip on her, the more she tries to slip away.

It's not conscious on her part. But I can see that any time I try to get closer to her, she pulls away. She never rejects me outright. But she's always dancing away from me, just slightly out of reach.

It's a constant effort to keep her away from Leo. It takes foresight and planning.

I knew he'd try to do something for her birthday, so I got up early and staked out her dorm.

Sure enough, he came strolling up with a hothouse orchid right before breakfast. He left it outside her door, probably thinking she was still asleep, though in actuality she was in the cathedral across campus.

As soon as he left the solar, I ran up the stairs, grabbed the orchid, and chucked it down the garbage chute, pot and all. There was no card. Pity—I wanted to see exactly what Leo would dare to write.

I'd gotten her a box of handmade toffee from the sweet shop in the village. Anna thanked me, but she didn't try it right then and there, only tucked it in her bag.

She's been spending more and more time with Chay and Zoe,

which makes me feel that she's deliberately avoiding being alone with me. At the same time, whenever Bram or my other friends join us, she slips away as if she can't stand to be around any of them.

That part might be genuine—Bram is abrasive as fuck and in some kind of vendetta with Chay. They despise each other, and our two groups can't coexist in the same space for five minutes without a fight breaking out between them.

It probably has to do with the fact that neither of them has a filter between their brain and their mouth.

Today we've barely crossed paths on the commons before Chay says to Bram, "Did you notice I beat your score on the range today?"

"It's a fuckin' tornado out there," Bram replies, his expression sour.

"Yet I managed to make eight headshots," Chay smugly informs him. It's not as windy inside the castle walls as without, but she still has her arms crossed over her chest with her hands clamped under her armpits.

Anna comes hurrying through the gates as well, head ducked down so she doesn't see us until she's almost running into us.

"How about you?" I say to her. "Were you setting records too?"

As Anna looks up, startled, I realize that she's wearing someone's sweater. Someone very large, because the sleeves hang down over her hands and the hem comes down lower than her skirt, so it looks like she's naked underneath.

I already know without asking who it belongs to. The pink in her cheeks isn't just from the cold.

That jealousy I thought I'd conquered comes roaring up inside me like a fire-breathing dragon. It wasn't dead—only sleeping.

"No," Anna says. "It was too cold."

Even with that sweater on? I want to say, but I bite back the words before I let slip how angry I am.

I hate that she has classes with Leo when I'm not there.

I hate that she has eighteen years of history with him.

I hate that Leo Gallo was ever born.

"I need to see you tonight," I say to Anna abruptly.

"I…I've got homework." She won't meet my eye.

"I need to see you," I repeat. It's not a request.

Anna does look at me now, her thick black lashes sweeping up like a fan and ice-pale eyes piercing right through me.

"Alright," she says at last. "I'll meet you after dinner."

She takes Chay's arm, and they hurry off to their next class.

Bram cocks an eyebrow at me, unsmiling. His idea of handling a woman is bending her until she breaks. He thinks Anna has me wrapped around her little finger. And he might be right.

Anna has taken the soul out of me. She's holding it tight in those slim, pale hands.

It's time for me to take something from her.

CHAPTER 21
ANNA

I FELT LIKE I WAS MAKING PROGRESS IN MOVING ON FROM LEO. I'VE been able to attend classes with him without a sick feeling of dread every time I walk into the room. I've genuinely been having fun with Chay and Zoe. And I've even been relaxing a little with Dean—trying to focus on him as a person without constantly comparing him to Leo.

The only problem is that I'm not sure exactly how much I like Dean.

There are things about him that attract me, certainly. His intelligence primarily. His discipline. And his intense interest in me is, of course, flattering.

But other things I don't like. No matter what he says about the hierarchy of Heirs and everyone else, I simply don't like his elitism. Even in the Mafia world, there are two kinds of bosses: those who lead by fear and those who lead by loyalty. I know which one I want to be. I don't think Dean falls on the same side.

Then there's the constant pressure. I've told him a dozen times that I want to go slow, that I'm not ready to jump into a serious relationship. But he's incessantly pushing me for more time, more interaction, and especially more physical contact.

That part is my fault.

It's probably a mistake to date someone if I don't want to fuck them. Sex is what any boy will expect.

And I'm not against having sex. I've never been against it. It's just never felt right in the moment. It's like there's this barrier keeping me from taking that last, final step into adulthood.

I wish I could punch my ticket as casually as other people seem to do it. I'd honestly prefer if it were over and done with. I don't know why I'm afraid of it, but I am. I don't want it to mean something, but it does.

And then, on top of it all, right when I feel like I'm regaining a little equilibrium, Leo knocks me over again.

It was just a fucking sweater. I didn't even have to take it.

But it was cold, and Leo was looking at me with those amber-colored eyes that looked warmer than any flame, that seemed to light me up from the inside, making me weak and melting.

I took the sweater and pulled it over my head.

And oh my fucking god, it filled my whole lungs with his scent. Leo smells better than any human on earth. His scent is warm and sweet and spicy all at once. It gives me a head rush; it makes my heart pound and my skin throb.

It's linked to a thousand happy memories, almost all my best and brightest. They flickered before my eyes until even that gray and barren field looked golden.

I wanted to cry from how bad I wished I could stop feeling that way. But I have no control over it. My attraction to Leo is a supernatural force. It takes me over in an instant and wipes away months of progress.

Then I ran into Dean while I was still wearing that goddamned sweater, and I know he saw it. I was flushed and guilty, and he demanded that I come see him tonight, and I had to agree.

Now I'm on my way to meet him, wondering what the fuck I'm going to do about any of this.

It's nighttime, past ten o'clock on one of the coldest days of the year, so the castle grounds are almost empty. The vast spaces between stone towers and walls look bleak and wind-blasted. Only the greenhouses are still bright and lush, their windows steamed up from the warmth of the plants within and the verdant green visible through the foggy panes.

The black dome of the sky is dark and starless.

I feel low.

As hard as I've been trying to fight it, a deep depression has been taking hold of me.

This is something I've fought all my life. I'm afraid I inherited it from my father. Often and not always for a good reason, sadness takes hold of me. I have to actively battle it. I have to try to focus on the things that are bright and stimulating and interesting in the world or else depression wraps its tentacles around me and begins to drag me down.

My mother is the opposite. She has a bright, shining joy inside her that can never be extinguished. Because of that, she's been the North Star for my dad—always guiding him back out of the darkness when it threatens to swallow him whole.

I'm beginning to realize that Leo used to fill that function for me. I didn't know how dependent I was on him because I saw him so frequently. I didn't realize it was his cheerfulness, his irrepressible charm that was buoying me up day by day.

Now that's gone, and my thoughts are taking dark turns, my dreams are becoming more violent and disturbing, and the things that usually make me happy aren't having quite the same effect anymore.

Even dancing is losing its shine.

That's the one thing I thought would never let me down. The one escape I could always turn to.

But this morning when I woke early and went to the cathedral and laced up my shoes, I felt heavy and dull. My movements were labored and lacking in grace. The music didn't vibrate through my body the way it's supposed to. The choreography didn't flow through my brain like a river. In fact, I kept stumbling, unsure of what to do next.

I feel lost and so alone.

I'm walking to the most distant corner of campus where the old icehouse sits. It's a squat stone hut, unused and far away from anything else.

That's why it's become the favored spot for students who want "alone time" with each other.

I know what it means that Dean ordered me to meet him here.

And it was an order. I could see that if I refused, we were about to have a serious fight. I didn't have the energy for that. I was already tired to my bones.

The door is unlocked.

I pull it open with a groan of unoiled hinges.

Dean is waiting for me, as I knew he would be. He's got a blanket, drinks, and snacks spread out on an old mattress as well as several candles burning. Not all the buildings in Kingmakers have electric lights, especially those that aren't supposed to be accessed at night.

He's even got music playing, a remix of "Crazy in Love" I've never heard before. Not as cheerful as the original, it has a mournful and almost menacing sound that sends chills down my body.

The tiny blond hairs on my arms stand up, and I can feel my nipples stiffening, not from arousal but from something much more uneasy.

Dean's eyes sweep down the front of my blouse. He mistakes my reaction. His eyes gleam, and his tongue darts out to moisten his lips. He's galvanized, the tendons standing out on his bare forearms where his shirtsleeves are rolled up to the elbow.

Without speaking a word, he closes the space between us in one swift stride. He reaches around me, yanking the door shut, and then pulls me hard against his body.

Already I'm panicking, my heart stuttering in my chest, my whole body shaking. My hands are clammy cold, and I feel the sick sinking sensation I always had to endure in our scuba classes when I would drop down, down, down to the bottom of the pool, the shimmering surface of the water fading away overhead, impossibly far out of reach.

I don't know what I'm doing.

I don't have my North Star anymore.

Dean seizes my face between both of his hands. He holds me there, forcing me to look directly into his eyes. There's a kind of madness shining there. I feel like I'm falling into it, losing all control.

He kisses me ferociously. He's biting my lips, sucking the breath from my lungs. I stand there, letting it happen to me.

He rips open my blouse, the buttons pinging off the stone floor and rolling away in all directions. Then he grabs my bra and tears it open too, my breasts bouncing out in the chilly air.

I make a sound something between a gasp and a sob.

Dean pushes me down on the mattress, the abrupt movement snuffing one of the candles so the room is almost dark, lit by only one faint, guttering flame.

He's kissing and grinding against me, pinning me down so my body sinks into the mattress like it's quicksand, so I can barely breathe, let alone move.

I can feel his cock, harder than iron, battering against my thigh with only his trousers between us, because my skirt has already bunched up around my waist.

He's not going to stop tonight. I know that already.

I know he's barely been holding himself back all along.

If I want this to stop, I have to tell him right now.

"Dean—" I start, but he clamps his hand down over my mouth.

"Don't," he growls.

He shoves his other hand down the front of my underwear and starts rubbing me again, trying to force me to reach his level of arousal, trying to lure me into doing what he wants me to do through sheer physical coercion.

It feels good. Whether I want it to or not, it does.

But it doesn't make me happy. Instead, it fills me with a kind of sick, sinking panic. I feel trapped and desperate. I know what Dean's trying to do. He wants me. He thinks if he takes my body, he'll own my heart and soul too.

But they already belong to someone else. I've tried to ignore it, tried to deny it, tried to kill it even. It doesn't work. It will never work.

I grew up with Leo. He shaped me every day of my life. I never learned how to love anyone but him.

I wrench Dean's hand away from my mouth.

"I can't do this, Dean," I cry. "I still love him. I tried to make it go away. I swear I tried every day. But it won't. I can't stop."

He looks down into my face, and I see his jaw working, his upper lip twitching. A Möbius strip of emotions whirls across his face.

I expect him to rage at me. Or kiss me again.

I could never have guessed what he does next.

He rolls me over on top of him so I'm straddling him. Then he blows out the last candle, plunging us into darkness. All I can hear is the low, insistent beat of the music and my own thundering heart.

Dean says, "Pretend I'm him."

"Wh-what?"

"Pretend I'm him," he repeats, his voice low and insistent. "I want you, Anna. I need you. If you can't forget him, then don't forget him. Picture him while you fuck me. Pretend it's him you're riding. Call out his name while you come all over my cock. I don't give a fuck as long as I have you."

It's insane.

Yet I'm tempted.

I've had this longing inside me for so long. I can't kill it, and I can't do anything about it.

If I do what Dean asks, at least I'll have a moment of relief.

Who knows? Maybe it's what I need to exorcise this fixation once and for all.

I lean forward to kiss Dean, my bare breasts pressing against his warm, hard chest.

Before our mouths can meet, I smell the clean scent of his skin. It's fresh and pleasant. But it isn't Leo.

I jump off him as if I've been electrocuted.

I run for the door, not even stopping to try to find my clothes in the dark.

"Wait!" Dean calls after me.

I don't wait, not for a second.

CHAPTER 22
LEO

I'm worried about Anna.

She's not looking well. She seems to be folding in on herself, like a star collapsing. Getting even more quiet than usual in class. No hint of a smile on her face.

I think she might have broken up with Dean. I haven't seen them sitting together at lunch or walking together across the grounds.

Granted, I've barely seen Anna because she seems to fade away the moment class dismisses, and she must be eating at odd hours because I haven't seen her at the dining hall.

I'm embarrassed to ask her friends. They might not know what's going on anyway—Anna has always been reticent about her romantic life.

The main reason I think Anna might have split with Dean is because Dean is in a foul temper. I saw him snarl at Bram over breakfast to the point where it looked like the two of them were about to come to blows, and then the next day his knuckles were swollen and bruised from hitting the heavy bag.

He's stomping around campus just hoping that somebody is stupid enough to get in his way.

A few months ago, I probably would have taken the opportunity to do exactly that. But I'm not as interested in butting heads with him anymore.

What I want to do is talk to Anna. I want to talk to her the way we used to—when we communicated before we even opened our mouths and everything in the world seemed like a joke between the two of us that only we could understand.

It's hard to find her because she seems to be avoiding me. Or maybe she's avoiding everyone.

We don't have as many classes together this semester. And the course work is getting more and more difficult. I have to spend several hours a night on homework.

We're in Marksmanship at the same time, though not much chatting can occur while we're all wearing protective ear and eyewear, taking aim at targets. Psychological Interrogation has assigned seating and we're on opposite sides of the room. So chemistry is probably my best chance to speak to her.

Our chemistry class is more like a lab. Last semester, we were studying undetectable poisons. This semester, we've moved on to explosives.

The desks are rectangular tables that fit two people. Anna's been sitting with Zoe generally, but Zoe has fallen prey to the flu that's been sweeping through Kingmakers, so I take my opportunity to slip into the seat next to Anna while Professor Lyons is still writing a list of ingredients on the chalkboard.

Anna gives a little jump when I sit down next to her, and I see her hand clench convulsively in her lap.

"Hey," I say.

"Hello," she murmurs.

"Zoe still sick?"

It's a stupid question. I already knew she was before I sat down, having already asked Chay that question over breakfast.

"Yeah. I think I might be getting it too. My head is killing me."

She presses one slim, pale hand against her temple, trying to ease the headache apparently throbbing beneath the skin.

"They probably have aspirin at the infirmary" is my genius suggestion.

"Probably," Anna agrees.

I should have offered to get her some. Too late—Professor Lyons is already starting the lecture, and I wasted those precious moments talking about Zoe and fucking aspirin.

Now we just have to sit here listening, while I'm painfully aware of Anna's slim frame next to me, the strand of her hair tickling my arm, and the soft puff of air that runs across my knuckles when she lets out a silent sigh.

The lecture seems interminable. I want to look at Anna, not at the professor, but I can't turn my head without her noticing, not when we're sitting side by side like this.

She's not taking notes like she usually does. Her notebook sits closed in front of her, her pens lined up next to it untouched.

Her black nail polish is chipped—unusual for Anna, who is careful with her appearance. She really must be sick. Or upset about Dean.

My stomach clenches painfully.

When the class ends at last, I blurt out, "What do you have next?"

Anna says, "Contracts and Negotiations."

"I'll walk over with you."

Her blue eyes flit up to my face, and for a moment I feel a hint of that old spark, that connection between us.

"Alright," she says.

We descend the long, spiraling staircase on the south end of the keep, then go out into the February sunshine. It's still chilly outside, but you can taste the first hint of spring in the air—the fresh grass coming up on the commons and puffy white clouds in the sky that are friendlier than the thick gray fog we had all through January.

The wind seems to remind Anna of the last time we spoke. She says, "I never returned your sweater."

"It's alright. I have three."

"That was kind of you to lend it to me." The unspoken part of her sentence is *considering we're barely friends anymore.*

My chest is aching, and I wonder how I can keep this conversation going without fucking it up somehow. I used to never worry about what I said to Anna. Now all I seem to do is make mistakes.

"It was nothing."

Wrong. That was wrong. It came out sounding like I didn't care about giving her the sweater, like I would have done it for anyone. I erased the meaning of the gesture and made it seem like there was no emotion behind it. When the truth is that I was *compelled* to help her. I can't bear watching Anna shivering or cold or unhappy in any way.

Frowning slightly, she switches the subject. "The next challenge is coming up."

"Only a week away."

"Are you excited?" Anna asks.

She's talking about the old Leo who loved competition more than anything.

I still feel some of that anticipation, but I'm not nearly as cocky as I used to be. I've been at Kingmakers long enough now to understand how brilliant and ruthless and experienced the older students are, how much they've learned in the three years they were here when I was not.

"I wish we knew what the challenges were going to be ahead of time. So I could better prepare."

Anna says, "You've always been good at thinking on your feet."

I hear a hint of her old confidence in me. It gives me a warm glow, buoying me up better than anything else could do.

Encouraged, I take a deep breath and ask her, "Are you okay, Anna?"

She throws a quick glance at me. "Of course," she says. "Why wouldn't I be?"

"I thought… I thought maybe something happened with you and Dean."

She's silent, walking beside me. We've almost reached the intersection where we'll part ways for our next class. It's now or never.

"Are you still dating?"

She turns to face me, her expression impossible to read. "Why do you ask?"

I feel like I'm traversing a thin layer of basalt over molten hot lava. How to navigate this? How to say the right things?

"I… I just wanted to apologize. For trying to tell you who to date. It's your choice, obviously, if you want to date Dean. I had no right to tell you not to."

Anna looks up at me, blue eyes like winter, cheeks like snow. No color in them at all.

"So you're happy for me," she says tonelessly.

No. No, I'm not fucking happy for her. I'll never be happy as long as Anna is with someone else.

But I don't own her. I thought I did. I was like a kid with a toy—careless and stupid. Until I lost her.

"Yes," I lie. "I'm happy for you."

I don't know if I've ever lied to Anna before. It doesn't feel good coming out of my mouth. In fact, it feels fucking horrible.

Anna regards me with a look I can't interpret. Maybe it's sorrow. Maybe it's contempt.

Without answering, she turns around and walks away.

I know I've fucked up all over again. But I have no idea how to stop.

CHAPTER 23
DEAN

ANNA DISAPPEARS FROM CLASS FOR SEVERAL DAYS.

She's barely spoken to me since that night in the icehouse.

I'm equal parts furious at her and desperate to see her.

After combat class, I sneak into her dorm tower, planning to break into her room again. Before I even put a hand on her door, someone pulls it open from the inside, and I'm met with the petite but stubborn frame of Chay Wagner.

"She's sick, and she doesn't want to talk to you," Chay says.

"Let me in." I try to push past her into the room.

Chay blocks the way, keeping the door mostly closed so I can't even peer around it to see if Anna's actually in bed or if she's even inside at all.

"Get out of the way," I growl at her.

"How about you get out of our dorm before I yell for Pippa," Chay retorts. "You're not allowed to be up here."

It's probably an empty threat. Pippa Portnoy is likely in class herself at the moment, but I don't particularly want to tangle with the famously vicious senior who wouldn't hesitate to report me if I annoyed her—or arrange an even more inconvenient run-in with one of her many minions.

"Anna!" I call around Chay's shoulder.

Chay just scowls at me. "You broke up. Get over it," she says and slams the door in my face.

Technically Anna and I can't break up, because technically we were never boyfriend and girlfriend.

But that's irrelevant.

I claimed Anna the moment I saw her.

I thought she might run back to Leo as soon as she fled the icehouse. But she hasn't done that—not yet at least.

I have a few theories as to why.

First, though she'd never admit it, I know that seeing Leo getting a BJ from Gemma Rossi cut Anna deep. The continued presence of Gemma and her obvious interest in Leo have been salt in the wound ever since. I've seen Anna carefully refusing to look at either of them when we're all in class together.

She avoids Gemma's whole cavalcade of Spies—luckily for me, because that nosy redhead Shannon Kelly is the only person who could possibly throw suspicion on what happened that night. Gemma obviously has no idea, and it seems like Leo doesn't either. He just thinks he was smashed and made a bad choice.

Anna may still be hung up on Leo, but she hasn't given up on her resentment from that party either. My little scheme was more successful than I ever could have dreamed.

I assume it wasn't the first time Leo fucked around with some random girl, but as far as I know, it was the first time it happened here, at Kingmakers, and apparently that means something to Anna. She must have thought things would be different once they went away to school together.

Maybe she would have forgiven him if Leo begged and groveled. As far as I know, he never did. He's probably too proud, the fucking idiot. Or else he knew it wouldn't work.

Anna is intense. She loves hard and hates harder. That's exactly what I like about her.

I want her to take all that misplaced affection for Leo and turn it on me instead.

For all the pleasure I've had with Anna—holding her hand,

walking with her, talking to her, touching that silky skin and those full lips—I've barely sipped from that cup yet. I want to drink her down all the way to the bottom. I want all of her, every last bit. Not a scrap left for Leo.

I made a mistake though, that night when I finally had her alone.

I was desperate. I tried to do whatever it took to take her virginity. I thought that would connect her to me whether she wanted it or not.

But it was a miscalculation.

What I actually have to do is make her choose. I have to show her indisputably that I'm the better man. Smarter than Leo, stronger than him. I have to humiliate and destroy him. And then when she sees how pathetic he really is, she'll come back to me. Willingly and fully.

For that reason, I look forward to the second challenge in the Quartum Bellum almost as much as Leo himself.

He thinks it's his chance for redemption.

I know he's about to fail, publicly and spectacularly.

At least if I have anything to say about it.

With the sophomores ignominiously defeated in the first round, the freshmen are facing off against the juniors and the seniors. They're confident in their ability to crush us. But there's a certain frisson in the air—the uneasy acknowledgment that this contest isn't quite as lopsided as they'd hoped.

Damari Ragusa tells me there's an alliance between Calvin and Pippa. They've agreed to finish Leo off quickly so they can face off against each other in the final round.

The problem is that Calvin doesn't really want to clear the way for Pippa to sail through to the finals. As arrogant as he is, he must know that Pippa is smarter than him, and she runs her crew of seniors like a generalissimo. She'll use Calvin to get rid of Leo, then slaughter him in a head-on match.

I know all these things. I wonder if Leo knows them too.

I see him holed up with Ares and Hedeon, strategizing.

Despite moping around about the loss of Anna, Leo is still the darling of most of the freshmen. Through his friendships with Hedeon and Kenzo, he's got the Londoners and the Yakuza working with him enthusiastically. The Paris Bratva seem to like him too, despite the fact that he abandoned Jules Turgenev in enemy territory.

It's only my crew who despise him almost as much as I do. But even they feel the allure of an unprecedented freshman victory.

"Do you think we could beat Pippa? If we made it through to the end?" Bram asked me one night with pretend nonchalance.

"No," I say flatly. "And it doesn't matter anyway. We barely made it through the first challenge. We're not going to win the second."

The weather seems to agree with me. The morning of the second challenge is lightning-stricken with thundering rain. The fields around Kingmakers are soaked and muddy as we take our places at the three vertices of a triangular pitch marked out with bleeding spray paint.

We're all wearing pinnies to show our class colors—white for the freshmen, green for the juniors, and black for the seniors.

Squinting across the field, I see Calvin Caccia staring back at us, his hair plastered to his skull with rain and his gray gym attire already soaked through and clinging to his bulky body.

Pippa's team looks even more intimidating. The seniors on average are significantly bigger than us and more muscular. Pippa stands in front of them, the smallest of the bunch but the most unsettling. With her dark, wind-blown hair, she looks like a witch commanding an army of giants.

I watch Leo, trying to gauge his mood. He's pacing back and forth, not in nervousness but in prowling strides like an animal. He looks like his father. I don't see anything of my aunt in him.

I know what Sebastian Gallo looks like. He's not careful to scrub his image online. Not like my father. You won't find a picture of Adrian Yenin anywhere, not even in our own house.

There used to be a wedding photo on our mantel—my mother trim and pretty and laughing in a short '50s-style wedding dress, my father also smiling, his face turned toward her so that only the handsome side of him showed.

I think he burned that photo after she left.

You'd think he'd be afraid of fire, but he isn't. Fascinated by it, more like. I've seen him burn plenty of photographs of himself from his younger years, letting the flames take both sides of his face.

The rain pounds down on my head. My rifle is slung over my shoulder on a strap.

Professor Howell has already explained the rules of the second challenge.

Each team has a bomb. Not a real bomb—it's a metal sphere tripped by a pull tab and loaded with paint.

Likewise, our rifles are only paintball guns. But not the usual type of pellets—these paintballs are the size of a chicken's egg, and they fucking hurt. They're closer to the rubber bullets shot at rioters. A direct shot could easily fracture a rib and will certainly raise a bruise bigger than your fist.

Unlike in the first challenge, being shot doesn't mean you're out. You can keep going if you're able. But a paintball to the wrong spot—to the balls, for instance—will knock you out of commission pretty quick.

I'd fire one right in Leo's eye if we weren't wearing safety glasses. They're not much use in the rain—I can barely see out of mine, and they're not even fogged up from running yet.

The goal is simple: get your bomb to one of the opposite corners and detonate it. First two teams to succeed are the winners.

Leo is muttering orders to our team, laying out his strategy. It sounds like he intends to make a spearhead to take the bomb across to the juniors' corner.

"Why the juniors' corner?" Hedeon says. "Shouldn't we wait to see which side is easier?"

"That *will* be the easier target," Leo says with supreme confidence.

Hedeon nods, going along with the obvious assumption that the seniors will be harder to get past.

I'm not so sure he's right. Pippa Portnoy is aggressive as hell. Speed and intimidation are her favorite weapons. I think there's a good chance she'll try to rush us again, like she did in capture the flag.

"Once we get through, our little battalion will split," Leo explains. "I need the fastest runners to stay with me. Erik, Kenzo, and Thomas, you stay right up front. Hedeon and Silas, you flank us and run their defenders over if you have to. I want the best long-distance shooters to stay behind us. Chay, that's you for sure. Why don't you take Anna, Ares, and Zoe along? I know you all work well together."

Anna gives Leo a quick nod but doesn't say anything. Her pale skin looks almost translucent in the rain, and the botanical tattoo on her forearm stands out like a brand. She's stubbornly refusing to meet my eyes, though I know damn well she can feel me watching her.

"We got you covered," Ares says to Leo. He's got his arms wrapped around himself because despite the rain, he's only wearing a thin white T-shirt, no pullover. Probably because he can't afford half the things he was supposed to bring to school.

He may be from one of the founding families, but nowadays the Cirillos are a disgrace. It pisses me off that his name still carries clout when he's a fucking pauper, while I had to trade two years of my life to even get into this school.

"Dean, Bram, Valon," Leo says, fixing me with a direct stare.

"Keep your people here as defense, picking off attackers. Jules and the rest of the Paris kids will act as snipers on the edges. Remember to stay inside the lines."

He thinks if he leaves the Paris Bratva with us, it'll ensure we don't let the attackers through too easily. Mafia honor dictates that you obey the orders of your boss, regardless of your opinions or feelings on the matter. Even if you didn't pick this particular boss. Even if you hate his fucking guts.

I'd like to fire my full clip into Leo's back the second he turns around.

But it is true that I can't let anyone see me sabotaging the team. For one thing, most of the freshmen genuinely want to win. Even the Bratva and Penose, who have no love for Leo.

The other issue is that the Yenin name isn't exactly shining with honor right now.

My grandfather was KGB before he turned Bratva. And what Leo said on the ship had a kernel of truth to it—my grandfather did breach his blood oath with the Gallos. It's a grave offense. One that would have ensured that he was shunned by the other Mafia families until his dying day, had that day not come so swiftly after.

The part Leo wants to forget is that his family fucking deserved it. They lied, murdered, and stole from us for years. They transgressed every rule of our people, including when Sebastian Gallo defiled my grandfather's one and only daughter. So they had it coming.

But it's still a black mark on my name. I want to rebuild my reputation at Kingmakers. Not show myself as a traitor all over again.

That doesn't mean I'm going to help Leo win, though.

I'll do the bare minimum I can get away with.

And if I get the chance to stab him in the back secretly, without anyone knowing, I'll take it.

Leo's still staring at Bram and me, waiting for a response.

Bram grunts his reluctant consent.

I just give a half smile that could mean anything. Leo narrows his eyes at me and turns away, the bomb cradled under his arm like a football.

All three teams crouch in our respective corners, our soaked sneakers making a squelching sound.

Professor Howell stands in the center of the triangle, starter pistol raised to the cloudy sky. The raindrops shatter as they hit the unyielding surface of his poncho, and his pistol looks slick and shining. He fires, signaling the start of the match.

Immediately, almost all the seniors and a third of the juniors rush toward our corner. They've obviously collaborated ahead of time, planning to take us out before they attack each other.

I assume Pippa had to agree to send out the bulk of her force and allow Calvin to keep most of his people on defense, because he wouldn't trust her otherwise. It won't matter. If they work together, they'll destroy on us.

They converge in the center of the triangle, charging at us in one mass, planning to overwhelm us with their superior size and numbers.

"Tighten up!" Leo bellows, shouting for his group of freshmen to form a phalanx.

Instead of giving in to the temptation to run at the other teams, Leo orders his team to hold their ground, tightly bunched together.

"Aim and fire!" he shouts.

The freshmen at the front of the spearhead start firing at the onrushing juniors and seniors. Because the aggressors are running and the freshmen aren't, Leo's team has better aim. And because the freshmen are in a close formation, the juniors and seniors can only shoot at the freshmen on the exterior of the pack.

Leo's positioned some of his best sharpshooters right at the apex of the phalanx. They're wreaking havoc on our aggressors in tandem with his snipers. Paintballs smash into their chests, limbs, and even their faces, leaving garish spatters of bright red paint that drips and runs as it mixes with the rain.

Subtly, Pippa's seniors fall back, allowing the juniors to take the brunt of the hits. A dozen juniors stumble and fall, and the rest falter, looking to Calvin for direction.

"Keep going, you fucking idiots!" he shouts.

He's got his bomb in his hands, and he looks like he plans to plant it in our corner. But I notice that Liam Murphy, Pippa's right-hand man, is likewise carrying their bomb. I have the sneaking suspicion that Pippa will make sure to detonate hers first, no matter what else might happen.

Sure enough, Pippa gives a sharp whistle, and her seniors split off, trying to flank Leo's phalanx. Leo takes the opportunity to charge right through the center, his group staying tight and swift with Leo at the head of the spear, the bomb protectively cradled under his sweatshirt to keep it out of the rain.

I expect Leo to try to cross the field to the seniors' side instead—it's barely guarded. But Pippa has been careful to force him the other way toward the juniors' corner.

It's a fool's errand. There's no way Leo can make it through. I expect him to turn, even if he has to cover more ground. Instead, he continues sprinting right at the wall of juniors, thinking he can bash his way through.

As Leo passes center field, the rear portion of his phalanx splits off, huddling down and raising their rifles to provide cover for Leo as he charges. I see Anna, Ares, Chay, and Zoe far off on the pitch, trying to clear a sideline for Leo. They're out of position and not doing much good.

Leo barrels forward with his remaining soldiers, ducking and dodging, trying to avoid as many of the defending juniors as he can. It's not working. Leo is hit with paintballs again and again in his chest and legs, almost all the shots aimed at him as his freshmen do their best to shoot, tackle, and pummel as many guards as they can.

Meanwhile, Pippa's and Calvin's teams are still attacking our corner. I shoot a couple of incoming juniors, just for the fun of seeing them jolt and stagger as the oversize paintballs explode, staining their shirts with garish scarlet spatter.

I steer clear of the seniors, because I don't fancy making enemies among the upperclassmen. I'm perfectly happy to let Pippa set her bomb. I'd help her pull the pin myself if nobody was watching.

I can see her stealthily creeping along the sideline, right behind Liam.

Calvin Caccia is plowing down the middle, thinking he's got a clear shot at our goal. Like Leo, Calvin is carrying the bomb himself, but he's not as willing to take shots from our defenders. For that reason, his progress is slower as he's forced to huddle in the center of his knot of protectors. Still, he advances on us steadily in a straight line.

I continue firing now and then just for appearances, barely aiming. I don't particularly care whether Calvin or Pippa makes it to the corner first. All I want is for Leo to fail.

I keep my eye on him as he continues his mad, desperate onslaught on the juniors' corner. He gets shot again and again in the shoulder, in the thigh, then right in the gut. He doubles over, stumbles, almost falls. He takes a paintball to his right leg just above the knee, and this time he does fall.

The juniors are laughing and jeering at him, taking great pleasure in firing at this cocky little shit who had the audacity to think he could beat the whole school. Even some of the few seniors guarding their own corner have drifted closer so they can watch.

Leo lurches up once more, but he's facing a veritable wall of juniors. There's no possible way he can make it to the corner. He should just give up.

With a roar, he charges at them anyway. They raise their rifles and fire their paintballs en masse.

The barrage drowns out the shouts from the other side of the pitch. In the pounding rain, the thundering rifles, and the jeers and yells, I don't realize what's happening. Until one high-pitched scream cuts through the noise:

"They've got the bomb!"

In slow motion, we all turn to the seniors' corner. Ares is sprinting for the vertex, carrying the bomb tucked under one arm. Anna, Chay, and Zoe are right behind him, firing at any remaining defenders. They're aiming for the seniors' hands, hitting them right in the fingers so they drop their rifles, howling and shaking their paint-splattered hands.

In disbelief, I look back at Leo Gallo sprawled out on the soaked grass, covered almost head to toe in red paint. He groans and rolls over on his back. He's grinning as he pulls a wadded-up sweater out from under his shirt.

The last two seniors try to physically block Ares's way, but even seniors are no match for his size. He barrels through them, shouldering them aside with such force that they go flying out of bounds. He sets the bomb right in the corner and yanks out the clip. It erupts like a volcano, belching white paint straight up in the air.

Calvin Caccia stares stupidly at Pippa Portnoy for a moment as the enormity of his situation washes over him. Only now does he realize why Pippa agreed to send her team out, leaving her end zone unprotected.

Almost all the juniors are clustered in their own corner, while Pippa's seniors have reached their goal. Calvin has twenty men around him, while Pippa has fifty. They run at us like swift, dark shadows, and we let them through. It's already a foregone conclusion.

The seniors detonate their bomb, the pitch-black paint securing their place in the finals. Calvin watches it happen, his face contorted in fury.

The freshmen pour across the pitch, physically hauling Leo up off the ground so he can hobble over to Ares and join in the wild celebrations. Their elation is twice as high as it was in the first challenge. The first win seemed like a fluke. This one is much more real.

They're slapping each other on the back, Leo wincing anytime he's touched on his bruised and battered flesh. They're all laughing and shouting, every one of them.

Except me.

I'm watching, silent and motionless, as Leo and Anna slowly push their way toward each other through the crowd.

They stand there facing each other, the rain pouring down on their heads harder than ever. They look into each other's faces, Leo covered almost head to toe in red, dripping paint, Anna with only two bright splotches on her body: one on her bicep and one on her hip.

Leo says something, and Anna replies. I'm too far away to hear or even to read their lips.

But I clearly see Leo sweeping Anna up in a hug, his arms wrapped tight around her.

CHAPTER 24
ANNA

Every shower in the castle is in use.

Chay and I run down to the armory, but even there, girls are clustered two or three under a showerhead, trying to scrub the red paint off their skin.

Our flesh is a map of welts, cuts, and bruises. The huge purple lump on my bicep looks like there's something growing under the skin, ready to burst out. My hip hurts even more. I'm hobbling around like a grandma, wondering if it might be broken.

"Why in the fuck did they use weapons-grade paintballs?" I ask Chay, dousing my head in shampoo and trying to pick out the bits of dried paint in my hair.

"'Cause they like to see us suffer," Chay says, stripping off her gray pullover that has a sleeve almost torn clean off. "Did you see Erik? He got hit in the mouth, and he's missing two teeth!"

"Leo was a mess." I shake my head at the memory of his banged-up face.

He had a black eye, a lump on his forehead, a split lip, two gashes on his cheek, and a huge bruise on the side of his neck, to say nothing of the parts of him covered by clothes. Still, he was grinning when I ran over to him.

"I dunno," Chay says slyly. "He looked pretty happy to me when he was hugging you."

I turn my face into the shower spray so I don't have to look at her.

In the elation of the victory, Leo and I lost all our awkwardness.

I ran right up to him, shouting "That was fucking incredible!" and he said "I knew you could do it," and we were both smiling at each other like nothing bad had ever happened, like we were old friends again. And before either of us could say anything to ruin it, he hugged me hard, his body like a furnace compared to the freezing rain.

Then we were swarmed by other students, and there was no time for anything else. All Leo could do was shout "Are you coming to the party tonight?" and I called back "Yes!" though I don't know if he heard me.

I actually hadn't heard about any party, but I knew there was sure to be one. Freshmen haven't made it to the final round of the Quartum Bellum in twenty years. We all want to celebrate.

"Did Leo tell you what he was planning ahead of time?" Chay asks me.

"He told Ares, then Ares told me, and I told you. It had to look real, him going for the goal. Everybody has to be looking the wrong way, or it's not a proper diversion."

"I thought we were fucked still." Chay scrubs her arms with a loofah. "Wouldn't have worked if Ares wasn't such a monster. Who knew he had it in him?"

I say, "He may be a sweetheart, but he isn't soft."

"No, he's definitely not *soft* anywhere." Chay gives a lascivious smirk. "Did you see him in that soaking wet T-shirt? Fucking hell, he's got a body under those clothes."

"Don't get any ideas," I warn her. "He doesn't need his heart ripped out."

"What are you talking about? I would never!"

There is no way she should be that offended.

"You already have. At least three times this year."

"When?"

I list the names off on my soapy fingers. "Sam…"

"Sam's an idiot. He thought narwhals were made up. Like unicorns!"

"Reggie…"

"He had terrible breath. Even gum didn't fix it."

"What about Thomas York?"

"He got mad when I beat him at target practice."

"Doesn't matter the reasons. They were all moping around for months after you dumped them. I don't think Ares could survive that. He may look big and strong, but he's got a vulnerable side."

"I know," Chay says, totally undeterred. "That's what I like about him. He's humble—not like the rest of the arrogant shitheads at this school."

"Including you," I tease her.

"Of course including me!" Chay cries. "But I have a right to be arrogant. Because I'm fantastic."

I laugh. "Can't argue with that."

We head back to our dorms to change clothes. As we pass Zoe's door, I poke my head inside and say, "You coming to the party?"

She shakes her head. "I don't think I should."

She hasn't showered yet, and her face is still spattered with a fine mist of paint like scarlet freckles.

There's a letter open on her bed. From the look of the rigid, formal writing and her expression of unhappiness, I'm assuming it's another joy-gram from her father chewing her out for whatever his spies have reported.

I mutter, "Fuck what he says. He's in Spain, and you're here. He can't stop you having fun."

"There's only two months left in the semester." Zoe sighs. "He'll have his chance to punish me soon enough."

Chay and I exchange unhappy glances. We want Zoe to come with us, but we don't want to get her in serious trouble.

"Let's have a drink together in our room, then," Chay says. "Nobody will see you in there."

"Alright." Zoe smiles just a little. She pushes herself up off the bed, leaving the unwanted letter abandoned, and follows us to our room.

Chay and I haven't had time to tidy up this week, so there's a jumble of shoes and clothes that have to be tossed off the beds before we have anywhere to sit down.

I love our room, even when it's messy. It finally feels like home.

Though Zoe's reminder that the school year is passing by swiftly does give me a little pang for my actual home so far across the ocean. I've never been away from my parents and siblings so long. I wonder if they'll think I've changed when they see me again.

Leo has changed.

I didn't realize it in the heat of the competition, but thinking on it now, that was very unlike him to pass the bomb to Ares and to trust him to take it all the way to the end while Leo provided the diversion.

Leo did what he had to for the good of the team, not caring if it was Ares who got the lion's share of the glory. And he took an absolute beating doing it. He was the leader we needed.

He wouldn't have done that a year ago.

I wonder if he sees the change in himself.

Chay is getting out the bottle of vodka that came in her Christmas package.

"Don't they search all the packages?" Zoe asks curiously. Her parents only sent three fresh school uniforms and a copy of *Atlas Shrugged*. They certainly wouldn't mail her contraband.

"They don't care if your mom sends you a bottle as long as it's sealed," Chay says carelessly. "They only care about the really sketchy shit. Knives or guns or poison or whatever. Which is hilarious because we have all that on campus."

"It's all locked up in between classes," Zoe points out.

Chay rolls her eyes. "Right, and none of us know how to pick a lock."

She unscrews the cap on the Iordanov, which has a grinning pink skull on the front and is already three-quarters gone since this isn't the first time we've all shared a nightcap. Three shots glug into water glasses stolen from the dining hall.

"To our covert operation," Chay says, grinning and raising her glass.

I drink the vodka down, promising myself it will be my only drink of the night. I want to talk to Leo if I get the chance, and I don't want to say anything stupid if I get too tipsy.

"We made a great team." Zoe smiles. "Us and Ares—like Charlie's Angels and Bosley."

"Who?" Chay frowns.

"They—never mind." Zoe shakes her head.

Zoe is a passionate fan of old TV shows. Her greatest disappointment came on the day when Chay confessed that she had never heard of Lucille Ball.

"I still think you should come to the party," Chay says.

Zoe soberly shakes her head. "I'm going to stay in and study. I missed too many chemistry classes, and now I don't know anything about secondary explosives."

She stays with us while we get dressed, however.

I pull on a black silk camisole and a pair of velvet pants. It's a softer and more romantic look than what I usually wear, especially once Zoe brushes my hair out and plaits it in a long and intricate braid with a black ribbon woven through.

"You're so beautiful," Zoe says without jealousy.

"So are you," I tell her.

It's true. With her coal-black hair and light green eyes, Zoe has a kind of ethereal loveliness that is only enhanced when she looks unhappy, as she does right now. She looks like an elven princess trapped in a dark fairy tale. Which in a way she is. She'll have to stay locked in this tower all night by the decree of her father while the rest of us are free to go where we like.

"What about me?" Chay says, more to break our melancholy mood than because she actually cares about compliments. Chay's sense of self-worth is a perpetual-motion machine that needs no fuel.

I survey her cherry-red pants and cropped T-shirt.

"You look like Mick Jagger."

"Oh," she says and pouts. "I was going for David Bowie."

I give Zoe a quick hug before we part ways at the door.

"Come down later if you change your mind," I tell her. "When everybody is too sloshed to tell on you."

Chay and I cross the courtyard quickly, holding our school blazers over our heads as makeshift umbrellas because it's still raining. We're heading to the stables where the havoc of a party underway is audible even over the sound of the rain.

The stables are on the far west side of campus and are a popular place for revelry when the weather is bad. It's been a long time since any animals were kept here, but you can still find traces of hay between the wooden floorboards.

One end of the stables is used for storage of odds and ends—broken desks and chairs, moldy textbooks, worn-out mops and brooms, stacks of filing boxes containing the records of students long dead. The still-living students have cleared the opposite side so we can gather here without attracting attention.

The most functional of the broken furniture has been repaired and repurposed to give us somewhere to sit. This includes a large sofa that apparently used to reside in the chancellor's office until two of the legs snapped off. Now its green velvet is stained and torn, and it groans beneath the weight of a half dozen Enforcers.

Music is playing from a speaker that looks like the same one Dean borrowed the night I met him in the icehouse. The sound quality is tinny, but nobody cares. It's turned up full volume, blasting Mac Miller.

I don't see Dean himself, which is a relief. I doubt he'll come. The last thing he'll want to do is watch Leo celebrate his victory.

Bram, however, is over by a hollowed-out watermelon turned into a makeshift punch bowl, pouring in a foul-looking combination of liquors.

My eyes keep roaming until I spot the person I most want to see: Leo. He's surrounded by a crowd of ecstatic freshmen, assuring them that he thinks our chances of winning the Quartum Bellum have never been better.

As if he can feel me looking at him, he glances up and breaks into a grin, then immediately winces because the smile reopened his split lip.

I've never seen him so beat up in my life. His right eye is almost swollen shut, and his entire face is a map of cuts and bruises. His bright eyes and huge grin shine through all the same, showing that nothing in the world can keep Leo down for long.

I wish there weren't so many people around. The smell of alcohol and the noise of the party and the press of excited freshmen crowding around Leo are bringing back painful memories. This is very like the night three months ago when he became captain.

I went into that evening full of hope and anticipation.

I'm afraid to allow myself to feel those same emotions over again.

Leo and I have been recovering our friendliness bit by bit. But I don't know if we can ever go back to where we were.

Actually, I'm sure we can't. Too much has happened since then. It's just like I was thinking, up in my room—Leo has changed. And so have I.

The night of that other party, when we walked down the path to Moon Beach, all I wanted was for Leo to kiss me. I wanted to see if the thing I'd been feeling could take physical form. I wanted to see if the attraction I felt would bloom if his lips met mine.

Now...now I want something much different than that.

I think of the trust, the companionship, and the connection we had. I want all of that as love, not just friendship.

But I don't know if that's possible. How could Leo and I truly give ourselves to each other after what happened? He hurt me, and I hurt him back. He fucked some girl almost in front of me, and I dated his worst enemy.

I know I made mistakes too. It wasn't just Leo. I had a lot of growing up to do this year.

But it still jabs at me, thinking about it. My hopes that were so high that night, dashed on the rocks when I saw Leo with Gemma...

Can you ever really forgive something that hurt that bad?

Does Leo even want to forgive me or to be with me?

The other day, he practically gave his blessing for me to date Dean. It seemed like he didn't even care.

Well, that's all over now one way or another. I told that to Dean a few days after his disastrous attempt to fuck me. He cornered me outside my dorm, and I told him it was over. He narrowed his eyes at me and said, "No, it isn't."

"That's not up to you." My fingers shook, though I willed them not to. "I don't want to see you anymore."

He stared at me, not answering. Then he said, "We'll see about that."

I don't know what the fuck that was supposed to mean, and I don't care.

Maybe I should have told Leo that Dean and I broke up, but it hurt my feelings all over again, the way he didn't seem to give a shit anymore. The way he almost seemed to be promoting it.

That's why I don't run over to Leo right now, pushing my way through the crowd of people around him. Because after all this time, I still don't know how he feels about me.

It may be that he just wants his best friend back.

As badly as I've missed Leo, I don't know if I can be that for him anymore. Not with the way I feel. It would be torture.

"Hey!" Chay says, seeing the unhappy look on my face. "Come dance with me!"

She pulls me out onto the uneven wooden boards before I can answer, elbowing her way through the press of kids who are jumping around, singing along to the music without knowing the lyrics, grinding against each other, and doing everything else short of actual dancing.

Chay knows how to move. She has that effortless sensuality that draws every eye in the room toward her—not just the guys but plenty of the girls too. She knows how to use her hips and her hands, how to bite her lip and toss her hair in a way that has four or five different dudes trying to cut in within five seconds.

"No, fuck off! I'm dancing with Anna!" she shouts, shoving them away unceremoniously.

But I can sense Chay's eyes drifting over to Ares on the opposite side of the room. He's leaned up against the wall, hands stuffed in his pockets. Plenty of people want to come up and congratulate him. He shrugs them off in the nicest way possible. I can practically hear him saying, "It was nothing. It was Leo's idea."

Ares is allergic to attention—probably because so much of the attention he gets from idiots like Bram is negative. Also I just don't think he likes it. If he weren't friends with Leo, he'd probably never come out of his room.

Chay views that as a challenge. Now she's turned to face Ares directly, showing him some of her best moves. She winks at him and beckons for him to come on over and join us. Ares blushes and shakes his head, determinedly turning his eyes somewhere else.

"How could he turn this down?" Chay scowls, gesturing to her tight gymnast's physique.

I laugh. "Must have hit his head in that challenge."

"Who wouldn't want to dance with the two prettiest girls in the school?" a deep voice says.

I spin around, seeing that Leo has snuck up behind us. It was a silly compliment, something that could mean nothing, but already my skin is burning just from how close we're standing.

"Fuck, you're a mess!" Chay laughs, looking up at Leo's battered face.

"Don't I know it." He grins. "Worth it, though. You girls were fucking flawless. All that target practice paid off."

"It was your idea." Screwing up my courage, I add, "I'm proud of you. Trusting Ares like that. Trusting all of us instead of just doing it yourself."

Leo looks down at me, his brows drawn together in a way I can't interpret.

He says, "Sometimes the harder thing is to let go."

My stomach drops like a rock.

Does he mean that about us?

Did he let go of the idea of what could have been between us?

He could have given up on it months ago. He could be miles past it now.

The music switches from upbeat pop to the mournful opening bars of "Wicked Game."

Chay says, "I need a drink!" and abandons us on the dance floor.

Leo and I look at each other awkwardly.

Then it's not awkward as his hands encircle my waist and I reach up around his neck. We fit together like we always have, Leo just the right amount taller than me even when I'm wearing heels.

He holds me, and it's easy, so easy, to move as one to the music.

I look into his eyes. They're golden and clear in his deeply tanned face. I see that hunger burning in them—that expression when Leo sees something he wants desperately. When there's a prize he'll give anything to win.

My heart is swollen and hot in my chest. My cheeks are burning. I'm battling the tears.

Leo swallows hard, making his throat contract. His lips part, and I'm both terrified to hear what he's about to say and wildly anticipating it. Everything in the world hangs on this moment.

"I missed you, Anna," he says thickly. "I've missed you so bad."

I blink, and two tears run down my face, searing the skin in parallel tracks.

"All the light went out of my life," I whisper. "I've been so dark without you."

"Really?" Leo says, and his voice cracks.

I nod, dropping the tears to the ground.

Leo hugs me hard against his chest. I smell his scent—the thing I love most in the world. I don't want to go one day without it.

Then someone shoves us hard, breaking us apart.

Dean snarls, "Get your fucking hands off my girlfriend."

CHAPTER 25
LEO

Dean faces me, fists already raised, Bram and Valon Hoxha right behind him.

Dean never turns red when he gets angry. His skin blanches paler than ever and becomes as stiff as a mask. The only light in his face is the glint of his incisors as his upper lip draws up in a snarl.

"I'm not your girlfriend," Anna says, furious.

Dean ignores her completely. His eyes are fixed on me and me alone.

So I say it again, to be sure he heard it.

"Anna doesn't belong to you."

"The fuck she doesn't," Dean hisses. "If you so much as look at her, I'll cut your fucking throat."

"Leo..." Anna says warningly.

She's probably worried that Dean's out of his mind, because he certainly looks crazy enough to try to kill me. Or she might be concerned that it's three against one. Until Ares materializes beside me, silent but staring at the Penose in a way that makes it very clear that he'll back me up whatever happens.

"It's okay, Anna." I give her a reassuring look.

Apparently Dean was serious about me keeping my eyes to myself, because that's all it takes. He charges at me, fists up in his boxer's stance. I barely have time to get my own hands up before he sends a flurry of punches directly at my face.

I'm not in the best condition for a fight. Those paintballs were no fucking joke. My head was already throbbing before Dean clocks me with a hard right cross, rattling my brain in my skull.

Vaguely, I'm aware that Bram and Valon have likewise charged at Ares, and the three of them are rolling around on the floor kicking and punching each other. But I can't pay any attention to that, because Dean is still attacking full throttle. He's no easy opponent even when I'm in peak condition.

He slams his fist into my ribs, ribs that might already be fractured from half a dozen paintballs. The yell that comes out of me is strangled and hoarse.

Exchanging blows with Dean while he's fresh and I'm beat is a bad idea. I've got to follow Ares's example and take this motherfucker down to the ground.

Diving under Dean's next blow, I drive my shoulder into his chest and knock him backward. He goes down hard, all my weight on top of him. He tries to roll out of it, but I've already seized the front of his shirt, and I use that to hold him in place while I pummel him with my right fist. I've got the longer reach, and I hit him three or four times hard in the face while his punches can only barely make contact.

Valon gets free of Ares and punches me hard in the left ear, knocking me off Dean.

Furiously, Anna knees Valon right in the face, but she's grabbed around the waist by another Penose who drags her backward out of the fight.

At this point, it's an all-out brawl. The mood of celebration has splintered into a dozen different fistfights, mostly between Dean's Penose and Bratva and some of my closer friends, including Kenzo and Hedeon.

I can't see Anna. While I'm distracted looking for her, Dean hits me with a left hook that sends blinding flashes of light across my vision. I hit him back in the nose and jaw, and soon we're rolling around again, kneeing, hitting, and elbowing every inch of each other we can reach. Our blood patters down on the bare boards, some from Dean but more from me.

Dean tries to stick his thumb in my eye, and I boot him off me with a heel to the chest. We both scramble upright again, Dean bleeding heavily from his nose and me leaning hard to the side because my ribs are a flaming ball of agony.

We're about to rush each other again when I hear Anna screaming, "Stop! Please stop!"

Dean and I stare at each other, breathing hard, our blood dripping down.

I don't want to stop. I want to fucking kill him.

But I'll do anything for Anna.

"Alright." I hold up my hands. "I'll stop."

I turn to look at her.

That's when Dean's fist comes crashing down on my jaw.

CHAPTER 26
DEAN

Anna screams for us to stop fighting, and Leo holds up his hands, signaling his willingness to stop.

He doesn't get to decide when we stop.

This isn't over until I say so.

Leo looks over at Anna, looks at *my* fucking Anna, after I just fucking warned him. I pull my fist back and sucker punch him from the side, the hardest punch of my life, with every ounce of my fury and bitterness behind it.

The lights go out as soon as I make contact. That was too much for him in one day. His knees buckle, and he keels over. He would have crashed all the way down if not for Hedeon Gray catching him from the side, stumbling back under Leo's deadweight.

I only have a second to enjoy it before Anna slaps me hard across the face. And I mean really fucking hard—it makes my ears ring and my eyes water. I have to blink to make her pale and furious face swim back into view.

"*You asshole*," she seethes.

Anna is burning with fury. I can almost see the sparks of outrage popping off her skin.

And I feel exactly the same. Why doesn't she see that she and I are the same at our core? I know she has the same capacity for obsession, extremism, violence that lives inside me. If we were to combine our strengths, we'd be unstoppable.

But she insists on turning back to Leo Gallo again and again.

What will it take to show her that I'm the better man?

"I am an asshole," I tell her. "A brute. A killer. I do what it takes to win the fight. And I won't ever stop fighting for you."

I look at Leo, supported by Hedeon Gray.

"He's soft," I sneer. "And he has betrayal in his blood. You deserve better."

I walk away from her, Bram and Valon in my wake.

Bram is chortling as we exit the stables. "That fucking idiot. Didn't see that coming!"

For me, the elation of hitting Leo was short-lived. Already I'm swirling with bitterness again, the image of Anna dancing with Leo burned in my brain. The way she looked up into his eyes. The expression on her face that I've never seen when she's looking at me, not one time.

Leo got knocked out because he was distracted by her. Because he listened to her when she asked him to stop.

That's how you make a fool of yourself. That's how you make mistakes that can get you killed—by allowing a woman to twist your judgment. To make you weak.

I've already made a fool of myself over Anna. I know Bram and the Penose think so. It's eroding my authority. They still answer to me, but they don't respect my fixation on Anna.

They expect me to control my woman. Even if she is an Heir herself.

I certainly can't lose her to another man.

Most of all not to Leo fucking Gallo.

What is it going to take to beat him?

He's the thorn in my side. The arsenic that's poisoning everything I want to taste.

The root of all evil in my life comes down to the Gallos.

If Sebastian Gallo hadn't murdered my grandfather, then I would have grown up in Chicago instead of Moscow.

If he hadn't burned and mutilated my father, then my mother never would have left.

And if my aunt had never betrayed our family and married the enemy, then Leo Gallo wouldn't even exist.

It would be *my* father who was best friends and allies with Mikolaj Wilk. It would be Anna and me who grew up side by side. We might have had a marriage pact by the time we were teens. We would have come to Kingmakers already betrothed.

Anna and I were meant to be together. It was only a diversion of fate that split us apart.

I can see this clearly. Why can't she?

Because of Leo, that's why. He's blinded her. Confused her. Seduced her away from me.

The only way to right the wrongs of the past is to set things back the way they should have been.

Leo Gallo shouldn't exist.

Bram is ruminating on his own irritations. "Who the fuck does that Greek peasant think he is, taking a swing at me?"

It looks like Ares took more than a swing. Bram's nose isn't nearly as straight as it was before, and he's got the start of a hell of a black eye. Valon doesn't look any better.

"I guess I needed three of you to handle him," I snarl.

"He's a fuckin' ogre," Valon complains.

"And what are you? A debutante?"

Bram and Valon both glare at me.

I don't give a fuck. They need a reminder of their own shortcomings. It infuriates me that Leo's friends are better than mine at fighting. Why in the *fuck* does he have everything, while all I have is shit?

"He's not winning the last challenge," Bram says, having apparently decided that his hatred of Leo and Ares outweighs his desire to be freshman champions.

Quietly, I say, "He's not surviving the last challenge."

Now the look that Bram and Valon exchange is distinctly uncomfortable.

Valon says, "What do you mean?"

"I mean I'm going to kill him."

A long silence stretches out in which we can only hear our feet treading on the sodden grass and the rain still falling down all around us. The courtyard is dark and empty, the rain insulating us from the possibility of being overheard by anyone else. I wouldn't even say this out loud, except to my two closest allies.

"You're doing it here?" Bram says. "At Kingmakers?"

I answer with a nod.

"What about sanctuary?" Valon asks. "What about the rule of recompense?"

He means that if we're caught, we'll be executed ourselves.

I say, "There's no recompense unless we get caught."

I can tell Valon doesn't like this idea at all, but he's no rebel. He may be an Heir by title, but he's a soldier by nature. He'll do whatever Bram and I tell him to do.

Bram considers the idea for a moment. I see him accept it, anticipate it even, his mouth twisting up in a smirk.

He says, "Accidents happen all the time. Especially in the Quartum Bellum."

"Exactly." I nod. "That's exactly right."

CHAPTER 27
ANNA

HEDEON GRAY AND ARES HELP ME CARRY LEO TO THE INFIRMARY. Leo's a fucking mess, and not just because of Dean. I'm pretty sure he had a hefty concussion going already before he even got in that fight. Now he's coming to in fits and starts, mumbling things that don't make any sense.

Even though we're soaked in rain crossing the courtyard, Leo's skin is burning.

The infirmary is located in a long, squat building that used to be used as a slaughterhouse for all the poultry, pigs, and cattle that provided meat for the castle. It's hard to know if the lingering scent of iron in the air is from those long-dead creatures or from all the students who have shed blood on the floorboards since then.

We hammer on the door, waking up Dr. Cross, who has his offices and apartments at the back of the building. Even after I see his light flick on, it still takes him a long time to pull the door open because he's about a hundred years old.

Finally, he cracks the door, peering up at us through his inch-thick glasses, wrapped up in a paisley dressing gown with his feet in gardening clogs.

"Why must you students always get yourselves in trouble at such inconvenient hours?" he says by way of a greeting.

"Sorry," Hedeon says. "Leo got pretty beat up in the

challenge earlier. And then...he fell down the stairs and hit his head again."

Hedeon isn't dissembling for Dean's benefit. While Dean would be in trouble for injuring Leo, Leo would be punished for fighting too. There's an unspoken agreement among students that fights are covered up at all costs, as long as both students remain alive.

Dr. Cross just rolls his eyes, opening the door wider to let us inside. He's heard too many feeble excuses to bother even pretending to believe ours. The truth is glaringly obvious, since both Ares and Hedeon likewise show clear signs of a fight—Ares with blood in his teeth and Hedeon with a deep tear in the neck of his shirt that shows the tattoo on his chest.

"Bring him in," Dr. Cross croaks, shuffling across the uneven floor.

Ares and Hedeon haul Leo inside. Because the roof is so low, Ares knocks his head against the overhead lamp, sending it swinging so the shadows in the room veer wildly from side to side.

"Careful!" Dr. Cross says. "I don't need any more patients at the moment."

He shows Ares and Hedeon the cot where he wants Leo placed.

Hedeon throws Leo down hard enough that Leo lets out a groan.

"Watch it!" I say.

"He's not exactly light!" Hedeon retorts. He has come a long way in improving his temperament this year, but he's still sulky and quick to anger.

Swallowing my irritation, I say instead, "Thank you for carrying him. You guys can go if you want. I'll stay with him."

"Don't mind if I do." Hedeon smooths back his rain-soaked hair. "There was a pretty little Accountant eyeing me. She probably ran away during the brawl, but if not..."

Ares looks like he's going to offer to stay, but then he glances between me and Leo and thinks better of it.

"I'll head off to bed," he says. "See you at breakfast."

The two boys file out, leaving me alone with Dr. Cross and Leo.

"Where's everybody else?" I ask.

I saw plenty of injured students hobbling over here after the challenge.

"Patched 'em up and sent 'em off," Dr. Cross says grumpily. "That's why I'm tired—only finished with the last of them an hour or two ago. I was just settling down to sleep when you so rudely interrupted me."

"Sorry," I say humbly.

Dr. Cross is checking Leo over for broken bones and particularly nasty scrapes and bruises. He presses Leo's right side, causing Leo to wince and groan and mumble something incoherent.

"Those are broken," Dr. Cross says matter-of-factly. "And this needs to be stitched." He points to an ugly gash on Leo's forehead.

Gathering the necessary supplies, he washes his hands carefully at the industrial sink, then rolls over a steel trolley bearing antiseptic, bandages, ointment, nylon thread, and a wicked-looking curved needle.

Watching Dr. Cross attempt to thread that needle is one of the most nerve-racking experiences of my life. His hands are shaking so badly that I can't see how he's ever going to get the thread through the near-invisible hole, let alone how he'll stitch up Leo's flesh. But after three attempts, he manages to line up the needle and pull the thread through.

He mops Leo's cut with iodine, then without bothering to anesthetize the wound in any way he jabs the needle right through, pulling together the edges of the torn skin.

That wakes Leo up real quick.

"Ow, Jesus!" he cries, jolting awake.

"Hold him down so he doesn't squirm around," Dr. Cross says dispassionately.

Gently, I push Leo back down against the pillows, saying, "Hold still. This will only take a minute."

It takes a lot more than a minute, because Dr. Cross is painfully slow, but I'll admit that the stitches are surprisingly even when he's done, and the cut looks clean and closed.

"Why'd you bring me in here?" Leo murmurs to me.

"Because you were a damn mess," Dr. Cross says before I can respond. "Those ribs are broken, boy, which I can't do anything about, so you just behave yourself for the next six weeks and don't be falling down any more stairs."

Leo smiles at Dr. Cross's unimpressed tone. "She pushed me, Doc," he says.

"If she did, I'm sure you deserved it." Dr. Cross snips the end of the thread and sets down his needle. "Now, you can sleep here tonight. Just you, boy, not the girl. I'll check on you in the morning. But you, young lady, tell the rest of the hooligans that I'm taking out my hearing aid and going to bed, so I don't plan to respond to any more banging on the door."

"Right," I say. "No problem."

While Dr. Cross is cleaning up his tray and washing his hands once more at the sink, I take the opportunity to squeeze in a few more words with Leo before I'm kicked out.

"Are you really okay?" I ask him, taking his hand and searching his eyes for the lingering effects of concussion.

In reply, Leo seizes me behind the neck and pulls me in to him, kissing me hard.

His lips are swollen and split, and I can taste blood in his mouth.

But I also taste Leo—that sweet, warm breath that I've felt on my face a hundred times when we laughed and talked with our heads close together.

He's warm, so incredibly warm, despite the rain and the chilly night. His lips are soft and full yet firm and strong against mine. It's been a long time since his morning shave; the hint of stubble on his upper lip rasps over my skin in delicious contrast to his tongue, which slips into my mouth, massaging my own.

I'm kissing my best friend. After all this time, I finally know what it feels like to kiss Leo.

It feels shocking and enlivening and absolutely fucking wonderful.

It feels like two puzzle pieces clicking together. It feels like finally remembering something I forgot. It feels like coming home.

For all the times I imagined it, this is better.

This is exactly right.

Leo releases me, only enough that I can look into his eyes from a few inches apart.

Smiling at me, he says, "I've never felt better in my life."

Dr. Cross clears his throat, wanting me to leave so he can get back to sleep.

"I'll come back in the morning," I promise Leo.

"You better," he says.

I leave the infirmary with my heart soaring.

My senses are heightened to a fever pitch. I can feel every single raindrop bursting on my skin. It's cool and effervescent, like I'm swimming through soda. The grass smells fresh and alive, and even the limestone walls of the castle seem to give off the scent of the ancient ocean in which they were formed.

I can still taste Leo on my lips. I can still feel his strong, warm fingers gripping the back of my neck.

I'm floating weightlessly over the ground. If I were to go to the cathedral to dance right now, I think I could give the best performance of my life. I think I could literally fly.

Without thinking, I turn in that direction, crossing the dark campus mostly by memory.

I force open the heavy double doors, stepping into the space that I haven't visited in weeks because I've been too heavy and depressed.

It's pitch-black in here. I find the candles I left stowed in the old altar and fumble with the matches that have grown damp from the humidity and the rain. The first two matches break, but the third sparks alight, and I light a half dozen of the uneven and heavily melted pillar candles I stole from the keep.

I set the candles all around the nave and then strip off my sodden camisole and pants so I'm only wearing my underwear. It doesn't matter. There's no one to see me.

I have no speaker, but I don't care about that either. I can clearly hear the music playing in my head: "Love Chained," the song that I know so well that it plays in my dreams.

The moment I start to dance, I feel that lightness again, that sense of lifting, floating, soaring across the stone. My brain and body separate, so I can almost watch myself dancing, whirling, spinning, dipping, while my mind is free to float around the cavernous space, untethered from the earth.

I missed this almost as much as I missed Leo.

I understand now that they're connected. Dancing is my way to connect with my deepest thoughts and emotions, and most of those center around Leo. When I was trying to deny my feelings for him, I couldn't dance at all.

Even this song...my favorite song...it was always about him.

I'm chained to Leo. I am and I always have been. We've been bound together since birth. Even when we die, the atoms of him and the atoms of me will find each other.

I dance until sweat runs down my skin like the raindrops sliding down the stained-glass windows overhead.

Then I sink down on the floor of the church, listening to my heart beat in the echoing silence.

The candles have burned down to stubs, the flames drowning in the last pools of melted wax. It must be two or three o'clock in the morning—the witching hour. The time when almost everyone in the castle will be asleep.

Leo will certainly be asleep in his infirmary cot, his body trying to heal after the repeated damage it took today.

I can almost see his face glowing in the candlelight before me. I want to see it in person, even if only for a moment. I want it immediately and intensely.

Snatching up my soggy clothes, I slip out of the cathedral once more.

Every window in the castle is dark, not a single sound to be heard over the relentless rain.

Oh—actually, that's not true. There is one light burning high up in the attic of the library tower. Up in Ms. Robin's room. She must be reading, unable to sleep.

Her light feels friendly to me, as if she lit it just to help me find my way across the dark grounds.

It's a long way back to the infirmary past the dovecote, the bakehouse, the stables, and the old wine cellar.

As I'm nearing the dining hall, I see something strange: Hedeon Gray descending down into the undercroft where the Spies have their dorms. I'm sure it's him, because he's wearing the same shirt that was torn in the fight.

Why is Hedeon going down there?

He said he was meeting a girl, but the girl was an Accountant.

His brother doesn't live down there either. Silas is an Enforcer, with his rooms in the gatehouse.

Could Hedeon have made plans with a different girl instead?

I've reached the infirmary, so all thoughts of Hedeon exit my mind.

I'm longing to go inside, but I hesitate outside the door. I'm not worried about waking Dr. Cross—we had to pound on the door for ages to get him out of bed the first time. It's Leo I'm thinking of. I shouldn't wake him; he needs his sleep. Still, I want to see him so badly.

Pulling a pin out of my braid, I slip it into the lock and work the heavy old tumblers until I hear them click into place. Then I push the door open, wincing at the creaking hinges.

As soon as I step through the door, I can smell the warm scent of Leo's skin and hear his heavy breathing.

I creep across the floor, feeling that same sense of heady anticipation I used to feel on Christmas morning running down to the tree.

There he is—passed out on his side, his broad frame stretching the limits of the thin infirmary blanket, his feet almost hanging off the edge of the cot, his dark curls messy on the pillow.

As I draw closer, I only intend to look at Leo, not to touch him or risk waking him up. But as I come around the side of the cot to look at his face, I see the gleam of his eyes looking up at me and the white glint of his teeth as he smiles.

His voice husky with sleep, he says, "Took you long enough. I've been waiting."

I laugh quietly. "You didn't know I was going to come back. I didn't even know."

Leo says, "I know you better than you know yourself."

There's no teasing in his voice now. He means that. And he's right.

"Get in this bed," he growls.

"I'm all wet and cold."

"I don't give a fuck." He lifts the blanket, showing me the perfect little hollow of warmth underneath, the space he's been saving for me.

I strip off my wet clothes once more, dropping them on the floor. Then I slide into the softest, most welcoming space I've ever encountered, with Leo's broad chest up against my back and his long, powerful thighs cradling my legs. Leo wraps his arms around me and pulls me tight against him, his face pressed up against my neck.

"Mmm," he sighs. "That's what I need."

A wave of warmth and sleepiness rolls over me. Sleep never comes easy to me—it's a battle every night. But I could sink down into oblivion right now, into the deepest and most comfortable rest of my life.

Except that I can feel Leo nuzzling his face against my neck and hear him taking deep, full inhales of my scent. He's breathing me in.

As he does so, I can feel something hard pressing against my lower back. His cock is stiffening and swelling with every breath.

I arch my back just a little, pressing my ass back against him, testing to see if that's really what I'm feeling. Leo lets out a low growl, deep and thrumming, and his cock gets twice as hard, like an iron bar between us.

All my sleepiness burns away in an instant. My blood rushes through my veins as Leo turns me over roughly so we're facing each other, his cock pressing against my belly now.

We're face-to-face, looking into each other's eyes. Slowly, Leo runs his tongue over my lips, tasting me. Then he kisses me, fully and deeply. I've never kissed someone like this, our mouths wide open, our tongues delving deep, our breath mixing together. I feel like I'm melting into him and he's melting into me. I've never felt so connected to another human, as if we were becoming one person.

I know Leo so well that I can feel what he's feeling. I know what he's thinking. I feel like I'm becoming him and he's becoming me, that even our consciousness is blending.

It's surreal and almost spiritual. Fuck it, it *is* spiritual—the most enlightened experience of my life. This is nirvana. This is soaring above the earthly plane. This is the epitome of human existence—two souls combining as one.

And that's just from a kiss.

It goes on for a long, long time. The better part of an hour. Until my lips are just as swollen as Leo's and more sensitive than they've ever been, all the input of my body focused on lips, tongue, mouth, and my hands fiercely gripping Leo's face.

At last we break apart, just an inch or two apart. Leo is looking into my eyes. All the confusion, the resentment, and the misunderstandings between us have burned away. I've let go of all of it. I don't blame him for anything. I see him, all of him—a person who is young and growing, who makes mistakes but who is the best human I know, who can't do anything but get better every single day.

I hope he sees the same in me. Because I'll do anything to make Leo happy.

"I'm sorry," he says.

"I'm more sorry," I tell him. "But it doesn't matter. You don't have to be perfect to be the perfect person for me."

"But I did fuck up, Anna. I want you to know I never cared about any other girl. Not Gemma, not anybody. I've only ever felt this way about you."

"I know," I say. "It's the same for me."

"And I don't care that you slept with Dean. It doesn't matter—"

"I didn't," I say immediately, interrupting him. "I never slept with Dean. We never actually...you know. Went all the way."

"It's okay if you did," Leo says. "I don't care."

He thinks I'm trying to spare his feelings.

"I didn't," I tell him firmly. "We got close one time, but I couldn't do it. I was thinking about you."

Leo is quiet for a moment. A long moment. Then he says, "That's what happened to me."

I look at him, at his still and sober expression that I can barely see in the dark infirmary.

"What do you mean?"

"Any time I was about to do it...I just...couldn't."

Now I'm the one frowning in confusion, not understanding him.

"Leo, are you trying to tell me you're a virgin?"

There's an embarrassed pause, and then he says softly, "Yes."

I almost want to laugh. That seems impossible, ridiculous even. But I would never laugh at him when I can tell he's feeling so distinctly uncomfortable.

"How is that possible?" I think of the endless parade of girls who threw themselves at Leo in high school.

"I mean, I fooled around a lot. But when it came time to actually do the deed, it just never felt right. It never felt like the right girl.

I didn't want to think about it. I never admitted to myself that the right girl…had to be you."

I think if I could see Leo clearly, he might actually be blushing for the one and only time in his life.

"I felt the same," I say quietly. "I'm a virgin too."

"Yeah?" Leo says, and now I hear something else in his voice: deep relief.

It hits me at the exact same moment.

I'm about to have something I never thought I could have.

Leo and I are about to experience sex for the first time together.

CHAPTER 28
LEO

I can't believe Anna's a virgin too.

I really can't believe it.

My heart is hammering against my chest, and I'm trying not to squeeze her too hard in my arms.

I never even let myself picture this scenario.

But now that it's happening, it seems like it could never have worked any other way.

Fate has orchestrated every confusion, every hesitation, every failed relationship that came before so that Anna and I could experience this precise moment, coming together when we were finally and fully ready.

Anna is lying in my arms, dressed in her damp bra and panties. We're completely alone in the infirmary, Dr. Cross too old and too far away to hear us, and every other person on campus fast asleep.

There's nothing to stop me taking her right here and now. Nothing except my own fear of fucking this up.

I've never been so scared in my life.

I know what I need to do, but I've never actually done it. Of course I know how sex works. I've seen plenty of porn. But that's not the same thing as experience.

It's Anna's first time too. This has to be perfect for her. I don't want to fuck it up. I don't want to let her down.

She feels the pressure of the moment just as much as I do—I can feel her pulse jumping wildly under my fingertips where my hand caresses the side of her throat.

Wanting to help her relax, I slide my hand down and start to knead the tense muscles where her neck meets her shoulders. As I feel the stiffness ebbing away, I move my hands down farther, massaging her shoulder caps and pressing my thumbs into the tight muscle just above her breasts.

I know she must be aching from all the running, fighting, and shooting earlier in the day. Sure enough, she can't resist my touch. She goes limp and docile in my arms, like a rabbit turned on its back.

The thought of Anna helpless in my arms is strangely erotic. Anna is fierce and stubborn. She's never helpless. But I'm suddenly aware that as strong as she is, I'm much stronger.

This is what it means to overpower a woman—it means that when you touch her the right way, she literally falls under your control. Her body is putty in your hands.

Reaching around behind her back, I unclasp her bra and pull it free, dropping it down on the floor. I curse how dark it is in the infirmary because I want to see her naked. Only a faint bluish light emanates from the digital clock on the wall. It's just enough to see the silvery glow of Anna's skin and the firm, full swells of her perfectly sculpted breasts.

I can see her nipples standing out, slightly upturned and aching to be touched.

Gently, I run my hand over her breast, feeling the butter-soft expanse of her skin with the single hard point of her nipple dragging across the center of my palm. Anna groans, arching her back to press her breast harder against my hand. I cup her breast and then slide my fingers down to caress and tug on the nipple itself, seeing how much stiffer it can get.

That obvious sign of arousal acts like an electric shock to my cock. It jumps up, jabbing against Anna's hipbone.

I wrap my arms around her whole body, crushing her against my chest so my cock can press hard against her, so I can feel how small she is compared to me.

I growl in her ear, "I told myself if I ever got you back, I would never let you go."

I squeeze her tight to let her know that I'm strong, that I'll protect her, and that I'll never let go of her.

I squeeze until I feel her relax against me, giving in to the embrace because she can't do anything else.

"I'm yours, Leo," she whispers. "I've always been yours."

She's giving herself to me. Every part of her. Even the parts that have long been the most secret and forbidden.

With that pervasive sense of taboo still hanging over me, I reach down her flat belly, sliding my hand under the waistband of her thong to touch the achingly soft skin of her pussy. How many times did I watch Anna dancing in a leotard and the thought crept into my mind to wonder how tight and perfectly shaped that little pussy must be beneath, covered by only the thinnest and smallest strip of material…

I have never in my life felt skin as soft as her bare pussy lips. My fingers glide over the surface like satin. I reach a little lower, down the narrow cleft between her lips, until I find the wetness around her entrance. I dip my fingertip inside, using the lubrication to slide my fingers up and down her pussy.

I lift my finger to my lips, tasting her wetness. I've never tasted a girl before. I've gotten plenty of blow jobs, but I never reciprocated on anyone. I never wanted to.

This is completely different.

I don't just *want* to eat Anna out. I *need* to do it.

I need it more than I need to draw my next breath.

I slide down her body, bracing myself on her thighs with my hands. I pull off her underwear, dropping it down on top of her bra.

Her legs open up like a flower, knees pointing out, because Anna is flexible. I love the way it opens up her pussy to me. I can just see the pale pink folds inside, the tiny nub of her clit exposed at the top, and then her opening, which doesn't look open at all. It looks like it wouldn't even accommodate my pinkie finger, which gives me a twinge of concern as to how we are actually going to fit together.

For now, I do what I know I can do. I lick her pussy softly and carefully, running my tongue all the way up her slit at what I hope is the right speed. I'm licking her like you'd lick ice cream—tasting her carefully, trying to reach every last bit of her.

Anna responds at once, moaning and writhing her hips on the sheets. She isn't pulling away from me but rather pressing her clit against the flat of my tongue. I assume she likes that.

Instantly, I get that competitive fire, that desire to perfect my technique. I want to test to see what's most effective. So I start using different strokes with my tongue, different levels of pressure, carefully analyzing the sounds she makes and the way she moves, being sure to only continue what elicits the softest moans and gasps of pleasure and not to do anything that seems too intense or uncomfortable.

Soon Anna's breath becomes a steady pant like she's running. She's whimpering, and I can tell she's ramping up. Gently, I slip one finger inside her. I'm shocked how firm her flesh is inside, how tensely she grips around my finger, like a hand grasping me.

I can't believe how close I am to putting my cock in there. I'm desperate to do it, yet I don't want to rush because I want all this to last forever.

I definitely want to make Anna come before I even put my cock inside her. If I can't control myself, if I blow instantly, I want to make sure she got off first.

Based on how tightly she's squeezing my finger, I have no confidence in my ability to hold back my orgasm.

I've found the right rhythm, gently sliding my finger in and out of her while I lick her at the same tempo. As she pants harder and harder, she seizes me by the hair and holds my head right in place while she grinds her pussy against my tongue, wordlessly telling me to hold my face still while she applies exactly the pressure she needs.

I'm obsessed with the way she smells. I've heard men criticize women's scent—they must be out of their fucking minds. I'm breathing in her scent purposely, and it's as rich and sweet as her sleep-heavy neck. Like the pheromones of skin but at a much wider and deeper amplitude. It's a natural scent, like summer grass in the sunshine.

I'm ferociously eating her pussy, unable to get enough of it.

Anna starts to come, which makes me more excited than I've ever been in my life. Her orgasm is more intensely arousing to me than anything I've experienced myself.

As she shakes and shudders, falling back against the bed, I rise up on my knees, towering over her, looking down on her. I want to see the whole length of her gorgeous nude body.

Of all the parts of her I've seen or imagined, I never could have imagined the perfection of her completely naked form. If it were made into a painting, it would be the most famous art in the world.

I take my cock in my hand. It fills the whole of my hand, throbbing and heavy. Kneeling between Anna's legs, I lean forward and rub the heavy, burning head of my cock against her still-sensitive clit. Anna moans and squirms, barely able to stand it. It feels incredible to have the most sensitive part of me rubbing against the most sensitive part of her.

As I rub her with my cock, I use my free hand to massage her breasts and pull on her nipples. Her nipples look so sexy that I lean over and take one in my mouth, amazed at how soft that skin is too. Every part of her is softer than anything I imagined.

I nuzzle my nose against her neck, kissing her soft throat, inhaling her scent.

"I want to be inside you," I tell her.

"Yes," Anna gasps.

I position myself on top of her, leaning on my elbows, and I shift my hips so that the head of my cock presses against her pussy. I expect her to have loosened up a little now, from my finger and her extreme wetness and the fact that she had an orgasm. But as my cock presses up against her opening, nothing has changed. It barely feels like there's any hole at all, and I'm not quite sure what to do.

Anna is urging me on, holding her legs spread wide, grinding her hips against me to try to help me get inside.

"It won't fit," I say, slightly embarrassed. "Do you want me to push harder?"

"Yes!" she pants.

I shove and thrust, with a guilty sense that this must be hurting her. It's working, though. I feel intense heat and warmth as the head of my cock slides inside her, millimeter by millimeter.

That sensation does something to me. It's far beyond simple arousal. It unleashes a monster inside me. A beast that is single-minded in its lust.

There's no stopping now, no holding back. I'm actually enjoying the feeling of her pussy tearing around my cock. The warmth and wetness increase, and I don't care if it's blood or lubrication.

I bite the side of her neck, and the monster inside me growls, "I'm going to dig a hole in you with my cock. I'm going to sculpt that perfectly tight pussy to fit me alone, and I'm going to tear a path to make it fit."

With that, I give one last thrust all the way inside her so I'm buried up to the hilt, and Anna gives out a cry more like a scream that would certainly wake Dr. Cross if he weren't halfway to the grave.

I slow down just a little—partly to give Anna a breath but mostly because I want to savor this exquisite sensation: my cock gripped tight inside her from the very tip of the head all the way down to the base.

Then I start fucking her again, speeding up the penetration, sliding all the way in and out as my every stroke jolts her body.

As Anna seems to get more comfortable, I rise up on my knees again, holding her legs open wide at the ankles and driving deep inside her. I think of all the times I've seen her stretching and bending on the floor, her legs wide open in the splits, her body bent all the way over. I remember the lust that percolated inside me every fucking time, how impossible it was to keep it buttoned down.

No—I can't think about that. I'm going to blow if I picture pulling her leotard to the side and fucking her. I'm going to blow right now if I don't stop driving into her so deep.

Hastily, I switch positions so I can cut off the urge to come.

I scoop Anna up, sitting her on my lap, lowering her down on my cock like she's sliding down a pole. Even though Anna is on the taller side, she feels tiny and light in my arms. She's so strong that she can support her own weight with her arms around my neck, and I can easily bounce her up and down on my cock with hands under her ass. The control I have over her body, her utter vulnerability, is intensely arousing. I can feel my orgasm building again. I'm barely holding on to it, like a rabid dog about to burst from its leash.

I try rocking her on my lap, my cock no longer sliding in and out but just bumping up against her cervix in shallow thrusts, her clit grinding against my lower belly right above my cock.

She presses her face against my neck and starts inhaling deep breaths like I did to her before. She loves my scent just as I love hers. It makes her ride me harder, like I'm a pony in a race. She goes from canter to gallop on top of me.

Then she shoves me down on the bed, biting and sucking on my neck.

This has a strange effect on me. I was already ninety-seven percent hard, and all of a sudden I'm at a hundred and ten percent. My cock swells beyond where it's ever been before. Bizarrely, this seems to reset my orgasm, just for a moment. But immediately, I can feel it building again, like a brake check followed by increased acceleration.

Anna sits up partway, her palms spread on my pecs, her fingernails digging into my skin. She's still riding me, bucking her hips hard. I never could have imagined how erotic this would actually be, having this gorgeous girl ride me so desperately. I feel like a fucking billionaire with a girl like this wanting me so bad, taking pleasure from my cock.

I've hit buzzer beaters in an arena full of people, but I've never felt a rush like this. Anna's animalistic attraction to me is better than any win, any triumph, any high.

Anna is feline, and my pheromones are catnip. She's going wild, biting and scratching my chest.

We have years of built-up frustration between us, sexual tension we couldn't even acknowledge, let alone dispel. The harder we fuck each other, the more we give and receive these bites and scratches, the more catharsis we feel.

We're fucking out all our hurt and frustration, all the time of waiting, all the agony of being apart. We were pent up beyond endurance.

Every time Anna starts to slow down a little, she leans over and inhales the scent of my skin and attacks me all over again, wilder than before.

My cock is throbbing and throbbing. I can't believe I haven't come yet. Only my body's confusion is holding it back, not any kind of willpower I could possibly muster.

She's biting and sucking my neck, lightly licking my earlobes.

Oh my fucking god, I've never felt that before. Of all the things she's done, it's the fucking ears that tip me over. I'm not going to be able to hold it anymore. I'm gonna fucking explode.

I grab her by the hips, my fingers digging into her ass. I pull her close so her bare chest is tight against mine.

Without meaning to, I groan, "I only ever want to come inside you."

And then I completely let go.

It's like I've been hanging on to the edge of a cliff for hours.

That orgasm is the most instant, perfect release, the throbbing pain of holding back instantly washed over with the intense relief of letting go.

It's a massive pheromone release. Chemicals flood through my brain and then through my whole body, emanating off my skin. They hit Anna like a wave, and her entire body vibrates like a music note. She starts to come again, shaking and thrumming on top of me, our bodies trembling along every last neuron.

The feel of her pussy clenching and pulsing around my cock while I shoot spurt after spurt of cum inside her is the purest form of bliss.

Nothing can match this moment. Nothing ever will.

CHAPTER 29
DEAN

THE LAST TWO MONTHS AT KINGMAKERS ARE A LIVING NIGHTMARE.

Every day, I watch Leo and Anna fall more and more in love.

They go everywhere together, side by side, hand in hand. The whole school could be crumbling down around them and they wouldn't notice. They only have eyes for each other.

Anna doesn't feel when I'm watching her anymore, even when I'm staring at her. She's lost all sense of anything that isn't Leo.

And Leo himself is even more insufferable. I hear his laughter echoing across campus, his stupid jokes and the sycophantic response of the friends that cluster around him.

My hatred for him is a living thing that I feed every day.

Every day, it grows stronger and more powerful.

I don't really believe that I can get Anna back. I never really had her to begin with. But there's one thing I'm determined to do: cut the fucking cancer that is Leo Gallo out of my life.

My grandfather deserves his revenge. So does my father.

Three weeks before the end of term, I call my father on the phone, using the bank of student phones that are only accessible on Saturdays and Sundays.

The phone rings and rings for a long time without an answer. He could be meeting with the *pakhan*. The Bratva certainly don't respect the Sabbath. Or he could simply be holed up in his room, refusing to answer.

Just as I'm about to hang up the receiver, I hear him rasp, "What is it?"

"Hello, Father."

"Dmitry."

A shiver runs over my skin.

That's what he always called me. When I came to Kingmakers, I used the name my mother gave me. Perhaps that was a mistake.

"To what do I owe the pleasure?" my father says.

I need a reason to call him. There's no such thing as a "chat" between us, no such thing as "checking in." Certainly not "missing you" or "wanting to hear your voice." Those are ridiculous Western concepts.

My father is still waiting on the other end of the line.

I take a deep breath and ask him, "What matters more? Honor or revenge?"

There's a long silence in which I can only hear my father's breath, which has a hollow, echoing tone. He was an athlete once—a swimmer, a polo player, a runner. Now he gets winded on the stairs.

At last, he says, "There is no honor. And there is no revenge."

I grip the receiver tight in my hand, pressing it against my ear as if that will force him to explain, to give me some sense of direction.

"What, then?" I say desperately. "What am I supposed to be doing?"

Another long silence, and then a sound that I can't quite believe.

Is my father actually laughing?

His strange, breathy chuckle turns into a cough. "Do you think *I* know, Dmitry?" he says with deep disdain.

I slam the receiver back down, my face burning.

Fuck my father. He's weak, I've always known that. Weak, broken, and lost.

I won't be like him.

I won't look to him any longer.

Only my grandfather had the right idea. What would he do if he were here?

He would do whatever it took to achieve his goal. No matter the risk, no matter the cost.

I can't plan anything until I know what we'll be facing in the third challenge. It's a secret, of course—none of us are supposed to know ahead of time. No one is supposed to have an advantage.

But I can assume that Professor Howell will be organizing it, as he did with the first two challenges.

So for the final weeks of the term, Valon, Bram, and I shadow Professor Howell everywhere he goes. We watch and we wait.

Finally, three days before the competition, I see him begin to make preparations. I follow him as he leaves campus, scouting out locations. And then I trail him again as he goes down below the armory and begins to fill the scuba tanks.

CHAPTER 30
ANNA

DATING LEO IS AS EASY AS SLIPPING INTO A WARM BATH.

I wondered if it would feel strange holding hands with him, kissing him, being openly romantic with him. Instead, it's the most natural thing in the world.

Even Miles doesn't seem to find it odd.

The first time he sees us holding hands, he just rolls his eyes and says, "Fucking finally. Are you both gonna stop tragically moping like somebody died?"

"You don't think it's weird?" I ask him nervously.

"Hate to break it to you," Miles says, "but you two ain't subtle. You've had a real *Sweet Home Alabama* vibe since you were about twelve."

"Why didn't you ever say anything, then?" Leo demands.

"'Cause of my finely honed sense of delicacy," Miles says. "Also I don't give a shit. Fuck each other or don't. Just stop sulking about it."

"That makes me feel a little better," I say. If Miles thought it was gross, he definitely wouldn't hold back in saying so. He's about as delicate as a stampeding bison.

"So you think everyone will be cool about it?" Leo says. "We haven't told our parents yet."

"Oh, hell no," Miles says. "Papa Miko isn't gonna be cool about this at all. He's gonna fuckin' murder you, Leo. I thought that was obvious."

"Really?" Leo looks slightly green.

"Oh yeah. Like, slowly and painfully. We're gonna find little pieces of you all over Chicago. So definitely enjoy your last week at school. It's probably all you've got left."

I can tell Leo's life is flashing before his eyes. He's staring at Miles blankly, not laughing at all.

I grab his shoulder and shake it. "He's joking, Leo."

"I'm not joking."

"Miles—"

"Totally serious."

"Cut it out."

"That's what Papa Miko's gonna say. Talking about your liver, Leo."

I punch Miles hard on the arm.

He just laughs and saunters off, calling back over his shoulder, "I want your Jeep, Leo! Leave it to me in your will!"

I look up at Leo, whose eyes are taking up half his face.

"He's joking, baby. My dad loves you."

"He *did* love me. Before I deflowered his daughter."

"I deflowered you right back. You think Uncle Seb is gonna be mad at me?"

"No, he's in too good a mood to be angry about anything."

"Why?" I say.

"Oh, I forgot I haven't told you this," Leo says, his face lighting up.

"What?"

"No, it's too good. I can't say."

He's as gleeful as a kid in a candy store now. There's nothing Leo loves more than teasing me on the rare occasions when he knows something that I don't.

"Spill it."

"What'll you give me if I do?"

I bite my lip, trying not to laugh. "I don't negotiate with terrorists."

"What about a barter?"

I glance around. We were walking to our chemistry class, and we've just climbed up to the third level of the keep. There are plenty of empty classrooms on this floor.

"Alright," I say. "I'll make it worth your while. Now tell me, before I make use of all those handy torture techniques we've been learning."

"My mom's pregnant."

I stare at him, mouth open. "Get the fuck outta town."

"It's true. They told me back in January, but I was…you know. Kinda depressed."

I hesitate, knowing this is a big upheaval for Leo. One that I wasn't always sure he'd actually enjoy.

"Are you…excited?"

"I really am," Leo says. I can see the truth of it in his face. "My mom always wanted another kid. Maybe if she'd had one sooner, I wouldn't be such a spoiled shit." He laughs. Then more seriously, he adds, "She deserves this. And I'm excited too. I'd love a little brother or sister."

"That's incredible!"

"Yeah, it is," Leo says. Then grabbing my hand and pulling me into the currently deserted classroom belonging to Professor Holland, he growls, "Now pay up."

"We're gonna be late for chemistry."

"I don't give a fuck."

He pushes me up against the chalkboard, not caring if we get chalk all over the backs of our uniforms. He kisses me ferociously, his fingers already unbuttoning the front of my shirt.

The whole length of his oversize body is pressing against me, crushing me into the wall. I love how huge Leo is because it makes me feel small by comparison.

What is it about sex that banishes all feminism from my brain?

In real life, I like to be strong and capable. But as soon as I'm turned on, I want to be lifted up, flipped over, and fucked by a man much bigger than me.

Well...one particular man, at least.

I drop down on my knees in front of Leo. I love how gigantic he looks when I'm in this position. His shoulders are a mile wide, impossibly high above me. And his cock...it already looks enormous, bulging out against the fly of his trousers.

I unzip his pants, letting his cock fall into my palm with a heavy *thunk.*

Leo's cock is fucking beautiful. I mean, I don't have a lot to compare it with, but it's as smooth and brown and healthy-looking as the rest of him, thick with veins like his forearms. The head looks heavy and powerful.

It's completely masculine, until I run my tongue up the shaft to the velvet-soft head. And then I taste that skin more delicate than any other place on his body.

The head of his cock fills my mouth, lying heavily against my tongue. I can feel it throbbing, several degrees warmer than his body.

Kneeling is a subservient position, but the power I have over Leo when his cock is in my mouth is incomparable. I can make him groan and shake. I can make him beg me to keep going. And I can make him explode any time I want.

I like to lick and suck until he's right on the point of orgasm, then pull back, moving down to his balls to tug and tease, then bobbing my head on his cock once more to build up his climax all over again.

It's a game of submission and control, giving and taking. I could do this for hours, except that the classroom door isn't locked and I know someone could walk in on us at any moment.

Plus Leo has no patience today. He's hungry for me, ravenous even.

I'd planned to take him all the way to climax, but he isn't having it. After only a minute or two of sucking his cock, he pulls me to my feet and bends me over the teacher's desk. He yanks my skirt up around my waist and pulls my panties to the side.

Then he thrusts his cock, still wet with my saliva, into my aching, throbbing pussy.

It makes me so wet sucking him off. It's almost more arousing going down on him than when he goes down on me. I'm more than ready to be fucked, and the feeling of that thick, hard cock driving into me is instantly and intensely satisfying.

Each thrust slams my thighs into the desk. I'll probably have bruises across the tops of my thighs tomorrow, but I don't give a fuck. I've gotten plenty of sex-related bruises in the last couple of weeks, and every single one of them has been more than worth it.

Everything I do with Leo seems to lead to sex. When we spar in combat class, I have to fuck him after. When we're laughing and teasing each other, there's this extra edge of aggression now, this tension that can only be dispelled one way. We've been sneaking off to every possible corner of the campus to satisfy the compulsion that neither of us has to hide anymore.

The warm spring weather helps us. We can find quiet places off campus, out in the fields or down on the beaches, where we can lay down a blanket and strip each other naked in the sunshine to lick and kiss and touch each other for hours.

It was on an afternoon like that when Leo found my last tattoo, the one I've never shown to anybody.

It's a constellation on my ribs, just below my heart.

Leo traced his finger over it, saying, "What's this one? You never showed me this."

"I know," I said.

"Why not? What does it mean?"

"It's Leo," I said. "The lion. I got it last year, when I thought you might not be coming to Kingmakers with me. So I'd have you with me either way."

Leo looked down at my face, his eyes golden with sunshine. "Why didn't you tell me?"

"I…I don't know. I had already started to realize that I might be feeling something for you…something that you might not feel for me."

"I did, though," Leo said fervently. "I did feel it. Long before I knew it." After a moment, he said, "What's your constellation?"

I laughed. "You know I don't believe in that stuff. I got this because that's how your mom named you. Not because I really believe in astrology."

Leo looked at me intently. "There is fate, though," he said. "There is you and me, brought together at this one time in this one place, out of all the billions of years and infinite miles of space in the universe. Do you believe in that?"

"Yes," I said softly. "I do."

"Then tell me."

"I'm an Aquarius."

"Then that's the first tattoo I'll get," Leo said. "As soon as we get home. Just tell me where you want me to put it."

Now Leo turns me around on Professor Holland's desk, turning me to face him so my legs are wrapped around his waist and he can kiss me while he fucks me.

He's got my long rope of hair wrapped around his hand, and he's crushing my lips under his, driving into me so hard that the desk is shaking and I'm afraid its legs will snap off.

As I start to come, I think that I'll tell him to get his tattoo in the same place as mine. So they'll be touching when our bodies are pressed together just like this.

CHAPTER 31
LEO

It's the last challenge of the Quartum Bellum and the last week of school.

In three days, we'll be boarding the ship to go back to Dubrovnik, the splinter point where the Kingmakers students will fly to every possible corner of the globe.

Anna and I will be flying home to Chicago together, to tell our families in person that we're in love and we intend to be together.

I look forward to that and to a whole summer with nothing to do but spend every possible moment with Anna.

Before I can do that, however, I've got to win this fucking challenge.

My desire to win has come roaring back. It's stronger than ever but different than it was before. It's not for me anymore. I want to make Anna proud.

She told me she doesn't care if we win or lose, saying, "You already did better than anyone could expect."

But Anna deserves a champion.

The juniors are out. It's just the freshmen against the seniors now.

As with the previous challenges, I have no idea what we'll be facing today. Even so, I'm not nervous. I'm not afraid. Anna will be with me, right by my side. I can do this.

The freshmen assemble on the field just south of Kingmakers, the same place that the second challenge took place. This time, there's no triangular pitch marked out in spray paint. In fact, there's no sign of any challenge about to commence, other than a simple wooden box set on the grass—the sort of box that could hold athletic equipment, pinnies, or almost anything, really.

Professor Howell, dressed in his usual olive-green fatigues with a silver stopwatch hanging around his neck, looks keen and expectant as the seniors join us.

Pippa Portnoy is standing at the head of her team, with Liam Murphy right beside her. Liam is an Heir in his own right, tall and fit, with a flaming red beard and a shock of hair in the same color, tied back with a thong.

Liam is well-respected by his IRA soldiers. He's quick and competent, one of the best marksmen in the school, yet he defers to his betrothed, Pippa. Which tells you everything you need to know about how clever and ruthless she must be.

She's watching me now with her dark eyes as bright as a magpie's. She shows no irritation that she's facing us in the final round of the competition or that we stole her flag in the first challenge. If anything, she's smiling in anticipation.

"Welcome, freshmen. Welcome, seniors," Professor Howell says pleasantly. "What a perfect day for the final challenge."

He's right—the sky is clear and cloudless, the sun brilliant, and only the faintest hint of a breeze stirs the grass around our feet.

"For this final challenge, you won't need your entire team. Instead, you'll be selecting six freshmen and six seniors to perform the final task."

"Six including ourselves?" Pippa clarifies.

"Six in *addition* to yourselves," Professor Howell says, smiling so that his pointed incisors show.

I ask, "Will you be telling us what the task is first?" The parameters of the challenge would, of course, influence who I'd want to select.

"No," Professor Howell says, smiling even wider. "You'll have to pick first."

Pippa and I both turn toward our respective teams, our eyes sweeping the eager and nervous faces before us.

I'm torn, because my natural inclination is to pick the fastest, strongest, and most physically gifted individuals. But what if the challenge is to build a pipe bomb or decode an encryption? Then I'd want someone with more technical skills.

"Make your selections," Professor Howell prompts us.

"Liam, Sam, Johnny, Sven, Mikhail, and Marcelline," Pippa rattles off without hesitation.

"Excellent. And you, Leo?" Professor Howell says.

"Ares, Hedeon, and Anna," I say. Those three are easy. But for the other three… Without knowing the challenge, I think I should pick one student from each specialty: an Enforcer, a Spy, and an Accountant. "Silas. Isabel. And I guess…Matteo."

Matteo looks shocked at being chosen and not particularly happy about it. I hope I'm not making a huge mistake.

By contrast, Dean's face instantly darkens when he sees that he's been snubbed. He's right to be pissed, in the sense that his practical and academic performance certainly warrants inclusion. But if he thinks I'm going to trust him to carry us to victory in the final challenge, he's out of his fucking mind. The fact that he won't be part of this at all is the best news I've heard so far.

I'm only moderately confident in my last three choices. I picked Silas because if there's a challenge that requires pure, raw strength, I don't think anyone can beat him. On the other hand, he's vicious and not particularly strategic. Picking him could easily blow up in my face.

Isabel Dixon has some of the highest marks out of all the Spies, and I know she's good with her hands too, particularly in assembling bombs, guns, and machinery.

Matteo is brilliant with numbers, codes, and research. But he's clumsy and physically weak. If he ends up in some sort of combat challenge, we're fucked.

"The rest of you can return to the castle," Professor Howell says, dismissing the students who weren't selected. They head off, some clearly irritated at not being chosen and others laughing and talking excitedly now that they're free to simply enjoy the outcome without any pressure of performing.

Only once we're alone—the seven freshmen, seven seniors, and Professor Howell himself—does he rub his hands together in anticipation and say, "Excellent. Now, this is what we'll be doing. This challenge is split into seven parts. Each teammate will have one task to complete. At the end of the task, you'll receive a puzzle piece. Assemble all your pieces, solve the puzzle, and you'll know where to find the final prize."

"So it's a scavenger hunt," Pippa says.

"Essentially." Professor Howell smiles in a way that makes me think it won't be quite that simple.

He kneels down to unlatch the wooden box, taking out a stack of hand-drawn and hand-lettered maps. He hands seven to Pippa and seven to me.

"These are the maps noting the location of the challenges. Give one to each of your teammates, and then we will begin the race. You have five minutes to divide your maps."

He starts his stopwatch, and my team gathers around me to examine the maps.

"That's the library." Matteo points to the first map.

"Yes, obviously." Hedeon rolls his eyes.

"That's the shooting range, so that will probably be a marksmanship challenge." I look at the second map.

"This one's in the armory. Bet it's combat," Isabel says.

"This one here looks like the river bottom," I say. "What kind of challenge could that be?"

Ares shrugs, mystified.

"And that one's down in the village." Hedeon frowns.

It's hard to know how to divide the maps without actually knowing what the corresponding challenges will be. I can almost hear the seconds ticking away on Professor Howell's stopwatch.

"Matteo, you can have the library." I thrust the map into his hand, hoping there's not some kind of trick involved, like the library challenge is actually a feat of strength. "Hedeon, you take the shooting range, Isabel, go to the river bottom, and Silas, you take the armory."

Silas grunts, his face as stony and expressionless as ever.

"Ares, you go down to the village," I say, thinking that it might possibly be something to do with sailing. Ares is the only one I know for sure can pilot a boat.

"What are these last two?" Isabel asks.

"That's the sea caves." Anna points.

I say, "How do you know that?"

She flushes. "I've been there."

"Do you want to take that challenge, then?"

She hesitates. "No. I'll take this one...on the cliffs."

I take the last map. "I'll do the caves, then."

I mostly chose them because the caves are right next to the cliffs, and I'd rather stick close to Anna if I can. Just in case she needs my help.

"Time," Professor Howell says, clicking his stopwatch.

I was so engrossed in dividing the maps that I didn't pay any attention to what Pippa was doing. Maybe that was a mistake. Maybe I should have tried to match up my players with hers. It won't be good if Matteo has to face off against Liam or Silas against Pippa.

I grit my teeth, thinking that most of Pippa's team looks older, wiser, and more prepared than mine. It doesn't matter who I pair up. We're already at a disadvantage.

I shake my head hard to clear it. That's not the way to think. We can do this, or we can't, and we'll find out soon enough.

"Never mind about them," I say to my team. "We're not competing against them. We're competing against ourselves. Don't hesitate, don't second-guess yourself, and whatever else you do, don't you fucking quit."

"We won't," Ares says firmly.

Professor Howell raises his starter pistol to the sky.

"Ready...go!"

I don't even hear the pistol shot because I'm already off and running with Anna at my side. We're sprinting east to the spot marked on the map—the place where she'll have to ascend the steep limestone cliffs and I'll have to go the other way, down into the underground sea caves.

Anna looks fresh and eager, running across the field as swift as a deer. Her hair streams behind her, golden in the sunshine, and it feels like it's only the two of us in a race against each other.

Off to our right, I see Johnny Hale and Mikhail Agapov jogging in a parallel direction, apparently having received the same maps as Anna and me.

"Which challenge do you think Pippa chose?" I pant.

"Who knows!" Anna pants. "How is she so terrifying when she's so tiny?"

"Are you scared of her too?" I laugh. "I thought you'd get used to her, living in the same dorm."

"Fuck no!" Anna cries. "It only gets worse. The other day, she said Angelique's perfume reeked, and she threw the bottle out the window."

"Did it reek?" I laugh, pressing my hand against the stitch in my side.

"Well, yeah," Anna admits. "Guess she did us all a favor. But she didn't have to make her cry."

Anna and I have reached the point where we have to scrabble down a steep path to the beach below. I hold out my hand to help her, and Anna ignores it, laughing and sliding down on her heels faster than I can follow.

"Come on, slowpoke!" she shouts.

I skid down after her, not caring if the loose gravel tears the shit out of my gym shorts, because after all, I'll only be using them a couple more days.

When we reach the beach, Anna and I have to part ways—her to scale the steep cliffs and me to enter the caves.

I look up at the cliffs, which seem impossibly steep and sheer.

"I don't see any ropes."

"I don't need any." Anna tosses her hair back over her shoulder.

"Anna—"

"I've got this, Leo!" she says, shaking her head at me. "Just go!"

I feel a strange hesitation to leave her, but I know Anna won't tolerate me babying her just because we're dating now. Besides, Johnny and Mikhail are right behind us. I really do need to hurry.

"See you soon."

With that, I run into the limestone caves, my sneakers splashing in the shallow pools of seawater that quickly deepen the farther in I go.

The map gave no indication of what I'd find in here. Even in the middle of the day, the sunlight fades within twenty yards of the entrance. I have to feel my way along, until I notice that the faint light up ahead isn't sunshine at all but rather the glow of a lamp.

I follow that light, hearing the pants and splashes of Mikhail right behind me.

We reach the lamp almost at the same time.

There, at the edge of a deep, dark pool, sit two sets of scuba diving equipment.

"Oh shit," Mikhail says.

Without answering him, I sit down and start to pull on the fins, weight belt, and tank.

Mikhail looks distinctly nervous, but he follows suit.

"You think we have to go in there?" he asks.

"Must be," I say.

"Just...don't get grabby," he says.

"Professor Howell didn't say anything about fighting for puzzle pieces. You stay out of my way, and I'll stay out of yours."

"No problem," Mikhail agrees with relief.

I hope this puzzle piece isn't as tiny as a standard jigsaw. Otherwise, I don't know how in the fuck I'll ever find it down in a pitch-black sea cave, even with a headlamp on.

Pulling my mask down over my face, I drop down into the water.

It's cold, especially with no wet suit. My headlamp illuminates only a tiny column of space ahead of me.

The limestone walls of the cave look pale and ghostly, like they're carved from bone.

I can only guess which direction I'm supposed to go. As I swim along, carefully kicking my fins, I realize this is not a single cave. Instead, I see openings branching off on all sides. It's a honeycomb of passages and caverns, all interconnected and all horribly alike.

Some of the passageways are narrow. I have to squeeze through, fighting the awful sense of claustrophobia and the knowledge of what will happen to me if I get wedged in a space I can't escape. I only have one tank of air.

I swim and search, trying to hold on to my sense of direction. This is a labyrinth. If I'm not careful, I'll search the same caverns over and over, passing right by the place where the puzzle piece is hidden.

I have to assume that it's not tiny, that it's something a person could reasonably find with only an hour's worth of air.

As I kick through one particularly large cavern, I see Mikhail swimming in the opposite direction. He checks my hands to see if I've found anything, and I shake my head. He makes an irritated gesture, like he's already tired of looking, and we pass each other by.

Twice, I'm scanning for the puzzle piece and accidentally hit my head on limestone. The second time, I pop up in surprise and my head breaks the surface of the water, though I'm still deep down underground. I realize that some of the caverns have air at the top—just a couple of inches between water and stone. I scan that area too, in case that's where my prize is hidden, but I suspect it will be deeper down.

The swimming helps to keep my muscles warm. Still, as the minutes pass, I'm getting slower and stiffer. I'm a long way from the entrance now. I hope I find the puzzle piece soon, or it's going to be difficult to swim back.

The caverns are all beginning to blur together. I have to trust the imperfect map in my head that I haven't seen this one before.

Right as I'm turning, a glint of gold catches my eye.

There…there at the bottom, where I suspected it would be…

I dive down to the sandy cavern floor, closing my hand around a hunk of metal the size of my fist. It's smooth on one curved side, uneven on the others. It looks like it might be a sphere when it's all put together.

I tuck the piece in my pocket, then turn around to swim out of the caverns again.

I'm running low on air now, but I probably have ten or twenty minutes left, depending how hard I'm kicking. Plenty of time to get out of here.

I only saw one puzzle piece, which means that either Mikhail already found his, or the two pieces were hidden in separate caverns.

Pondering this, I accidentally take a wrong turn at a branch point and run into a dead end.

"Fuck," I mutter into my regulator. I can't make mistakes like that. Every second counts.

As I'm about to turn around, something seizes me from behind. My regulator is wrenched out of my mouth, blinding me with a spray of silvery bubbles.

I whip around, thinking that Mikhail has run into me or for some inexplicable reason has decided to attack me. Deep down in my brain, the less rational part of me is conjuring up images of sea monsters.

Instead I see something much worse: a boy in a wet suit and goggles, with a shock of white-blond hair floating above him like pale seaweed and a knife clutched in his hand.

Dean Yenin.

I expect him to attack me. To stab me with the knife.

Instead, he slashes my air hose with his knife. He slices off the regulator in one swift cut, then kicks hard with his fins, swimming away.

I chase after him, knowing that he's holding the one and only thing that can keep me alive: his air tank.

He's swimming with all his might, trying to get away from me, and I'm doing the same, stroking with my arms and kicking hard with my fins even though my lungs are already burning.

I seize him by the leg. He kicks me in the face, his heel connecting with my nose. Doggedly, I grab hold of him again. We're tussling, fighting, the twin circles of light from our headlamps sweeping wildly around.

Our underwater punches are dull and dreamlike, and Dean's violet-colored eyes are crazed behind the glass lenses of his scuba mask. His bared teeth grip the mouthpiece of his regulator.

I expect him to try to stab me with the knife, but strangely he shoves it in his belt instead so he can pummel and throttle me with both hands. I realize with a sick and chilling certainty that it's because he doesn't want any stab wounds on my body. He wants this to look like an accident when they find me drowned.

My lungs are screaming, convulsing as they try to force me to draw a breath that will only flood them with seawater.

I manage to rip Dean's regulator out of his mouth, but before I can take a breath, he hits me again, breaking free from my grip and swimming away with the only working air tank.

I could try to grab him one last time, but I know I only have a few seconds left. So instead, I turn and swim as fast and hard as I can for the one thing that might save me.

No time for wrong turns now. Black spots are already flashing in front of my eyes, and the insistent gulps of my lungs won't be denied much longer.

I've got five seconds at most.

Four…

Three…

My head shoots up, hitting the top of the cavern. I press my face against the stone, gasping for air.

I've found the two inches of space at the top of the cavern. I can breathe, but only by staying right here with my face tilted up into the tiny bit of space between the limestone and the water.

I'm trapped.

I could try to take a deep breath and hold it while I swim to the next cave, but I already know it's too far. I can't go forward or back.

I have no idea how long this air will last. There's only a couple of inches. How much oxygen does a person need every minute, every hour? I haven't saved myself; I've only delayed the inevitable. This air will run out, and I'll suffocate just as surely as I would underwater.

The salty seawater laps my face, colder than ever. I have to lift my chin higher to keep it out of the water.

Another cold burst hits my legs, and I tilt my chin higher still.

The space is shrinking.

The tide is coming in.

CHAPTER 32
DEAN

I SWIM OUT OF THE CAVERNS AS FAST AS I CAN, LOOKING CAREFULLY around to be sure that Mikhail Agapov is nowhere nearby.

No one can see me.

I wore gloves. I dropped Leo's regulator in the passageway. It will look like it tore off while he was swimming through, and he panicked and drowned.

As I climb back out of the water, I see only the lantern standing next to the pool. No discarded tank or flippers—Mikhail isn't out yet.

I hesitate, wondering if there's any possibility of him finding Leo down there. No… Leo was almost out of air already. He must have drowned within minutes. Whether Mikhail finds him or not, he's already dead.

I carry my own wet suit, flippers, and tank out with me. I've got to smuggle them back up to the school, into the storage room next to the underground pool.

It's essential to hide all the evidence. There can't be any missing equipment, any hint that what happened to Leo wasn't an accident.

I had Bram and Valon staked out at the shooting range and the river bottom. Those were our only chances to attack Leo in secret. If he'd gone to the armory or the library or even the village, there'd be too many witnesses around.

It was fate that he picked this part of the challenge. Fate that I found him down in the underwater caverns.

Finally, the stars are aligning for me.

He's dead. Leo is dead.

I press my palm against my chest, expecting to find my heart beating a thousand miles a minute.

I can't feel it. No pounding, no pulse.

I feel nothing at all. Just a dark, empty space where my heart used to be.

That's better, I suppose.

I was tired of hurting.

CHAPTER 33
ANNA

THE START POINT AND END POINT OF MY CHALLENGE ARE CLEARLY marked on the map, so I know I have to scale this cliff.

As Leo noted, there are no ropes waiting for me. No anchors, no safety harness.

I don't mind. I've never been afraid of heights.

I like being up in the air, be it dancing, climbing, or flying. The feeling of weightlessness is freeing.

It's the opposite of scuba diving, where the water crushes you and holds you down. I never liked that class, and I'm glad it's over.

As soon as I reach the base of the cliff, I start to climb.

I can see Johnny Hale right next to me. He's a stocky, powerful dude, heavy with muscle, and he starts out fast, hauling himself up hand over hand.

He should use his legs. Arms tire out much faster.

I'm not climbing as fast as him, but I'm steady. Leo always said I had an engine that just wouldn't quit. I've never been the fastest sprinter or swimmer, but it's true that I can keep going almost forever.

So I'm not surprised when Johnny starts to slow down a third of the way up the cliff, and I begin to catch up with him.

I haven't increased my pace. I'm just moving onward and upward, using all my body, my fingertips dug into the crevices of the rock and the strong muscles of my quads and calves helping to shove me up.

I've drawn almost level with Johnny when we reach the halfway point. The sun is beating down on us, glinting off his piercings. His face is dripping with sweat. His chest and arms too. I doubt that's helping his grip.

Wickedly, I call out to him, "Isn't this fun?"

"Get fucked," he growls back at me.

"It's not so bad," I say. "As long as you don't look down."

Irresistibly, Johnny drops his gaze to the sea-battered rocks below. His face blanches, and his eye starts to twitch.

You don't feel the sense of height until you look down. Then the vertigo hits, and you spiral.

I would never look down. Only up.

"See you at the top!" I laugh, climbing faster than ever.

My shoulders are burning, and my palms are raw as they grasp and hold the rough stone over and over. Once, a handful of the soft limestone crumbles away in my left hand, and my weight drops onto my right arm with a painful jerk.

I shake it off and continue climbing. This is a one-way trip—once I get to the top, I can run back to the school through the sheep fields. The distance is farther, but I think it will be faster than trying to climb down again.

When I'm four-fifths of the way up, I spot an albatross nest on a narrow ledge of stone. The nest is huge, added to year after year by diligent birds until it must be four feet in diameter.

My pulse quickens. I'm sure that's where I'll find the prize.

I haul myself up on the ledge, peering into the roughly woven nest of twigs and mud. Sure enough, I find two hunks of gold, identical in shape and size. I tuck one into the front of my shirt, inside my sports bra, where it makes an unwieldy lump a little smaller than a softball. I leave the other in place for Johnny.

I told myself I wouldn't look down, but I can't help checking to see how close he is getting.

He's paused about three-quarters of the way up the cliff, trying to shake a cramp out of his arm. All that muscle is weighing him down. There's a reason the best rock climbers are lean and wiry.

I'm about to turn around and start climbing again when I see a bright flash down by the entrance to the sea caves: sun glinting off metal. For a moment, I think it might be Leo coming out, but I realize it's someone going in instead. Someone wearing a tank. Someone with white-blond hair.

My heart stops dead in my chest.

He's gone in an instant, so quick I might only have imagined it.

There's no reason for Dean to be here. He's not even competing.

I can hear Johnny grunting and puffing right below the ledge. He's going to climb up here any minute. I only have a short lead ahead of him.

I'm supposed to take this puzzle piece and run back to the castle. That's what Leo entrusted me to do. He's counting on me.

But my skin is sweating, and I taste acid in my mouth, the adrenaline burst telling me that something is wrong.

I swing my legs over the ledge and start to climb down.

"What the fuck are you doing?" Johnny says. "Was it in there? Is it in the nest?"

I don't answer. I just keep descending, trying to watch the entrance of the cave for anybody else going in or out.

It's much more difficult climbing down than up. I have to feel for my footing, and again and again I miss the placement of my feet and they slip out from under me.

My hands and arms are horribly exhausted. My fingers are cramping up. I'm terrified that any second they'll simply let go.

I didn't expect to come back this way. I didn't save anything for the climb down.

I can't keep an eye on the entrance. At some points on the cliff, I can't see it at all because of the way the rock bows out. I don't know if Dean's come out again or if Leo has. For all I know, Leo could be back at the castle already. I can't constantly check because I have to watch what I'm doing, or I'm going to slip and fall a few hundred feet and then I won't be helping anybody ever again.

It's maddening how slow this is. It's taking me twice as long to go down, the minutes ticking away while my brain screams at me that something bad is happening, that I have to hurry.

Time stretches out, my shoulders and back throbbing, my hands so raw I can barely feel them anymore. The sun is too hot, sweat is burning my eyes, and my head is spinning with what might be heatstroke or only vertigo.

At last, I see the ground beneath me.

I'm afraid to let go of the cliff in case it's only an illusion and I'm still high up in the air. I can't let go with my hands until I feel my soles touching solid ground.

I press my feet against the flat ground, reassuring myself I've actually made it.

Then I run to the cave entrance, my legs shaking so hard beneath me that I slip and stumble over the rocky ground.

As I'm dashing inside, I slam into somebody coming out. We both fall back on our asses.

"What in the hell—"

I scramble up again, seeing only Mikhail. He's wearing a pair of scuba goggles pushed up on his head.

"Where's Leo?" I shout.

"How should I know?"

"Did you see him? Is he in there?"

Mikhail is trying to get past me so he can run back to the castle, but I won't let him pass.

"Is Leo down in the water?" I cry.

"It's a maze down there," Mikhail says. "I have no idea where he went."

"Give me those!" I snatch the goggles off Mikhail's head.

He shoves past me, holding a lump of gold in his hand. He got his puzzle piece.

I run into the cave, following the distant glow that I hope is a flashlight.

Instead, I find a lamp and the sodden, tangled pile of Mikhail's discarded scuba equipment. There's no sign of Leo anywhere. Or Dean either.

I pick up Mikhail's tank. There's only a small amount of air left in it—maybe ten minutes' worth.

I pull it onto my back anyway.

I may be making a huge mistake. But I'm not leaving until I've looked for Leo.

I drop down into the pool, which is much deeper and colder than I anticipated. Switching on Mikhail's headlamp, I see the sickening truth of what he was trying to tell me: it is a maze down here. A huge, rambling, impossibly confusing tangle of tunnels and caverns.

I have no idea which direction to go.

My chest is rigid with fear. If I get lost down here, I don't have the air to find my way back again.

I don't care. I know I saw Dean come in here. And I know it wasn't for nothing.

I swim hard, checking each cavern I pass, trying not to get turned around in the gloom.

I'm looking for Leo but also for Dean. Or possibly the two of them together.

The time is slipping by too fast—I've already used up half the remaining air. I've got to swim faster, though that makes me take deeper breaths.

As I kick my way down a narrow limestone tube, I see something that pulls me up short: something black and metallic. I dive down to retrieve it.

It's a regulator, attached to a short length of hose.

The dread I feel then is vast and suffocating.

Someone is down here without any air.

I'm trying not to sob as I keep swimming forward. I know in

my heart that the only thing I can find now is a body—either Leo or Dean. I turn one last corner and I see it—someone bobbing awkwardly against the roof of the cavern, their face twisted up. Someone tall and tan and long-limbed. Someone I love more than anything on this earth.

I swim to him, choking on my mouthpiece, sobbing behind my mask, sure that Leo is dead. I grab his body.

And it grabs me back. The hands gripping me are alive and warm. I can't believe what I'm feeling until Leo puts his face under the water and looks right into my eyes.

He gently takes the regulator from my mouth and sucks in a deep lungful of air. Then he puts it back between my lips and hugs me hard.

The dial on the tank beeps furiously. We're almost out of air, and there's two of us now.

But we know where we need to go. Hand in hand, kicking hard, Leo and I swim out of the caverns. We only pause to pass the regulator back and forth so we can share the last dregs of the air.

It's getting harder and harder to draw breath. The tank is beeping continuously, the dial far past the red line.

Leo and I keep swimming. My muscles are cramping, and my head is getting light. I don't think we're close to the last pool. It's impossibly far away. We're not going to make it.

I'm slowing down. Like a nightmare, no matter how hard I paddle, my progress is nil. The water is thick as oil. I can barely kick my feet.

I gesture to Leo to take the tank.

Instead, he grabs my hand and kicks with all his might. He's pulling, dragging me along. I can't see the light of my headlamp anymore. I can't see anything. Everything is black…

Leo wrenches me out of the water and throws me down on the limestone. He presses hard on my chest, forcing the water out. Then he covers my mouth with his, breathing air into my lungs.

I roll over on my side, vomiting seawater.

Leo covers me with his body, trying to warm me up. Then, thinking better of it, he picks me up in his arms and carries me out of the caves, into the sunshine.

Gulls are wheeling and cawing overhead. The waves wash rhythmically against the rocks.

I squint up at Leo's face, at the brilliant drops of seawater glinting in his eyelashes.

"Did you get the puzzle piece?" I ask him.

"Oh my god. Is that what you're thinking about right now?"

"I got mine." I fish it out of my bra. "You could still win, Leo."

He pulls his own puzzle piece out of his pocket, holding it up so it blazes in the sun.

"Do you think you can run?"

CHAPTER 34
LEO

When Anna and I reach the field south of the school, legs shaking and lungs burning from our hobbling run back up from the sea caves, we find Silas and Hedeon already waiting for us, each holding their piece of the puzzle. Hedeon had been looking anxiously in all directions for the rest of our team, while Silas simply sits on the grass, as taciturn and expressionless as ever.

On the opposite side of the field, I see that Mikhail and Johnny have of course already returned, both having completed their tasks far ahead of Anna and me. Likewise, Sam and Liam seem to have retrieved their puzzle pieces.

"I beat him back," Silas grunts, jerking his head toward Sam on the opposite side of the field. "We each had to fight three opponents. I beat the third before he was even done with the second."

The evidence of Silas's battles is clear on his face. His left eye is almost swollen shut, and his nose is making a strange whistling sound. He doesn't seem bothered by his injuries. I'm not entirely sure Silas is human.

"Liam finished before I did," Hedeon admits. "He's such a fucking good shot."

Hedeon is a decent marksman but not even top five in our year. If I had known what the challenges were going to be, I would have picked someone like Chay or even Gemma Rossi, as awkward as that might be.

"It's alright," I say. "They can't put their puzzle together without the rest of the pieces."

"What took you so long?" Hedeon says, frowning. "Mikhail's been back a long time and Johnny even longer."

"Sorry to keep you waiting!" Anna snaps at him. "We were just drowning ourselves while Liam was showing you up at target practice."

"It wasn't stationary targets—" Hedeon starts, but I hold up my hand to cut him off before he and Anna can get into it. I put my arm around Anna's shoulders for good measure, pulling her against my side. She's still pale and shaking, not at all recovered from our ordeal.

"It doesn't matter," I say. "Give me all the pieces. Let's see if we can put any of them together."

From the way Mikhail, Johnny, Sam, and Liam are bunched together in a tight circle on the opposite end of the field, I suspect they're working on the same thing.

"What is this?" Hedeon says, turning the irregular metal lumps over in his hands. "How are these supposed to fit?"

"I don't know," I say.

At that moment, I see Marcelline running out through the Kingmakers' gates, the sun glinting off the gold in her hands.

"She got hers," Hedeon says.

"Where's Matteo?" Anna asks.

We fix our eyes on the gates, hoping to see Matteo following close behind. Every second that ticks past feels interminable. I understand now why Hedeon looked so strained when we finally ran up.

Three or four minutes later, Matteo comes puffing across the field, his round face flushed from running.

"I'm sorry," he pants, shoving his puzzle piece into my hands. "We had to solve a code. Fuck, it was so hard. I've never seen anything like it. That Marcelline is a goddamned android."

Before I've even added Matteo's piece to our pile, Pippa likewise comes sprinting up from the direction of the river bottom. She throws her puzzle piece triumphantly to Liam.

"*Fuck*," Hedeon mutters under his breath. "If Pippa's back, we're done."

"They're still missing one piece," I remind him, but I feel the same sense of impending doom. There's no sign of Isabel yet, and if Sven beats Ares, I doubt it's going to take Pippa long to solve the puzzle.

"Let me see those." Matteo takes the pieces from Anna. He turns them over, examining all sides. "Ah!" he mutters, managing to click two of the pieces together.

His early success is deceptive. After another five minutes, he hasn't made any progress on the other four.

I'm watching for Isabel and Ares. I expect to see Isabel first, since Pippa is already back, but instead Ares comes limping up the road from the village, hunched over and deathly pale.

I run down the road to him, shocked by the sight of his gray face.

"What the fuck happened to you?"

In answer, he leans over and vomits up a large quantity of water.

Wiping his mouth on the back of his arm, he groans, "They fucking waterboarded us. We had to last two minutes. I know that doesn't sound like much, but it was—"

His body convulses, and he retches again, this time nothing coming out.

I throw his arm over my shoulder so I can help support him the rest of the way.

"They told us we could stop any time. And we could rest if we wanted. But we had to do two minutes straight…to get the piece. I'm sorry…it took me so long."

"Sven isn't back yet," I say. "Maybe he won't be able to make it."

"I almost didn't," Ares groans miserably.

He presses the second-to-last puzzle piece into my hand.

"That fucking thing better be real solid gold for what I had to do to get it."

I help him back to the others, Anna staring in horror at Ares's sweating, shaking frame.

"What happened to you?" she cries.

"Just…the worst afternoon of my life." Ares laughs weakly.

"Gimme that!" Matteo cries, grabbing Ares's piece and swiftly slotting it into place. "I needed that one."

I'm scanning the field in the direction of the river bottom, anxiously waiting for Isabel. She's our last teammate and our last puzzle piece. If she can get back here before Sven, we might actually do this. We might actually win.

Anna is helping Matteo with the puzzle. She aligns the fourth piece, but then there's a long and agonizing break while they can't seem to find how the other two fit.

"This should be easy!" Anna cries in frustration.

"Why do they all look the goddamn same and still don't fit?" Hedeon snarls.

Silas doesn't attempt to help. He's glaring moodily across the field at the seniors, who are likewise working on their puzzle under the fierce observation of Pippa, who's barking orders I can't quite hear.

I see motion at the end of the field. My heart swoops up as at long last Isabel pushes her way through the trees. But at the same moment, Sven limps and lurches his way up the road, a lump of gold clutched in his hand.

"Goddamn it," I mutter.

I don't have to tell Isabel to run—she's already sprinting at top speed, quicker than Sven can manage. She's a mess, hair tangled and muddy, fingernails broken off, hands and arms scratched raw. She thrusts the last puzzle piece into my hands, saying, "God, I'm sorry. That fucking Pippa."

Matteo and Anna seize the last piece, but it doesn't elucidate how they're supposed to finish the puzzle. Whatever they're building is oddly shaped, and Matteo removes one of the other pieces that was already in place, not sure it's in the right location.

Still breathing hard, Isabel says, "We had to get through this fucking mess of snares and trip wires. She was setting them off on me on purpose."

I'm only half listening. On the other side of the field, Sven has added his piece to the pile, and the seniors are feverishly working to assemble their puzzle. I can't tell whether they're further along than we are. All I know is that every second that passes of Matteo turning the uneven golden lumps over in his hands seems torturous and interminable.

We're so fucking close. If we lose the whole thing because of this goddamned puzzle…

"No, that's wrong," Anna says, taking the puzzle from Matteo. "It goes this way, I'm sure of it."

Anna manages to slot one more piece into place.

"Wait!" Isabel breathes. She grabs the last piece, twisting and turning the puzzle in her hands like a Rubik's Cube. Two of the pieces rotate, leaving a gap. She slips in the last piece and gives a final twist, the two halves of the puzzle finally coming together in one solid whole.

We stare at the golden skull in her hands.

"What the fuck does that mean?" Hedeon says.

A split-second whirl of images whips through my brain. The chancellor, the banners, the announcement of the Quartum Bellum…

"The keep!" I hiss, careful not to call it out. "The grand hall!"

Seizing the skull in my hand, I start to run. The rest of the team chases after me.

As we pass Pippa's team, I can see Pippa herself holding the puzzle in her hands, one single piece out of place.

She stares at me in wide-eyed disbelief as I sprint past her, her shock quickly turning to fury.

I'm not looking back at her. I'm staring straight ahead as I dash through the gates, between the greenhouses, right toward the keep.

My team dashes inside the grand hall in a tangled knot, sweating and panting, hoping we're at the right place...

As soon as I see Luther Hugo standing in front of the fireplace, I know that we are. He's beneath his own black banner, the grinning golden skull floating above his head like a crown.

He smiles at us, his dark eyes glittering in his deeply lined face. It's the sort of smile the devil might give you if you managed to fiddle his tune.

"Well, well, well," he says softly. "Do my eyes deceive me? Or am I looking at the freshmen?"

I take the heavy gold skull and press it into his hand.

CHAPTER 35
DEAN

I WATCH FROM THE COMMON ROOM WINDOW AS LEO AND HIS TEAM of freshmen run into the ground floor of the keep. They're followed less than five minutes later by the seniors. I can tell from Pippa's expression of fury and their lack of haste that they already know Leo won.

For me, it's like watching a demon be resurrected for the sole purpose of torturing me all over again.

I fucking killed him. I drowned that motherfucker. How is he still alive?

I had him trapped way down deep in those caves with no air.

It's impossible.

Yet there he is, not just alive but triumphant.

I go into my room and lock the door and sit down on my bed.

Outside, I hear the ruckus as the other freshmen realize that we won the Quartum Bellum for the first time in anyone's memory. They're all celebrating, loudly at first, and then the noise fades away as they leave the Octagon Tower and head out onto campus so they can hear the whole story.

I don't care about the details. I only care what this means.

For one thing, I might be in a fuck of a lot of trouble. Leo knows I tried to kill him. If he tells the chancellor what happened, if he has proof... I don't know exactly what they'll do to me, but it won't be good.

That should be my primary concern. But it isn't.

I have an entirely different realization occupying my brain.

I sit alone on my bed, reliving everything that happened this year. What I tried to accomplish and how I failed every time.

I was wrong in thinking that there are good and evil people in the world.

There's no good and evil.

There's only the people blessed or cursed by fate.

Fate smiles on Leo. It gives him everything he wants. I killed him, I know I did. Yet somehow, he was saved. I loved Anna. She loved Leo instead.

"Good people" are simply favored by fate.

"Evil people" understand that the world works against us. So it doesn't matter what we do. We have to survive by any means necessary. We have to fight and claw to take a tiny fraction of what fate denies us.

I thought I could have love. It was impossible from the start. The universe doesn't want me to have love. I've never been given it, not from my father or mother, not from friends or lovers.

I give up on love. I give up on kindness, friendship, integrity, mercy.

If all I can be is brutal, vicious, cruel, if that's what I'm meant to be, then I'll be the most brutal. The most vicious. The most cruel.

In a way, it's a relief.

I'm tired of fighting it.

It's time to be who I really am.

CHAPTER 36
ANNA

THE PARTY THAT TAKES PLACE THAT NIGHT DOWN ON MOON Beach is the most epic of the school year. Almost every single freshman is there, along with most of the sophomores and even a good portion of the juniors. The seniors, of course, are entirely absent, furious that their final week at Kingmakers was marred by such a humiliating defeat.

Leo is laughing and telling the best parts of the story to anyone who wants to hear, which is a constant stream of students. He makes everything sound amusing and suspenseful, even the parts that were fucking awful, but I notice he's leaving out one key detail.

He hasn't told anyone that Dean tried to kill him. He admits that his regulator was torn off and that I had to dive down to help him. But he's acting like it was an accident.

When I get the chance, I pull Leo aside and ask him, "What the hell are you doing?"

He smiles at me, slipping his arm around my waist and pulling me close against his body.

"What's wrong, beautiful? You mad 'cause I haven't danced with you yet? Come on. I've still got plenty of energy. I'll spin you around all night long."

He's pulling me toward the crowded mass of students dancing around the bonfire, already starting to sway me to the music.

"That's not what I'm talking about," I say, but he's got his hands on my hips, his whole body pressed against mine, making me grind with him. Leo has such a smooth and enticing way of moving that I find myself putting my arms around his neck, dancing along with him before I even know what's happening.

"There you go," he growls in my ear. "Isn't that so much better?"

I laugh and nuzzle my face against his neck, breathing him in, feeling his warmth against my cheek. Leo's heat radiates out of his whole body, flowing into me, warming me to my core.

"Now," he says, "ask me what you wanted to ask me."

I say it to him quietly, right in his ear, so no one will hear over the noise of the music. "Why haven't you told anyone what Dean did?"

Leo looks down into my face. His eyes are glowing and alive from the reflected flames. "You think that I should?"

"Of course you should! He tried to kill you. He probably will again!"

Leo frowns slightly. Not from anger—it's something else.

"What?" I say.

"I just…feel bad."

I stare at him like he's lost his fucking mind.

"You feel bad for the person who tried to murder you?"

Leo gives a low laugh. "I mean…yeah," he says. "I kinda do."

Just when I think Leo couldn't possibly surprise me again.

"Pity is a dangerous emotion," I tell him. "It won't be reciprocated."

"I know," he says. "And I'm not saying we're going to be friends or that I'll lower my guard. But, Anna, if I lost you, and he was the one dancing with you right now… I'd be so fucking devastated. I might have tried to kill him too."

"You still have to tell the chancellor. You can't just let this slide."

"I won, Anna. I won you. That's punishment enough."

I don't entirely like that answer. I'm afraid of what Dean might still try to do. If Leo thinks their grudge is over, I highly doubt Dean agrees.

Leo can tell I'm not convinced.

He wraps my hair around his hand and gently tugs to force me to look up into his eyes. He holds me pinned in place, one arm wrapped around my waist, the other hand cradling the back of my neck. He turns the full intensity of his gaze on me.

"Anna," he says. "He's not a threat to me. No one is. When I have you, I'm fucking invincible."

All Leo's power and determination burn in those golden eyes. His face is terrifying in its beauty. His body thrums with strength. I can't do anything but believe in him when he's like this.

"Alright," I say. "I trust you."

Leo gives me a wicked grin. "I don't know. I think you need a little more persuading."

He takes my hand and pulls me back through the crush of students, over the uneven sand. He takes me all the way off the beach.

For a second, I think he's going to lead me into the trees where everyone likes to sneak off and hook up. I pull up short, feeling an irrational aversion to the place where I saw him with Gemma Rossi not so long ago.

"Not in there," I say.

"Of course not," Leo agrees.

Instead, he takes me back up the path away from Moon Beach, all the way to the fields on higher ground. It's a warm night; the grass is tall and fragrant, sprinkled with patches of pale blue wildflowers. The breeze makes a soft whispering sound all around us.

Only when we're far away from anything else does Leo lay me down in the grass and gently remove all my clothes.

I've never been completely naked in the outdoors like this—not since we were little kids skinny-dipping. Strangely, it brings me back to that time when I had no fear or shame, when Leo and I seemed like one person, having never been apart.

I've loved him through every stage of our lives. And I love him most today. I'm amazed at the man he's becoming. Overcoming his weaknesses. Amplifying his strengths.

"You're a goddess," Leo says, looking down at my nude body glowing in the moonlight.

He lifts my foot, which he's just stripped of shoe and sock, in his hands. He presses his thumb into the arch of my foot, massaging it. I groan from how good it feels.

Leo kisses my foot, then he runs his tongue from my heel all the way along the instep up to my toes.

"Don't!" I laugh, trying to pull my foot away, but he's got it locked tight in his grip, and he's looking down at me with that hunger, that fire that I know means he's about to do something kinky to me.

"You think I care about licking your foot?" he says. "I'll run my tongue over every fucking inch of this body."

To prove it, he starts sucking on my toes.

I give a little shriek from how strange that feels—I've never had my toes in someone's mouth. It makes me shiver and squirm. But there's also something erotic about Leo's warm lips and tongue on such a sensitive part of my body and something even more sexy in the proof of how rabid he is for me. Nothing about me could disgust him. He wants all of me.

Leo starts licking and biting and kissing his way up my leg, up the calf to my inner thigh. Now I can hardly stand it. I want him to go higher still. His mouth feels indescribably good, and I want that tongue on my pussy. I fucking need it. I'm spreading my legs, begging him to give me relief.

Leo's teasing me, getting closer but torturously slow.

"Please..." I moan.

"Please what?"

"Please fuck me."

Leo buries his face in my pussy, licking me everywhere I want. He uses his fingers and tongue like a maestro, playing me like an instrument. He shoves my thighs wide open and thrusts his tongue inside me, fucking me with it, making me scream out loud from how good it feels. I grind my pussy against his face, wave after wave of pleasure crashing over me, sudden and hard.

I could cry. That's how powerful it is—it makes me want to sob like a baby.

But there's no time for that. Because Leo is already climbing on top of me, freeing his cock from his trousers with one hand, gripping the back of my neck with the other so he can kiss me ferociously.

I can taste myself in his mouth, and I love it. I love all parts of us mixing and combining.

I'm longing for him to shove his cock inside me. I'm waiting for it, but it still takes me by surprise. It does every time. He thrusts into me, and the sensation is brutal, intense, and right on the edge of pleasure and pain—as powerful and acute as it can possibly be.

Leo feels enormous on top of me. He blocks out the moon and stars overhead; he envelops me in his warmth and his scent. I can feel his strength as his muscles flex with every thrust.

I can't get enough of him.

I'm obsessed.

"This is the best thing," I gasp. "It's better than dancing."

Leo laughs. He wraps me up tight in his arms and fucks me even harder. "Like that?" he growls. "You like that?"

"I fucking love it."

He squeezes me so hard that I can't move. He fucks me so deep that I can't feel anything else. I love the way he takes me over, the way he draws this pleasure out of me.

I can feel another climax building, and I don't have to do anything to make it happen. I couldn't make it stop if I wanted to.

"You ready?" Leo groans.

"Yes. Yes."

We come together, me tipping over the edge first, Leo following right after so we're both crying out together, both clinging to each other, both clenching and squeezing each other as hard as we can.

Then we're lying together in the trampled grass, and I realize how silent it is without our heavy breath and the blood pounding in my ears. It feels like Leo and I are the only two people in the world.

The next morning, we have to pack our bags. The ship is coming to take us all back to Dubrovnik.

Chay is wondering how the hell she's going to fit all her stuff back in her suitcase.

"How did you get it in there in the first place?" I ask her.

"I don't know! For one thing, I didn't have this blanket, but I want to keep it. Fuck it. I'll just throw away my uniforms and buy new ones in the fall."

"I should do that anyway," I say, examining the skirts and blouses that have become increasingly distressed over the course of the school year. The hem of my green plaid skirt is nothing but ragged threads.

I definitely have to throw away my ballet slippers—they're beat to shit from dancing on the rough stone of the cathedral. I have more at home.

I can't believe I'm going to see my house again and my parents and brother and sister.

I still haven't warned them that I'm dating Leo. I don't know if it's cowardice or if I really think they'll take it better in person.

I'm hoping they'll understand that Leo and I were meant for each other from the beginning. But I'm afraid that they won't be able to shake off the taboo of falling in love with someone you were raised with as family. Mafia families can be so stubbornly traditional. Our cousins are treated as close relatives, whether linked by blood or not.

"If you folded your clothes, they'd fit better," Zoe says to Chay from her perch on the end of my bed. She's watching us pack, having already filled her suitcase and spotlessly cleaned her tiny room.

"You could fold them for me." Chay bats her eyelashes at Zoe.

Zoe gives her a stern look but stands up from the bed to come over and help.

"Thank you, love," Chay says, putting her arm around Zoe's waist and laying her head on her shoulder.

Zoe sighs, her expression unhappy. Unlike Chay and me, there's no anticipation for Zoe in the journey home.

"You should come visit me in Berlin," Chay says sympathetically. "Come see me over the summer."

"I don't know if my parents will allow that," Zoe says. "I expect they'll want to spend the full three months pressuring me to drop out of school and marry Rocco sooner."

I say, "You're not going to do that, are you?"

"Absolutely not." Zoe shakes her head. "No matter what they say."

It's not what they'll say that I'm worried about. It's what they might do.

"Come on," Chay coaxes. "I bet Anna will come visit me too."

"Sure." I nod. "Leo would love that trip."

"If you're gonna bring Leo, you better bring a hot guy for me." Chay smiles mischievously. "What about that cousin of yours? You think Miles would fancy a trip to Germany?"

Zoe gives a haughty sniff.

"What?" I laugh. "You don't like Miles?"

"Not particularly," Zoe says.

"Why not?"

"No offense, but I find him arrogant and reckless. I can't understand anyone who gets into trouble deliberately. He thinks everything's a game, like there's no real consequences."

"I'm not offended." I shrug. "That's accurate."

"He's funny, though," Chay counters. "And pretty fucking sexy."

Zoe shakes her head silently, not impressed by those particular qualities.

"Well, I wouldn't mind giving him a try," Chay says. "Before he gets himself expelled."

"I'll put in a good word for you," I tell Chay. "No promises, though. Miles listens to me about as much as he listens to anyone else. Which is zero."

"No worries." Chay shrugs. "I've got a few options at home waiting for me." She grins, picturing these friends with benefits that she hasn't fucked in almost a year. "It's like a cute dress you forgot about way in the back of your closet…good as new again."

I laugh. "I'm excited for you."

I finish packing my own suitcase—not as neatly as Zoe but with more room to spare than Chay. That done, I haul it downstairs so I can leave it with the wagons that have pulled into the bailey, ready to carry both us and our luggage back down to the harbor.

As I throw my suitcase onto the pile of waiting bags, I hear a heavy thud right next to me. I turn to find Dean dropping off his own bag.

We haven't spoken since the night he fought with Leo. And I haven't seen him since the day of the final challenge.

We straighten up slowly, staring at each other. I can feel my blood rushing with pure, unadulterated fury.

It's hard to tell what Dean is thinking. His shoulders are hunched and his eyes narrowed almost to slits. His face looks pale and tight.

"I know what you did," I say quietly. "I have proof. I've got the regulator you cut."

"You have a broken regulator?" Dean says coolly. "What does that prove exactly?"

"Stay away from us," I hiss at him. "If I decide to kill someone, I'll actually succeed."

Dean just laughs.

"It's you who will come find me again, Anna. Once you realize what a mistake you made."

"I'd rather swim back to Dubrovnik."

"Maybe you'll get your chance," Dean says softly. "Watch your step on that ship."

I turn and stalk away from him, feeling irritated and unsatisfied. He's right—the regulator is flimsy evidence. It's my and Leo's word against his. And I'm sure he's got some asshole friend who would provide him with a fake alibi.

I head into the dining hall so I can grab a quick lunch before it's time to board the ship. The meal is simpler than usual—bacon sandwiches, fresh fruit, and unpasteurized milk. No other options. That suits me fine—the bacon cured on the island is the most delicious I've ever tasted.

I take two sandwiches and sit down with Matteo and Paulie to eat. Hedeon plops down next to us a moment later, his plate piled high with food. He's not a big fan of Matteo or Paulie, but apparently he likes us better than eating alone.

"Excited to get back?" he says to me, mouth full of an enormous bite of sandwich. He ignores Matteo and Paulie.

"Yes," I say.

I'm not really thinking about heading home. I'm remembering the night I visited Leo in the infirmary. When I saw Hedeon sneaking down to the undercroft.

"Did you ever meet up with that girl after the second challenge?" I ask casually. "The Accountant?"

"Yeah, I did," Hedeon replies smoothly. "She was quite the wildcat too. Don't be fooled by those shy little Accountants. They like the kinkiest shit."

It's so odd watching him lie. If I didn't know what I'd seen, I'd be completely fooled. His expression is as calm and confident as ever, and he answers without hesitation.

I press just a little further. "I thought I saw you later that night, going down in the undercroft."

Now I spot it—an infinitesimal twitch at the corner of his right eye. But his smile only widens.

"Must be some other tall, dark, and handsome guy," he says. "I've never been down there."

"Ah," I say, as if I believe him. "It was pretty dark."

Hedeon changes the subject to our final grades, a topic on which Matteo and Paulie can't resist chiming in.

The whole exchange is over in a matter of seconds.

I haven't clarified what Hedeon was up to. But I have discovered something interesting...

He's a practiced liar. And he's hiding something.

As we climb up into the wagons, there's an air of nervous excitement and also a strange kind of regret. Kingmakers was our home for almost a year. Isolated as we were on the island, it feels strange to leave.

Plenty of students are doing a last-minute exchange of numbers, which we have to scribble down on paper since we don't have our cell phones back yet.

We ride down to the harbor where the ship waits, much larger than any of the fishing boats moored next to it.

"I forgot how big it was," Leo says. He's sitting next to me on the bench seat, his arm loosely draped behind me to protect my back from the jolting of the wagon.

Ares sits across from us, looking up at the ship with a strange expression. I thought he'd be excited to see his family again. Instead, he looks almost as if he's dreading it.

Noticing the same thing, Leo says, "You gonna come see us in Chicago?"

"I'd like to," Ares says. "But I'll be working over the summer."

"I've got a fuck ton of air miles," Leo says, trying to indicate that he'd pay for the flight without embarrassing Ares.

"Thanks," Ares says noncommittally. "I'll miss you guys."

"Well, don't miss us yet," Leo says. "You still have to tolerate a long voyage back to civilization with us."

By the time we board the ship, the main deck is already packed with students. Unlike the voyage over, we're all going home on the same day. The net strung between the masts is already full of raucous juniors, and there's barely a place to lean, let alone sit down. We end up jammed in the bow with a bunch of freshman spies.

Everyone is talking over their plans for the upcoming summer. I hear Shannon Kelly tell her friend Jean Hamilton that she plans to stopover in Spain before going home to Dublin. I had a contracts class with Shannon first semester, but we don't cross paths much, being in separate divisions. Plus she's best friends with Gemma Rossi, who I don't hold a grudge against but prefer to avoid.

Throwing her mane of curls back over her shoulder, Shannon spots me standing behind her and gives me a strangely guilty look.

"Hope there won't be so many people seasick on the way back," I say to her. "We can't all fit along the rail."

"If anybody pukes on me, I'm throwing 'em over," Shannon says. She hesitates, then leaves her friend, drawing closer to me instead. She glances over at Leo, engrossed in his conversation with Ares. "So you're with Leo now, are ya?"

"Yes," I say. "I am."

She nods, chewing on her lower lip.

I can tell she has something on her mind. My father always told me that the best interrogation method is silence. If you want to hear what someone has to say, then shut your fucking mouth.

So I just look at her, calmly and quietly.

"I didn't want to say anything...when you were with Dean," she says, her voice low so it won't carry beyond the two of us.

I stay silent, waiting.

"I don't even know if I even saw anything."

She takes a deep breath, tucking her hair back behind her ears. This is a useless maneuver, since the curls spring free again immediately.

"You remember the night we had that party down on Moon Beach?" she says. "The first party we had down there."

"Yes," I reply in a neutral tone.

"Well, I was standing there talking to Gemma. She had a bit of a thing for Leo, and he had just been named captain, so she was wondering if she should go congratulate him. Then Dean came up to us, which was sort of weird 'cause he never talks to us. He had two drinks with him. And he passed one to Gemma, just one. And he told her she should give it to Leo."

I swallow, my throat making a clicking sound.

"Did she?" I say. "Did she give it to him?"

"Yeah." Shannon nods. "Leo drank it. Then a little while after, Gemma said he seemed really fucked up..." She trails off. "I didn't want to get in the middle of it. Gemma's my best friend. She didn't mean any harm. I thought it wasn't my business, especially once you started dating Dean. But now that you're with Leo..."

"Thanks for telling me," I say faintly.

"No problem," Shannon says, her cheeks flushed pink. She turns away quickly and rejoins her friend.

The ship is pulling away from shore, heading out into open water. The deck rocks gently with the waves. I feel like I'm reeling far more than the motion of the boat would cause. I feel like I might fall right over.

I forgave Leo for that night. But now a much more sinister possibility is striking me: the idea that Leo might not have required forgiveness at all. The idea that he might have been drugged.

Drugged by Dean.

Shannon's story has the ring of truth to it. It's more sensical than what I thought happened. After all, it was unlike Leo to get out-of-control drunk, especially so quickly. If I hadn't been emotional and upset, if I'd actually analyzed the situation, I might have realized the truth. Instead, I lost my temper. And Dean was right there to capitalize on that moment.

I want to find him and rip his fucking face off.

I'm already scanning the deck, searching for a glimpse of his white-blond head.

I must look crazed, because right as I spot Dean on the opposite end of the ship and I start rushing forward to confront him, Leo steps in front of me, grabbing me by the shoulders.

"Where do you think you're going?"

"To stab that motherfucker," I snarl.

"Who?" Leo says, bemused.

"Dean of course!"

"What happened?" Leo says, trying to pull me aside to calm me down.

I give him a brief and painful recitation of what Shannon told me, my throat constricted with guilt. I'm realizing more and more by the minute that Leo was a victim, that it wasn't his fault. Which means that everything that happened between us is *my* fault instead.

I'm so ashamed that I can barely get the last few words out. My face is flaming, and I can't look Leo in the eye.

"I'm sorry," I whisper.

Leo wraps his arms around me and pulls me hard against his chest. He's squeezing me with all his strength. I can feel his body shaking slightly.

"I'm so relieved," he says.

"What?" I pull back from him just a little so I can look up at his face.

"I'm relieved," Leo repeats. "I can't tell you what a weight that is off my mind."

"Aren't you angry?"

"Yeah, of course I'm fuckin' mad. That devious little shit. But, Anna, I thought I made the biggest mistake of my life that night. And I still did! 'Cause I should have kissed you the moment I had you alone on that walk down to the beach. I should have never let you out of my sight at the party. I should have told you what you mean to me way before any of that even happened. But at least I didn't fuck around with Gemma on purpose. I couldn't stand that I did that. I couldn't stand the pain I caused you."

I'm looking up at him in total disbelief.

"You're not mad at me, Leo?"

"God no," he says, kissing me quickly. We're still on Kingmakers property, and we're not supposed to show open affection.

I say, "I don't understand how you can let things go so easily."

I'm a grudge holder. When someone's wronged me, I never forget. It eats at me if I don't do anything about it.

"Everything that ever happened to me before today brought me to this point," Leo says. "Right here, right now, with you in my arms. I wouldn't change anything. Because I'd never risk not being here with you."

I can't help laughing.

"I think you might be becoming a Buddhist," I say to Leo. "You're shockingly Zen."

"Yeah," Leo growls, raising an eyebrow at me. "Unless someone fucks with my baby."

The flight home with Leo is the most blissful experience of my life. I'm thirty thousand feet up in the air, floating over the clouds, cuddled up in the arms of the man I love.

We're so exhausted from the school year that we sleep almost the entire time, only waking when the flight attendants bring us snacks and drinks.

Miles is on the same plane as us from Dubrovnik to Vienna, but then he takes a different exchange, planning to stop in Los Angeles before coming back to Chicago.

"What's in Los Angeles?" Leo asks curiously.

"So many things," Miles says. He loves being mysterious.

"Are you meeting someone?" I ask him.

Miles holds up his phone. "I have to play a song for a guy. Just one song."

"Why don't you just send it to him?" Leo asks.

"It's called striking while the iron's hot," Miles says. "Deals get done face-to-face, while emotions are high."

"Well, make sure you tell your parents," I remind him. "I don't want to see your mom waiting at the airport for you all sad."

"I already told them," Miles assures us. "And I'm gonna bring my mom home some pumpkin bread from the Monastery of the Angels, so don't you worry your pretty little head about her. She'd much rather have that than me."

Leo and I finally touch down in Chicago in late afternoon, knowing that both our fathers will be there to meet us.

We haven't discussed how we'll make our announcement. We were too sleepy and happy to stress about it on the way back.

In the end, we do the thing that feels most natural—we walk out of baggage claim hand in hand, as if we've always been lovers.

My father and Leo's father are standing right next to each other, forming an amusing study in contrast. Uncle Seb is in a linen sport coat, deeply tanned, with threads of gray at his temples and a stylish pair of dark-framed glasses perched on his nose. He's relaxed and happy as he leans on his walking stick. Next to him, my father appears more fair and pale than ever, wearing dark clothes with no hint of summer in them, scanning the crowd keenly for any sight of us. He holds his hands clasped loosely in front of him, his tattooed skin like patterned gloves.

When they spot Leo and me and the way we lean against each other as we walk, our fingers intertwined, their reactions are equally opposite.

Uncle Seb's mouth falls open. He appears confused for a moment, then he breaks into a slow grin that brightens to pure delight.

By contrast, my father comprehends in an instant, and

his expression becomes rigid and furious, eyes burning in his blanched face.

"Anna," he says through thin lips. "What is the meaning of this?"

I take a deep breath, holding my chin high. This is the crucial moment. I can't show a hint of weakness or my father will tear me to shreds.

"Leo and I are in love," I say calmly. "And we're going to be together."

Uncle Seb wisely stays silent, understanding my father well enough to know that this needs to sink in.

"Leo is your cousin," my father says in his most chilling tone.

"Papa," I reply, looking into those eyes that are as cold and blue as my own, "you know as well as I do that while we can choose our family, we cannot choose who we love."

There is a long silence in which Leo's fingers grip mine with an intensity that tells me he's not ever letting go, no matter what happens next.

Leo tells my father, quietly but firmly, "No one will love her better than I can. No one will cherish and protect her as I will."

There's a terrifying intermission that feels like two heavily weighted scales teetering back and forth. A breath of air in the wrong direction could send it tumbling down.

Uncle Seb is brave enough to break it. He says, gently and sincerely, "Come now, Miko. Where did you ever expect to find someone good enough for Anna?"

We're ganging up on him, not that it matters. My father will fight a thousand people when he feels he's in the right.

But in this particular instance, he isn't sure.

"We will discuss this more at home," my father says, snatching up my suitcase. His dark back is a rebuke to all of us. But as he strides toward the car, he pauses and calls over his shoulder to Uncle Seb, "Will your family join us for dinner?"

Uncle Seb hides his grin. "Of course. I'll bring the wine."

"Not that shit cabernet," Papa says.

"Never the cab, always the merlot," Seb agrees, tipping a wink in my direction.

EPILOGUE
LEO

TWO MONTHS LATER

I wake early in the morning because I can feel that Anna isn't in bed next to me. She snuck into my room after midnight and lay curled up in my arms for hours, her breathing heavy, deep, and peaceful.

While our parents have finally accepted that we're in love and intend to be together, they're not quite ready for shared rooms on our joint family vacation.

This cabin belongs to Uncle Miko. That of course means that it's located in the darkest and loneliest bit of forest imaginable, tucked up against the mountains. We're on a little spit of land, surrounded on three sides by a lake as black and glossy as a mirror and on the other by towering pines.

The cabin could be a witch's house with its steeply pitched roof, rough-hewn logs, and continually smoking chimney. It's large enough to fit both the Wilks and my branch of the Gallos quite comfortably.

Still, Anna and I can never be completely comfortable when we're apart. That's why she's crept into my room every night so she can get the rest she needs asleep on my chest.

It almost makes me dread going back to Kingmakers. I asked

Anna if we should get married instead and start our lives together. She considered for a long time.

"I want to be married to you," she said at last, her clear blue eyes fixed on mine. "I want it desperately. But I also want to be the best wife for you, the best partner. The empire we'll build together…it will eclipse anything anyone has done before. If we finish our education first."

I knew she was right, though I hated to admit it.

"Three more years…" I sighed.

"We'll be there together," Anna said, intertwining her fingers with mine.

Now she's wandered off before the sun is up, and I know that means she's troubled. My restless love can never be still when there's something on her mind.

I slip out of bed, pulling a thick sweater over my bare torso and shoving my feet in battered sneakers. I creep downstairs and out onto the wraparound porch, where I spot Anna sitting on the edge of the moss-covered rocks, her bare toes dipping in the lake.

She looks pale as a ghost, dressed only in a nightgown with her long sheaf of silver-blond hair trailing in the water.

I take the woolen blanket off the porch swing and bring it down to her, wrapping it around her slim shoulders. She tilts her chin up and kisses me, her lips cool against my warm mouth.

"We go back to school in only a few weeks," she says.

"Did you change your mind?"

"No." She shakes her head. "I just wonder what will happen."

"What do you mean? What are you afraid of happening?"

"I don't know." She gazes out over the black water blanketed with mist. "I think this year will be different. When we started out at Kingmakers, it was difficult, but it was new and exciting. I have a feeling things are about to get a whole lot darker."

"Darker than almost drowning the last week of school?" I laugh.

Anna looks at me, somber and serious. "Yes," she says.

I kiss her again, longer this time.

"I'll be right by your side," I tell her. "I'll always protect you."

"I know," she says. "I'm not afraid of anything when I have you, Leo."

We sit side by side with my arm around her until the first morning light burns the mist away and the lake turns from black to navy to pink, the sky streaked with orange. The birds make strange and mournful cries across the water.

I can smell bacon sizzling in the kitchen—probably my mother wide awake and instantly hungry.

By the time Anna and I return to the cabin, hand in hand, my mom has pancakes on the skillet, coffee percolating, and eggs poaching too.

"Good morning," Anna says, hugging my mother from behind. She has to reach much farther around than usual to do it because my mom's belly now keeps her arm's length away from the stove. "How's Baby Frances doing?"

"She doesn't like that upstairs mattress," my mom says, "but she's very excited for breakfast."

"That makes two of us," I say.

"No breakfast for you until you set the table," my mom tells me sternly.

"I have to set the table," I say. "I'm the only one who can reach the plates way up here."

I lift them down from their perch on the impractically high shelves above the sink, then pass them to Anna so she can set them out on the table.

Once I've grabbed the glasses, I join her in arranging the place settings. She's leaning way over the table to reach the other side, her nightgown stretched tight across her cute little ass. I can't resist pinching her bottom.

It's the worst possible timing, since my father and Uncle Miko have just come strolling into the room. Uncle Miko's expression goes from calm to homicidal in an instant.

"Young love!" my dad says cheerfully. "Can I get you some orange juice, Miko?" And then in an undertone, "Please don't murder my son."

"Everybody sit down!" my mom says. "The pancakes are ready!"

As we arrange ourselves around the table, Anna and I make sure to take the seats farthest from her father. My mom deposits a huge platter of crispy golden pancakes in the center of the table. My dad brings the bacon and toast a moment later.

I can hear Whelan before I see him, thundering down the stairs at full speed. There's a tumbling, banging noise that sounds like he might have fallen down the last four, but he comes sprinting into the kitchen looking perfectly recovered.

"Where is your sister?" Miko asks him.

"Coming," Whelan pants, plopping himself down at the table and seizing a fistful of bacon. "She's gotta get all fancy first."

"Use the tongs," Miko says sharply, rapping Whelan across the knuckles with them.

"Right," Whelan says, grabbing another pile of bacon with the tongs.

Aunt Nessa floats into the kitchen, as graceful as Anna and barely looking any older than her, even in an old T-shirt and ponytail with no makeup on her face. She gently takes the majority of the bacon from Whelan, dividing it onto Miko's and her plate.

"But I'm starving!" Whelan complains.

"Eat that first, and then we'll see," she says.

Cara follows Nessa a moment after, wearing a clean flannel shirt and denim shorts, her dark hair brushed and braided into two plaits. She sits down on the other side of Anna, giving her sister's hand a quick squeeze.

"It's so nice to be all together," my dad says. "May not happen again for a while, once the baby's born. Traveling with an infant is awful."

"Are you scared to start it all over again?" Nessa asks my mom.

"No," my mother says with her usual bluntness. "It never felt right, having only one. I never felt done."

"I'm sorry I was so unsatisfying," I tease her.

A year or two ago, I would have been annoyed hearing that my mother was unhappy with me as her only child. She probably wouldn't have admitted it. But she can see how happy I am and how little I need that kind of flattery.

"You'll understand soon enough," my dad says. "The desire to have children with the person you love can be overpowering."

"Not *very* soon, though." Uncle Miko frowns.

"Don't worry, Papa," Anna says. "We're not in a rush."

She lays her hand on my thigh under the table. Then, wickedly, she slides it a little higher, inside the leg of my shorts. I stiffen up, trying not to show the slightest sign of enjoyment on my face. I can feel Uncle Miko's frozen stare drilling into me, as if he can see right through the table to his daughter's wandering hand.

"Maybe we should draw up the marriage contract," my father says. He grins at Miko. "Will there be a dowry or a bride price?"

He's only joking. My dad and Miko have run their empires generously and equally, side by side. There's no difference in "value" between Anna and me, at least not from a business perspective.

Without taking his eyes off me, Uncle Miko replies, "You will be bankrupted, my friend."

Anna's fingers steal farther up my shorts toward my crotch. I try to trap her hand without visibly moving, but she slips my grasp and continues on until she's brushing the side of my cock. Perversely, preposterously, right under her father's stare, I feel the rush of blood as I start to get hard. I swear to god, he knows exactly what's happening. Miko always knows.

Trying to hold my lips as still as a ventriloquist, I mutter, "*Anna...*"

Anna smiles serenely, taking a sip of her coffee with one hand and teasing my cock with her other.

I want to jump up and run to the bathroom, but it's too late now; I'm already hard. I'm trapped here while the love of my life attempts to bring down the wrath of the devil on my head.

There's only one thing I can do.

I knock over my own glass of orange juice, right in my lap.

Then I grab a napkin, press it over my crotch, and jump up from the table.

"Oops!" I say. "I better clean up!"

I run upstairs to shower and change, and I don't dare go back down for breakfast until I'm sure Uncle Miko has safely engaged himself someplace else.

I hear Anna coming up to shower shortly after, when I'm already in my room. She's skipping up the stairs and down the hallway, probably laughing to herself.

That's fine with me. I want her cheerful and unaware when I punish her.

It's not easy to capture Anna. She's fast and wary. She'll know that she has it coming after her stunt at breakfast.

So I leave the house as soon as I'm dressed, telling my mother that I'm going to chop a few more cords of wood for the stove.

I take the axe from its place leaned up against the porch, and I head out into the woods to the stand of birch trees ten minutes away that we've been felling, chopping, and stacking in the woodshed.

This part of the forest is dense and nearly silent. You'd think I was hours away from any other human. You can't hear the loons on the water anymore. Only the soft buzz of bees and the occasional creak and groan of the breeze knocking the pine branches together.

I set the birch logs up on a ready stump and begin to split them. It's relaxing work with a smooth, steady rhythm. The swing of the axe, the heavy thunk as it hits, and the clean split of the wood breaking apart. Then I pick up the pieces and throw them neatly on the pile, to be carried over to the woodshed when I'm finished.

Despite the shade and the cool morning, I soon start to sweat.

I unbutton my shirt and take it off, enjoying the breeze on my bare skin.

Swish, thunk.

Swish, thunk.

Swish, thunk.

I'm listening to the wood split. Listening to the wind. And listening for the sounds of Anna approaching.

I know she'll follow me. She can't resist the sight of me chopping wood. She loves to watch me do anything athletic. She always has.

She's quiet and stealthy. But I've learned to hear even her light footsteps over soft, loamy ground.

I hear the snap of a twig. Instantly, I drop the axe and sprint toward her.

She tries to run away, fleet as a white deer in the forest, but I grab her around the waist and throw her over my shoulder as she hits and pummels my back with her fists.

"You crossed a line, baby girl."

Anna doesn't waste time arguing. She's saving her breath for squirming and struggling.

"Do you know what they used to use woodsheds for?" I ask her as I carry her inside, carefully ducking so I don't hit her head on the low doorframe. "That's where they used to take naughty children when they misbehaved. And, baby girl, you've been very naughty."

As soon as I set her down, she tries to run again, but I was expecting that. I seize her by the hands, then take off my belt and wrap it around her wrists. I pass the end of the belt all the way through the buckle, cinching it tight, then I hoist her arms up over her head and tie the other end around the rafter.

"Let go of me!" Anna demands, her cheeks already flaming pink and her eyes brilliant blue in the gloom.

"I don't know why you always have to poke the bear." I walk around her slowly as she stands on tiptoe in the center of the woodshed. Anna can stand in that position for a very long time. "I think you like to see how wild the bear really is."

Anna bites back a smile. She's enjoying this a little too much. I'm going to have to punish her harder than usual. She's too tough—she'll barely feel it otherwise.

I grab the front of her shirt and tear it open, baring her chest. She isn't wearing a bra. Her nipples instantly stiffen up as if in defense of what I'm about to do.

"That was my favorite shirt!" Anna cries.

"Keep quiet or I'll have to gag you."

When Anna opens her mouth to retort, I use the remains of her T-shirt as a gag, tying it tight behind her head. The outrage at this action causes many muffled shrieks.

"That's probably better anyway," I say. "Your dad already wants to kill me. Imagine if he heard you screaming off in the woods."

I run my tongue over Anna's helpless lips, spread apart and held open by the gag. Anna twists and squirms, rotating on the end of the belt. I grab her nipple and pinch it hard, making her shriek at a much higher frequency.

"Can you tell me, baby," I say. "Why do you love this so much?"

I shove my hand down the front of her jeans, dipping my middle finger inside her soft, tight pussy. When I pull it out, my finger is soaked all the way up the second knuckle. I hold it up to show her.

Anna narrows her pale blue eyes, passing over from fear to rage. That's all part of it—part of making her feel every last acute sensation blended with her arousal.

I know what my girl needs. She's no common princess, wanting to be stroked and pampered. Anna is a Mafia queen. That means she would never tolerate a civilian or a soldier. She only submits to the motherfucking king.

She needs the boss of bosses.

The only man who can tame her.

She needs me.

"Do you know what a switch is?" I ask her.

She watches me silently through those narrowed eyes, refusing to nod or shake her head.

I take the switch down from the wall. I cut it off a birch tree and stripped the bark off it. It's long and flexible, with just the right amount of whip.

I slowly slide my fingers down its length, testing its flexibility. Then I bring it down sharply on my palm, making a loud cracking sound that makes Anna flinch.

"When someone needs to be punished, you take them to the woodshed and you fetch the switch," I say to Anna softly. "Baby girl, you need to be punished."

I walk around her again, trailing the switch lightly across her bare back. Her flesh trembles, and her fists tighten in the loop of my belt.

Swiftly, I reach around her and unbuckle her jeans, yanking them down around her knees. Her underwear comes with them. Now I can see the smooth twin globes of her ass, flawless and unmarked.

Not for long.

I bring the switch down hard on her ass. It leaves a thin red line, right across both cheeks. Anna's muffled scream is the highest yet.

I whip her again and again, until her ass is striped with red lines and both cheeks are glowing pink, no hint of creamy skin left.

She stops shrieking, but her body still flinches with each hit. Her nipples are so hard that they stand out an inch from her chest.

I'm sweating harder than when I was chopping wood.

I reach around and test Anna's pussy. She's wet all the way down the inside of her thighs. She moans helplessly as I slide my fingers over her warm and throbbing clit.

I stand in front of her, her nipples brushing against my bare torso. I rip down her gag and plunge my tongue into her mouth, kissing her like an animal, without gentleness or technique. I bite her lips, I suck on her neck, and I fuck her with my fingers until she's sobbing and begging for relief.

I rip her jeans the rest of the way off, tossing them aside. She grabs the belt in her hands, pulling herself up higher so she can wrap her legs around my waist. I free my cock, stabbing it all the way into her with one thrust.

Her pussy is a thousand degrees, the hottest I've ever felt it. And my cock is an iron brand, fresh out of the fire. I hold her by the hips, and I fuck her violently, intensely, until the sweat pours down my chest.

It's exactly what she needs. In seconds, she's coming, screaming out so loud that for the first time I think she might actually be heard all the way over at the cabin, and I clamp my hand over her mouth. I hold it there as I blow inside her, a rush of boiling hot cum that sears my cock as it pours out of me. I'm roaring too, biting down hard on her shoulder.

When she collapses against me, I undo the belt, both of us falling down on the floor, our legs too weak to support us. I'm covered in sawdust and sweat, but Anna doesn't care. She lays her cheek on my chest, still breathing too fast, her heart like a running rabbit.

"That was a good one," she says when she can speak again.

I press my face into her hair, inhaling her scent.

"Best ever," I say.

"Best so far," she replies.

READ ON FOR A SNEAK PEEK AT MILES AND ZOE IN *KINGMAKERS: YEAR TWO*

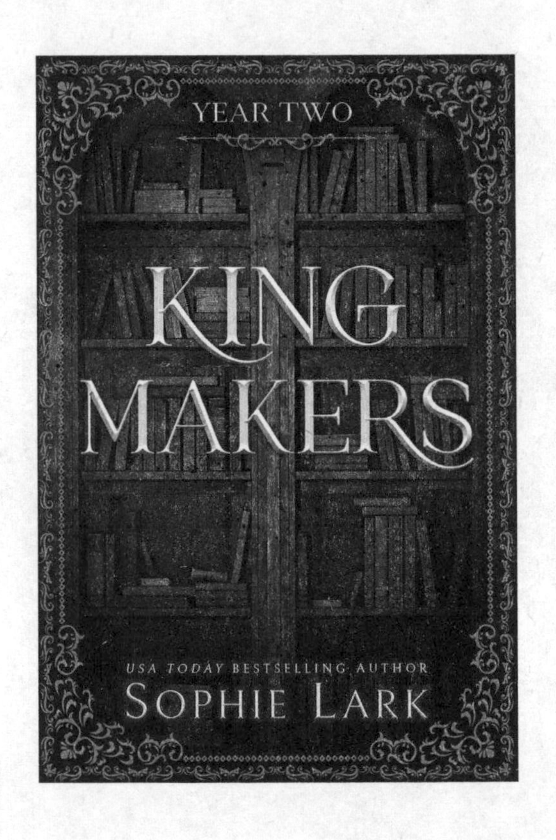

CHAPTER 1
ZOE

It's my engagement party tonight.

I've never been less excited to celebrate something.

My stepmother Daniela sends her team of specialists to ensure that I'm in peak form, so Rocco and his family can be sure they're getting their money's worth.

They come into my bedroom at three o'clock in the afternoon and spend the next four hours scrubbing, exfoliating, waxing, moisturizing, painting, and primping every square inch of my body.

The fighting starts immediately when I demand to know why they're waxing my bikini line.

"It's an engagement party," I tell Daniela. "Not the wedding night. I don't expect anyone to be checking under my skirt."

I glare at my stepmother, who is already partway through her own exhausting preparations for the night ahead. She has a mud mask on her face and her hair up in rollers the size of soup cans. Far from looking ridiculous, it only makes her appear all the more imperious as the curlers encircle her head like a crown, and the mask obscures the few hints of emotion Daniela ever betrays. I can't tell if Daniela actually lacks all human feeling or if she's just very good at hiding it.

Daniela is only ten years older than me.

I was nine when my mother died, nine-and-a-half when my father remarried.

He used my mother up like an old sponge, putting her through fourteen pregnancies, ten miscarriages, two stillbirths, and the shameful arrival of me and my sister Catalina, none of which produced a male heir.

That last stillbirth was the death of her. She hemorrhaged on the gurney. The darkest part of me suspects that my father held back the doctor, allowing the life to drain out of my mother as punishment for the fact that even that final breathless baby was a girl.

My father went into a rage.

There was no comfort for Cat and me, no time to mourn our mother. Instead he ordered flower girl dresses.

He was already making arrangements to marry Daniela, the youngest daughter of rival Galician clan chief. Her sisters had produced two sons each for their husbands, proof in my father's eyes that Daniela would likewise be fertile and useful.

Daniela fell pregnant on the honeymoon, but an anatomy scan showed that the fetus was female yet again. My father forced her to abort it.

I only know this because I heard him shouting at her for hours, berating her into doing it. She was sick for several weeks after, pale and unable to walk from room to room without hunching over.

I don't know how many more times she was coerced into repeating that process.

Eventually, my father stopped trusting in fate and turned to science.

They saw fertility specialists. Daniela went through several rounds of IVF, harvesting her eggs for the sole purpose of selecting the gender ahead of time.

None of these attempts were successful. Daniela bore no babies at all.

I'd feel bad for her. But the sympathy wouldn't be returned.

Daniela hates me. She hates my sister, too.

Her loyalty is all to my father, no matter how he abuses her.

She's his constant spy, acting as jailor to Cat and me and helping carry out all my father's most insidious plans for us.

Like this engagement.

It was Daniela who brokered the deal with Rocco Prince and his family. She told Rocco's mother that I was intelligent, studious, obedient, submissive. And of course, beautiful.

When I was only twelve years old, she sent the Princes photographs of me laying by the pool in my swimsuit.

The Princes' first visit soon followed. Rocco was thirteen—just a year older than me—but I could already tell there was something very wrong with him.

He came out to the garden where I was sitting on a bench under the orange trees, reading *The Witch of Blackbird Pond*. I stood up when I saw him approach, smoothing down the white muslin skirt of the summer dress Daniela had selected for me.

Back then, I was innocent enough that I still had fantasies of a better life. I had seen movies like *Sleeping Beauty* and *The Swan Princess* where the prince and princess were betrothed by their parents, but their love was genuine.

So when I heard that Rocco was coming to see me, I imagined he might be handsome and sweet, and maybe we would write letters to each other like pen pals.

When he approached me in the garden, I was pleased to see that he was tall and dark-haired, slim and pale with the look of an artist.

"Hello," I said. "I'm Zoe."

He gave me an appraising look, not answering at first. Then he said, "Why are you reading?"

I thought it a strange question. Not, "What *are you reading?*" but "Why *are you reading?*"

He tilted his head, looking me up and down, unsmiling. "Are you trying to impress me?"

I shook my head, confused and wrong-footed.

"I always read on Saturdays when there's no school."

I didn't tell him there was nothing else to do at my house—Cat and I weren't permitted to watch TV or play video games.

He picked my novel up off the bench, examined the cover, and contemptuously tossed it down again, losing my place. I was annoyed but tried not to show it. After all, he was my guest, and I was already aware that our futures were meant to entwine.

"You're pretty," he said, dispassionately, looking me over again. "Too tall, though."

If that meant he wouldn't want to marry me, I was already starting to think that might be a good thing.

"You live in Hamburg?" I asked, trying to hide my growing dislike.

"Yes," Rocco said, with a toss of his dark hair that might have been pride or disdain—I couldn't yet tell. "Have you ever been there?"

"No."

"I didn't think so."

I noticed little black flecks in the blue of his eyes, like someone had spattered his irises with ink.

"What's that noise?" Rocco demanded.

A parrot was screeching in the orange tree, swooping low over our heads, and then returning to its branch.

"It's annoyed because it has a nest full of babies up there," I said. "It wants us to leave."

Rocco reached inside his jacket and took out a pellet gun. It was small, only the size of a pistol. I assumed it was a toy gun, and I thought it was childish of him to carry it around.

He pointed it up at the small green parrot, following its flight path in his sights. I thought he was play-acting, trying to impress me. Then he squeezed the trigger. I heard a sharp puff of air. The parrot went silent, cut off mid-cry, dropping like a stone into the flowerbed.

I cried out and ran over to it.

I picked the parrot up out of the earth, seeing the small dark hole in its breast.

"Why did you do that?" I shrieked.

I was thinking of its babies up in the nest. Now that the parrot wasn't squawking anymore, I could hear their faint cheeps.

Rocco stood next to me, looking down at the moss-colored bird. It looked pathetic in my hands, its wings folded and dusty.

"The chicks will wait and wait," he said. "Then eventually they'll starve."

His voice was flat and expressionless.

I looked in his face. I saw no guilt or pity there. Just blankness.

Except for the tiny upward curl of his lips.

Those little black specks on his irises reminded me of mold. Like there was something rancid in him, rotting him away from the inside.

"You're horrid," I said, dropping the bird and wiping my palms atavistically on the sides of my dress.

Then Rocco did smile, showing even white teeth.

"We're just getting to know one another."

Rocco has not improved on further acquaintance. Every time I see him, I loathe him more.

Tonight I'll be expected to dance with him, to hang on his arm, to gaze at him as if we're in love. It's all a performance for the guests.

He doesn't love me any more than I do him.

The only thing he likes about me is how much I despise him. That he enjoys very much.

That's the man for whom Daniela demands that I wax my pussy.

I stare at her with deep distrust, wondering what she knows that I don't. Why does she think it's important that I be perfectly smooth from the chin down? What does she expect to happen?

"I'm not doing it," I tell her. "He's not touching me tonight."

Daniela tilts her head to the side, eyes narrowed.

She's quite beautiful, I'd never deny that. She has the austere look of a saint in a painting. Like a saint, she worships a cruel and vengeful god: my father.

"You'd better learn to please him," she says quietly. "It will be so much harder on you if you fight. The things a man can do to his wife when she's trapped with him, all alone in a big house like this, with only his soldiers around..."

She blinks slowly in a way that has always reminded me of a reptile.

"You should learn how to flatter him. How to assist him. How to serve him with your body . . ."

"I'd rather die," I tell her flatly.

She laughs softly.

"Oh, you'll *wish* you were dead . . ."

She nods to her team of estheticians. With something approaching force, they push me down on the chaise, pry my legs apart, and spread hot wax over the entirety of my pussy, all the way up to my anus. Then they rip the wax off in strips, until I'm bald as an egg absolutely everywhere.

Daniela watches the whole thing, then examines the final result. She checks my bare pussy for any sign of deformity that might derail her plans. Then she nods her approval.

"When I was presented to your father, I was stripped naked in front of a dozen of his soldiers. They evaluated me like a horse at auction. Be grateful it's only Rocco you have to impress."

She leaves me with the aestheticians so she can complete her own beautifying.

Daniela has already selected the clothing and jewelry I'll be wearing.

The aestheticians carry out her orders, zipping me into a suffocating gown that hoists up my breasts and cinches my waist to a fraction of its usual size. The gown is long, gold, and sparkling, with the sort of sleeves that are not sleeves at all, but only fabric draped below the shoulders. My hair is piled up on my head with a gold band as a tiara.

It's all undeniably beautiful, in impeccable taste.

I'm a glittering golden gift.

A black shroud would be more fitting. I feel like I'm going to my own funeral.

I'm like those maidens the Incas used to sacrifice to the gods: the Virgins of the Sun. All year they were fed delicacies—maize and llama meat. They were bathed and beautified with feathered headdresses and exotic shell necklaces. And then they were carried to the mountaintop tombs, to be sealed inside as an offering to a god that craved their death.

Catalina comes into my room, likewise dressed for the night ahead.

Cat perfectly suits her name. She's small and lithe, and she moves as silently as a little black cat. She has a pretty heart-shaped face, large, dark eyes, and a dusting of freckles across her nose. She's dressed in a pale lavender gown.

Even though we're only a year apart, she looks much younger.

She's always been timid.

I can see how nervous she is for the party, for everyone staring at us. Lucky for her most of the attention will be pointed in my direction. And she doesn't have to worry about being roped into some hateful marriage contract, at least not yet. That was part of my agreement with my father: Cat doesn't have to get married until she graduates college, and neither do I.

My father and stepmother are allowing me to attend Kingmakers for all four years, as long as I agree to marry Rocco directly after graduation.

It was a last, desperate ploy on my part to delay the inevitable.

They only agreed because Rocco is also at Kingmakers, as are plenty of his cousins and mine, always around to spy on me, to make sure I'm not drinking or dating or breaching any of the rules of the betrothal.

Kingmakers is no normal school.

ACKNOWLEDGMENTS

I have to thank Line first, for all the incredible art she made for the re-release of Kingmakers.

Kingmakers was what brought us together in the first place. At the time, Line was working a media job she hated in Denmark, and she'd become quite miserable. A mutual friend introduced her to my books as a form of escape. Line identified with my gothic ballerina and started drawing fan art of Anna and Leo, Miles and Zoe.

When I saw Line's portrait of Zoe, I was stunned! No one had ever captured the essence of one of my characters so perfectly. It wasn't just a portrait; it was rich with symbolism from the story.

I bought several of Line's drawings to put in the books and soon hired her to draw more. Before long, she was working for me full-time, illustrating each of my new releases, and a beautiful partnership was born.

It will always make me so incredibly happy that the picture Line drew of Zoe escaping through reading is what allowed her to escape the job she hated and build a career doing what she loves. I'm so thrilled to have all new Kingmakers art to celebrate how much she's grown as an artist in the time we've been working together!

Thank you also to the other full-time members of the Sophie

team, Maya and Brittany, and also to Emily Wittig, who designed the gorgeous new covers.

And finally, thank you BD for being the love of my life, my best friend, and my soulmate. Enemies-to-lovers will always be my favorite trope, but the strongest relationships are between the closest friends.

ABOUT THE AUTHOR

Sophie Lark is the *USA Today* bestselling author of *Brutal Prince* and the Sinners Duet. She lives in Southern California with her husband and three children. Her favorite authors are Emily Henry and Freida McFadden, and she looks forward to Halloween every year.

The Love Lark Letter: geni.us/lark-letter
The Love Lark Reader Group: geni.us/love-larks
Website: sophielark.com
Instagram: @Sophie_Lark_Author
TikTok: @sophielarkauthor
Exclusive Content: patreon.com/sophielark
Complete Works: geni.us/lark-amazon
Book Playlists: geni.us/lark-spotify